LOVE'S SECRET BARGAIN

Elizabeth's eyes swept Andrew's face slowly, lingering over his deeply tanned features so she might always remember how handsome he was. The words she knew she should speak stuck in her throat, impossible to utter. Instead she replied calmly, her only choice suddenly clear, "My father insists I send you away, but I will not do it."

"Because we have a bargain?" He drew near, his voice low and tender.

"What is it you wish me to admit, Indian?" Elizabeth whispered hoarsely, sorry now she'd not chosen the safety of the porch.

"Only the truth, Elizabeth." Andrew reached out to enfold her trembling body in his warm embrace. His lips met hers lightly, tasting their sweetness, and she relaxed against him. He pulled her down into the cool grass, cradling her body gently in his arms. His hands strayed down the buttons on her bodice as he kissed her, caressing her tenderly. As he began to run his hand slowly up the inside of her slender thigh she struggled against him, finally realizing what he meant to do. . . .

MORE TEMPESTUOUS ROMANCES!

SAVAGE FIRE

PHOEBE CONN

ZEBRA BOOKS
KENSINGTON PUBLISHING CORP.

ZEBRA BOOKS

are published by

Kensington Publishing Corp.
475 Park Avenue South
New York, N.Y. 10016

First printing: June, 1984

Printed in the United States of America

Prologue 1758

The spacious bedroom was veiled in shadows save for the soft circle of light illuminating the massive four-poster bed. The pretty woman's hair shone with a bright golden glow as she read from a small leather bound volume of poetry. Her voice held a musical lilt, giving the romantic verses the richness of opera. She glanced up frequently to smile at the man who lay quietly resting among his pillows, but his eyes were closed, his once handsome face now far too thin.

Marie leaned forward as she took Phillip's hand lightly in hers. "I think that is enough for tonight. Go to sleep and I will see you when you wake in the morning."

The pale man stirred slightly then opened his eyes.

Their color was striking, a rich clear green which lit his whole face with warmth as he tried unsuccessfully to return her smile. "No, please do not leave me tonight, Marie. I do not want to waste what little remains of my life in sleep." He gasped hoarsely for breath as he spoke, the effort proving exhausting for him.

After carefully marking her place, Marie laid the small book aside. Then, lifting her long skirt gracefully, she climbed upon the high bed and lay her head gently upon Phillip's left shoulder. "I will stay until you have fallen asleep. You know I will always stay for as long as you need me."

Phillip raised his hand to remove the pins which held her fair hair in place. His slim fingers combed through the silken tresses with a lazy caress until he had spilled the curls about her shoulders in casual disarray. "I wish we could have danced together, my beauty. Just once I wish I could have held you in my arms and shown you off to all my friends."

"We will dance, Phillip. When you are well again we can dance the night through if you wish." Marie bit her lip savagely to force back her tears. They both knew he would never again be well but she could not admit that. It was far too sad a prospect to consider, let alone accept.

"For now I must be content to hold you like this. It is all I can offer."

"Oh, Phillip, you have given me so much, more than you will ever know. I am so happy to be here with you." Marie reached up to kiss his flushed cheek tenderly then touched his auburn hair. It was still so

6

thick and shiny despite his rapidly failing health. "Did I ever tell you about the first time I saw you?"

"Was it not here in this very room?"

"No, it was last spring. The first pretty day of spring and I was strolling through the park when you walked by with one of your friends. The gentleman had told some joke and—"

"Then that was no friend of mine, Marie, for none of them can be called gentlemen." A sly smile curved across his handsome mouth as he teased her.

"Phillip, just listen!" But Marie was laughing too. His sense of humor had never failed him and gave her all the courage she needed to finish her story. "The other man then, said something and you laughed. I stood and watched the two of you walk by then I followed you until I found someone who knew your name."

Phillip continued to stroke her soft curls lightly with his fingertips. "You came here then, just to be with me?"

"For no other reason, Phillip, I wanted only to be with you."

"I wish God had sent you to me sooner, my angel. I wish—"

"No, Phillip, we have tonight, tomorrow, all of eternity to spend together. Do not be sad for what we have missed."

"Yes, I do hope to spend eternity in your arms, Marie. That would be paradise indeed." Phillip pulled her mouth down to his and began to kiss her with a slow, sensuous abandon and she clung to him, her love spreading through him with a warmth that lit his

7

final hours with the brilliance of that spring day when first she'd seen him smile. That was the image which filled her heart, the way she saw him still, tall and strong, laughing, filled with the vibrant life which was now slipping away so rapidly she feared each beat of his heart would be the last.

One
Spring 1775

Elizabeth smiled wistfully as Jed bid her a good morning as he moved with a slow shuffle toward the back door. How could she have forgotten he was no longer young? With her father away visiting his brother in Philadelphia, the endless chores their farm required had fallen mostly to Jed and then to her. They were both tired to the point of exhaustion, but she knew she'd simply expected too much of the man who'd always been more of a dear uncle to her than a hired hand.

"Jed," she called softly, "let the fence go for a day or two. It's needed repair for weeks and a few more days won't make any difference."

The gray-haired man nodded thoughtfully. "That's true enough, but I can't let Olaf come home and find it not done."

"My father won't be back for two weeks at the very least, Jed, and you'll be no help to him then if you've worn yourself out now. We both worked much too hard yesterday. Do only what must be done today and no more," she ordered sensibly, her voice both confident and warm.

"I'll not argue with you, Miss Elizabeth." With a low chuckle and a merry twinkle in his blue eyes he closed the door quietly and left to begin his day's work.

As she moved about the kitchen, Elizabeth's mind was still occupied with what must be done to insure her father returned to the well-run farm he'd left rather than to the chaos she'd made of it. On the day he'd departed she'd been so confident she and Jed could handle the work alone. What a fool she'd been! Each day they had fallen further behind in their daily routine until she despaired of escaping her parent's wrath and had no hope of winning his praise. Daniel MacGregar would come and work for a day or two if she asked for his help, but she knew all too well what he'd expect in return. No, he'd become far too bold of late and she'd not risk encouraging any further advances from him by requesting assistance from him now. Her delicate features set in a determined frown. She hurriedly washed the breakfast dishes hoping she'd have time after her morning chores to do her baking for there was not a crust of bread in the house. When a loud knock rattled the front door she swore softly to herself, not pleased at having been interrupted when she was so terribly busy, but drying her hands on her apron she quickly crossed the braided rug and peered out the window before opening the door.

The black bearded man appeared to be a trapper from the looks of the furs piled high upon his wagon but it was the Indian, whose hands were tied by a rope tethered to the old vehicle, who intrigued her most.

They seldom saw Indians near their farm, thank God, as all knew they were lower than snakes, savages who

10

killed women and children as well as grown men. But this man was bound firmly as he waited on the dusty path. He stood with his feet slightly apart, his shoulders held straight in such a proud posture she could not imagine how the trapper had captured him. Since Jed was in the barn she knew he would come running if anything were amiss, so even though she were alone in the house she opened the door.

"Good morning, miss, name's John Cummins. I wonder if I might stop for a minute to water my mules, and I'm might parched myself now that I think of it."

Elizabeth gestured toward the well at the east side of the house. "Help yourself. I can let you have all you want to drink for the water is plentiful." She kept her eyes on the Indian while John Cummins continued to chat. The savage looked young and strong but he had obviously been so badly beaten she was surprised he could still stand. She remained at the open door while the trapper watered his mules and drank several cups of water himself but she soon realized the man meant to give none to his prisoner. "Surely the Indian is thirsty, too. Aren't you going to give him a drink?" Elizabeth found the young brave's glance most unsettling. The spring day was a cool one but he wore only buckskin leggings and a breechcloth. His moccasins were well-worn as if he'd been forced to walk a long distance in them. His bare chest and arms were covered with cuts and bruises of every size and shape. Whoever had beaten him had done a most thorough job. His long, dark hair might have been braided once. She couldn't tell. It hung in wild disarray, tangled over his shoulders, making him appear all the more fierce.

"Him? Hell no. Those bucks like to suffer. They enjoy being brave. It's what they do best, ain't it, Silver Hawk?"

At the sound of his name, the Indian looked up slightly but his expression didn't change. If the trapper had expected him to beg for water he was disappointed, as the savage did no more than sneer.

Elizabeth was fascinated by the disheveled young man. His muscular build, proud stance and defiant look simply mesmerized her and she hated to see the trapper leave. As he climbed back up on his wagon, she called out to him, "What has he done?"

"Done? Probably all sorts of nasty deeds, miss. I'm just turning him in at Oak Grove. There's always a reward out for one murdering Indian or another. Might as well collect one for this buck."

"But you don't know if he's wanted for any crime?"

"Look at him, miss, a murderer if I ever saw one. Thanks again for the water. Good day." The trapper touched the brim of his dusty hat and picked up the mules' reins.

"No, please wait!" Elizabeth ran to the well and filled the tin cup with water, which she carried to the Indian. When she got closer his wounds looked even worse. Some were obviously burns. She held the cool cup up to his lips and waited for him to drink as she spoke in a soft voice too low for John Cummins to overhear. "Being brave is one thing but dying of thirst is quite another. Please drink this for me."

The Indian gulped down the water as best he could. His lips were dry and so cracked she knew the effort must have hurt him terribly. When he spoke she looked up quickly, shocked by his words.

"Thank you."

The man's eyes were bloodshot and weary but they were of the same deep shade of green as her own and she gasped in surprise.

"Get away from him, miss, before he spits on you, or worse!" John Cummins laughed as he clucked to his mules.

"No, stop!" Elizabeth ran to the front of the wagon and grabbed the mules' harness with both hands. "That is no Indian! His eyes are as green as mine!"

"So? He's a half-breed, probably. Damn French father most likely. Half-breed or full blood he'll be worth the same."

"How can you be certain you'll get anything for him?"

"I will if I'm lucky." The man frowned suddenly. "That's why my partner went on ahead, but we're very seldom lucky."

"Then maybe you'd be wise to consider an alternative," Elizabeth offered with an enticing smile. She turned again to appraise the young man more closely. He'd been cruelly abused, that was true, but he still appeared to be strong and with a few days rest he should be able to work. Perhaps she could solve his problems if he solved hers. She approached him slowly, forming her plan as she spoke. "How much English do you speak? Can you understand all we've said?"

"I know English," the captive replied in a defiant snarl.

"Good, now listen carefully . . ." Elizabeth stopped abruptly as she realized the man's gaze was raking her slender figure with an all too appreciative glance.

"Stop that this instant! I am trying to help you escape the gallows. Can't you bother to listen?"

The tall man shrugged indifferently. "I was listening." He lifted his eyes to hers, his hostile stare no more respectful, but she obviously had his full attention.

Ignoring his insolence for the moment, Elizabeth continued. "Mr. Cummins here plans to turn you in for any unsolved murder or theft. He'll collect the bounty no matter how remote the possibility you committed the crime."

Silver Hawk straightened up to his full height, his already proud posture growing militant. "I am no criminal."

Elizabeth believed him readily for although his manner was a menacing one, he appeared to be too incensed by the trapper's treachery to be lying. "I'm glad to hear it. Now I think I can help you, but if I do, you'll have to repay me by staying here to work."

"You want me to work for you?" Silver Hawk asked disdainfully. "For a woman?"

In a flare of temper Elizabeth replied with equal sarcasm, "You find the prospect of the gallows preferable to such a humiliation?" She turned away, not bothering to wait for his reply and nodded to the trapper to continue his journey.

John Cummins howled gleefully. "Cut your own throat that time, chief. She'll not have you now!"

Silver Hawk watched the girl's proud grace as she moved away. She was tall for a woman, her head nearly even with his shoulders and he could tell by the length of her stride that her legs would be long and elegant, as beautiful as the rest of her. Realizing the depth of his

14

error, he called out, "How long must I work?"

Elizabeth turned back toward the wagon, ignoring the Indian as she made a bargain with the trapper. "I have a fine mare. I'll trade her for your prisoner. She's worth more than any bounty you might receive. Wait here while I fetch her."

As John Cummins examined the chestnut horse carefully, Elizabeth remarked casually to the Indian, "She is sound, a beauty too. I say she's worth three months of your time. Will you agree to that?"

Silver Hawk's deep green eyes smoldered with hatred. "You are no better than he! I'll be no woman's slave!"

Elizabeth responded impatiently, "I am buying your freedom, not you, you dolt! I'm setting you at liberty, not making you my slave. The horse is mine, all I own of value, but at present I need a farm hand more than I need a fine mount. If you'll not give me your word that you will stay here with me and work at whatever task I assign you for three full months then you may take your chances with the magistrate in Oak Grove." Elizabeth stood waiting for the man's reply, her arms crossed over the soft swell of her breast as she tapped her foot rapidly. "I'll warn you now, an Indian with no way to prove his innocence and no friends to speak in his behalf can expect little mercy."

Silver Hawk looked over at John Cummins. Then, after a long moment's pause, held out his bound wrists to Elizabeth. "Untie the rope. I will stay."

"And work? You must give me your promise that you will work before I'll release you," Elizabeth insisted sternly.

"I will work!" Silver Hawk growled, his fury at the

15

wretchedness of his fate unhidden.

John Cummins completed his inspection of the horse and seemed very pleased. "This is a fine mare, miss. What will your pa say about this trade?"

"I am the mistress here. The horse is mine to do with as I please. She is yours if you'll give me this Indian."

"Well, seeing as how he might die on me, or get away, knowing what a murdering dog he is, I will gladly take your horse. Write me up a bill of sale and I'll make you out one for Chief Silver Hawk here."

"He is a chief?" Elizabeth looked back at the young man. She had never imagined a chief to be either so young or in such a sorry state.

"Says his father is. He's one of the Iroquois. That's all I know about the murdering thief."

"Who is it he murdered?" Elizabeth had grown weary of the trapper's incessant insults, but as she glanced back at the Indian she had to admit if any man had ever looked capable of foul deeds this one surely did.

"Who knows, someone for sure though. They're all murderers ain't they?"

Elizabeth gave up on that discussion and hurried back inside her home to fetch a scrap of paper upon which she wrote out a bill of sale for Lady and one for the Indian since she doubted John Cummins could write. He signed the paper with what looked something like his initials then untied the rope which bound Silver Hawk to his wagon.

"Here you go, miss. I'd keep him tied up if I were you. He's a mean one."

"He's half dead is what he is. Who beat him so

cruelly? Was it you?"

"Aye, me and my partner. We had quite a bit of sport with him. Good day again to you, miss." John Cummins tied Lady in the Indian's place, then climbed back up upon his wagon and headed his mules down the narrow trail.

Elizabeth watched Lady being led away and bit her lip anxiously. Her father would never forgive her for this. She knew she would be in deep trouble when he returned home, but with any luck the farm would be running smoothly again and that accomplishment would have to be enough to stay his anger. When she turned, the Indian was watching her closely, frowning as if he were puzzled by what she had done.

Elizabeth dropped the rope and tried her best to untie it, but the man's wrists were already bleeding and she was afraid she was only adding to his pain. "I'll call Jed to help me. Can you walk to the barn?" When the man did not respond she was perplexed. "Look, I gave that horrid man my horse for you so you now work for me. When I tell you to do something you will do it. Now come with me to the barn and you can rest there."

"Am I to live in the barn like your horse?" He stared down at her defiantly, his gaze daring her to try and dominate him if she thought she could.

Elizabeth put her hands on her narrow waist and stamped her tiny foot. "At least my horse had the sense to come when I called her, now come!"

"I will come." But Silver Hawk had taken no more than two steps before he stumbled and fell against her.

Elizabeth grabbed his waist but he recoiled from her touch. There was not an inch of his back that was not

17

cut and bleeding. "Oh, Hawk, I am so sorry, please try and walk to the barn with me." She moved her arms down to hold him around his hips and called for Jed to come and help for if the man fell she was far too slight of build to catch him and the last thing he needed was to fall in the dirt of the barnyard.

The hired hand came out from behind the barn then broke into a frantic run. "I'll get the musket, Miss Elizabeth!"

"Jed, you come here and help me this minute!"

It took the badly frightened man a few seconds to realize his mistress was calmly walking toward the barn with her arms around a savage's waist but he did then begin to approach them cautiously.

"Have you your knife, Jed? Use it to cut the rope which binds his hands, please."

"No, I'll not venture that close, Miss Elizabeth. Oh, no." Jed appeared to be terrified their lives would be over the instant he cut the man's bonds.

Elizabeth looked up at Hawk and winced. "Will you just look at this poor creature, Jed. He is cut to ribbons. Now give me your knife and be quick about it." Elizabeth spoke calmly to Silver Hawk as she took the knife from Jed's hand. "Give me your hands, yes, that's it. I'll cut the rope." She slit the coarse rope with the small knife but passed it immediately back to Jed. She would take no chances on being stabbed either, for in spite of her trusting nature, she was no fool. "Jed, please go into the house for a blanket, some water for this man to drink, and something to clean his wounds. I want to be certain he recovers swiftly from this brutal beating."

"Miss Elizabeth, he is a savage. Your father will just

18

shoot him the minute he arrives home," Jed argued forcefully.

"He will not. I traded Lady for this man, so he is now my responsibility and I'll not have him so badly abused." She took Silver Hawk's right hand by the fingertips so as not to hurt him again and led him into the barn. Fresh straw lay in the first stall and she motioned for the Indian to sit down. "You will rest here for the time being."

"I am no horse!" His glance had not softened as he surveyed his surroundings with disdain. He looked every inch the cutthroat John Cummins had sworn him to be and was obviously displeased by her command.

Elizabeth sighed sympathetically. "No, Silver Hawk, you're no horse. I can see you are a man. That's why I am trying my best to help you."

The Indian hesitated a moment as if considering her words, then sank to his knees in the straw and Elizabeth knelt down beside him. When Jed returned with the soap and water, she tried to decide how best to tend his numerous injuries. "I don't know where to begin to get him clean, Jed."

"We could just douse him in the horse trough, Miss Elizabeth."

"Jed, will you stop making jokes. I am serious! Look how badly he has been treated." But as she squeezed the soapy water from the rag Jed had brought, the Indian grabbed it away.

"Fine, you do it. You think I'm enjoying this? Go ahead, clean up by yourself and I'll just sit here and watch. When you need help with your back just ask." Elizabeth moved away from him, but watched closely as he rinsed off his arms and chest. The pain must have been horrible but he did not cry out, or even whimper.

"We should put something on them cuts, Miss Elizabeth. Your pa has a bottle of medicine he uses for the horses. Shall I bring that?"

"Horses? Oh, well, why not if it will work. Go and get it, please." Elizabeth read the label carefully. The directions were simple enough and she remembered her father using the medicine on Lady once when the mare had gotten a bad scratch. "This won't hurt the man any and it might help to heal the wounds." She set the bottle aside and waited for him to finish. When he had, she held out her hand for the rag. "Please let me clean your back. It is the worst and you can't do it yourself in spite of your pride."

Elizabeth moved to sit behind him when he put the rag in her hand, but she could scarcely bring herself to touch his shredded back, and shuddered with revulsion. "Wait until your wife sees you, Silver Hawk. She'll weep even if you won't."

"I have no wife."

"And why not? You're old enough to have a squaw, aren't you?" Elizabeth waited, but he did not respond, only sat, his shoulders straight as she tried to clean the dust of the trail from the long bloody cuts. "How did they do this to you, Hawk, with a whip?"

He nodded slightly and Elizabeth continued in a soft sympathetic tone. "I am sorry to hurt you again, but I am afraid you will become ill if we don't get you cleaned up properly. Now, I hope this medicine doesn't sting too badly. Tell me if it does and I'll stop." Elizabeth poured a tiny amount of the amber liquid upon a clean rag and held it to the Indian's lacerated shoulder. Silver Hawk did not even flinch. He simply fainted across her lap in a heap.

"Oh, no! Have I killed him, Jed?"

The hired hand bent down and felt for the pulse in the Indian's throat, then shook his head. "It might be better if you had, Miss Elizabeth, but he's just passed out from the pain."

"Well, help me and we'll put this all over him while he can't feel it." With Jed's help Elizabeth managed to treat all of Silver Hawk's wounds thoroughly and then they spread out the blanket and rolled him over upon it to rest.

"Loosen his belt, Jed, then he can sleep more comfortably." As Elizabeth watched her friend, she grew thoughtful. "If this man were white, and just burned brown from years in the sun, would he be dark all over, Jed? Indians wear clothes like his all the time, don't they? Surely they don't go about naked, so if he is white shouldn't we be able to tell by looking at him?"

"Miss Elizabeth, you want me to pull off his britches!" Jed appeared astonished by her question and backed away.

"No, Jed, let's just undress him part way. Just lower his buckskins a few inches past his waist, please."

Jed hesitated a moment then slipped the breech-cloth down the man's hips to reveal a line of fair pink flesh which was a surprising contrast to the bronze skin of his well muscled back. "Well, he's not that brown all over is he, miss?"

Elizabeth reached out and touched the soft skin of the Indian's exposed hip. "No, he is quite fair for an

Indian I'd say. I think he must be a white man, not a half-breed either but all white. What do you think?"

"I don't know what he is, miss, other than trouble and I don't want him to wake and find me pulling off his britches!"

"Put his clothing as it was, just leave his belt loose." Elizabeth cleaned off the man's face, then tried to pick the leaves and twigs out of his long hair. As she pushed his hair back from his forehead she remarked upon the stubble on his chin. "Do all Indians have such heavy beards, Jed?"

"I know naught of the creatures, Miss Elizabeth."

"Well, in spite of the bruises on his face he is quite handsome, isn't he? Let's leave him on his stomach to sleep and give his back a chance to heal since it's the worst." She raised his right arm to cradle his cheek, then sat back.

"I think we should tie him up real good. We know nothing of this man and what he might do." Jed looked at the young brave's powerful build and shuddered. "I've never been so close to an Indian before and I find I do not like the feeling at all."

"I'll not keep him in chains, Jed. Why should he wish to harm people who have been kind to him? He'll not hurt us," Elizabeth replied optimistically.

Jed coughed nervously, then forced himself to speak. "Miss Elizabeth, forgive me for saying so, but he is a young man and you are a very pretty girl. There are no Indian women as fair as you. You have hair as yellow as the straw here and—"

Elizabeth's clear green eyes sparkled with amusement. "You think he might scalp me, Jed?"

"No, miss, I think he might do worse."

22

"Worse? What could possibly be worse than that?" Elizabeth was puzzled, then suddenly understood. "You mean he might rape me? Well, I doubt he has the strength to do it, Jed. I know I could outrun him. He could not have walked much farther behind that wagon."

"No, miss, he looks done in, but he might be stronger tomorrow."

When Silver Hawk awoke late that afternoon he appeared to be too weak to move. He lay just staring with an insolent gaze as Elizabeth brought him some supper.

"I am happy to see you were comfortable enough to sleep the day through, Hawk." Elizabeth placed the bowl of soup by his side and smiled with a teasing grin. She was relieved to see he had not found the confines of the barn unbearable.

"Silver Hawk." His voice was no more than a whisper and Elizabeth disregarded Jed's stern warning to bend down to hear his words and he grabbed her long hair pulling her down upon him in the straw.

Elizabeth lay sprawled across him, her legs entangled with his. "Forgive me, Mr. Hawk, Silver Hawk it is then. Now let me go."

The young man made no move to release her and Elizabeth peered up at his defiant gaze through the screen of her own hair, which he held firmly in his left hand. She put her hand over his gently and pulled her curls free. Her voice was sweet, very pleasant as she spoke to him, "Let me go please, Silver Hawk. I did not mean to insult you."

The Indian frowned as he released her, then watched her draw away. "I do not frighten you?"

"No, of course not," Elizabeth lied courageously. "I cannot believe a man who would say thank you, as you did this morning, would want to hurt me now. I'm glad you are feeling better, but even if you have only a small portion of your strength back I know you could kill me. But it would be so unfair of you to harm me after I have undoubtedly saved your life. These are troubled times and strangers here are often dealt with harshly. Surely I do not deserve to die for showing you kindness."

"Why did you do it?" Silver Hawk attempted to sit up but failed. He fell back upon the straw and lay exhausted by his effort to rise.

"Why? First let me help you eat, then we can talk." After a brief hesitation she offered, "If I sit behind you I think your head will fit quite comfortably in my lap." She waited to see if he had any objection to her plan and when he remained silent she moved behind him. "Now I hope you like my soup. It is one of my best recipes."

The man grimaced at the taste but was apparently too hungry to protest more forcefully. He opened his mouth again as she brought the spoon to his lips but clearly he was not pleased.

"You do not like this? Well, when you are better I'll prepare other things, but this is at least warm and I hope it is nourishing. I thought it tasted very good but then I am used to my vegetable soup, and perhaps Indian food is very different."

Elizabeth continued to spoon the soup into the young man's mouth, carefully wiping his chin with a towel. His teeth were even and very white. She was positive he would have a wonderful smile, if Indians ever smiled which she wasn't at all certain they did. She knew nothing more about them than Jed. She recognized an Indian when she saw one and that was all the expertise she possessed.

"You've finished that bowl. Shall I bring you some more?"

"No more, Elizabeth." He said her name slowly, pronouncing each of the four syllables separately.

"You remembered my name? Now I am surprised. Where did you learn to speak English so well, Silver Hawk?"

"I speak English."

"Yes, I know that. We are talking now, aren't we? But where did you learn? Who taught you to speak English? Do you recall who it was?"

The young man frowned again. "I did not learn, I know."

Elizabeth remained seated with his head upon her knees, even though there was no longer any need for such an intimate pose. "Do you mean you have always known English, since you were a small boy?"

"Yes, I have always known it."

"I have heard Indians sometimes take white children and raise them as their own. Were you such a child?"

The man snarled his reply, "I am Silver Hawk, son of the great Seneca chief, Flaming Sky!"

"Are his eyes as green as yours, his skin so fair?"

"What is fair?"

Elizabeth took his hand, lacing his fingers in hers. "Look, your skin is brown but mine is not. I am pale, fair, my skin is light and you are dark but only where your skin is tanned from the sun."

Silver Hawk's eyes widened noticeably. "You looked at me?"

"No, not all of you, certainly not. But your skin is as fair as mine, Silver Hawk. I do not believe you are an Indian at all."

"I am Indian. Silver Hawk, son of Flaming Sky!"

Elizabeth continued to be patient and ignored his temperamental outburst. "Yes, I understand, but does Flaming Sky have eyes as green as yours and mine?"

"His eyes are black like the night, like my mother's eyes."

"I see, well, tell me then, how many of your tribe have green eyes? Are there many Seneca braves with eyes so green as yours?"

The young man was silent for a long while then at last answered, "Only Silver Hawk."

"Only you?"

He nodded this time and Elizabeth realized he still held her hand in his. His grip was relaxed though, not forceful, and she did not pull away. She touched his long hair lightly with her fingertips. It was a rich deep brown which curled softly, not black and straight as she thought an Indian's hair would be.

"Can you remember being small, Silver Hawk? Are you certain you are not an adopted son, a white man, not truly an Indian?"

His hand tightened upon her wrist until she would have cried out in pain had she not willed herself to be silent. "Does that upset you? To remember, or to think you might be white, which is it? Do you hate us so?"

26

"I am not hurting you?" Silver Hawk was puzzled. He could feel her delicate bones under his fingers, a little more pressure and they would snap like twigs in his grasp.

"Yes, you are hurting me badly. Please stop."

Silver Hawk did not release her but he did not increase the strength he had exerted upon her wrist either. "I am Indian."

"Is that what you want me to say? All right then, you are a fair skinned, green-eyed Indian. Does that satisfy you?" When he released her wrist she rubbed it briskly but it was too late. The dark purple blotches would not go away. "Do you want me to look as gruesome as you do? How did John Cummins capture you, Silver Hawk? How did he catch a young man as strong as you? Now tell me the truth. Don't be embarrassed."

"I have forgotten, what is embarr—?"

"Embarrassed? Ashamed, don't think I will laugh at you. Just tell me how he did it."

"He and his partner jumped from a tree," he explained.

"I see. They must have hit you over the head to knock you out, then tied you up. Is that how they did it?"

"Yes, they tied and beat me."

"With a whip obviously, but they burned you too, didn't they? Took wood from their camp fire and burned you?"

"One wanted to burn my eyes."

Elizabeth felt sick. He might be able to describe his ordeal calmly, but she could not bear to imagine what he must have suffered, and for what? Was being an

Indian a crime in itself? She was the one who felt ashamed then, for she knew it had been the unusual shade of his eyes which had led her to trust him.

"I will work three months and no more," Silver Hawk declared firmly, their bargain still weighing heavily upon his mind. He had no interest in discussing his misfortune any further.

"Yes. I will count ninety days from the first one you are able to work. At the end of that time you may simply tell me good-bye and be on your way."

"What must I do?" As he looked up at her the green of his eyes was dulled by pain, their color now a soft slate gray.

"We grow wheat and corn on our farm. The crop has been planted but there is still much to be done to see that it thrives and the harvest is a good one. We raise a few pigs each spring to have meat for the winter and they need tending. The horses are my father's pride. He raises them to sell, so they must be well groomed and cared for. I tend the vegetable garden myself, milk the cow, feed the chickens and gather their eggs. I'll not need your help. You'll be working with Jed but I won't expect you to complete any task alone until you've learned how I want it done." Elizabeth paused, attempting to choose her words to make her point clear. "Jed has worked for my father since before I was born but he is not as strong as he once was, which is why I needed another hand to help him."

"He cannot work and still you pay him?" the Indian asked with amazement.

"Jed will always have a home here with us, but he

can work. I didn't mean to make it sound as if he couldn't. He might work at a slower pace than he did in years past, but he earns his pay."

"And I must earn mine?" Silver Hawk moved so swiftly Elizabeth had no chance to escape him as he sat up and, catching her in an easy embrace, pulled her down across his lap where he held her captive in his arms. His mouth found hers soft and pliant beneath his own. Her lips parted to protest his unexpected action, but she could not stop his warm tongue from filling her mouth as easily as if she'd always been his woman. He ran his fingers through her bright curls as his lips caressed hers in a kiss he had no desire to ever end, for her taste was too sweet, delicious and he savored it to the fullest before finally drawing away with a wicked grin. "Is that not what you really want of me?" Yet where he'd expected acceptance he saw only the wildest rage.

As she leapt to her feet, Elizabeth screamed a hostile denial, "No! Don't you ever touch me again or I'll take a whip to you myself and give you the thrashing you deserve! I'll make what Cummins did to you look like a child's prank! I don't have to buy men, far from it. I have many fine suitors without the likes of you!" She turned and fled swiftly to the house, slammed the door and shoved the bolt in place, her chest heaving with the effort of her flight. What had made that Indian brave think she wanted him to kiss her? Her knees felt weak and she sagged back against the sturdy wood, grateful for the protection of her well-built home. She'd never let Daniel put more than a light kiss upon her cheek. What had made Silver Hawk think she'd be so eager for his affection that she'd accept the kind of kiss he'd dared give her? Raising her fingertips to her lips she wondered outloud, "Was that no more than a kiss?" Hot tears of anger poured down her cheeks. She'd issued no idle threat. Should he so much as touch her again she'd thrash him soundly.

Two

Early the following morning Jed stood aside to allow Silver Hawk to precede him through the back door. While still apprehensive, he'd found the Indian not nearly so frightening as when he'd first encountered him. "I did what I could to make the lad presentable, Miss Elizabeth. He seems well enough to work today."

Elizabeth clenched her fists at her sides as she turned, not eager for another confrontation with the man whose fate she now wished she'd left to the whim of the magistrate in Oak Grove. She could only stare in astonishment however, for freshly shaven, his hair neatly brushed and tied at his nape, wearing one of Jed's soft muslin shirts with his buckskins, he was obviously a white man and an extremely handsome one at that.

Seeing her surprise, Jed spoke up quickly, "My shirt's a poor fit I know. Perhaps Olaf might have an old one. He's more Silver Hawk's height and size than I am."

"What? Oh, yes." Elizabeth forced herself to look solely at her old friend rather than at his distracting companion. "I'll see what I can find. I'd forgotten he'd need clothes but at least my father can't complain I've allowed a half-naked Indian to dine at his table."

"I will be Indian still," Silver Hawk offered slyly, apparently greatly amused by her remark.

Elizabeth glanced down at the deep purple bruise which circled her wrist and readily agreed. "We need not debate that issue any further. Everything's ready for your breakfasts. I'll tend to the milking while you men eat." With that hurried explanation Elizabeth slipped past them and picking up her pail ran toward the barn.

By the time she returned to the house, Elizabeth had regained her composure and coolly explained what she wanted the men to do that morning. "Jed has been meaning to replace some fence posts. Do you truly feel well enough to work, Silver Hawk?"

"Yes, I can help him." He shrugged, then forced himself not to let the pain that gesture had caused him show in his face but his back still felt as if it were on fire. "I want you to begin counting the days today."

"I have the posts cut and loaded on the wagon, Miss Elizabeth. At least that much is done," Jed explained helpfully.

"Good. I didn't realize you'd gotten that far with the project." Yet as they walked out into the yard Elizabeth hesitated to send the men off alone, for the Indian had taken unfair advantage of her kindness the previous afternoon and she would not be taken for such a fool ever again. "I think I will come with you. There's plenty of room for the three of us to ride together."

"Do you work on fences, Elizabeth?" The Indian could not believe Jed would ask the young girl to do such hard work. "Must you do a man's work on this farm?"

Elizabeth's bright curls shone with the sparkle of the morning sunlight as she shook her head. "No, never. I just thought I'd go along to watch. You say you are well, but perhaps you are not."

Silver Hawk's green eyes smoldered with contempt. "I told you I would do your work here. Why did you accept my word yesterday if you were going to doubt it today?"

Surprised by his question, Elizabeth realized she had no choice but to trust him. She glanced over at Jed and he nodded reassuringly. "All right, but do not push yourself past what you can comfortably do, for if you should fall ill you will be worthless to me." With a spritely turn she left them on their own and went about her own business.

The sun was high overhead when Elizabeth heard a familiar voice calling her name loudly. She leaned her hoe against the back of the house and left her garden to greet Daniel MacGregar. He was smiling proudly, obviously greatly pleased with himself for he was seated astride her favorite mare, Lady.

"Good day, Daniel. What brings you this way?" Elizabeth inquired nonchalantly, longing to hug her dear horse but not wanting to give the smirking young man that satisfaction.

"I've come to see you, of course." Daniel slipped down from the mare's back and strode toward the pretty blonde. "I believed none of the tale that trapper spun, but he showed me a bill of sale with your signature, so I knew Lady had not been stolen."

"No, it was a fair trade." Elizabeth lifted her hand to shade her eyes from the afternoon sun. Daniel's face was as familiar to her as her own. His features were even but as usual posed in too sarcastic an expression for him to be considered truly handsome. His black hair shone with blue highlights and his brown eyes taunted her with a sweeping glance. He was of medium height, a scant two inches taller than she, with a solid, muscular build the power of which she'd too often seen him use against those he could not dominate by his wits alone. His family was prosperous, their farm more than twice the size of her father's, but although Daniel was regarded as the most eligible bachelor in Oak Grove, she had grown weary of his attentions.

"Where is the savage? I'd like a look at him."

"He's working with Jed repairing the fence along the western boundary."

"Ah," Daniel grinned smugly, showing off slightly crooked teeth. "Then we are alone here."

"What of it?" Elizabeth demanded. She placed her hands on her slender hips and said pointedly, "State your business and be gone, Daniel. I have work to do and must see to it."

The young man reached out, placing his hands upon her shoulders to draw her near. "Why do you treat me so badly, Elizabeth? I thought it would please you to know I'd bought your mare."

Tolerating his touch for no more than an instant, Elizabeth pulled free. "I am grateful to learn she'll have a good home, that is true."

Daniel frowned dejectedly, hurt by her curt rebuff. "I meant to give her back to you as a gift."

"Did you now?" Elizabeth looked behind him. "And how did you expect to return home since you brought no other mount with you?" That was just like him, she thought to herself, for Daniel had far more bravado than brains.

"I mean her for a wedding present," Daniel admitted reluctantly, scanning her expression for some small sign of acceptance.

"Then you may have to keep her for many years before she can be such a gift, as I have no plans to marry in the near future, none at all. Now I am very busy and must bid you good day."

As Elizabeth turned away Daniel reached out to catch her arm in a firm clasp. "You're wrong, Elizabeth. You'll be my wife before the summer is out if I have my way!"

Struggling to get free, Elizabeth smiled broadly as the wagon rolled into the yard and Jed and Silver Hawk leapt down from the high seat. The Indian had cast off his shirt, loosened his hair and looked thoroughly fierce as he stood staring at his young mistress and her companion.

Daniel released Elizabeth swiftly. "My God, is that the man?"

"Why, yes." Elizabeth motioned gracefully. "Please come here a moment, Silver Hawk. I'd like you to meet one of our neighbors, Daniel MacGregar. Daniel, this is Silver Hawk, my new field hand."

The Indian crossed the short distance in three long strides, but did not offer his hand. He stood at Elizabeth's side and glared resentfully at her visitor.

Daniel backed away, grabbing hurriedly for Lady's reins. He pulled himself upon her back. "Until the Sabbath, Elizabeth. I will speak with you then."

"Good-bye." Elizabeth waved briefly, then spoke to the Indian. "You have completed the fence already?"

"Yes, it is done. When my people build a fence, we

35

use the whole tree. It is little work to dig holes for the slender posts you have. Do you wish to go see it?" Silver Hawk challenged hoarsely.

"No, not today." Elizabeth continued to watch as Daniel rode away at a gallop, her throat tightening into a painful knot as she saw her horse disappear into the distance. She'd quite forgotten the man at her side until he spoke again.

"One of your fine suitors?" he asked sarcastically.

"Perhaps." Elizabeth saw no reason to explain more to the arrogant young man since he was little more than a stranger.

"When is the Sabbath?"

"That is another name for Sunday, three days hence. We go to church rather than work. It is the Lord's day and we worship him and rest."

"I may not work?" Silver Hawk asked defiantly. "You said I must stay ninety days, but if I may not work one day in seven I will have to stay here one hundred five days rather than ninety and that is not fair!"

"What?" Elizabeth's eyes widened in surprise. The man was clearly furious with her again and she had done him no wrong. "Come inside for a moment. I had not even considered the Sabbath when we made our agreement and I should have done so." She entered her home and, taking her slate from the small table in the corner, sat down at the dining table and quickly made her own calculations, astonished to find he had made his so rapidly in his head. "Yes, you are right. Thirteen weeks is ninety-one days, but if I do not count Sundays, you must stay here fifteen weeks." Glancing up she saw him watching her closely,

36

apparently fascinated by her columns of neat figures. She pushed the slate across the table to him. "You were correct. I wrote exactly what you said."

"Yes, I can see. I can still read numbers as well as words."

"Why do you say still?" Elizabeth asked curiously.

"I know how to read and write," Silver Hawk proclaimed proudly, annoyed she did not believe that he could.

"Show me." Elizabeth erased the slate and handed him the thin pencil.

Silver Hawk fingered the instrument awkwardly for a moment, then leaned down and printed one word in neat block letters, ANDREW.

"Do you know what that says, what that word is?" Elizabeth was stunned. It had to be his name. It just had to be, but Andrew what?

"Andrew. It is my name." He looked up at her, his expression one of amazement. The word had apparently startled him even as he had written it.

"Do you see these ugly purple bruises on my wrist? You are a fair skinned, green-eyed Indian named Andrew, are you? You are no Indian, Silver Hawk, and you know it! Would you have broken my arm just to hear me repeat your lies?" Elizabeth spoke angrily, but he had hurt her and so needlessly too.

Silver Hawk snarled his reply in a tone that left no further room for argument. "I am Indian. I did not lie!"

Elizabeth jumped back, startled by the ferocity of his response. She drew in a deep breath and attempted to make him see reason. "Yes, you were raised by the Seneca so you are one. Anyone could see you are an

37

Indian, Silver Hawk. Forgive me, but if your name was Andrew, can you recall the rest? Your last name too? If you can then maybe we can find out what happened to your family if they weren't all killed when you were taken."

The green-eyed man shook his head. "My family is Seneca. My parents and three sisters are all living."

Seeing her efforts to discover his true identity were futile, Elizabeth held her temper and returned to their original topic. "I will leave the decision to you. If you wish to work only six days each week you may do so, or you may work seven and go home that much sooner. The choice is yours to make."

His expression still serious, Silver Hawk inquired softly. "Do all your suitors go to your church?"

"Yes, of course, but why should that concern you?" Elizabeth responded in a puzzled tone.

"MacGregar is a coward. Are the others fools also?"

Elizabeth grabbed the slate and pointed toward the door. "I'll not allow you to insult my friends, Andrew, or Silver Hawk, or whomever you might be! Now go and find Jed. Get back to work. I have no more time to waste with you!" She got up and marched to the stove, intent upon checking the fire in the oven, although she had nothing cooking. When she looked back over her shoulder ready to insist he leave, she was amazed to find he'd already gone and she was quite alone in the house.

Sunday morning Elizabeth dressed in her prettiest dress, a pale blue linsey-woolsey she'd made herself, and picking up her bonnet and Bible went out the front door expecting to find Jed waiting with the wagon ready to drive her into Oak Grove for church. Instead she found Silver Hawk neatly groomed and dressed, ready to accompany her.

"You should not go alone," he explained reasonably. "If I go to see you are safe and watch the team, that is work." He took her hand to help her up, then leapt up beside her and taking the reins clucked to the horses.

Elizabeth was annoyed. The ride was not a long one but she'd expected Jed to go with her. He was not a churchgoer himself but drove the horses whenever her father was away. "Jed is not ill, is he? He seemed fine when I saw him earlier this morning." Elizabeth looked around the yard, hoping to see the older man.

Silver Hawk drew the team to an abrupt halt. "Are you afraid to go with me, or ashamed to?"

Finding his contempt-filled gaze difficult to return, Elizabeth looked away. "No, neither. I am only worried about my friend, that is all." In the past few days they had enjoyed an uneasy truce and she had no desire to upset the delicate balance which existed between them.

Starting the team again, the young man nodded. "He is well, but how can he rest if he must escort you into town?"

Elizabeth stole a glance at her companion, her thick fringe of lashes disguising her curiosity. "That is kind of you to consider his comfort. I will count this as work for you then."

"Good." After a long silence he spoke again, his tone far less demanding as he asked, "Will you call me Andrew?"

"Andrew is an unusual name for an Indian," Elizabeth remarked drily, not daring to watch his reaction.

"It is my name," Andrew answered softly, not offended. "I want you to call me Andrew."

"It is a small matter. I do not mind." Looking out over the fields Elizabeth felt only the beauty of the spring morning and did not mind granting such a small favor.

"Jed told me your father will return home soon. Do you know when?" Andrew asked casually.

"I'm not certain. In a week or two perhaps. It depends on how he found his brother and his family. Sometimes he stays longer than a month."

"He leaves you alone for so long?" he inquired incredulously.

"I am not alone!" Elizabeth laughed out loud at his question. "Jed is with me and now you are here, too."

Andrew frowned, not pleased by her frivolous mood. "How will you tell your father about me?"

"Why, I'll tell him the truth, of course. What else could I say?"

Andrew predicted calmly, "He will not want me to stay."

"Your bargain is with me, Silver Hawk, Andrew, I mean. He will have no choice but to let you remain. Are you worried about meeting my father? You needn't be. He is a young man and a very nice one."

"I am not afraid!" Andrew scowled, insulted by her question.

Elizabeth placed her hand lightly upon his sleeve, then removed it quickly when he shot her a disapproving glance. "I did not say frightened. I said worried. There is a great deal of difference between the two words. It is obvious to me you are a brave man. Now do you see the fork ahead? Oak Grove is to the left." Elizabeth opened her Bible and tried to read, although the dirt road was too uneven to allow such an effort with any success, but at least Andrew did not bother her again with any more questions. He was an astonishing man in many respects, she realized. She'd bargained only for a strong back, but he was far too clever a man to be regarded solely as a laborer. When they reached the church, he swung her down from the seat as effortlessly as if she'd weighed no more than a small child, his hands spanning her narrow waist easily.

"Would you care to attend the service?" Elizabeth asked politely.

Andrew glanced over her head at the curious stares directed his way and shook his head. "No, I will wait here with the wagon."

"As you wish." Elizabeth turned away, scanning the gathering crowd for Daniel and his family, and seeing the young man making his way toward her, made no effort to elude him. She took his arm as they started for the door, but before they could enter the small wooden building, Andrew brushed by her side.

"I have decided to come with you," he whispered, bending down slightly so only she could hear.

Elizabeth hid her amazement as best she could, but as they reached their pew Andrew slipped behind her so Daniel was left sitting beside him on the aisle. She covered her smile with her fingertips so as not to laugh

41

out loud, but Daniel's outraged expression was almost worth it. When she looked up at Andrew, his gaze was quite innocent as he glanced about the stark interior of the church but she knew better. He'd sat down beside her to deliberately provoke the young man he'd called a coward and she hoped he knew what he was doing. He might enjoy fighting for sport. She'd heard Indians did, but he'd not do it while he was in her employ. Her smile faded as she realized what a scene he might create, and she heard little of the Reverend Williams' sermon although she heard serveral of those seated around them remark it was the finest he'd ever given.

By the time they were ready to depart, Elizabeth was beside herself with anger, so livid she could scarcely see. She enjoyed attending church because it provided an opportunity for her to see all her friends, but whenever anyone had approached her, the tall man by her side had moved to block their way. Without ever speaking a word his proud stance and hostile stare kept everyone away. Daniel had simply sulked, his gaze black, as he'd glared at her from a distance, surrounded by his friends. She'd expected better of him, and frustrated beyond endurance, she returned to the wagon and climbed up into the seat unassisted. She said nothing until they'd left the small town far behind. Then she put her hands over Andrew's, taking the reins from him and pulling the team to a halt.

"How dare you behave in such a fashion? I am not some precious bit of property that must be protected! You had no right to frighten my friends away so rudely, you are not my—"

"Husband?" Andrew offered slyly.

"No! I was about to say father! Is there no end to your conceit?" Elizabeth was thoroughly disgusted by his obnoxious smirk.

"I am too young to be your father." Andrew found her comment amusing and laughed heartily at her distress. He had a very pleasant laugh, rich and deep as if he enjoyed good jokes and laughed often.

Elizabeth stared at him for a moment, her mood turning from anger to curiosity. "Just how old are you, Andrew?"

After a moment's pause he decided to reply truthfully. "Twenty-eight. Far too young to be your parent."

"How old do you think I am?" Elizabeth asked caustically.

"Eighteen, I think, or nineteen. No more." Andrew looked her up and down slowly, his appreciative glance lingering upon her shapely curves just a moment too long.

"Well, you're wrong. I will not even be sixteen until September. Now let us go. We've wasted enough time sitting here."

"I did not stop the team," Andrew protested immediately.

"Oh!" Elizabeth shrieked in frustration, then slapped the reins upon the horses' backs before thrusting them into his hands. "Here, you drive the team."

Andrew closed his hands over her fingers, catching them in a tight clasp. "If I may not touch you, then you must not touch me."

Elizabeth's eyes smoldered with contempt. "I am

not touching you, not pawing you. I merely handed you the reins!"

Andrew ignored her attempts to pull free. His hands covered hers firmly and she could not escape. "Does MacGregor kiss you as I did?"

Elizabeth felt her cheeks redden with a bright blush at the impertinence of that question. "How he wishes to kiss me is none of your business!" Finally yanking her hands from his in a burst of fury, she jumped down from the wagon and sprinted away, running across the fields toward her home, not daring to spend another second with the man she was fast learning to despise. A whipping would be too good for him, but she could think of no other punishment should he dare to take advantage of her again.

Elizabeth spoke not one word during the midday meal, a fact which was not lost on Jed. He'd seen her come home alone which was a curious circumstance indeed, but when he'd asked the Indian what had happened, the young man turned away to unhitch the team, obviously unwilling to discuss the subject. He did not enjoy sitting with the two attractive young people when their dislike for each other created such tension. At his first opportunity, he excused himself and went outside to sit on the porch.

Andrew found he had no appetite either and pushed his plate away. "I am no farmer, Elizabeth. I will do your work because I gave my word, but I would rather hunt. The forest which runs beside your fields is filled with deer. I can provide meat for your table. Would that not be more useful?"

Surprised by the mellow tone of his voice, Elizabeth

looked up slowly. "I cannot allow you to take my father's musket, but when he returns he may loan it to you for he loves venison and has little opportunity to hunt himself."

Andrew shook his head emphatically. "No! Cummins and his friend burned my bow and arrows, but I can make new weapons. I do not want your father's musket." Clearly he thought the idea ridiculous. "I have already gathered strong branches, but Jed's knife is but a small one and I need another."

"A knife?" Elizabeth swallowed with difficulty, then thought herself foolish. Even if Jed's knife were not suitable for fashioning weapons, Andrew had had ample opportunity to steal it and kill her with it had he wished to do so. For that matter, he could undoubtedly snap her neck with his bare hands. He needed no weapon to dispatch her should he so desire. She got up and went to look through those she used for cooking and came back quickly. "Will this knife do? The steel blade is well made and very sharp, or if not there are others." She placed the knife on the table then turned back to see what else she could find.

"Elizabeth?" Andrew called softly.

"Yes?" As she turned he threw the knife with astonishing speed. It lodged in the wall beside her, no more than four inches from her cheek. She pulled it out with a forceful tug and commented flippantly, "I'm sorry to see you're no better than that with a knife. Not only did you miss me, but that was too high to kill me with any certainty either. Try again." She thrust the point of the blade into the table top a hair's breadth from his hand. If he'd wanted to see her go

45

shrieking hysterically from the house, his plan had failed, for her gaze was as defiant as his, a blazing green fire reflecting his own inner light.

Andrew stood up slowly, then circled the table to face her. "You are a very brave girl, Elizabeth. If you are not afraid of Indian braves, nor of knives, why did a kiss terrify you so?"

"That was not terror, but disgust! Now take the knife and make whatever you need and I shall expect to see venison upon the table before the week is out!"

Andrew nodded slightly. "I will not disappoint you."

"You already have. See that you don't do it again." Turning abruptly, Elizabeth picked up her milking pail and got halfway out the back door before realizing it was far too early to bring in the cow from the pasture. To avoid looking foolish, she left the bucket on the back steps and went out to her garden to see what had grown ripe enough to pick for supper.

In the days that followed, Elizabeth kept her conversations with Andrew to a minimum. Each morning she and Jed would decide what the young man should do that day, then the older man saw the work was completed satisfactorily. Not only were they able to keep up with their daily chores, but Andrew also enlarged Jed's living quarters so he could move out of the barn. While he joked easily with Jed as they worked, he had become as silent as Elizabeth during meals, speaking only when Jed spoke to him and making no effort to initiate any conversation himself.

By the end of the week Elizabeth had grown weary of Andrew's sullen silence. She'd begun to feel strangely guilty, as if she'd said or done something wrong even though she knew she had not. Still, a nagging sense of remorse grew within her until she could no longer bear it. When Andrew sat down on the porch after supper to work on his arrows, she went outside to join him, determined to be friendly. He had been working diligently each evening since she'd given him the knife and was now cutting slits in the ends of the smooth wooden shafts for feathers. She picked up one of the slender arrows and admired its precision. "I had no idea these would be so difficult for you to make but they are perfect."

Andrew looked up, surprised by her interest. "They are worthless if they are not straight."

"Yes, I understand why." Elizabeth lay the arrow aside and watched him work awhile longer. His fingers were long and slim, his touch light as he fit the feathers into the three grooves he'd made. When he did not speak again, she tried another tack. "Before my parents married, my mother worked in a fine home in Philadelphia. She used to tell me amusing stories about the city and its people so I'd know there was a world far different from the one here on our farm. But I know little of Indians and what your life has been. It was unreasonable of me to expect you to make weapons and go hunting in one week's time. Please forgive me for demanding it."

Without breaking the rhythm of his handiwork, Andrew responded confidently, "I will do it."

"But you needn't, Andrew. I was angry with you.

Go hunting when you have the time and are ready, not before." Elizabeth was disappointed he'd not accepted her apology but continued to sit silently by his side.

When he realized she was going to stay, Andrew admitted hesitantly, "I should not have thrown the knife, but I was angry too."

"No, you most certainly should not have done that, Andrew." Her father would shoot him without hesitation if he ever heard about that stunt, she realized with a sudden chill. "Why were you angry with me? You had no reason to be."

The young man laid the knife aside while he got to his feet and gathered up his arrows, then slipped the steel blade carefully under his belt. "A woman cannot tell any man, Indian or white, that she does not want him and be surprised when he is angry. Are you too young to know that, or simply too foolish?"

Elizabeth had noted on more than one occasion that Andrew's English was flawless when he wished to insult her. He might reply in monosyllables all day and then unleash his temper without warning. She rose also and faced him squarely. "I have made it plain from the day we met that all I want from you is a good day's work. That's all I'll ever want and I've made no secret of it."

Andrew stepped closer, his voice honey smooth as he whispered, "A whipping will be a slight price to pay for what I want from you, Elizabeth." He watched the light in her eyes change from defiance to fright and smiled with deep satisfaction. "You will give me what I want, and willingly too!"

"Never!" Elizabeth struck him with a force which

48

left the print of her small hand plainly visible upon his tan cheek, then turned and walked into her house. She was appalled, infuriated by his boastful promise and vowed never to speak another kind word to him ever again. She would die first!

Sunday morning Elizabeth dressed slowly, trying to think of some excuse to avoid another impossible journey to church with Andrew by her side, but Jed came into the house for breakfast alone.

"Your Indian's gone hunting. He left before dawn."

"He is not my Indian!" Elizabeth responded fiercely then, seeing the gentle man's shock at her harsh rebuke, apologized. "Forgive me, but he is neither Indian nor mine."

Jed slid into his place at the table. "I say he is both and Olaf will be far from pleased about him. You know that, don't you?"

Elizabeth's pretty lips were set in a thin line as she moved toward the door. "I know nothing of the kind. I will wait on the porch. We'll leave after you've eaten."

The church service seemed interminable that morning. Elizabeth's head throbbed with a steady ache as the prayers continued past the usual time for dismissal. Daniel was fidgeting nervously at her side, no more able to concentrate than she was. She glanced up at him frequently, as if they'd just met rather than having known each other all their lives. She'd always regarded his interest in her with a bit of pride. He was nineteen and she'd considered him a grown man until . . . She sat up abruptly, forcing Andrew's attractive image from her mind, but it continued to taunt her. He was so different from Daniel, far more

49

handsome, tall and lean, yet powerfully built. His proportions as well as his features as perfect as a pagan god's. His mind was far keener than Daniel's too, for he had a ready wit which unfortunately was too frequently turned against her. Had he truly gone hunting, or had he simply left, walked out on their bargain rather than staying to see it through? Her cheeks paled at that prospect, that he could be gone, vanished from her life as swiftly as he'd entered it, never to return. But no, he'd been far too insistent in his vow to take her to leave. That was obviously all he wanted from her, to satisfy his lust at her expense. Daniel was no less obvious in what he wanted, she realized suddenly, but he had spoken of marriage on more than one occasion where Andrew certainly never would. That thought shocked her. What a husband that man would make!

She listened with scant interest to her friends' chatter after dismissal. Their trivial concerns bored her and while more than one had asked where her Indian might be, she'd said only that he'd gone hunting and turned their other questions about him aside. With any luck, he'd hunt every Sunday and she'd never have to bring him into Oak Grove again.

"May I call at your home this afternoon, Elizabeth?" Daniel took her elbow as he escorted her to her wagon and helped her up to the seat.

"You know that would not be proper with my father gone. I cannot invite you today." Elizabeth was glad for the excuse for she was not in the mood for his company.

"Then when?"

"Perhaps he'll come home this week and next

Sunday you could come home with us for dinner. Would you like that?"

"Yes, of course, but only if that savage does not share your table. I'm glad you did not bring him today. Leave him home after this."

"What gives you the right to tell me who may sit at my table and who I may and may not bring to church?" Elizabeth nodded to Jed who clucked to the horses, leaving Daniel choking in a cloud of dust as the animals struck a brisk pace. "Jed! I did not mean for you to do that!" She turned and waved jauntily, hoping Daniel would think Jed's haste mere carelessness rather than the rudeness it had been.

"Well, I have never liked that one, Miss Elizabeth. He is not fit to wipe your shoes, he isn't."

"And you know a man who is?" Elizabeth teased him, wondering whom he might have in mind, for Daniel was clearly the best of the lot in Oak Grove.

Jed gave the pretty blonde a sidelong glance and nodded. "That I do, but he is the bashful sort and may not be able to speak up for himself."

"Bashful? What do you mean, for I have known all the boys in Oak Grove since I was small. None would be too shy to approach me, although I've no doubt Daniel would fight any one who did."

"No, he'd not dare challenge Andrew for you. You know he hasn't the courage to do that."

"Andrew!" Elizabeth shrieked the man's name. "Andrew is not in the least bit bashful, Jed, and should I repeat some of the things he's done and said to me, you would skin him alive!"

Jed laughed, scoffing at her feisty response. "Don't you know a real man when you meet one, girl? Has that young MacGregar pup spoiled your judgment so badly as that?"

"Enough of this topic, Jed. Andrew is no better than the crudest of ruffians. Do not suggest his name to me ever again." She faced straight ahead, seething with anger. Bashful? Why the man was a satyr!

Three

When Olaf Peterson returned home Sunday afternoon he was leading Lady on a rope behind his mount and Elizabeth could scarcely contain her joy as she ran to hug her mare's neck.

"You should kiss me first, Elizabeth!" As a small child Olaf had come to the Colonies from Sweden and his speech still held the musical tones of his first language. He was glad to be back home as his journey had been a long and tiring one. "I do not care for the city of Philadelphia nor it's political intrigues which my brother so enjoys. I much prefer the simple life here on my farm with my beautiful daughter, but you love that horse more than me! I might just as well have stayed away for all you missed me."

"I'm sorry, Papa, but you don't know how thrilled I am to have Lady back." Elizabeth hugged him warmly then. Her father was as blond as she, but his eyes were a deep blue and his fair skin tanned dark by years in the sun. He was not yet thirty-five, a young man still and a handsome one. "How did you talk Daniel into giving Lady to you?" Elizabeth held her breath, hoping her engagement had not been settled without her consent.

"He did not give her to me, child. I bought her and

for a high price indeed."

"You bought her for me? What a wonderful present! Thank you!" Elizabeth gave him another affectionate squeeze. "You know I love you. You are the best of fathers!" She did love him dearly and they had grown very close since her mother's death. She knew several women who were most interested in becoming his second wife, but he still seemed far too much in love with her mother to consider remarrying.

"Jed, take the horses. I want to speak to Elizabeth alone." Olaf led his daughter into the house and turned to face her. "Now, I want to hear why you purchased an Indian brave, of all the outrageous things, Elizabeth! What happened to the savage? Where is he? You were lucky not to have been murdered, to have been butchered as you slept! I simply cannot believe you would trade your mare for an Indian. Whatever possessed you to do it?"

Elizabeth took a deep breath and tried to imagine how he felt. The story did sound ridiculous, she had to agree, but it had all seemed so sensible at the time. "Would you like some tea, Papa? This is a long story."

"With you telling it, I've no doubt that it will be. Just get on with it!" Olaf was completely exasperated with her. "You continually think of things to do which get you into all sorts of mischief, but I thought you had more sense than to buy a young Indian brave!"

Elizabeth put the kettle on for tea and ignored her father's temperamental outburst as she tried to describe the circumstance which had inspired her to swap Lady for Andrew. "Jed and I worked so hard, but there was simply too much for the two of us to accomplish alone. It was really the most remarkable thing that the trapper stopped here with Andrew just when I needed another hand so badly, but I didn't truly buy the man. I simply bargained for his freedom."

"Who is Andrew? I thought we were talking about an Indian!" Olaf was used to Elizabeth's tales. She was bright, but a handful for him and he tried to keep his patience with her in order to listen more calmly, but it was difficult. Had she not been so lovely to look at he might never have been able to do it.

"Andrew is the Indian, but that tells you little for he is an extremely complex individual." That was an understatement, she thought bitterly. "He is actually a white man but he was raised by a Seneca chief as his son. He can read and write English as well as speak it, so he must have been tutored or gone to school when he was small. He's agreed to work for me for three months, and I have to admit, he is industrious. He's accomplished more than I ever dreamed he would. Since we had no place for him to sleep, he and Jed enlarged the shed behind the barn to accommodate them both. He built a bunk for himself and a new one for Jed as well as a table and two chairs. Jed says his home is as snug as a captain's cabin now. Apparently the Seneca build homes of wood and the work comes easily to Andrew."

"How old is this Andrew? About your age?" Olaf pursed his lips thoughtfully. He was getting more worried by the minute. "A young Indian brave is one thing, Elizabeth, a young white man quite another, but I don't like the sound of this one bit."

"He is twenty-eight, a full grown man, not a youth. He's gone hunting today, but he should be home

55

soon." Elizabeth thought perhaps she should say something more to prepare her father to meet him and continued with the only information she dared relate. "He is very intelligent, tall, his appearance quite pleasing. His eyes are as green as mine."

"Green-eyed, you say?" Olaf pondered that thought for a moment, then spoke. "That might be an unusual enough characteristic for him to find out who his family was, and I'd think he'd want to know. He's not told you his last name. He uses only Andrew?"

Elizabeth licked her lips anxiously, not relishing the memory of her bitter confrontations with Andrew over his heritage. "He says only that he is Seneca, the son of Chief Flaming Sky. If he knows more he won't tell me. Perhaps he would tell you, though."

"Likely as not he won't." Olaf turned as Jed entered the house carrying his luggage. "Jed, how could you have let Elizabeth trade Lady for some Indian? I cannot understand how you could have been so derelict in your duty to take care of my daughter in my absence." He was clearly annoyed with the man for both his tone and glance were fierce.

"I did not know she had done it until it was too late, sir. But he was beat up something awful, and had I been there I would not have let him be led off to die. You would have done something yourself to help him had you been here."

"That's undoubtedly true, Papa," Elizabeth agreed promptly. "The trapper was going to turn Andrew in for a bounty when he had not a shred of proof he was guilty of any crime."

Olaf's frown deepened. "Why are you two so sure he isn't?"

Jed responded quickly. "I've worked with him for two weeks, sir. He is a fine man. Once you get used to the fact he's more Indian than white, you'll like him too."

"I doubt it."

As if on cue there came a loud rap on the door and when Elizabeth opened it, she found Andrew standing on the front porch, a magnificent stag slung over his shoulder and a wide grin on his face.

Olaf was too shocked to speak. The man looked completely Indian to him. Every inch of him from the eagle feathers braided into his long hair to the moccasins on his feet, he was Indian. As their eyes met he gasped, shocked as Elizabeth had been by the familiar stare for the light in the man's green eyes was both wild and determined sending a chill down the blond man's spine. He could scarcely call the savage before him Andrew when what he was was so very plain.

Elizabeth watched the surprise in her father's expression turn to alarm and moved swiftly to head off an unfortunate scene. "Bring the deer around to the back, Andrew. There will be plenty of time for you to meet my father once you've had a chance to clean up." She closed the door behind them and whispered rapidly, "Skin the beast. I'll want to roast a quarter and make jerky of the rest. When you've finished cutting the meat, bathe and dress in the most gentlemanly fashion you can manage. I don't mind at all if you wish to look like the Seneca you are when you hunt, but for my father's sake, please try and look like a white man tonight."

Andrew laughed as he carried the carcass around to

the rear of the house. "I brought your deer, Elizabeth, but I do not think your father likes venison after all."

"Will you stop making jokes? I am serious! I want my father to like you. Won't you make some effort to impress him?"

Andrew's smile vanished as he replied calmly, "I believe I already did."

"Yes, you most certainly did, but he'll get over his initial shock after he speaks with you and sees what a sensible man you can be. I have the right to expect that much of you tonight, Andrew. I want to see your very best behavior."

Andrew raised an eyebrow quizzically. "Will he demand I leave if he thinks me a savage?"

Elizabeth did not like the evil gleam in Andrew's green eyes, not one bit she didn't. "It matters not at all whether he likes you or not since your bargain was with me and not him."

"Then why must I work so hard to impress him?" Andrew asked logically.

"Because it would make my life, all our lives, so much easier, that's why!" Elizabeth realized she'd been a fool to expect his help and turned away, ready to abandon the effort.

"All right, I will do my best to make him like me, but first you must kiss me as a reward."

"Kiss you!" Elizabeth's long lashes nearly swept her brows, she was so shocked by his demand. "How dare you ask such a thing? I'd sooner kiss the devil himself than you!"

"If that is your choice," Andrew remarked casually. "I will come to dinner as I am, feathers and all." He crossed his arms over his bare chest and glared menacingly, suddenly withdrawing behind the stoic exterior he'd displayed when first they'd met.

"Damn you, Andrew! Come here, and this is no reward but a bribe!" Elizabeth stood on her tiptoes and placed her hands lightly upon his shoulders. She knew better than to turn her cheek and lifted her lips to his, her whole body tense with expectation as she waited for what was to come.

Andrew stared down at her, his gaze critical. "No, you must kiss me as I kissed you."

Elizabeth looked around quickly, wanting to be absolutely certain her father and Jed were still in the house and wouldn't catch her with Andrew. His skin was warm to her palms but he was not making her task any easier and she hated him for it. Slowly she lifted her hands to his neck, winding her fingers in his thick chestnut curls to pull his mouth down to hers. She traced the outline of his lips with a tantalizing caress with the tip of her tongue before invading his slightly open mouth with an assault as deft as his. She felt his whole body shudder with a tremor of desire as his arms tightened around her waist and she clung to him, frightened by his passion, yet his kiss was like magic drawing her closer still and she made no effort to fight his affection until he pushed her away, his eyes filled with contempt.

"It is a shame you are no more than a pretty child playing at being a woman!"

Elizabeth backed away as he pulled the knife she'd given him from his belt. She'd no desire to watch him skin the deer for clearly he'd make a vicious job of it. She was confused by his startling change of mood for she had kissed him, exactly as he'd wanted her to. So why was he so angry? Exasperated, she told him precisely what she thought of him. "No, it is you who continually behaves childishly, for whenever I show you the slightest bit of kindness, you rebel instead of responding in kind. What is it, Indian, your fierce pride that won't allow you to trust a woman, or is it the fact I am a white woman that gives you no peace?" Without waiting for what she knew would be an insulting reply she returned to her father, hoping to coax him into building a fire outdoors so she could roast the venison for supper. At least they would have a fine meal to celebrate his homecoming, and he'd have to thank Andrew for that.

Later that same evening, Olaf Peterson sat nervously trying to eat his supper while attempting not to stare rudely at the stranger at his table. Elizabeth had insisted upon preparing the venison and he had to admit the meat was delicious but he had never felt so ill at ease in his own home. He had been astonished at the transformation in Andrew for he now saw a well groomed and neatly dressed white man in the Indian's place, and for some reason he found that change all the more disconcerting. The man had described his hunt in colorful language and then had politely asked him about his journey to Philadelphia. He had further surprised him then by actually seeming to have some grasp of the situation between England and her colonies, but despite his obvious intelligence, Olaf did not look forward to the man's presence in his home for the next two and half months. Clearing his throat, he continued their discussion. "Events have taken an alarming turn this spring, Andrew. Last month General Gage led seven hundred men from Boston to

Concord to capture a store of arms and munitions. They were fired upon by Minute Men at Lexington Green. The reported casualties were nearly three hundred to the British forces and less than a hundred to the colonials. Such an act of aggression cannot go unpunished by the King."

"The Seneca fought with the British against the French. I was young then, but I know the stories are true."

Olaf had to agree. "Yes, that is correct. The Iroquois did aid in the defeat of the French. The Colonies remained under British rule in part due to the fine warriors of the six Iroquois tribes."

Elizabeth was always eager to join a discussion on politics. "Andrew, what will happen now? The King has sent ten thousand more soldiers here to the Colonies to put down the threat of a rebellion. Many men say the Colonies must be independent of the Crown and perhaps the war was really begun when General Gage's troops were fired upon at Concord. We'll never be free without a long fight. Everyone knows that. If the Iroquois helped the British soldiers before, what will they do now?"

Olaf was aghast at that question. "Elizabeth, I am sick of the talk of war. There was no other subject in Philadelphia! War is not a fit topic for young ladies to discuss!"

Elizabeth disregarded her father's comment. "I am serious, Papa. I really want to know. What will happen, Andrew?"

The handsome young man smiled at her for a moment, then shrugged. "It is a matter for the Council of Chiefs to decide. I do not know which way they would go, what would really be to our best advantage. I will have to consider it for I have not."

"Yes, you really must, Andrew, but I can think of no good reason for your people to be loyal to King George. He is too far away and wants only our taxes, never our happiness. Why, do you know that we may raise sheep, cut their wool and make yarn, but we aren't allowed to weave it into cloth to make our clothes? We are forbidden by the King from weaving! We must send our yarn to England to be woven into cloth which we must then buy back and at a high price, too! What would your people say if the King told them to send all their hides to England to be made into buckskin which they would then have to buy back to fashion their clothes!"

Andrew laughed. "They would say no, Elizabeth. That would be a stupid thing to do. There is no need to send to England for things we can make here ourselves."

Olaf threw up his hands in despair. "Now do you see why I cannot take you to Philadelphia, Elizabeth? Not only do you calmly speak treason, but you incite others to do so as well! Now hush." He could imagine his daughter arguing all night with the Indian and, having no desire to hear it, suggested they all prepare for bed instead.

With her father's return, everyone's burden was lightened, and when Elizabeth found her gardening unbearably tedious, she wandered to their small apple orchard and climbed upon a low limb as she'd done as a child. She'd come there often to be alone with her thoughts after her mother's death, for it had broken her father's heart to have lost the beautiful, young wife he adored and she had not wanted to add to his grief by letting him see her own. Her parents had been so deeply in love, surely her mother had never had the problems she faced with the men she knew, but Elizabeth still longed to ask her advice. Her mother had been dead for more than three years though, so she had no one in whom to confide and was dreadfully afraid she was making life difficult for her father when that had been the furthest thought from her mind the day she'd made her bargain with Andrew.

Andrew paused, bending down to see more clearly through the trees, then changed his course to cross the orchard. Elizabeth did not hear him approach and his voice startled her so badly she nearly fell to the ground, yet when he reached out to grab her waist, she pushed his hands away.

"Oh Andrew, you frightened me. What is it you want?" She smoothed out the skirt of her soft cotton dress as if sitting in trees were one of her usual pastimes rather than an attempt to find comfort in the games of her childhood.

Andrew leaned back against the trunk of the apple tree, his gaze even with hers. "You have your mare back. I saw your father with her just now."

"Yes, he bought her from Daniel yesterday. She is mine once again."

Frowning, Andrew's handsome features slipped easily into his usual stern expression. "If you have your horse, why must I stay?"

"You promised me you would, that's why!" Elizabeth responded indignantly. "I will not allow you to go back on your word." Yet even as she spoke she thought only how attractive he was. He'd tied his hair securely at his nape which gave him something of a civilized appearance, but as usual, he'd gone without a shirt. The long scars from the beating he'd suffered were healing rapidly, growing fainter each day as his tan deepened. He was a handsome sight, young, virile, and impossibly troublesome.

"You have no other reason?" he inquired pointedly, his mood somber.

"No, of course not. What other reason could there possibly be?" Elizabeth drew her hand across her cheek, pulling a stray curl back into place. As she looked up he held her gaze locked in his, insolent, taunting. She knew in an instant what he wanted her to say. "Do all the Indian girls like you, Andrew?"

"Of course they do. Why wouldn't they?" He laughed at her question for it was greatly amusing. Women always liked him, very much indeed. All women that was, except her.

"Well, I am no Indian maiden." Elizabeth stated the fact clearly, hoping he'd see the folly in his incessant pursuit of her.

Andrew reached out to take her hand. His touch was light as his thumb drew lazy circles upon her palm. "I know you are not an Indian girl, Elizabeth. I have always known that."

Daniel had held her hand, shyly, hesitantly, but never had his touch brought the exquisite torture Andrew's now evoked, and she stared at his deeply bronzed fingers and tried to summon the breath to speak. "I still know nothing of you."

"I am what you see," Andrew insisted softly. "There is nothing hidden." Glancing down at his buckskins, he grinned slyly. "Well, very little hidden."

Elizabeth blushed, his teasing as difficult to accept as his hostility but inspired by his intimate mood she spoke sincerely. "It pains me to call you Andrew when I knew you first as Silver Hawk, an Indian brave. That is the way I think of you still. It's as though we're tearing you in two, neither Indian nor white. It would be different if only we knew who you really were, who your true family might have been."

Andrew released her hand abruptly as he straightened up proudly. "I know exactly who I am and my name is the least of it. Why do you understand so little?" He left her to her solitude then. As swiftly as he'd joined her, he slipped through the trees and was gone.

Elizabeth remained perched on the low limb, amazed by the turn of her own thoughts. How would things be any different if they knew Andrew's family name, knew for certain who his people had been? Would she trust his motives then instead of taking offense at each word he uttered? What did it really matter, when he'd be gone so soon? She counted the days absently. She'd known him little more than two weeks and yet the thought his maddening presence in her home would soon come to an end brought a curious sense of loss. He'd only been sweet to her in hopes she'd release him from his promise and when she wouldn't he'd turned on her again, dismissed her as if she were a naughty child rather than his mistress. Well, she'd show him how little she cared what he thought of her!

Despite her resolve, Elizabeth found it impossible to ignore the handsome Indian brave, for after supper her father produced a map and began to interrogate him, and her natural curiosity drew her into their conversation.

"What Elizabeth has told me about your background leads me to believe we might be able to locate your family, Andrew." Seeing the young man's posture stiffen noticeably, Olaf hastened to reassure him. "Are you not curious about your past?"

"Why? It cannot be changed," Andrew replied philosophically.

"That is true, but what if you have family still living? Had I lost Elizabeth, I know I would never rest until I found her again. It is possible your parents have spent the years you lived with the Seneca combing the Colonies for you. I cannot bear to think of such heartbreak. Can you?"

Andrew sighed softly, his interest slight, but when he saw the thoughtful light in Elizabeth's eyes, he gave in. "All right, let us try."

Olaf turned his attention to the tattered map he'd unrolled upon the table. "We are here, Andrew. Our farm borders this forest. Here is the Susquehanna River. If we trace it south we reach the Chesapeake Bay and the Atlantic Ocean. If we follow it north it extends clear to the Seneca lands below Lake Ontario. This map is old. There are many new settlements along the river but the land itself is unchanged."

Andrew regarded the drawings with keen interest. He understood the symbols for he knew the land of the Seneca as well as the territory over which they roamed to hunt and to carry out raids upon their traditional enemies, the Algonquin. "I understand your map. I know where I live now, but I was small when I became Seneca and do not recall the name of my home or of my people."

Elizabeth let her eyes move slowly over the Indian. As always she found the sight of him impossibly distracting but forced herself to concentrate on the purpose at hand. "Can you remember how old you were, Andrew? Then we might pinpoint the year when you were captured."

Andrew turned to face Elizabeth, his gaze growing dark. "I was not captured by the Seneca. I was lost, wandering alone in the forest when my father found me. He took me in, cared for me himself until I was strong. He taught me his language and all I would need to know to be his son."

"Andrew, can you recall nothing before Flaming Sky found you? Nothing about your parents or perhaps brothers and sisters? If you lived on a farm or in a city, you have no memories of either? There is nothing you can tell us to aid in our search?" Elizabeth persisted in her questioning, hoping to find clues to locate his family, but it seemed to be an impossible task. She watched his eyes fill with pain and knew he did remember something, an incident perhaps too horrible to relate, but she wanted him to go beyond that, to the part of his past that would help them find out who he really was, or at least, had been.

Andrew shook his head slowly. "I have tried, truly I have, Elizabeth, but I remember nothing before Flaming Sky's presence. I was no more than eight years old and—"

"Eight!" Elizabeth's pretty green eyes lit with

happiness. "You see, you do remember something important after all! Your age is a valuable clue, Andrew. Are you certain you're twenty-eight years old now?"

"Yes, I do not know the day of my birth as you do but I know I have spent twenty winters with the Seneca, so I am twenty-eight years old."

Olaf printed 1775 neatly upon Elizabeth's slate, then subtracted twenty. "Yes, that makes sense. In 1755 the wars with the French had begun. Many families fled their farms to escape the fighting." He again pointed to the wrinkled map. "Many of the settlers in the western regions of the colonies of New York, Pennsylvania, Maryland, all the way down to Virginia, returned to the eastern settlements where they'd be safe. It is possible your family fell under attack either on their farm or perhaps as they made their way east and were scattered in the resulting chaos. That would explain how you came to be wandering the woods alone."

"Andrew, can you remember traveling with Flaming Sky? Did you cross a long distance before you reached his home? Many days or even weeks? Could he have found you so far south as Virginia?" Elizabeth traced a line across the map with her fingertips as she continued to probe his memory.

Andrew shook his head sadly. "I had been alone for a long time, finding what I could to eat. I remember only that he had food. That was what I needed then, not maps." The young man dismissed the one before him with a sweep of his hand.

Olaf frowned thoughtfully as he appraised the

obvious strength of the man who sat before him. "If you were eight in 1755, you would have been sixteen by the time the war with the French and Indians ended. Last night you said you'd heard stories of the war. I'll bet you heard a lot more than tales, Andrew. You were fighting yourself, weren't you? Isn't a Seneca considered a man when he is sixteen, old enough to be sent out to kill? How many white men are dead because of your skill as a warrior?"

"Papa! It was no crime to slay the French!" Elizabeth exclaimed heatedly.

Andrew looked first at the fair-haired beauty by his side then at her father. "Both the British and the French Armies had Indian allies. I did not count bodies, nor their color."

Elizabeth closed her eyes as the most horrid of images filled her agile mind. No terror could be worse than facing an Indian in battle, of that she was certain, but if Andrew were indeed the murderer John Cummins had claimed him to be, his grim deeds had all been done years before, in a war he'd helped the British to win. "Stop it, both of you. This is pointless. Papa, last night you said the Seneca braves were to be praised for their part in keeping the Colonies for England and now tonight you'll call Andrew a killer for being one of those valiant men? How could you be so unfair?"

Olaf pointed a warning directly at his feisty daughter. "I'll send you to your room if you can't keep a civil tongue in your pretty head. I want you to see this man for whom you so calmly swapped a fine mare for the butcher he is. It matters not upon which side he fought. He is no better than a mercenary, a man hired to kill, and I'll wager he'll do it again at his first opportunity."

Elizabeth grew pale at that prospect, but persisted. "Why shouldn't he have fought the French? His parents, whatever family he must have had were no doubt slaughtered by those villains. Why shouldn't he avenge their deaths as a dutiful son must?"

Olaf opened his mouth to refute her argument, then realized she was right. "Yes, a son has such an obligation, that I will admit, but I want you to see Andrew for what he is, Elizabeth. There is a limit to revenge and I doubt he knows it."

Andrew watched Elizabeth lift her chin proudly and was again impressed by her courage and spirit. He was amazed to hear her defend him so readily, but that she had so little respect for her father confused him. Would she fight any man just for the sport of it? Turning to Olaf he hoped to end their argument. "The war is long over, all revenge taken. How might I find my white parents should I wish to do so?"

Olaf nearly strangled on his own frustration. The young man was staring at him coolly, ignoring his insults and he was forced to give the help he had offered. "Let us first concentrate our efforts in New York since that is closest to Seneca lands. Write to the newspapers in the larger settlements and ask for information concerning the identity of a green-eyed boy named Andrew who disappeared in 1755. Hundreds of children must have perished, or been captured, but their relatives will remember them, if any of those who survived the atrocities of that war are living still. It may be weeks before we hear any word, but I'll not have you living on this farm as an Indian, Andrew. Elizabeth trims my hair. She may cut yours or you can do it yourself, but I want it done within the hour. Next Sunday I shall expect you to attend church services with us also as I'll not have heathens under my roof."

Elizabeth watched the light change in Andrew's eyes, the green brightness in their depths turning hard, and she interrupted quickly, hoping to prevent a bitter argument. "Andrew should not be forced to attend church, Papa, nor to trim his hair. He promised only to work and he does so diligently. We should not demand more of him than that. I know he must find our church service tiring and it is not necessary that our beliefs be his." Pausing for a moment, Elizabeth remembered her invitation. "Oh, yes, I told Daniel he might come for dinner on Sunday if you had returned home."

"Did you now?" Olaf's face lit with a pleasant grin. "It's about time you began to appreciate that young man and what he can provide for your future."

Andrew snorted derisively, then brought his fist to his mouth to cover his gesture with a forced cough. "I want to go to church with you, Olaf. I did not find the service so difficult to understand, and if it would please you I'll allow Elizabeth to trim my hair."

Elizabeth stared, mouth agape, unable to respond as Andrew sat, politely accepting her father's completely unreasonable demands with the greatest of ease where only moments before she'd seen him on the verge of an explosive burst of temper. What in heaven's name was the man doing? He detested their bargain, fought her at every turn and now he would calmly volunteer to

71

attend church and cut his hair? It made no sense at all to her, but she brought her scissors from her sewing basket and offered, "Let's go outside on the front porch. The light is still good enough for me to see what I'm doing."

As Andrew drew his shirt over his head and tossed it on the porch rail, Olaf winced. "Elizabeth said you'd been abused. I did not realize how badly."

"Just sit down on the steps, Andrew, and I'll kneel behind you. Actually I think your back looks very good. The slashes are healing nicely." Elizabeth reached out to touch the scars which crisscrossed the muscular bands of his broad back then dropped her hand quickly when she saw her father's disapproving frown.

Andrew laughed at her unexpected compliment for he cared little how badly his back was scarred. "You were a good nurse, Elizabeth. You could not have taken better care of me had I been your horse!"

"Oh, Andrew, you hush." The pretty blonde knelt behind him as he sat down on the top step. She untied the black ribbon which held his hair in place and tried to decide how best to begin. The curls felt soft to her fingertips, their brown color rich and glossy with a faint auburn sheen, and she found it difficult to concentrate on her task and at last leaned down to whisper to Andrew. "You'll want to wear your hair tied back since most white men do. I will leave it as long as I can so when you go home you will not be embarrassed."

"It will grow, Elizabeth. Just cut," Andrew chuckled, surprised she would consider his feelings as she never had. Yet as he sat in the pale light of the gathering dusk enjoying her gentle caress, his agile mind begin working upon a plan. He had to appear the most willing of workers, the most responsible of men to impress her father or the man would force him to leave and he was not yet ready to go. He watched Olaf slyly through his thick fringe of eyelashes, judging his height and weight accurately with his keen powers of observation, skills he had been carefully taught, for to misjudge an opponent could prove to be a fatal error and one he did not intend to make. Elizabeth had said her father was young. Why had he not believed her? Olaf might fight well to keep his beautiful daughter, but Andrew knew the man would never win. A slow smile played over his mouth, betraying the sensuous theme his thoughts had taken but Olaf saw only the growing heap of dark curls and satisfied Elizabeth was doing a good job, walked back into the house.

Four

Believing her father's presence would discourage Andrew from disgracing her again, Elizabeth rode to church seated between the two men, her heart light and free of care. She would speak sweetly to Daniel, perhaps flirt with him a bit. He'd accompany them home for dinner and then Andrew would be able to see firsthand what a charming and popular young woman she truly was, not simply a child posing as a woman as his insults continually claimed. Her plan went even more smoothly than she had hoped, for Daniel drew her aside to sit with his family while her father followed Andrew into their usual pew. When after the service Daniel escorted her out into the sunshine, she saw Andrew walk away rapidly, apparently preferring to wait at their wagon rather than meet any of her father's friends.

Engrossed in conversation with several of her girl friends, Elizabeth laughed happily at their gossip until she turned to speak to Daniel only to find he'd left her side. She glanced about the various groups remaining in the tree-lined courtyard and soon discovered that not only was Daniel missing, but his best friends Ian and Mark Campbell were gone as well. Excusing herself politely, she lifted her skirt and rushed toward the back of the church where the wagon was tied. Expecting the very worst, she was not surprised to hear voices raised in an argument. As she rounded the corner, the fight had already turned vicious, and dazed by Andrew's punishing blows, Daniel MacGregar went sprawling in the dirt and stayed there. Elizabeth ran to her friend's side, ready to tear into Andrew herself when she saw Ian Campbell grab a heavy branch from beneath a fallen tree and circling behind the wagon he approached Andrew stealthily, clearly intending to swing the wooden club at the tall man's head. "Andrew, behind you!" Elizabeth screamed a warning and he spun, catching Ian with a brutal kick to the groin which dropped the hapless youth where he stood, a cry of agony his only response.

Andrew backed away toward the wagon, protecting himself from another unexpected attack and hissed at Mark Campbell, his challenge uttered in the Seneca dialect, but clearly understood. Never as bold as his brother and Daniel, he shook his head and stuttered a shaky refusal before he bent down at Ian's side.

The noise of the fight had attracted a considerable group of onlookers and Andrew turned toward the other young men, silently daring anyone else fool-hardy enough to fight him to come forward and try, but none did.

"Andrew!" Elizabeth pointed at the wagon as she issued a stern order. "We are leaving immediately. Get in the wagon unless you wish to walk home!" She turned to help Daniel rise, but he shoved her away and snarled angrily as he got to his feet.

"It's true! You are that Indian's squaw, no better than his whore!"

Andrew tore past Elizabeth to pluck Daniel up by the front of his shirt. He lifted him clear off the ground and shook him until he was limp as a rag doll, his dangling feet kicking up a dense cloud of dust which flew all around them. He smacked the young bully's already bloody face with the back of his hand as he set him back upon his feet and demanded, "You will take that back, now! Apologize to Elizabeth and then to me!"

Daniel was so dizzy he could scarely stand let alone speak, but as he tried to find the words, he saw Elizabeth leap into her wagon and taking a whip to the team she started toward home, her bright curls flying in the warm spring sunlight. She had never looked more beautiful and he called her name but it was too late. She was gone and his voice was lost on the wind.

By the time she reached home, Elizabeth's fiery temper had not cooled. She called to Jed to take the horses and, tossing her bonnet upon the porch, ran past her garden and through the orchard. On and on she ran so furious she wanted to scream the foulest words she knew. How many people had heard what Daniel had called her? A dozen, maybe more? How many would believe his vile lies? How could she ever hold her head up again when the gossip was sure to be flying all over Oak Grove by now? What would her father do to her, or to Andrew if he believed such ridiculous nonsense to be true? Oh, no! In her haste to leave she'd completely forgotten her father would have no choice but to walk home! Stumbling toward the newly rebuilt fence, she sank down in the tall grass, too exhausted to worry over the discomfort she'd caused him when the good name she'd always had had been ruined by Daniel's jealous lies. What had possessed him to say such dreadful things about her when she had given him so much attention that morning? Was he so great a fool he did not appreciate her interest in him when she freely gave it? Was that the sort of husband he'd be, a man so jealous he'd fight men whom he had no reason to regard as rivals? She was thoroughly disgusted with him for he didn't own her and he never would.

The afternoon sun cast deep shadows across the path as Andrew came over the ridge carrying two pheasants in his left hand and his bow and arrows in his right. He approached Elizabeth slowly and, calling her name softly to wake her, knelt down at her side. Her expression was so sweet he was tempted to lean down and kiss her before she could awaken and fight him. While her hair was blond, her lashes and brows were dark, accenting her finely shaped features with the delicacy of an exquisitely painted China doll. Forcing her beauty's distracting tug upon his emotions to the back of his mind, he called her name once again more loudly.

Elizabeth saw the pheasants immediately and squealed with delight. "Oh Andrew, pheasants. How wonderful for surely there is nothing better to eat this side of paradise!" She sat back then, suddenly embarrassed by her burst of enthusiasm for his dark stare was murderous.

"You should not have left me, Elizabeth. I know you care nothing for me, but Daniel must apologize to you and you were not there to hear it."

The fire of anger swept across Elizabeth's emerald gaze as she hastened to dispute his word. "I will never speak to Daniel MacGregor ever again, so he will have no opportunity to apologize! And as for you . . ." Suddenly lost in the depth of his steady gaze she faltered, uncertain what to say. His heavy fringe of dark lashes cast shadows upon his bronze cheeks and the line of his lips seemed far too sensuous, neither smile nor sneer, but impossibly inviting and she was drawn toward him, captivated by the strength of his muscular body which he'd scarcely bothered to clothe. Tearing her eyes from his she continued, "And as for you, I had no desire to watch you kill or maim Daniel! You deserved to walk home!"

"He will know better than to try and fight me again, but why would he call you my squaw? How could he be so stupid?"

Elizabeth folded her hands calmly in her lap. Daniel frequently behaved in a stupid fashion, but she'd not admit that to Andrew. "He was merely jealous for he has always considered me to be his future bride, but that possibility no longer exists for I shall not wed a man who has so little respect for my good name."

Andrew persisted, still puzzled. "Was this matter settled before I came here? You wanted to marry that buffoon?"

"Andrew, really!" Elizabeth could not help but laugh. "No, nothing was settled. Daniel had not spoken to my father for his permission to marry me, but he has always made it known that he intended to do so."

"Is that all a man must do here to have a wife, just ask a man for his daughter?" Andrew asked incredulously.

"No, it's not quite so simple as that. First, the man

usually tries to impress the young woman he hopes to marry. He wants her to want him for a husband and when he is certain she does then he'll ask her father's permission to marry her."

Andrew looked away, his glance traveling over the rolling field of growing grain. "What if the father says no, then what happens?"

Elizabeth shrugged. "I suppose the young man would have to find another bride, unless—"

"Unless what?" Andrew demanded, turning his intense gaze upon her as he waited for her reply.

Elizabeth's throat grew so dry she could scarcely swallow. Why was Andrew so curious about such a thing? Did he have some young woman in mind and wished to ask her advice? Slowly she attempted to explain. "Unless the young man changed the father's mind somehow, or if the young woman loved him so dearly she could not bear not to be his wife. In that case they might simply run away together. To elope it's called, when a couple runs away to be married."

Andrew nodded, then rose to his feet and extended his hand. "You must go home first. I will follow. The pheasant will be proof enough of where I've been, but you must not tell your father you have seen me for he is very angry with us both."

Relieved he had changed the subject, Elizabeth agreed. "I understand, and Andrew," she paused, hoping to apologize, "I am truly sorry about this morning. It is a long walk home and you shouldn't have been forced to make it when I know Daniel must have started the fight thinking with Ian and Mark's help he could give you a beating."

"I did not walk. Your father and I rode home with

Angus MacGregor. He was so ashamed of his son's deeds he would not allow us to walk."

"And Daniel?" Elizabeth whispered softly.

"He had to walk home," Andrew admitted with a sly wink.

"You are a devil, Andrew!" Elizabeth laughed as she lifted her skirt and ran lightly toward her home. He was a very handsome devil too, she thought, but whom could he wish to marry, for what sane father would give his daughter to such a rascal?

Olaf was seated upon the front porch, his Bible open on his lap but he was not reading, merely staring off into space when Elizabeth arrived back at the house. He motioned to the chair at his side and spoke sharply, "Sit down here with me, Elizabeth. I've something important to say to you."

As she complied with his request she hastened to make him see reason. "I am sorry to have left you at the church, Papa, but it was Daniel's fault. Truly it was."

Olaf looked askance at his only child. "The less said about this morning's disgraceful behavior the better. Andrew is a young and handsome man. I should have foreseen the problems his being here would cause. There is only one thing for you to do now, Elizabeth. Tell him he is free to leave and send him on his way in the morning."

"But Papa," Elizabeth gasped sharply, "I can't do that!"

"And why not?" Olaf inquired sternly.

Elizabeth looked down at her hands, twisting the fabric of her skirt anxiously between her fingers as she searched her mind frantically for some reasonable excuse. "I simply can't. I gave my word and he gave his. He must remain here the full ninety days. He must."

"Elizabeth!" Olaf hissed reproachfully. "I will not have tongues wagging over this! From what I've seen all week, you and Andrew barely tolerate each other, but what others may imagine is a different matter entirely. After supper you will tell him to leave. No more arguments, girl. Now see to your cooking for I am hungry!"

Not even the prospect of something so delicious as pheasant could lift Elizabeth's spirits that night. She moved through her tasks slowly, her mind preoccupied with the impossibility of her father's demand. When Andrew brought the pheasants to her, she took them without comment, but he touched her arm as she turned away.

"If someone must take a beating over this it will be me, Elizabeth, not you."

Elizabeth shook her head, her expression wistful. "Don't be ridiculous, Andrew. My father does not beat me and I will not allow him to beat you either."

Andrew lifted an eyebrow quizzically. "I had forgotten. You wish to do that yourself?"

"I am not in the mood for your jokes, Andrew. Which do you want to do, milk the cow or pluck these birds? I want to save the feathers for they are so very pretty."

Andrew scowled bitterly. "I do not milk cows!"

"Fine, then you prepare the birds. The water's boiling. See if you can be finished by the time I return

81

with the milk."

"Is it to be a contest?"

"Andrew, stop it!" Elizabeth stamped her foot for emphasis. "Just do it!" She thrust the birds back into his hands and slammed the back door on her way out, frustrated beyond endurance by his constant teasing. She would not miss that!

While she had never tasted more delectable food, Elizabeth had seldom enjoyed a meal less. Jed made several attempts at conversation, not understanding why his companions should be so glum when he was in such high spirits. He'd spent a most relaxing day and now had the finest of suppers.

"I do not know how we got along without you, Andrew. Elizabeth is a fine cook but it helps for her to have something so tasty as this to prepare. Yes, indeed." He helped himself to another portion of the tender meat and washed it down with ale.

Elizabeth placed her fork on the side of her plate and tried to think of some way to send Andrew away, but as she glanced toward him her mind went blank and she felt only the spark of excitement which had always flowed through her when he was near. His presence made her uncomfortable, for he was nothing like the boys of Oak Grove. Of course he was no mere boy she knew, but a full grown man with all the appetites such a splendid being as he would possess. Her face flooded with color as he looked up, as usual his gaze mocking hers as if he could read her mind with the greatest of ease. Seeing he was finished eating too she turned to her father. "Will you please excuse us? I'd like to speak with Andrew outside if I may."

Olaf paused briefly, then nodded, understanding her desire to keep the matter private from Jed who made no secret of his regard for the Indian. "As you wish."

Andrew closed the front door quietly behind them then gestured toward the chairs. "Do you want to sit here on the porch or would you rather go for a walk?"

"Walk I think." Elizabeth stepped lightly down the path away from the house, glad not to have to face him as she spoke. "As you know my father was not pleased about what happened this morning and although it's clear Daniel and his friends went after you, that fight has put us all in an embarrassing predicament. We have to live here, you see, while you will soon be gone."

Andrew reached out to take Elizabeth's hand and led her through the orchard. When he reached the tree where he knew she liked to sit he stopped and swung her up upon the low branch, waiting to see she was comfortable before he took his hands from her waist. "Oak Grove is only a tiny part of the world, Elizabeth. Do you not long to see more of it?"

"Yes, of course I do. I hope someday to visit Philadelphia at least, if not go far beyond, but that is not the question here."

Andrew leaned back against the tree, his face set in an impassive mask as he waited for what he was certain she would say. Her long shimmering curls fell in gentle waves around her face, framing the sorrow in her expression with an exquisite glow. He had never seen a more beautiful or desirable woman and ached that the surge of passion which filled his loins could not be spent as nature had intended. "What is it you are trying to say?" he snapped angrily, attempting unsuccessfully to redirect his lust into another emotion.

Elizabeth's eyes swept his face slowly, lingering over his deeply tanned features so she might always remember how handsome he had been. The words she knew she should speak stuck in her throat, impossible to utter and she replied calmly, her only choice suddenly clear. "My father insists I send you away, but I will not do it."

Andrew laughed with relief, his good natured chuckle ringing against the trees with a warm echo. "And why not?"

Once begun, Elizabeth found a ready explanation and gave it. "People are too quick to gossip. If you were to leave it would only incite more rumors, not stop them. We have a bargain and it should be kept. I cannot obey my father this time. I will not."

"Because we have a bargain. There is no other reason?" Andrew drew near, his voice low and tender.

"What is it you wish me to admit, Indian?" Elizabeth whispered hoarsely, sorry now she'd not chosen the safety of the porch.

"Only the truth, Elizabeth. You warned me this morning, called my name or I might have been badly hurt. Why did you do that unless you want me as desperately as I want you?" Andrew reached out to enfold her trembling body in his warm embrace. His lips met hers lightly, tasting their sweetness while he waited for what seemed to be an eternity for her to respond. She slipped from the branch to stand in his arms, every inch of her supple form pressed against his, her will subdued this time by tenderness rather than strength. She relaxed against him, lifting her arms to encircle his neck as she accepted his sweet kiss, drawing him more and more deeply into her enchanting affection until he pulled her down into the cool grass, cradling her body gently in his arms. His hands strayed down the buttons of her bodice as he kissed her, caressing her tenderly until he lowered his head to the rosy tip of her soft, full breast.

Elizabeth laced her fingers in his soft curls as she felt his mouth move over her tender flesh. His lips were hot, his tongue a flame upon her cool skin and she gasped with pleasure, holding him still more tightly in her arms. She was lost in the delightful sensation he brought. She simply lay upon the soft bed of grass, enjoying his touch, loving his sweet affection but as he began to run his hand slowly up the inside of her slender thigh, she struggled against him, finally realizing what he meant to do. In that same instant she heard her father calling her name, compounding her terror to impossible proportions. She leapt to her feet, frantically struggling to button up her dress before her father could catch her in a flagrant abuse of his wishes.

Andrew rose, chuckling softly at her haste. He lifted her chin with his fingertips and gave her one last kiss. "Tell him I have refused to leave and have gone off into the woods. Well, run. Do it!" he ordered, his voice still slurred with desire.

Elizabeth smoothed out her clothes as she ran, stopping only momentarily to comb her curls into place with her fingers before she entered the house and slammed the door. "The man is impossible, Papa. He refuses to leave, saying it will make him appear a coward."

"What? Oh, damn it all, Elizabeth. Why should he care what anyone calls him when he is gone?" Olaf crossed the small house swiftly and yanked open the door. "Where is he? Gone to Jed's shed?"

"I doubt it. He just sprinted off into the woods. Maybe he'll change his mind and keep on going." Elizabeth tried to breathe deeply, slowly. She was fortunate her father had not looked at her more closely as she'd come through the door. She gathered up the supper dishes and began to clean up the remains of the meal with hands which still shook with the passion Andrew had so easily aroused. She was neither ashamed nor sorry now, simply filled with wonder at the sweetness he'd shown her and she found it difficult to hide her smile as her father continued to fume over Andrew's perversity.

"Tomorrow I will insist he go, Elizabeth. I will demand it!" Olaf slammed the door as he went out into the deepening night, muttering still about his willful daughter and her damn Indian.

Elizabeth splashed her face with cool water, then ran into her room and brushed her hair with furious strokes. When her father returned she smiled sweetly, knowing her appearance was again quite proper. "Perhaps it will be best if Andrew stays, Papa. He is a willing worker even without pay and there is so much for you to do here."

"Aye, that is true, but not it if costs you a husband." Olaf sank down into his chair and sat back, weary of the whole matter.

"Daniel, you mean?" She asked with a saucy toss of her curls. "I'll not have him now that he's had the audacity to call me Andrew's squaw." As that word passed her lips she realized what she'd done, nearly traded a few moments of pleasure for a lifetime of respectability for no matter how white she might know Andrew to be, he wished to live his life as an Indian, but could she? Chilled to the very marrow she kissed her father's cheek tenderly and bid him good night. "Do not stay up too late, Papa. We have both had a trying day."

"And tomorrow will be no better!" Olaf grumbled under his breath then relented. "Good night, my dear. We'll try and make the best of things. Perhaps it would cause more gossip if Andrew left than if he stayed. I will speak to him in the morning and tell him I have changed my mind. If he is still here in the morning, that is."

Elizabeth nodded numbly. "Oh, I feel certain he'll be here. Good night." She went quickly to her room and closed the door as she whispered, "Damn you, Andrew. What have you done to me now?"

The morning broke with a splendid brightness but Elizabeth had gotten little sleep. She avoided Andrew's gaze at breakfast rather than attempt to hide the confusion of her feelings and sat silently listening as her father told him his decision to ask him to leave had been the wrong one. She found her troubles compounding then, for Andrew readily agreed to stay as he'd originally promised and even went so far as to ask if he might ask Elizabeth to help him write the inquiries to the newspapers since he'd been unable to find time to complete the task on his own.

"I'm certain Elizabeth will be happy to help you, won't you, dear?" Olaf asked confidently, pleased to find Andrew in so reasonable a mood.

Elizabeth nodded for he'd given her no choice really. "Yes. Perhaps we could work on them some night after supper." Seated at the table she told herself, with her father in his chair so she'd have no more temptation to yield to Andrew's intoxicating kisses. A fine mess she'd made of things. He'd sworn to take her and she'd nearly given herself to him with no thought of the consequences.

As they prepared to leave the house to begin their morning chores, Daniel MacGregar appeared at the door, a fragrant bunch of spring flowers clutched tightly in his hand. Andrew glared fiercely as Olaf let him in, his dislike for Daniel clear in his expression, but he left the house without voicing his opinion.

Daniel shuffled his feet nervously as he walked to Elizabeth's side and held out the brightly colored bouquet. "I have come to beg your forgiveness, Elizabeth. I embarrassed you and your father needlessly and hope you will be generous enough to grant me your pardon." He rushed through that speech, having rehearsed it many times and wanting only to have the humiliating ordeal over.

Elizabeth looked at the pretty flowers then lifted her bright glance to the dark eyed young man. She'd always known him to be proud, at times arrogant to the point of being a vicious bully but he'd obviously met his match in Andrew for his face was swollen, his chin cut and badly bruised where the Indian had struck him. Curiously, she felt not the slightest twinge of sympathy for him since he'd brought all his misery upon himself. She took her mother's crystal vase from the cupboard, filled it with water and bringing a knife returned to the table and began to trim the stems of the blossoms before placing them in an attractive arrangement. "These flowers should not go to waste. I'll thank you for them. It's a pity you never thought to bring such a sweet gift to me before today."

"Elizabeth, please!" Daniel pleaded, his bloodshot eyes filling with tears. "Won't you please forgive me?"

"No, I will not. I'll simply ask you to leave and not come here ever again for I no longer count you among my friends."

Seeing her implacable mood and knowing it well, Daniel turned to Olaf. "Sir, I would like to marry Elizabeth, as quickly as it can be arranged. You know I am well able to provide for her. I have no excuse for my actions yesterday other than to plead frustration because she has kept me waiting for so long, far longer than any man could endure with patience."

Olaf pursed his lips thoughtfully. "She is my only child, Daniel. I'll not force her to wed against her will but she is young to contemplate marriage even if you are not. She will give you her answer on her sixteenth birthday. That will give her time enough to consider your proposal seriously."

Elizabeth opened her mouth to argue. She'd give him her answer right then, but seeing her father's warning glance she remained silent. For as long as she could remember she'd expected to marry Daniel, to reside on his farm, to live a life similar to the one her mother had known, but her mother had married a man she adored and had found each day they'd shared filled with pleasure. But now as she looked at Daniel she knew she didn't love him and never would. Suddenly she understood what Andrew had been trying to tell her. It was what a man was himself that was important, not his last name or what he owned. Daniel might have a fine family, wealth, an admired position in their small community but he was weak, a bully who'd not fight for what he wanted without several friends to back him up. He offered an easy life, but an empty, joyless one and she'd not have him, not that day and not in September.

Daniel nodded, knowing Olaf offered the only hope he had left. "May I still come to call, sir, until then?"

Elizabeth shook her head and seeing her gesture Olaf spoke sternly. "No, you may not. It is obvious to me you need time to think this matter over also, Daniel. You may speak to my daughter should you meet her in town or on the Sabbath, but she will not accept your calls here until September. If you truly want her for your wife, you should consider the wait a small sacrifice to make."

Scowling angrily, Daniel had no choice but to accept Olaf's conditions and leave but the moment he was gone the blond man exploded in a fit of anger. "That was Angus MacGregar's only son, as you well know. You'll find no better! I'll not have you live as your mother did, worn out from work, dead in her grave when she was no more than thirty-one!"

"She loved you, Papa. She never complained, not

once did she say she had too much to do or that the work was too hard! I'll not marry Daniel, I won't. I don't care how many servants he might have or what fine clothes he can buy for me. I care nothing for that. I want a husband I can admire and respect, a man who is bright, honest and brave." Elizabeth's voice caught in her throat as she realized whom she was describing. The prospect of marrying an Indian brave, no matter how fine a man he might be, appalled her and dear God, that was what Andrew was.

"Elizabeth?" Olaf stepped close, his deep blue eyes filled with concern. "We'll argue no more about this now. It is several months until your birthday and by then I'll wager you'll come to your senses. Now I must go. The stock can't wait to be fed just because we have so many problems."

As her father left by the front door, Elizabeth ran out the back but she had not taken two steps into the yard before Andrew grabbed her hand and swung her into his arms. He pulled her into the shadows at the rear of the house and whispered hoarsely, "What did you tell MacGregor?"

Elizabeth placed her palms on his chest to put more space between them but he moved back only slightly. "If you were so very curious, why didn't you remain to hear it?"

"Tell me!" Andrew demanded, his gaze dark, his tone insistent.

Seeing it was pointless to argue, Elizabeth replied calmly, "He apologized and I sent him away." That was not the complete truth she realized, but all she'd reveal.

"Why did your father change his mind about

sending me away?"

"You are too fine a worker to dismiss, Andrew. I convinced him he'd be foolish to make you leave."

"You did not tell him the truth then?" Andrew asked with a puzzled frown.

Elizabeth swallowed with difficulty. With him so near she could scarcely think at all, let alone discern what was the truth. "That is the truth. You are the best of hands, Andrew. He could not ask more of you than you already give." That was the type of man he was she realized. He always gave his best when they had no right to expect it.

"That was not what you told me last night," Andrew murmured softly, bending down slightly to brush her fair curls with his lips.

Blushing deeply at that memory, Elizabeth stammered, "What did I say?"

"It was not in words for you talk constantly and say little, but your love for me is plain in your kiss."

"My love?" Elizabeth was astonished by the arrogance of his assumption. "You think that I love you? Well, I don't!" she vowed with a determination borne of terror.

Andrew chuckled, locking his hands behind her back to hold her captive in his arms. "I have no time to argue with you now. Tonight when your father is asleep I will meet you. Come to the barn and I will be waiting for you there."

"No! I will not!" Breaking free of his grasp she ran back into the house, back to the safety the solidness of the structure provided, but there was no escaping the emotions which tore away at her innocent heart. What was the matter with her? Why hadn't she sent Andrew away when she had the chance? Numbly, she sat down at the table and inhaled the flowers' heady perfume. Whatever was she to do with her life? She was faced with an impossible dilemma. She could either marry a man she'd never love, or love a man she could never marry.

Five

Elizabeth spent the rest of the day rehearsing possible dialogues in her mind, planning what she could say. It was always difficult to talk to Andrew for his glance was too direct, his purpose always so damn clear and she felt trapped in a snarl of her own creation. Her father seemed convinced there was a good chance they could find his family and she seized upon that hope as her best option. For were Andrew to find his parents, no matter who they might be, or where they might live, he would have no reason to return to the Seneca. He'd be obligated to go home to his natural parents and most likely they were farmers or merchants, something respectable for he was too fine a young man to have sprung from people of low repute. Determined to learn his identity, after supper she brought paper, ink and pens to the table and attempted to help Andrew compose the most compelling queries she could summon to mind asking for information as to the possible identity of an eight-year-old, green-eyed boy named Andrew who had been separated from his parents in 1755. He seemed faintly amused by her efforts, but after they had decided upon a brief format he wrote several letters himself while she wrote the others.

"There, although Papa suggested we begin with New York, we have enough letters written to send a few to newspapers in Pennsylvania too. That should give us a better chance of finding your people, Andrew. If it doesn't, well, we'll just try farther south." Elizabeth gathered up the sheets of stationery and addressed the envelopes in a neat hand. "My father can mail these when next he's in town and then all we shall have to do is wait for some reply."

"I am not a patient man, Elizabeth. I do not enjoy waiting." Andrew got to his feet, ready to leave the house then bent down slightly and whispered, "Do not keep me waiting tonight."

Elizabeth's cheeks flooded with color as she watched him leave. She had not even made up her mind to meet him and he had the nerve to caution her not to be late! Yet her anger was futile for as her father went to his room and she went to hers she was too restless to disrobe and go to bed. She paced her room, endlessly moving up and down the confines of the small space until she realized her footsteps matched the rhythm of her father's deep snore. He was sound asleep, and he never woke before dawn. Why shouldn't she go out and meet Andrew, tell him exactly what she thought of him, too.

Andrew stood up when he heard the door of the barn slide shut. He waited silently for if Elizabeth had sent Olaf with his musket, he had no intention of speaking and giving the man a target. When he heard her call his name softly he stepped out from the shadows. "Another few minutes and I would have come for you."

"What? You mean you would have come to my

room?" Elizabeth cried out indignantly. "You have no right, none at all and yet you continually behave as though I were some tasty morsel you couldn't wait to devour!"

"My thoughts are as transparent as yours, it would seem," Andrew replied with a wide grin. "Since you know your fate, I am glad you did not waste any more of our time by trying to escape it."

In the darkness his taunting words held a warmth which stole over her like an intoxicating liquid, flooding her senses with desire although he had not reached out to touch her. Her voice sounded hollow in her ears, coming from a long way off as she whispered, "What is it you want, Andrew, to take all I have and leave me unfit to be another's bride?"

"No! You will be no man's bride but mine!" He responded bitterly, his vow a pain-filled snarl as he drew her into his arms, crushing her against his chest as he wound his fingers in her curls, holding her mouth captive beneath his own as he kissed her again and again, no longer able to contain the fire her slender body kindled within his own. He swept her up into his arms and carried her to the stall where she'd first brought him. He lowered her slowly onto the soft woolen blanket he'd brought from his bed then stretched out beside her. He put his right leg over her left and slipped his hand under her skirt to the bare thigh above her stocking. Her creamy skin was so cool to his touch and he felt a tremor course through her whole body as he moved his hand higher. She seemed to be wearing endless lengths of slips and lace and it was all he could do not to tear the garments from her body and satisfy his desire for her immediately. He forced back that lust with difficulty while he continued to caress her thigh gently and smiled as he heard her breathing quicken to sharp gasps. He meant to teach her well, to show her the pleasure a man could give a woman before he took his own. She was a delight to kiss, to lead further and further for her shyness soon disappeared as she returned his affectionate touch. He let her hands move over him for he thought surely she must be curious about how a man is made, but he was careful to keep his passion under control as he aroused hers. It would have been so easy for him to lead her into an intimacy from which she could never withdraw nor even want to, but she had not come to him willingly as he'd wished. He did no more than move his hands over her lightly, across her flat stomach, down her smooth thighs, the most tantalizing of caresses until she was completely his, languidly lying in his embrace so lost in pleasure he could have done whatever he wished but he did no more than touch her that night. He held her and kissed her until she was nearly asleep in his arms, drunk with the delicious sensations he gave with such generous affection.

Elizabeth had forgotten her fears the moment Andrew's lips had touched hers. The attraction was too strong, his taste too delectable and her lips parted easily under the pressure of his. She felt only the promise of pleasure more beautiful than any she'd ever known. It filled her veins with a heat which left her limp in his embrace and she was grateful for the strength of his arms around her as she could never have continued to stand on her own. The softness of his blanket enveloped her with the tenderness of a cloud and she surrendered herself completely, rejoicing as his touch carried her aloft into the realm of pure sensation where nothing mattered to her but being with him. It was not until her mind finally cleared that she realized he had not simply used her as she had feared he would, but he had treated her as if she were precious to him, as if her happiness outweighed his own and she asked him shyly, "Is this what it feels like to make love, Andrew?"

The innocence of her question amused him and he covered her face with light kisses before he answered. "Yes, but making love is far better, for we would share that joy together, Elizabeth."

Elizabeth buried her face in his warm shoulder and clung to him, desperate to feel his strong lean body next to her own. She wanted then to give him what he had given her but could not make herself say the words. If she let him make love to her then there was no turning back. She would indeed be an Indian squaw for the rest of her life. She pushed him away as she got unsteadily to her feet and made her way back into the house to sleep alone in her own bed. Her dreams were wild, as tormented as her thoughts and she awoke as unhappy as she had been when she'd gone to bed. She was terribly afraid she was falling in love with a man she ought not even to know and she could not decide what to do to stop the pain which tore at her heart.

While Elizabeth dreaded facing Andrew the next morning for fear her expression would betray her inner turmoil, he came bounding into the house in the best of spirits, smiling happily at a joke Jed had told him. He and the hired man kept up a steady stream of teasing while they ate breakfast, then he left without so much as a wink in her direction as if the day were too promising to waste in her company and she was thoroughly confused. She wanted to talk to him, to decide what must be done but as the week progressed Andrew came and went about his work with no effort to speak to her alone until Friday afternoon. He entered the house as she was ironing. She wiped the perspiration from her forehead and set the heavy iron back on the stove, glad for the excuse to take a break.

Andrew sat down at the table and stretched out his long legs to get comfortable as he grinned slyly. "Have you missed me?"

"Missed you!" Elizabeth shrieked. She picked up the hot iron, ready to hurl it at him but it slipped from her grasp and nearly crushed her toes as it fell to the floor.

"You must be more careful, Elizabeth. You might hurt yourself so badly Daniel MacGregor might not want you after all."

"What are you talking about?" Elizabeth sprinkled water on the shirt she'd been ironing and stretched it out flat ready to press. "Is that why you've ignored me so rudely all week, because of Daniel?" Were all men simply born jealous? she wondered.

"Your father did not tell me. I overheard something he said to Jed. Were you too ashamed to tell me yourself?"

Elizabeth looked up, her glance filled with confusion. "Ashamed of what? What are you talking about?"

Andrew found the innocence of her expression perplexing for surely she knew exactly what he meant. "I heard your father say he would not let you marry

Daniel until your birthday. Is that the truth or not?"

"Well yes, but—" Andrew had left the house and slammed the door before she could complete her sentence. Well no wonder he had been so aloof, but he might have been gentleman enough to allow her some time to explain!

Olaf stepped out of Andrew's way as the young man bolted past him when he climbed the steps and went inside. "What was Andrew doing in here just now? I thought he was with Jed."

Elizabeth replied with the first thought which entered her mind. "He just asked me what I'd planned to prepare for supper. Maybe he thought he might have time to go hunting."

"Oh, I see." Olaf sat down and watched his daughter work for a moment, damp ringlets clung to her forehead and he could tell by her expression she did not enjoy ironing. She was a very pretty girl, more than merely pretty really, a beauty as her mother had been and he felt a stab of remorse for the long hours of labor she put in each day. She had grown so serious, become so independent he despaired of ever finding her a husband and said so. "You've had far too much work to do here since your mother died and I have not been as thoughtful as I should have been. I've forced you to grow up too swiftly and I'm not pleased with the result. I'm the one who should be considering marriage, Elizabeth. Not you."

"Why, Papa? Are you serious? Do you have a woman in mind?" Elizabeth gave him her most charming smile. She knew he must be lonely but doubted he'd want to remarry.

Olaf blushed as he revealed his plans. "Well, yes,

100

you know Margaret Nelson. She has been a widow for more than a year. I have reason to believe she would welcome my proposal."

Elizabeth tried to hide her shock, but then asked too quickly, "Margaret has little children, Papa. Do you want to start all over again with such babies?"

"Her children are well behaved and quiet, Elizabeth. They will not give me the constant problems you have always presented," Olaf admonished her sternly, forgetting the concern for her which had prompted him to begin their conversation.

"I see." Elizabeth gave her full attention to her ironing for a long moment then could no longer contain her curiosity. "What makes you think Margaret likes you best? Each Sunday she is surrounded by handsome young men. Do you think you have a chance with her?"

Olaf responded angrily, "Those dandies? She'll not marry one of them."

Elizabeth laughed at his fierce determination. "I didn't realize she'd been alone for a year. Perhaps you should propose to her soon before someone else does."

"Yes, if Margaret were here then you wouldn't have to work so hard. You'd still be playing with dolls if your mother were alive."

"Dolls, Papa? It's been a long time since I've wanted to play with dolls, years and years." After a slight hesitation she inquired, "You haven't told anyone about Daniel's proposal have you? That would make things very awkward for both of us if the story were known."

Olaf rose slowly, a deep scowl drawing his brow into a thin line. "You know what we agreed, Elizabeth.

101

You'll not marry Daniel or anyone else for that matter until you've turned sixteen. Don't tell me you've decided you want to marry Daniel before then because I absolutely forbid it."

Elizabeth smiled sweetly, none of her resolve to avoid that young man showing in her innocent expression. "I'm in no hurry to marry him."

"Good, all I ask is that you'll consider the alternatives carefully so that your answer to him will be the correct one for you both. Now I think I'll go into Oak Grove this afternoon. Do you have your shopping list ready?"

"Salt is the only thing we need. Oh, and please mail those letters Andrew and I wrote. He'll only be here another two months so there's no time to lose."

"I'll take them. Why don't you leave the ironing for another day, baby. It's awfully warm in here this afternoon."

"Thanks, Papa. Maybe I will." Elizabeth returned his fond kiss affectionately. He was a sweet man, but she dared not confide her problems in him for he'd never understand.

When Andrew glared at her angrily that evening Elizabeth gave him her most dazzling smile, stunning him completely as she turned his angry stare aside. Now that she knew what had upset him she was no longer worried. He'd been jealous, that was all and no wonder if he believed she'd agreed to marry Daniel in the morning and then had met him secretly that same night. She licked her lips with a sensuous slowness and watched him turn away, apparently thoroughly disgusted with her duplicity. She had a choice she realized. She could let him go on thinking the worst of her, or she could tell him the truth, but to tell him the truth would be to invite his advances which was lunacy. Perhaps she should wait until they had gotten some response to their inquiries, for then they would know where he'd be going when he left their farm. She struck that idea immediately, however, for that would appear too calculated, as if she'd been more interested in who he was than what he was and she'd not have him think that of her. He got up to leave as she began to clear the table but, seeing her father had stopped Jed for a moment, she whispered softly to Andrew, "I must see you, tonight."

Andrew shook his head, warning her to be silent as he denied her request but she only repeated it and, not wanting to arouse Olaf's suspicions, he walked beside her through the kitchen to the back door. "No! You have made your choice!"

Elizabeth grabbed a large wooden spoon and began scraping her frying pan to cover the sound of her voice. "You will meet me tonight, or I will come and get you!"

"No!" Andrew stomped out the back door and off into the night. He'd not be her slave. She might own his days but not the nights, by God! He stopped then and laughed to himself. If she came to the barn, came to him willingly as he'd boasted she'd do, then he would not let her leave.

The full moon's pale light filled the barnyard with an enticing luminescence Elizabeth barely noticed as she approached the barn. She'd meant what she'd said. If Andrew weren't there she'd march right into the shed he shared with Jed and sit down on his bunk and tell him what she thought of him for thinking so little of her. Jed would be shocked of course, but what did that matter when Andrew was the one who truly mattered to her. Warmed by that thought, she slipped through the partially open door into the inviting darkness of the barn.

"Elizabeth?" Andrew reached out to take her hand and lead her into the hay-filled stall where he'd again left his blanket but she pulled away.

"We can talk here, Indian. Did you really think I would have agreed to marry Daniel last Monday morning and then nearly, well, nearly made love to you that night? Do I seem so fickle as that? So silly and empty headed that I would prefer him to you? I understand what you've been trying to tell me, that a man's character is more important than his name. I don't care that Daniel is wealthy and that you have nothing. I don't care one bit about that."

Andrew threw back his head and howled with laughter but she clamped her hands over his mouth to keep him from waking the animals and Jed, and probably her father too. "I am sorry, Elizabeth, but my tribe is rich. We have many horses, mountains of furs, fertile farm lands, more than MacGregar will ever own. Flaming Sky is a powerful sachem and I am his only son. I have—"

"Stop it! You're making me feel like I'm being sold to the highest bidder." Yet she was shocked for she'd never even considered the prospect he owned more than he'd had with him the morning she'd taken him from John Cummins.

"You are not planning to marry MacGregor in September. Is that what you're trying to tell me, Elizabeth?" Andrew's smile was a gleeful grin as he made no attempt to hide his pleasure.

"I'll not marry him in September or any other month either. He asked for me and my father said I would give him my answer on my birthday and not before because he will not allow me to marry until I am sixteen."

"I will be gone by September," Andrew replied softly.

Elizabeth forced back the sorrow which filled her whole being with dread. "You will not stay, Andrew, not even for me?"

"No, Elizabeth, I will not stay." He heard a sharp gasp escape her lips, as if he'd struck her and instantly he felt her pain. He pulled her into his arms, his mouth seeking hers in the dim light, his lips playfully teasing hers before he tightened his embrace. His kiss was far different then, deeper, lustier, filled with passion as he claimed her for his own. His slim tan fingers moved over her soft breasts. Her thin muslin dress offered no barrier to his touch and he held her with a slow sensuous caress which sent tremors of desire surging up her spine until finally she had to draw away simply to catch her breath.

Andrew stood with the loveliest creature he'd ever known in his arms and he was overwhelmed with the need for her, for her tender touch always brought the promise of delights he could no longer wait to sample. He stroked her silken hair and spoke in a voice filled with desire. "I will make you no promises which would only be lies."

Elizabeth relaxed against him, felt his loving warmth and knew if he would give her no more than that one night she would take what he offered eagerly. She could see his smile clearly in the soft light of the moon which filtered through the open loft. All her confusion, her anguish over her future melted away as she reached up to kiss him. "Promise me only this, Indian, only this."

Andrew needed no further encouragement to make love to the woman he found impossible to resist. He lifted her into his arms and carried her back to his blanket. As he placed her upon her feet he unfastened the tiny buttons on her soft dress and she let it slip to her feet. He cast her undergarments aside, his hands sliding down her smooth slender body slowly, his touch light yet drawing forth the sweetest of pleasures. That he knew a woman's body and knew it well was plain in the easy command he exerted over her emotions and yet with Elizabeth it all seemed new, filled with the thrill she could not describe but longed to enjoy again and again.

Elizabeth's knees grew weak. She clung to him as he folded her into his embrace. She wanted more of his tantalizing touch yet could no longer make her breath form the words to ask. He lowered her gently to his blanket then slipped off his buckskins quickly before dropping down by her side. His mouth covered hers as his fingers combed through her long hair, fanning the curls out over the soft bed in the freshly laid straw.

"Do not be afraid of me, Elizabeth. I will teach you all there is to know of love."

Elizabeth smiled as she ran her small hands over his lean body, slowly learning the strength of his muscular build. He was so warm, his touch gentle as he returned her affectionate caress. She nuzzled his neck with her lips, softly teasing him with playful nibbles before her mouth returned to his.

Andrew hugged her more tightly, pressed her lissome body along the length of his own. His touch was easy, his kisses deep as he savored her luscious taste. His mouth moved gently down her throat, slid over the soft rise of her shoulder. Then at last his tongue found the rosy crest of her breast. Her smooth creamy skin held the faint fragrance of flowers enticing his senses as his lips explored her delicate beauty. She was perfection, from her warm delicious lips, which clung to his so eagerly, to her soft full breasts, tiny waist and narrow hips. She was the most exquisite of women and not in the least bit shy as she lay in his arms, the warmth of her skin slight compared to the heat of his. His hand trailed across her flat stomach and down her smooth thighs. He loved the feel of her flower-scented skin and wanted only to give her pleasure, to bring her the full rapture of love as he taught her the most stunning of life's secrets. All his thoughts were of her as he whispered, "What did your mother tell you about making love, about the first time you would be with a man?"

Elizabeth was startled by the sound of his voice and puzzled by his question. His fingertips caressed her still, bringing an intoxicating sensation almost beyond her endurance, making any coherent reply nearly impossible but she tried to answer him calmly. "My mother taught me so many things, Andrew. She was so loving and sweet but I was very young when she died. She told me only that being with the man you love is something very special, very nice, but had I been older she would have told me more. I am sorry to know so little. What must I do to please you? Tell me what you would like me to do and I will gladly do it."

Andrew touched Elizabeth's fair curls lightly. "I am pleased with you already. You may do whatever you wish, hold me or kiss me, anything which gives you pleasure but you must not ask me to stop now that we have begun."

Elizabeth's fingertips moved slowly down his arm, tracing his muscles as she wondered out loud, "Why would I ever want to do that, Andrew?"

Andrew exhaled slowly and decided it might be far wiser to simply surprise her with what was to come than it would be to tell her the truth and make her dread what could not be avoided. He was uncertain which was the more cruel but his choice was quickly made. His lips found hers once more and he kissed her slowly as he let his fingertips wander down the soft swells of her body with a slow tantalizing touch which grew increasingly more intimate as he drew her into a closer embrace.

Elizabeth adored Andrew, loved him dearly though she dared not speak those words. She no longer hesitated to give herself to him fully. Totally surrendering herself to the touch of his lips and hands, she did not draw away but let herself drift upon the wave of pleasure which swelled through her loins. His dark, thick curls were loose, brushing against her cheeks as he kissed her. He smelled so good, like the spicy soap he'd used to wash, like the hickory smoke of the fire and she entwined her slender fingers in his chestnut curls to hold his head to hers as she returned his hungry kiss. His touch was as delicious as his taste, warm and sweet, so slow and easy her body seemed to glow with this newfound rapture. She moved against his hand, inviting his sensuous caress as she hugged him. His body was so different from hers, strong and sleek yet she felt completely safe in his arms, with no fear of the power she knew him to possess. He had such grace and charm, gave such happiness filled with tender excitement. He was all a man could ever be and she wanted only to return the pleasure he gave so lavishly to her.

The weight of his lean bronze body was slight as he shifted his position to cradle her in his loving embrace yet she felt his tension, sensed his impatience and whispered softly, "I want you, Andrew. I want you so very much." His manner changed swiftly then with her enticing acceptance and he released the fiery passion he no longer had to contain. She gasped sharply then, shocked as his first savage thrust seared deep within her but she forced herself to be silent as he continued to move with a slow forceful rhythm for she knew her father would kill him for what he'd just done. That danger frightened her far more than the handsome man in her arms. Her breathing was nearly as ragged as his but she had never expected making love to be what it was for gradually she became more Andrew than herself. She could feel the pleasure flood through his body, heightening in intensity until it burst within her and his ecstasy became hers. It was a fire which grew from the depths of her being and spread through her slender limbs with a sensation so exquisite and so unexpected she was lost in the power of his affection, swept away on the cresting tide of emotion which filled her heart. She knew she would be his forever if she did not die in that very instant from the boundless joy of knowing his love, but it would have been worth it to her. She would have paid any price for what he'd given her that night and she knew she'd given the same splendid gift to him.

When reason at last returned to Andrew's agile mind, he could not stop kissing Elizabeth's flushed cheeks, her tear-filled lashes, her delicate ears. She had amazed him with the depth of her response and he was the far more astonished of the two. "I did not need to teach you, Elizabeth. You know all there is to know of giving love." She had taught him a beauty he had never known, what it was like to truly make love with affection and joy. All that love was ever meant to be he'd found with her and it was a shock he could scarcely accept.

A slow smile spread across Elizabeth's lovely features. "You might have warned me what to expect, Andrew, for I did not know pain and pleasure could be so finely interwoven nor did I understand how close we would become, truly one being instead of two."

Andrew buried his face in her golden curls and kissed her throat hungrily. "I will never have enough of you, never. I am sorry to have hurt you, for I know that I did. I wanted to be so gentle with you but—"

Elizabeth stilled his apology with a lingering kiss. "I

110

want all you can give, Indian, all that a man can give to a woman I want from you. Pain is such a slight thing compared to the joy I have found in your arms." She lay with her small body still pinned beneath his, her fingers playfully twisting a strand of his hair. She had found a contentment with him she'd not known existed and had no desire to ever leave his embrace.

"Elizabeth." Andrew could say no more as his need for her captivated his emotions anew. This time he was far more relaxed, deliberately teasing and sweet for he knew now she was truly his and, that urgency satisfied, he had the whole night to devote to giving her pleasure while he enjoyed the warmth of her acceptance. Yet she too knew how to be enticing and he soon gave up all hope of being playful and let the driving passion she aroused so easily carry him once more. His kiss was wild, filled with the abandon he longed to express and his hands were no longer light but possessive as he dominated her body with expert swiftness. He was so entranced by her loving sweetness he could no longer reason at all but only feel through every ounce of his powerful body the affection she gave so joyously to him. Her love was like the summer wind, surrounding him in a warmth like no other, better, stronger, richer, deeper. He could not find the words in either of the languages he knew to describe the joy her love had given him again.

Elizabeth embraced Andrew tightly, for her need was as strong as his. She was as desperate for his loving as he was to give it. The destiny she'd always seen in his deep green eyes was now hers and she was so filled with joy her passion stunned him once more. She was

111

a slender girl of no more than fifteen and he was a full grown man but they were a match so perfect she knew she was now his, but he was also hers. They lay entwined in each other's arms until the hour neared dawn, not wanting to miss a second of the closeness which enveloped them more snugly than the warmest of blankets. Elizabeth closed her eyes and breathed deeply. "I did not even dream making love could be this perfect. Thank you, Andrew. You are the best of teachers."

Andrew stretched lazily in her arms. "It is you who has taught me, Elizabeth, but now you must go." His lips moved over the swell of her breast in a final caress but he made no move to release her from his embrace.

"Yes, I know." Silently she prayed only that there would be other nights for them to share so that her memories would be many when he had gone. She ran her fingertips over his bare chest, but her expression grew thoughtful when he leaned down to kiss her lips again. His kiss was more loving each time and she held him, enjoying his affection so greatly she was unwilling to see the night end yet knew it already had.

Tears came to Elizabeth's eyes as she slipped from his grasp and quickly drew on her clothes. She ran from the barn and went soundlessly back to her room, but the first light of dawn was already streaking across the sky. We must be more careful, she thought anxiously, but she could not stop smiling as she washed thoroughly in the chill water from the white china pitcher on her wash stand. Andrew's scent had covered her fair skin from head to toe and she leaned back against the wall to keep from falling when she grew dizzy with the memory of what they'd shared.

She had never thought it would be so easy to give herself to a man, but Andrew was not just any man, but the dearest and best. She climbed back into her bed and although she had slept not at all that night she had never felt less tired. She lay her head upon her pillow and, dreaming she was still locked in Andrew's tender embrace, fell sound asleep.

Six

Elizabeth's heart leapt to her throat as Jed began to tease Andrew at breakfast. He chuckled gleefully, playfully describing how he'd awakened to find the Indian gone from his bunk.

"So when he comes in I says to him, 'Don't tell me you've taken up hunting by moonlight?' and he tells me he thought he'd heard something but it had only been an owl. Now I ask you, have you ever met an Indian who didn't recognize the sound of an owl?"

"Andrew is the only Indian I know, Jed, and if he wants to chase owls through the forest at midnight it is no business of mine. Now let's get to work." Olaf was clearly not amused by the older man's tale.

Andrew got up from the table and complimented Elizabeth on the breakfast before leaving the house with the other two men. His words were few but she understood his message. They would have to be doubly careful for, if Jed and her father were to put two and two together, they would be in terrible trouble.

Elizabeth tossed and turned restlessly in her bed that night, unable to fall asleep when her whole being cried out for Andrew's sensuous caress. Her father had stayed up later than usual. Perhaps he had only been reading, but she was worried he might be keeping an eye on her. He had stopped by her door on his way to bed and had stood there for a long while not realizing she wasn't asleep. Had he become suspicious that if Andrew left his bed at night he might be meeting her? They mustn't be caught together. They simply mustn't and, although she longed to go to Andrew, she did not for his life was precious and not worth any risk.

It was nearly dawn when she felt the kiss upon her cheek. Andrew's lips were light, honey smooth as they teased her from her sleep and into his arms but he gave her only a warm hug and then took her hand to lead her to the open window. He helped her out, then taking her hand again, made his way through the night's deepest shadows to the soft grass which covered the ground of the small apple orchard. He paused to pull her sheer gown over her head and then dropping to his knees, buried his face in her warm stomach, his lips caressing her firm flesh with kisses so inviting she soon slipped from his grasp and pulled him down upon the cool dew covered clover.

"Andrew, I cannot bear this game we must play, but should my father even suspect that we are lovers he will kill you."

Andrew covered her face with kisses, stilling her anxiety with the strength of the passion which flowed between them once again. "Never, he will never kill me. Do not be afraid for I am not." He had no intention of allowing Olaf to discover their secret. He rubbed his cheek in her tangled curls and kissed the length of her throat as he moved his hand down her splendid body, savoring her taste and contours until his heart was aflame with the desire only she could quench. She welcomed him as before, matching his fire with a consuming heat which left him shaken to the depths of his Indian soul. He told her over and over again how lovely she was, how exquisitely made and delightful to love, and although she understood not one word of his whispered praise, she let the sweet sound of his voice fill her with happiness and forgot all thought of caution in his delicious embrace.

The sight of Daniel MacGregor's ready smile gave Elizabeth a moment's pause for as they filed out of church, he and his father came up to join them. The MacGregors shook hands awkwardly with Andrew, as if unwilling to make the gesture of friendship, but once that formality was over, Angus spoke up in his usual booming voice. Slightly taller than his son but of considerably more bulk, his words rang with the unmistakable sound of authority.

"I understand your concern for your lovely daughter, Olaf. I have reminded Daniel many times of her youth, but as most young men he has little patience. We are planning a party next Saturday. The spring is too glorious to waste without some celebration. Will it violate the terms of your agreement with my son if you and Elizabeth are invited?"

Olaf tried to stifle his smile, wondering just who had gotten the idea of having a party, but he was not opposed to attending it. "It sounds like a fine idea, Angus. Elizabeth and I will be there."

Elizabeth glanced at Angus' proud grin, Daniel's satisfied smirk and her father's confident smile and suddenly felt as though she were suffocating under

116

their thinly disguised efforts to throw her into Daniel's arms. She knew the MacGregars' parties well. There would be music and dancing, plenty for the men to drink and somehow Daniel would arrange to speak with her privately, only talking would be the last thing on his mind. Outraged, she found her voice. "What about Andrew? Isn't he invited too?"

Absolute silence met Elizabeth's query, as if she had spoken the vilest of oaths rather than suggesting something which seemed only right to her. Before the pause in the conversation became even more awkward, Andrew began to laugh.

"I know I'm not welcome in Daniel's home, Elizabeth. You needn't make him say it for I did not expect to be invited to his party."

Elizabeth straightened her shoulders proudly, unwilling to give in so easily. "I will not attend the party if Andrew will not be there, Mr. MacGregar. I'm sorry, but I must insist he be included in our invitation." She spoke calmly, her request a sensible one in her opinion for if she could never reveal the depth of her friendship with Andrew, she would not deny it existed.

Olaf took his daughter's arm as he turned away. "Elizabeth and I will be there on Saturday night, Angus. I promise you she will have learned some manners by then!"

Elizabeth tried to pull free but her father propelled her toward their wagon and nearly tossed her upon the seat. "Have you lost your senses completely, girl? Andrew works for us. He is no more than a bondsman and Angus MacGregar does not entertain servants!"

"Andrew is no servant!" Elizabeth cried out hoarsely, then seeing the Indian's warning glance, grew still. How in heaven's name did he expect her to continue to see him if she had to attend parties and flirt with other young men as if the one she loved did not even exist? Tears welled up in her eyes and she blinked them away with difficulty as her father and Andrew climbed up into their seats. She had been a fool to think she could keep such a secret when every fiber of her being cried out to proclaim the truth. Knowing all too well that truth would seal Andrew's fate as well as her own, she clamped her mouth shut and rode home in silence.

Olaf ushered Andrew and his daughter into the house the minute they arrived home. "Last Sunday it was a brawl and this morning you disgrace me by insisting Angus entertain the man who nearly killed his son! I have spoiled you dreadfully since your mother's death and see I must pay for indulging you now. Go to your room, Elizabeth, and stay there until time for supper. Maybe that will give you a sufficient opportunity to realize what you've done today." Turning to Andrew, Olaf continued in the same angry tone. "I want you to leave here this minute, Andrew. While I will miss your help, I can no longer afford the scandal your presence here continually creates. I know it must be a long way to your home. I will give you a horse and rations for the journey, but you must be gone within the hour."

"Papa, no! Punish me if you must but Andrew is blameless!" Elizabeth pleaded without success for her father's expression was stern, his mind made up on the issue.

"Elizabeth, you will go to your room this instant!"

Elizabeth looked up at Andrew, her beautiful green eyes brimming with anguish. She could not bear to go when she knew she'd never see him again.

"Do as your father asks, Elizabeth. I want to speak with him alone."

She could not imagine what he could possibly have to say, but walked slowly from the room, certain her entire world had come to an end. Knowing she couldn't bear that bravely, she fought to hide her sorrow until she closed the door of her room where she sat too numb to weep over the tragedy which had overtaken her so swiftly—she'd had no time to bid Andrew good-bye.

Half an hour later Olaf Peterson closed his daughter's bedroom door and leaned back against it. She was sitting primly on the edge of her bed, her hands folded in her lap and her green gaze as murderous as Andrew's. He closed his eyes for a moment to clear his thoughts, then asked in a voice he could barely control, "That savage of yours just calmly told me he'd heard our custom was to ask a man for permission to marry his daughter. He then had the audacity to ask for mine so he might marry you!"

"He did what?" Elizabeth leapt to her feet, hope filling her heart with a joy she'd thought never again to feel. "What did you tell him?"

"I was as astounded as you are obviously. I told him no, of course. He has no intention of living as we do. He wanted to take you home to the Seneca and I'll not allow that outrage. My God, the man must have taken

119

me for a complete fool!"

"Andrew said that he wanted to marry me and take me home to his tribe?" Elizabeth's lovely skin grew pale at that thought. She wasn't afraid of Andrew, but the prospect of living with Indians terrified her for she could scarcely imagine what her life might be.

"Yes, and I told him you deserved far better than that. I won't allow you to reside with savages, Elizabeth. My God, to whom would you talk?"

Elizabeth nodded numbly. "Andrew says I talk too much too." Well, that had not been exactly how he'd put it, but that had been his meaning all the same.

"Did he now? He's smarter than I thought then. He refused the horse I offered, as well as the food, saying he'd leave as he came. I swear to you, baby, if he comes back with his friends and tries to kidnap you, I'll do my best to kill him."

"Please, Papa, don't even threaten such an awful thing." Elizabeth sank back down on her bed. At least Andrew had asked for her. He'd been gentleman enough to do that and she was grateful for it.

Olaf frowned. His daughter's reaction had not been what he'd expected and he was worried. "Andrew had no cause to think you'd accept his proposal, did he? Tell me the truth, Elizabeth. If he so much as forced you to kiss him I'll go after him right now."

Elizabeth responded truthfully. "No, Papa, he did not force me to do anything I didn't want to do."

"Well, I'm glad he's gone. His presence here has driven me to distraction. Since we've always shared our meals with Jed, there was no way I could bar him from our table, but thank goodness that ordeal will be over. I always had the feeling he was waiting for something, watching for an opportunity of some kind. I did not trust his motives but perhaps his main interest has always been you and now that he knows he can't have you let's pray he does not return."

"Why do you dislike him so, Papa? He is a fine man. You can't deny how diligently he worked for you no matter what his motive. Why couldn't you have appreciated him for that if for no other reason?" Elizabeth had never been able to understand her father's attitude. Was he simply jealous as Daniel had been, too jealous to want his only daughter to fall in love with any man? At least Andrew had had the sense to leave calmly, for she knew a fight between the two men she loved could have had only one outcome and she shuddered at the thought of one of them lying dead because of her.

Olaf stared at his pretty daughter for a long while, his gaze piercing and troubled as he studied her delicate features in the soft light which filled the small room. She looked the same as she always had, no less innocent, no less dear, but he was frantic with worry and vowed to himself never to allow her to even meet such an unsuitable man ever again. "He had no last name and a vicious past, Elizabeth. That's exactly what I told him, too. I would be a lunatic to give you to such a man."

Elizabeth did not argue, for it was pointless now that Andrew had gone. She had cared too deeply for him to worry over such an insignificant flaw as his lack of family name and, that he had fought as the Seneca he was, mattered not at all to her. She knew in her heart

Andrew was the finest man she would ever meet and nothing would ever change her opinion of him.

"When I was in Philadelphia your Aunt Rebecca chided me for not bringing you to meet them. It might be a very good idea if after the MacGregars' party I sent you to stay with my brother's family for the summer. With any luck by the time you return, Daniel and his father will have forgotten there ever was a man named Andrew living here."

"I'll not forget," Elizabeth whispered softly. She'd always wanted to visit Philadelphia, but not like this, not to be banished to avoid gossip which had become the truth.

Olaf took a step forward. "What did you say?"

"I said I will go if I must." It mattered little to her where she went if Andrew would not be there.

"I wish to God I'd taken you with me when I went this spring, then that trapper would have had his bounty and that maddening Indian would have been taken care of for good!" He slammed the door on his way out, leaving his angry wish hanging in the air. It was a thought so obscene Elizabeth could scarcely cross her room to reach the porcelain wash basin before she was violently ill.

Hiding her grief as best she could, Elizabeth performed her chores slowly the following week, her heart too heavy with despair to give her any peace. She had gambled on having two more months to share with Andrew and had lost, yet as she looked back there was nothing she would have changed. The weeks he'd spent in her home had been the most exasperating of her life, but also the best. She drifted through the days forcing herself to wash and iron her prettiest summer dress so she'd have something attractive to wear to the MacGregars' party, but she could not seem to make herself prepare for a trip to Philadelphia the following week.

Friday afternoon she wandered out to the orchard and sat down wistfully dreaming of the night she'd spent there with Andrew. She closed her eyes and leaned back against her favorite tree, knowing if she lived forever she'd never forget the ecstasy of those stolen moments. Lost in the delicious daydream, she returned Andrew's light kiss readily before her eyes flew open in shock. "Andrew!"

He raised his fingertips to her lips and scanned the orchard hurriedly to be certain they weren't being observed. "How was I supposed to meet you if you never left your house? I dared not come to your room for fear your father now slept there. You have kept me waiting all week and I was beginning to think you did not want to elope with me after all!" Andrew whispered angrily, his tone greatly perturbed.

"But I thought you'd gone home. I had no idea I was supposed to meet you. How would I have known that?" Elizabeth didn't know whether to laugh or cry she was so thrilled to see him again.

Andrew swore softly to himself. She had pushed his patience to the limit as usual. "Did you not tell me yourself that if a father refused a couple permission to marry they would elope?"

Elizabeth reached out to caress his cheek sweetly. "I didn't know you really wanted me for your wife, Andrew. My father is planning to send me to

123

Philadelphia on Monday and I would have gone for I had no hope of ever seeing you again."

Andrew drew Elizabeth into his arms, crushing her slender body in a desperate embrace as his mouth claimed hers in a kiss which left her all the more shaken for the effect of his passion was too forceful not to evoke an undeniable response. When he lifted his head she could barely focus her eyes upon his. "I told you you'd be no man's bride but mine. Was that not clear enough for you? Hasn't what we've already shared made you my wife?"

"Yes, yes, of course it has." Elizabeth smiled readily, she should have known an Indian would regard the words of a marriage ceremony as a mere formality after the depth of their unspoken vows. Then the reality of their situation brought a sudden wave of fear. "If my father sees you here there will be hell to pay. If we are to go away together, how can we arrange it? Tell me quickly for Papa and Jed will be home for supper soon."

"We will leave tonight, but do not give your father any reason to suspect our plan. Follow the routine you always do, then pretend to go to bed and wait for me. I will come for you and we will leave for my home and never return. The journey will be shortest if we travel west as far as possible before turning north. You are not used to travel, but we will reach my home safely."

"Yes, I understand." Elizabeth nodded quickly but could not keep the tears from filling her eyes. "I should have known our only chance to be together was for me to go with you."

"Elizabeth," Andrew spoke her name softly but

with a command she could not dispute, "dress warmly. Bring only what you can carry in one hand and no more. I will hunt along the way, but bring whatever food you have handy. Do as I say and do not give your father any reason to watch you tonight for we will need every hour of darkness we can get to make good our escape."

Elizabeth brushed his lips lightly with hers, then ran back into her house. After supper she sang softly to herself as she often did, but her mind was busy sifting through her possessions trying to decide which would be the most useful to take. She wrapped jerky and biscuits in a napkin, then slipped a sharp knife into the pocket of her apron and carried everything back to her room before returning to sort out her books. Her Bible had been a present from her mother but that was precious to her father as well so she selected an older one, the leather cover worn with age, but it would serve her as well.

"Elizabeth? What are you doing there?" Olaf glanced up from a column of figures he was trying to add and regarded her with a curious eye.

"Just straightening up a bit, Papa. Sorry I disturbed you." When he returned to his work, she carried the old Bible to her room. She hated to leave home with no good-bye, but if nothing else she could leave her father a note so he would know she'd gone of her own free will. That message completed she returned to the front room to kiss her father good night and gave him a warm hug. "I love you, Papa."

Olaf looked up, surprised by her sudden display of affection. "I love you too, Elizabeth, but you've always known that."

"Yes, I have." She rushed then to finish what she wanted to say, hoping he'd recall her words when she was gone. "I hope Margaret is as smart as I think she is and says yes when you ask her. She'll make you a fine wife."

Olaf laughed and gave her a playful swat as she turned away. "Good night, Elizabeth. Margaret is not so clever as you, but she's almost as pretty and I think she'll do."

"Good night, Papa." Elizabeth went to her room, made a small bundle of the things she'd decided to take, then dressed carefully in her favorite dress, the soft blue linsey-woolsey. Remembering her father had given her her mother's wedding ring to keep, she slipped it on her finger. Indians most likely did not wear wedding rings, but perhaps Andrew would not mind if she wore her mother's. The gleaming gold band fit her finger perfectly as if it were a sign she was indeed Andrew's bride.

Turning her thoughts back to the practical, she slipped into bed but was too warm and lay worrying about what would surely happen should her father catch her with Andrew before they could get away. She focused her anxiety upon that very night and let her mind wander no further. The future had to be met one day at a time and she'd not allow herself to contemplate her life with the Seneca just yet. At last her father came to her door and stood silently watching for a moment before he went into his own room. She strained to listen as he prepared for bed and did not relax until she heard his deep snore and knew he was sleeping soundly. She got up then, straightened out her quilt and then sat on the side of her bed, trying not to faint as she waited for Andrew and when he appeared at her window she handed him her small parcel, then climbed over the damp sill. She lifted her lips to accept his soft kiss and taking his hand in a firm clasp moved silently by his side into the night.

Seven

Andrew led Lady at a steady pace through the forest without stopping once until the rising sun sent fiery streaks of crimson across the morning sky. He stopped then and helped Elizabeth down from her mare, then let the gentle animal graze in the tall grass while they sat nearby to rest.

"We are not traveling west, but north, Andrew. Why are we going this way?" Elizabeth unwrapped a piece of the venison jerky and handed it to him. "I was not certain of our direction until it became light, but I am sure now."

Andrew sat watching the sunlight turn her fair hair to gold for a long while before he replied. "I only told you that we would travel west in case there were a trap, Elizabeth. I did not want to walk into one. I had always planned to go to the north first. This way we will be in Iroquois territory when we must journey west."

Elizabeth put down her piece of jerky and stared intently at her handsome companion. "A trap?" Then she understood him. In an instant she knew what he meant and was appalled by it. "Oh, Andrew, you didn't think I'd lead you into a trap, did you?"

He shook his head slowly as he smiled. "It was only a thought I had, that perhaps you might tell your father you were leaving. It would have been a simple matter for him to lie in wait in the forest and kill me. Then all his problems with his beautiful but headstrong daughter would have been solved."

"Andrew, you cannot believe I would ever be a party to such a hateful plan! You simply can't believe that!" Elizabeth protested heatedly.

Andrew shrugged nonchalantly and took another bite from the strip of jerky he held loosely in his right hand. "It was only a thought. I did not say that's what actually happened."

Elizabeth responded angrily. "A very gruesome thought that was too! How could you accuse me of such a horrible thing? I would never betray you, Andrew. How could you ask me to be your wife if you do not trust me? If you thought I would help my father trick you, simply to provide a convenient excuse for your murder, why did you wait all week to speak to me? Why didn't you just go on home alone?" Elizabeth was astounded that he could have even come up with such a ridiculous idea, let alone have given it the consideration he obviously had.

Andrew's well-shaped mouth curved into a sly grin as he answered. "Because I have already tricked him. I have taken you, haven't I? He will never be able to find us now."

"You did not kidnap me. I have come with you willingly, but I hope he does not try and follow us. I left him a note. I told him never to attempt to find me, that I would come back to see him when I could. Still, he may come after us with soldiers. You know he wanted me to marry Daniel and I'm afraid he will cause trouble for us even when we reach your tribe."

"No, he is a farmer, not an Indian scout. He will not be able to track us through the forest. Do not worry." Andrew continued to chew on the jerky as if he had not a single care to disturb him on that clear spring morning.

"Andrew, he knows your name and that of your father. It will not be too difficult a matter to find your village if he really wants to search, which I am very much afraid he will."

Andrew enjoyed the sight of her pretty features in the soft morning light and smiled. "You are as smart as you are beautiful, Elizabeth, but there is one thing you do not understand."

"And what is that, or should I say thank you first?" Elizabeth smiled in return, happy to be with Andrew for his ready confidence gave her courage, yet she was still frightened her father would overtake them before they reached his home.

"He does not know my name or that of my father."

"What do you mean, Andrew? He knows you are Silver Hawk and that Flaming Sky is your father, a chief. He will tell the authorities and they will know where to find us." Elizabeth was exasperated that he was overlooking so obvious a point.

"Elizabeth, there is no Seneca chief named Flaming Sky and I am not Silver Hawk." Andrew observed her reaction closely as he saw the meaning of his words take shape in her mind. She frowned slightly, then began to draw away. She got slowly to her feet and backed away toward Lady, reaching out for the mare as if she could touch the safety of home in the animal's dark glossy hide.

Andrew's gaze did not falter but he did not stand up

130

to follow her. He stayed seated where he was and called to her softly. "Come back here, Elizabeth. Come here to me."

"You lied to me?" Elizabeth was terrified now. What had she done? If he had lied to her from the first day they'd met, surely he had lied to her about everything, about taking her home and making her his wife. He had been so very clever, gradually winning her trust until she believed in him completely. She was paralyzed with fright, positive now she was the one who had been tricked, not her father. She had been tricked into loving a man who told nothing but lies and she was sick with shame, filled with revulsion for her own stupidity. Her father had tried to warn her. Again and again he had tried to make her see what Andrew was. Why had she never believed him?

"Elizabeth, come back here and sit beside me again. I will explain."

"With what, more lies? I am your prisoner, aren't I? You have managed to make a captive of me and such a willing one at that. How your tribe will laugh when you take me home. What will happen to me then, Andrew, or is that even your name? Perhaps it is John or David, or some other name you can't even recall. Well, what have you planned for me, Indian? Will you give me to all your friends to rape until they have had their fill of a white woman? Was that your plan? To let all the braves have me as you have? Did you think I would be willing now? Well, I will never be willing. You will have to beat me senseless to ever come near me again!"

Andrew sprang to his feet and caught her around the waist as she tried to swing herself up upon Lady's back. He tossed her down upon the grass and pinned her slender body beneath his own where he held her captive, nearly crushing her delicate wrists in his strong grip. "You think I would let another man touch you? Or that I would ever harm you? My God, I should beat you for what you've just said!" But Andrew's anger left him swiftly as he saw her terror was real. She was shaking with fright, desperately afraid of him and it made him sick to think he had done that to her. He sat up then and pulled her into his arms, stroking her blond curls lightly as he called to her softly, speaking as he would to gentle any wild creature he wished to tame. He kissed her lips tenderly and at last she began to respond, hesitantly at first, but then her kisses grew more ardent and she wound her arms around his neck to hold him in her loving embrace. Andrew lay her down gently in the thick grass and kissed her slender throat as he unbuttoned her dress. He continued to kiss her as his hands moved down her shapely form. He knew her body almost as well as his own, the soft swelling of her breasts, the gentle curve of her ribs, the tiny waist his hands could span. He loved every inch of her beautiful body and he could not bear to think she had thought he would give her away, ever let another man touch her. He tried to make her understand as his lips caressed her creamy smooth breasts. His hands traced delicate patterns across her flat stomach and down between her thighs until the tremors which shook her lissome body were those of passion, not fright.

Elizabeth's tears made their kisses salty, but she clung to Andrew as her desire grew bolder. She wanted

132

him still, could not refuse him when he touched her as he did. His hands were like magic, drawing feelings which she could not deny as the longing swelled within her until she could not wait for him to take her again. She wanted only to give herself to him as the warmth grew within her. She was his as he was hers and there was no space between them as he took her, no space between either their splendid young bodies or ageless souls. They were each consumed with such passion for the other that they were truly one, bound forever by a love which radiated a sparkling light until it blinded them with its fiery brilliance, fusing their hearts with its flame.

The sun had traveled high in the sky but Elizabeth lay in Andrew's arms not wanting ever to move in spite of their earlier haste to flee her father's wrath. Her slender fingers traced the line of one of his scars along his chest and down his side, her touch easy, gentle. Once healed the scars were faint under his deep tan, but she knew each one distinctly and how it felt to her fingertips and lips. "I am sorry, Andrew. I should not have said what I did to you. It is only that I am so afraid we will never be able to share this loving peace as we long to, never find our home, or the happiness that should be ours."

Andrew turned on his side and grinned down at her. "When will you learn that you are mine and that I mean for my wife to always be happy? Your body knows you belong to me even if your mind does not, for I did not have to beat you, my love."

Elizabeth turned away from him as she began to rebutton her dress. "I am not in the least bit ashamed to be here with you, but I would prefer not to hear anymore surprises such as the one you gave me this morning."

Andrew sat up to hug her warmly, then drew her upon his lap. "Then let me explain as best I can. When the trappers caught me I did not tell them my name. They called me Silver Hawk to laugh at me. It was a joke because they hoped to collect a large bounty for me and I saw no reason to tell you the truth that first day you bought me."

"Andrew, please, I did not really buy you. You mustn't even think that."

"Yes, you did. Now just listen. I never made any secret of the fact I wanted you and it did not take me long to realize your father would not let you marry an Indian, so I knew I would have to take you and I saw no reason to give him the information he would need to find us."

"Then what is the truth, Andrew? Will you trust me with it now?"

"My name is Rising Eagle and I am Seneca as I told you. My father is Chief Six Bears, although I think Flaming Sky is an impressive name, don't you? I made that up since white people do not seem to understand our names. I knew you would believe whatever I told you. But all I told you of Andrew is true. That was all true. Now you must trust me as you have learned to. I did not mean to frighten you so badly by telling you lies. My only purpose was to keep you with me. That was all I ever wanted to do, just to keep you as my own."

"We should go, Andrew, or may I call you Rising Eagle. You are like an eagle, you know, cunning and swift but do not trick me ever again. I beg you. Do not fool me again."

"No, I will not, but you must promise not to try and fool me either, Elizabeth."

"How could I fool you, Rising Eagle? You are far too clever for a simple girl like me to trick." Elizabeth began to laugh as Andrew tickled her ribs as he helped her to her feet.

"You are sly too, Elizabeth, as clever as I am and you know it."

Elizabeth stepped back to look at the man she had chosen. She thought him perfect in every way. "I think I understand your name. I have seen eagles soaring on the wind, gliding on the breeze without the slightest effort until they swoop down to catch their prey. Rising Eagle is a fine name for you, for the eagle is handsome, perhaps as beautiful a bird as you are a man."

"Can men be beautiful? Is handsome not the better word?" Andrew helped Elizabeth to mount Lady, then again took the reins in his hands.

"Yes, men are called handsome, but you are more than that, Andrew. I wish we had found your people. Your features are perfect. You are so tall and well built, I cannot help but think you are someone very important if only we knew your real name. If only we knew who you really were."

Andrew stopped Lady as he turned back to face his wife. "I am Rising Eagle of the Seneca, Elizabeth. If that is not fine enough for you I will send you back home right now!"

Elizabeth shook her head. It was impossible for her to return home and she knew that even if he did not. "You must forgive me. I did not mean to insult either who or what you are. I am happy to be your wife, exactly as you are."

Breaking into a ready grin, Andrew leapt upon Lady's back and put his arms around Elizabeth's waist. "Your horse can carry us both for a while." He began to nuzzle her neck playfully with his lips, kissing her sweet smelling hair as they rode along. "I want to take you home, Elizabeth, to meet my parents, to make love to you in my own bed."

"Will a bed make any difference, Andrew?" Elizabeth giggled as his wandering lips tickled her throat. "We have shared a soft woolen blanket, fresh crisp snow, grass covered with sparkling dew and—"

Andrew hugged her so tightly she could not continue. "You will love my bed. Our beds are made of piles of furs. They are so soft and comfortable you will never want to get up ever again."

Elizabeth put her hands over his. "I care little where I sleep as long as you will be with me. I hope the fact you are bringing home a wife will not be too great a shock for your parents."

"They will adore you. Do not worry. It is time I took a wife and they will not argue about my choice."

Yet Elizabeth wondered if his parents would not be as hostile to her as her father had been to him. "Where will we live, Andrew? Do you have your own house?"

"No. The women own our homes, Elizabeth, not the men. When a man marries he goes to live with his wife's parents, in her mother's home. That is our custom. A woman's daughters live with her, her daughters and their husbands and all the children."

"Her grandchildren?" Elizabeth supplied the word she thought he might have forgotten.

"Yes, a woman's daughters, sons-in-law and grandchildren live with her in one house. Our homes are much larger than yours, longer and wider, but they are made of wood as yours was."

"I will have no mother in your village, Andrew, no relatives of any kind to take us in. Where will we live?" Elizabeth posed her question thoughtfully, for she knew so little of what to expect their life would be. "I am afraid as your wife your family is going to look upon me as most unsuitable if I cannot provide a home for you if that is the custom."

"I will build a house for us and a fine one. Do not worry. I know how to build a house," Andrew boasted confidently.

"Yes, I'm sure you do for you did such a fine job on the small house you shared with Jed. There seems to be nothing you can't do and do well, Andrew, but I know nothing of your tribe, your family. I don't want them to laugh at me, or at you."

Andrew scoffed at that impossibility. "Elizabeth, why would they laugh at us? You are so very pretty. Everyone will love you dearly. My mother's name is Rainbow, and she is like her name, pretty and sweet and my sisters are nice, too."

"Will you tell me about them, Andrew, but tell me their names in English for I doubt I can even pronounce your Indian words." Smiling shyly she turned to look up at him. "When we make love you speak to me in your own language and I've no idea what it is you are telling me."

Andrew laughed heartily at her complaint. "I did not realize I did that but even if you cannot understand my words, you must understand what it is I'm trying to say, can't you?"

137

Elizabeth nodded. "Yes, at least I hope I do. Now tell me about your sisters. You know I am the curious sort."

"Summer Moon is the oldest, the liveliest too. She was born the year after I became my father's son and I helped to raise her as I did Fawn and Blossom when they were born."

"That would make Summer Moon nineteen, wouldn't it?"

"Yes, Fawn is seventeen and Blossom sixteen. They have always followed around after Moon. They do what she does and copy her ways more than my mother's. They are like twins they are so close in age, but all three girls are pretty, very different from you, but pretty still."

"You are Chief Six Bears' only son though?"

"Yes, my mother had only the three girls and no more babies came to her. Had Chief Six Bears not found me he would have no son."

"It was a lucky thing for both of you that he found you when he did, for I'm sure he is very proud of you and it is clear you love him." Elizabeth was still worried about being accepted into Six Bears' family, or into Rainbow's if that were how she should think of it, but said no more about her fears.

Lost in their dreams of the future, they did not stop until after the moon had risen, but Andrew was certain he could elude Olaf Peterson no matter how many soldiers the man found to search for his daughter. Another day and they would enter land acknowledged as being Iroquois territory and he would feel safer still. He would be home then. On his own ground, the rest of their journey could be made more swiftly.

"These apples are filling if not so delicious as your dinners usually are, Elizabeth." Andrew had eaten several for he had brought plenty along with the dry biscuits and jerky she had provided.

"When will we be able to build a fire and cook something? Jerky has never been one of my favorite foods and I am tired of it, even though it has been our diet for only one day." Elizabeth sat opposite him, her back against an oak tree for support as she nibbled their sparse meal.

"In a day or two. I do not want to take the time to hunt or light a fire whose smoke would signal anyone following us."

Elizabeth shuddered. "I pray my father will not follow us, yet I know that he will. He will not let me go so easily as this."

"We will be safe. Had he taken you to Philadelphia I would have gone after you. It would have been difficult for me to find you in that city, but I would have done it."

"Yes. Somehow I think if such a feat were possible you would have been able to do it and I would not even have known you would attempt it. I am sorry I understood the depth of your feelings so poorly. Perhaps I am a child after all."

Andrew pointed to her small bundle and asked, "What did you bring, my pretty child?"

"I am embarrassed to show you. I'm sorry we had no time to talk about what I would need." Elizabeth untied the parcel and her small bottle of perfume caught Andrew's eye immediately. He reached for it and turned it slowly in his hand.

"What is this?"

"Perfume. Remove the lid and you will see."
Elizabeth was surprised at his ignorance, then
remembered he would have had scant opportunity to
meet ladies who used perfume in his village.

Andrew seemed genuinely surprised by the bottle's
contents. "This smells just like flowers, exactly as you
do."

"Did you think that pretty fragrance was only me?
Now I am sorry you saw the bottle for now you will
know it is only my perfume. There are many different
scents. This one is from France. They make some
wonderful perfumes there."

"The French do?" Andrew scowled. "I have no love
for the French."

"I can understand your feelings since you fought
them so fiercely when you were young. That war is
over now though, and some say the French will come
to help us defeat King George if there really is a
rebellion."

"Why would the French wish to do that?" He had
come to rely on Elizabeth for all sorts of information.
He had found her far different from an Indian girl in
that she knew so much about her world. She was
interested in things he had thought only concerned
men, and yet he trusted her judgment completely.

"My father could explain this better. All I know is
France and England are enemies. If we fight England,
then we can ask her other enemies to help us. They
would come to our aid in order to hurt King George, to
weaken his power in the world and thereby boost their
own."

"Now I understand." Andrew nodded but his

expression did not lighten. "You brought your Bible?"

"Yes. I want to teach our children to read, Andrew. I thought that would be the best book to use. There are so many wonderful stories we can read for years and never finish them all."

Andrew frowned. "I want our children to be Indian, to be Seneca as I am."

"Am I to have no say in how my own children are to be raised? Don't you want them to be able to read and write English as well as you and I do?"

"No, it will be better if they are taught as Indian children are, if they are raised to be Seneca, not white." Andrew was serious, his gaze sullen. "I am tired of trying to live as a white man does. I want to go home where I can return to the ways I know once more."

Elizabeth retied the ends of the cloth which held her few belongings. "Andrew, you are a white man and I am a white woman. Our children will only have to look at us to know they are white, too."

"They will believe what we tell them. I will teach you to speak our language and to learn our ways. You will be as Indian as I am in time."

Elizabeth clenched her teeth and looked away rather than fight with him but her effort was a futile one. She was too angry to keep still.

"Elizabeth? You will do as I say because you are my wife. Keep your Bible and read it to yourself, but do not try to teach my sons to be white men."

"Your sons! Will you just look at me? My hair is so light it is nearly white. My skin is fair and my eyes

141

green. No matter what language I speak your sons will know their mother is a white woman. What if your sons are blond like me? What then, Rising Eagle? Tall, green-eyed men with hair as white as the snow which covers Sweden where my Viking forefathers ruled. Their Viking blood will make them fierce warriors, but no one will think them Indian no matter what language you insist they speak!"

"No, they will be dark as I am. If it were not for my eyes no one would know I am not as Indian as my friend Red Tail."

"Your sons will resemble you because you say so? I do not think it will work that way. Why are there so many women in the world when all men pray to have sons! No man wants a daughter, not ever." Elizabeth got to her feet and threw down her half eaten apple angrily as she walked away from her husband. She had tried to hold her temper but it was impossible when he was being so stupid. She was angry, hungry, and so terrified her father would somehow overtake them and kill Andrew she could not bear to rest. "Let us go on. I'm not tired and Lady has rested long enough to continue. I don't want to stay here and fight with you. The moon is bright again tonight and you will not get lost."

Andrew watched as Elizabeth took her mare's reins in her hands. She hesitated, unsure in which direction to begin and had to turn back toward him. He got slowly to his feet and walked to her side, standing close as he ran his fingers through her pale yellow hair. "Forgive me, Elizabeth. I did not know you were not wanted. Why are you so afraid your father will come after us if he cares so little for you?"

"I was not talking about my father, Andrew. I was

talking about you! You want boys you can raise as
Indian braves. What if we have only girls? Do you not
care how I raise them? May I teach them to speak
English so I will have someone to talk to? May I teach
my daughters to read and write so I won't be ashamed
of them?"

"Ashamed? You would be ashamed of our children
if they could not read?" Andrew snarled angrily.

"No! Ashamed I let you tell me what to do when I
know you are wrong!" Elizabeth shouted right back at
him, too mad to care how willfully she was defying
him.

"You still do not understand that our children
cannot be both Indian and white? That they must
belong in one place or the other?"

"No, I don't for one minute believe that! If that
were true, then you wouldn't want me for your wife,
for clearly I will never truly belong to your tribe!"

Andrew's grip on her shoulders was firm. He could
have shaken her soundly but did not. Instead he
lowered his mouth to hers and began to kiss her
slowly, sweetly, very gently in a surprising change of
moods which confused Elizabeth completely. He
pulled her against his chest, pressed her slender body
tightly to his then moved his hands slowly down her
back. When he moved a step closer, he forced her
against Lady's flank but the mare stood still, allowing
them to lean against her without flinching. Andrew
placed his hands on the horse's back as he continued
to savor Elizabeth's marvelous kiss, holding her
captive easily between his strong arms. He simply
kissed her again and again until she was lost in the
passion he aroused within her, lost in the need her
own body felt for his.

Elizabeth felt her knees weaken as the tremor of pleasure slid down her spine. She could not fight him with words when he could take her very soul and hold it in his grasp. She had no way to argue when he conquered her body with such masterful ease. She could not escape his loving kiss as he leaned against her. His warmth and Lady's were the same, enveloping her with a heat which stifled all thought save one. She broke away from his lips when her need overpowered her and she begged him to finish what he had begun. Her small hands tore at his shirt. She could not wait when he moved with such deliberate slowness. "Please, Andrew, please." Her voice was no more than a whisper as she begged him to make love to her. He had taught her too well, made her bond to him too strong. Her need for him was too great for him to do what he had done to her, to tease her as he had and he knew it as he dropped down to the grass and drew her into his arms. He could use the force of desire to dominate her, to win any argument, yet when he took her it was his own heart he lost again, his own soul which was now more hers than his, and he knew that as he held her in his loving embrace. He kissed her face and whispered, "Will you not obey me because I am your husband and you love me so? Will you not give me children who will be truly mine as well as yours?"

Elizabeth said nothing in reply, but pulled his head down to hers again. She began to kiss him with a passion more wild than any he could ever have imagined. Her whole body seemed to caress his as her lips moved down his throat and along the length of a scar which crossed his chest. Her lips burned his skin. Her hands gave him no respite from her desire and he

144

pulled her tightly against his heart and tried to remember why they had been fighting when he loved her so intensely. They went no farther along their journey that night, too exhausted from their passion, too satisfied from the other's gift of pleasure. They fell asleep, each clasping the other warmly even in slumber.

Elizabeth kept her eyes closed as she lay resting in Andrew's arms, but she was not asleep. Her mind kept churning over their latest argument. They had always fought each other tooth and nail for neither could bear the other's domination and their relationship had perpetually been a stormy one. Why had she been so foolish to think their marriage would be any different?

Andrew was also awake although she did not realize it. He lay cuddling her close and watched her expressions change. When a tear escaped from beneath her long lashes to roll down her velvet smooth cheek, he leaned down and kissed it away. "Do not cry, Elizabeth. We should not have disagreed so about babies who may never be born. It was foolish. I will be so happy to have daughters, beautiful fair ones who look like their mother. Do not ever think I will not want your little girls."

"Truly you would?" Elizabeth wiped her eyes as she sat up. Her hair was all tangled and she remembered her hair brush was still tied up in her bundle.

"Yes, women are very important to us. I don't think you understand that. I told you it is our women who own our houses and also our fields, but they choose our chief, and have the right to say if a captive will live

145

or be put to death.''

Elizabeth grew faint. The nausea which swept through her made her gag and she turned away as she covered her mouth quickly. She felt dizzy and Andrew's face blurred before her eyes.

"Elizabeth, what is wrong? Are you ill?" Andrew grabbed her shoulders, ready to catch her should she faint.

"My God, do not ever speak to me of killing men for sport ever again! Can't you understand that thought makes me violently ill!" Elizabeth shuddered as she remembered the horrid tales she'd heard of the Indians' tortures.

"It is no sport, Elizabeth. A warrior knows how to die bravely."

"Andrew, to kill an enemy in battle is one thing, to torture him to a slow, gruesome death quite another and I will never be a party to such an atrocity!"

"Not all captives are killed. Many are adopted into our tribe."

"Who decides which it will be? The women?"

"Yes." Andrew answered calmly, the matter of little consequence to him.

"Then how many men may I take in, Andrew? Your tribe will never kill another prisoner if I am to be given a voice."

Andrew sighed as he got to his feet and pulled on his clothes. "You have a Christian soul, Elizabeth, but I can not fault you for that since you saved my life so willingly. I will have to build you a large house I fear."

Elizabeth found his teasing most offensive and her nausea did not abate. She felt awful, sick through and through but perhaps it was only their meager diet which had brought the wretched feeling in the pit of her stomach. She was afraid, hungry and still tired after a night of rest. No wonder she felt ill and pushed the sickness from her mind as they made their preparations to move on. She had no time to be ill now.

As they began their trek through the forest that morning, Andrew again talked about their argument. "I was foolish to believe you would not want to teach our children. Teach them all you can and I will do my best too, and perhaps they will be able to survive in the world. If you teach them the white man's ways and I teach them to be Seneca, then they will understand whomever they meet."

"Do you really mean it? You don't mind if I teach my babies to read?" Elizabeth was overjoyed by his words but scarcely believed they could be true.

"No, you are right. They will need to know how to read, Elizabeth. Every child should know more than his parents." Andrew gave his attention to their travels and Elizabeth understood he did not wish to discuss the subject any further. He was a proud man but a fair one, and she cursed herself for understanding so little.

The woods came alive again as the many creatures who inhabited the trees and burrows began their daily foraging for food. The earth still smelled damp from the dew of the night but Elizabeth found that aroma comforting, like that of her father's fields when freshly plowed. She found herself watching the squirrels as she rode along. Their squeaking was playful as they leapt from tree top to tree top in an endless game of pursuit. As they moved deeper into that section of the woods the trees became more dense

147

and the light grew dim even though the sun had risen high in the sky. Elizabeth shivered and patted Lady's neck affectionately to give the animal courage. Surely her horse liked the place no better than she.

"I don't like it here, Andrew. It is too dark and cold. Is your home in a forest so gloomy as this?"

Andrew glanced back at his wife's worried expression and chuckled. "No, we live in the most beautiful of forests. Do not worry about my home. It is nothing like this." He saw his advice was futile, for her anxiety was easy to see. "I do not like these woods either, but we will be through them soon." As he walked on, his practiced eye searched for signs of game. He was tired of jerky too and hoped to have something far better to eat for supper, but he saw no sign of deer nor even rabbit and hurried his steps.

Elizabeth felt the change in the forest and called in a hoarse whisper. "Andrew, stop. Something is wrong!"

"What is it?" Andrew drew Lady to a halt and stepped back to her side. When he placed his hand on her knee he could feel her trembling and gave her leg an affectionate squeeze.

"Listen, it is too quiet. The birds have grown silent and not without reason. I heard someone call, a man's voice I think." Elizabeth strained her ears but the sound did not come again.

"Elizabeth, there is no one here but you and me." Yet Andrew trusted her and listened more closely, too. If she had heard something he had missed he would have been surprised, for he missed little. Then he heard it. Yes, it was a call, a signal from one man to another and they were nearby. He pulled Elizabeth from her horse's back and led the animal behind a thick stand of birch trees and drew his knife.

Elizabeth watched Andrew's face anxiously and did not speak. He would not hide from friends, that she knew. The six Iroquois tribes did not prey on each other so he must have heard something which told him the voice was not that of an ally. She clung to him as they waited behind the trees. His breathing was steady and even but she felt the tension in his lean muscular body and held her breath, not eager to see who might be approaching.

The voices came near, calling back and forth as if the men wished not to lose contact in that dismal section of the woods. They passed by with steps so silent Elizabeth feared they would hear her heart beating and turn to see her. They were Indian braves, but did not resemble Andrew. Their buckskins were fashioned in a different style, their hair shorn leaving only a crest running across the crown of their heads, their faces darkened by the swirling patterns of their tattoos. They looked evil to her and she shuddered as she gripped Andrew's arm more tightly. He did not move or speak until they could no longer hear the men's calls.

Andrew slid his knife carefully back under his belt. "The Algonquin are my enemies, Elizabeth, but what they were doing so far south I do not know. We must be more careful, and we must hurry in case there are more hunting parties out." He helped her up on Lady's back and led the horse on through the forest at a much swifter pace. They continued until the mare grew tired but Andrew only slowed down. He did not stop to rest. At last the trees began to thin out and the sunlight poured down giving the day a brightness and cheer which was a welcome sight. When Andrew finally stopped to rest, they were well within Iroquois territory and he felt safe in coming to a halt.

Elizabeth could contain her curiosity no longer. "What would those men have done to us had they seen us, Andrew? Taken us prisoner?" She took one bite of apple and tried to chew but she was still too frightened to have any appetite.

Andrew sat down opposite her but looked away. He hesitated to answer but he did not want to lie to her again. Deciding the truth was better for her to know, he spoke slowly, his meaning clear. "I would never have let the Algonquin make a captive of you, Elizabeth. They would not have taken us alive."

Elizabeth's terror was ever greater then. "Andrew, you mean you would have killed me yourself rather than let those braves have me?" She could not believe that was what he had meant, yet the truth of his statement was clear in the depths of his deep green gaze.

"Yes. That is exactly what I would have done had they seen us. You would have died instantly, with little pain. I would have made your death swift, Elizabeth."

Elizabeth was stunned, horrified that he could have contemplated such an action, yet it was plain he would have done it. He would have snuffed out her life in a single stroke and when he tried to pull her into his arms, she shoved him away. "No! Don't you dare touch me! How could you have planned such a beastly thing? How could you want to kill me? Don't you love me at all?"

"It is because you are so dear to me that I would

have done it. I will never let another man have you, Elizabeth."

Elizabeth felt sick still, clear to her very soul. "What could they have done to me? Beat me? Raped me? If I were alive I could get away, somehow escape, but if I am dead I have no chance! No, Indian, you must never think of killing me ever again. Do you believe I have so little courage I would not survive to escape?"

Andrew shook his head. "Elizabeth, if they had taken you with them, back to their village, you would be a slave unless some brave took you for his wife, which is what would have surely happened. As a wife you would be one of them and not expected to try to escape. When an Indian is adopted into a tribe he does not try to go home. He becomes one of the tribe as if he were born into it. You would have been Algonquin, Elizabeth, for the rest of your life one of theirs."

"Why do you ignore the fact I am a white woman with no such beliefs as you hold? If I am captured I will run away! You must promise me, Andrew, you will never kill me in order to save me from another fate. I refuse to accept such a death. If another man kills me then so be it. But I will not die by your hand. You must promise me never to think of that again."

Andrew shook his head emphatically. "No, I will make no such promise. I will kill you rather than let you fall into the hands of my enemies."

Elizabeth got to her feet on legs that were trembling so badly she could barely stand but she willed herself to remain upright and did so. "I am going back to my father. I do not wish to be your wife if I must always fear you are about to plunge your knife into my heart.

I cannot live with you in fear for my life. Good-bye."
She grabbed Lady's mane to pull herself up on the
horse's back but Andrew was by her side instantly and
swung her back down to the ground. His face was dark
with anger. He was furious with her constant defiance
and said so through clenched teeth.

"I can see I am going to have to protect you most
fiercely, wife, so that you are never in danger of being
captured ever again! You are mine and I will not let
you go. I did not mean to frighten you. I have heard
white women have killed themselves rather than be
taken by Indians, or by a man they did not love. I
wished only to spare you such horror."

"You don't mean it? You thought I would commit
suicide rather than be captured when life with Indians
is paradise from the way you describe it?" Elizabeth
was as angry as he and threw her words right back at
him.

"Elizabeth, I swear you will learn to hold your
tongue if I have to beat you to make you understand
that! You will not argue with me in front of my tribe or
my family. Do you understand me? You will not defy
me as you have always defied your father!"

"I will fight you every time you are wrong, Indian,
with my dying breath I will fight you if you are
wrong!"

Andrew's hands tightened on her arms until he saw
the pain fill her eyes, but she did not cry out and when
he remembered how he had bruised her wrist he knew
that she would never admit he had caused her any
pain. He was disgusted with himself. She was no match
for his strength, nor could she resist his caress but he
had to make her understand. He dropped his hands to

152

his sides and stepped back. "Elizabeth, I have tried to live as a white man to please you and your father. I worked on the farm and did whatever task I was given without once complaining, but Seneca warriors do not tend crops! We clear the land for our women to plant yet I worked to grow wheat and corn for you and you did not hear me once say I would not do a woman's work!"

Elizabeth frowned as she listened, the cause of his anger a surprise to her. "I did not know we had insulted you so by asking you to work as a white man does since you are one! And why do you complain to me now when it is pointless? We have left the farm and will never return."

Andrew swore the vilest oath he knew, his words incredibly filthy, but he knew Elizabeth understood only his tone if not his language. "What I am saying is, if I can be white to please you, it is now your turn to live as an Indian woman does to please me."

"An Indian wife does not argue with her husband, not ever?" Elizabeth asked incredulously.

"No, she does not. She respects her husband too much to disobey him."

"That can't be true, Andrew. You've never been married so perhaps you do not know what really happens between a man and his wife. Surely when an Indian woman is alone with her husband she tells him what she thinks. Just because you have never heard an Indian woman fight with her husband does not mean she does not do so!"

"Elizabeth!" Andrew could bear no more, yet as he looked at her she was so pretty he could not stay mad. Her cheeks were flushed with bright pink, her green eyes flashing with an angry fire and he wanted only to dominate her in the only way he could. Not with his fist, but with his heart. "Will you agree to that then, to fight with me only in private? If you will but agree to that I will be most content."

"Andrew, I know you are twenty-eight and I am but fifteen. I know there are so many things I do not understand about you and your people, but I know enough not to embarrass you in front of them. I would never do that to you, never." She stepped into his arms then and her lips sought his with such eagerness he could not help but respond. When his kiss grew more passionate she pulled away gasping for breath while she could still think clearly. "Would you please give me your knife?"

"I will give you anything I own. Now come back here." Andrew pulled her down onto the soft mossy floor of the forest as his hunger for her overwhelmed him again.

"I want that knife first, Andrew." She pulled the weapon from his belt and tossed it near where Lady grazed in the tall grass before coming into his arms.

Andrew suddenly understood her action and leaned back, his disbelief plain on his handsome features. "You did not think I would kill you while we are making love!"

"Why not? It would be the best time, for then my last thoughts would be the joy of knowing you. I will never feel safe with you again, Andrew, not when I know of your plans for my death."

"Do not fear. I will promise you now as I did not before, I want only happiness in your heart when you are with me, Elizabeth, never fear."

"Truly you will promise me, no matter what happens, what awful thing befalls us, I will not die by your hand?"

"I promise." Andrew's kiss consumed her in his passionate fire. He would not cause her grief by such thoughts of death and thought only of their life which would stretch toward eternity with her endlessly in his embrace. He had known other women and although Elizabeth had never asked he knew she understood he had, but he had loved none of them and none had loved him with such eager devotion as she and none had been so exquisitely beautiful. He had not fully understood what love between a man and woman could be until he had found her and he would never release her from the bond their loving had forged. He would never let her go. Despite his promise, he would see to it she never knew another man's body as she knew his. The words ran through his mind with the swift rhythm of his powerful body as he took her again. She was his, his, only his.

Eight

Andrew and Elizabeth had eaten well for the first time in almost a week and were feeling quite lazy and content. The game was plentiful and Andrew would be able to hunt whenever he wished for they were near his home and he knew any men they encountered would be friendly. They were camped at the edge of a wide sun-drenched meadow and, when Elizabeth sat down and leaned back against the gnarled oak which shaded their small campground, Andrew stretched out and lay his head in her lap.

Elizabeth combed her husband's dark, thick curls with her fingertips as she listened to the tale he was telling. She loved to hear him speak. His voice was so pleasant and soothing with a rich, deep timber which made whatever he said all the more enjoyable to the ear. He had asked if she'd like to hear some Iroquois legends and she had been delighted to listen. The task was not an easy one for him as he had to put the stories into English as he told them. The old fables had always been told with the most beautiful of language and he struggled to make the poetry of the words come alive for her now. She had been surprised to realize how different the Indian way of thinking was from her own. There was a beauty and love for all of Nature's creatures which was totally foreign to her. She understood Andrew's purpose, however. He was attempting to teach her in a most charming fashion, with patience and love, teaching her to see his people with the same admiration he felt.

"Andrew, do you suppose I could write down your stories, save them for people to read in English? They are enchanting and who will share them with the world if we do not? You understand the Seneca better than any other white man ever will for you are Indian. It is not merely the clothes you wear but the way you think, your whole outlook on life which is uniquely Indian."

"Who would want to read such stories, Elizabeth? Who would care to learn what a savage believes?" Andrew looked up as he teased her. That she enjoyed the tales had pleased him enormously and as always he was delighted simply to look at her lovely face.

"I care! And if I would love to read your stories then surely there must be others who would enjoy them too."

"I do not think so, Elizabeth, but if you wish to learn the tales and write them down I will help you. Our children will read them even if no one else ever does. You can teach our children all the Indian stories you want. I know you will make them very smart if you teach them all you know."

Elizabeth shook her head, sending her bright curls flying. "Andrew, you must not flatter me so for I know very little. I had learned all the schoolmaster could teach me by the time I was ten. When my mother died I think the man was grateful for a reason to excuse me from further attendance at his school. I asked too

157

many questions and I soon realized he knew very few answers."

Andrew laughed at her confession, that she could be a woman of such passion and still so innocent at times greatly amused him. "What is it you wish to learn, Elizabeth? Is there anything of importance you do not know? You will know far more of the world than any of the other braves' wives, I am certain of that."

Elizabeth chose her words carefully. While the bitter arguments which had filled the first few days of their journey were now few, she was still cautious not to upset him. "History was what I loved best, but I know only what has happened in the world and not why, when surely that is the most important thing to learn."

"Yes, I see what you mean. To understand a man's actions is necessary in order to be able to predict them."

Elizabeth leaned down to give him a sweet kiss. "I was hoping you would appreciate my concern. Whatever shall I do until I can master the Seneca language? I do not want to offend your people unintentionally, especially since I will have no mother or clansmen to defend me should I get into trouble."

"I will never leave your side, Elizabeth. Do not worry. You will learn rapidly. You like to talk too much to be quiet for long." Andrew ducked out of the way of her fist and drew her into his arms as he rolled over in the thick grass. He lowered his mouth to her throat to kiss her slowly, enjoying the feel of her silken skin upon his lips.

Elizabeth looked up into his clear green eyes and smiled shyly, her concern real even if his was not.

"How much longer will it be before we reach your home, Andrew? Can you tell me?"

"It depends on how much we want to hurry," he whispered in her ear as he continued to kiss her with small playful nibbles.

"I don't want to hurry at all. I love it right here. The beauty of this meadow is perfection and the earth a lovely soft bed."

"Not nearly so soft as my bed of furs, my love."

Elizabeth shivered in spite of the warmth of Andrew's easy embrace. "I am sorry to be so apprehensive, Andrew, but all you tell me of your home makes me feel I will be out of place there."

Andrew stood quickly, then pulled Elizabeth up on her feet by his side. "Enough of your incessant worrying, Elizabeth. We can be home by nightfall and I was foolish to tarry here. The sooner we reach my home the sooner you will see how pointless your fears truly are. Now come. Let us hurry. There is enough daylight left to see us home." Andrew gathered up their meager belongings and swung himself up upon Lady's back then reached down for his wife.

"Isn't tomorrow soon enough, Andrew? Can't we wait here for the night and go to your home tomorrow?" Elizabeth hung back, unwilling to take the hand he offered.

"Now, Elizabeth. We are going home now!" Andrew's expression left no room for argument and Elizabeth stepped forward and put her hand in his. She rode behind him, hugging his waist tightly as she lay her head upon his back, the steady beat of his heart the only comfort she had.

"You see what an obedient wife I am, Andrew? Do I

not comply with your every request most eagerly?" Elizabeth tickled his ribs as she hugged him.

"Stop that or I will make you walk the whole way!" Andrew chuckled and took her hands in his. "You are the dearest wife any man could have, Elizabeth, and my family will love you as I do. You will see."

But Elizabeth was not reassured. Her dread grew as they traveled along and she did not speak again until they came to Andrew's village. The long wooden dwellings were surrounded by a tall stockade. Pine trees had been felled and their trunks then buried in the ground to make the strongest of forts. There was a welcoming shout as Andrew was recognized and Elizabeth tried to look confident as she held her husband's hand. She would not embarrass him by appearing frightened even though she was terrified and she held her chin high and walked proudly by his side to his mother's home.

After a hearty welcome they were given a warm corn pudding to eat and beautiful new clothes to wear. Elizabeth found the buckskin dress as soft as silk and so comfortable she wondered why every woman did not own such magnificent garments. But the way the women had touched her blond hair did not please her. They had examined her closely as she had dressed, as if she were some strange curiosity Rising Eagle had brought home to amuse them. The women stared at her and whispered amongst themselves, their dark brown eyes sparkling with delight, but not one spoke a word of English and although she tried, Elizabeth could not understand a thing they said to her in their own language.

Once dressed, Elizabeth found herself being ushered

outside where the entire tribe seemed to be gathered to greet them and to hear Rising Eagle's account of his long absence from his home. Andrew kept her hand in his, holding on to her tightly as if his touch would provide the reassurance his words would not. What he was explaining she could only guess, as it seemed to be taking him forever to relate his account of his time to his father. The chief's gaze did not falter from that of his tall son's, but Elizabeth's apprehension grew when the man did not once smile at her as he questioned Andrew again and again. Andrew's tone was calm, but she could not help but worry as time wore on. She was certain they were arguing and she could think of nothing which would cause a disagreement between the two men but her presence. The crowd of onlookers seemed totally absorbed in the discussion. They stood quietly nodding their heads to concur with one point or another and none seemed inclined to return to his own home before Rising Eagle and Six Bears were finished speaking.

As Andrew's expression grew tense, Elizabeth could no longer keep still. When he paused for a moment, she whispered quickly, "What's wrong? What is he saying?"

Six Bears gestured toward her and Andrew turned to face her, but his expression was not a pleasant sight. "I do not want to frighten you, Elizabeth, but my father does not want to give his consent to our marriage. Since I am adopted he insists I take a Seneca maiden as my wife and I have refused."

"But I am already your wife, truly I am. How can he demand that you take another?" Elizabeth whispered earnestly, what little hope she'd had of being accepted now dashed.

"Yes, of course you are." Andrew reached out to touch her fair curls with a sweet caress. "It will simply take me more time than I thought to convince him he must agree to my choice. Do not worry though, for I will win him over to my view eventually."

"Eventually? Andrew, whatever shall we do if he will not give his consent?" Elizabeth's pretty eyes filled with despair as she implored her husband to devise some clever plan.

"I will force him to if I must, but he will give his consent." But despite his optimism the hour grew late and Six Bears had not changed the decision he'd made within seconds of seeing Elizabeth. He used all the arguments she had given Andrew herself. She had no totem, no longhouse in which to live, no mother to advise her. She was unfit in every way to be a bride for his only son. Instead he made another suggestion which finally Andrew had to accept.

Andrew's scowl was easy to read and Elizabeth was devastated as he looked down at her. "He will adopt you as his daughter, Elizabeth. My mother will be yours and my sisters yours also. He will let you remain here under that one condition only."

Elizabeth stared up at him too shocked to speak for a moment for she was certain she could not have understood the chief's offer. "Would I then be your sister and not your wife?"

"Yes. He has forbidden me to discuss the matter any further tonight. He is the sachem, the chief of my village and my father as well. I cannot disobey him."

"Yet I disobeyed my father to come here with you!" Elizabeth was too outraged at the injustice of

Andrew's words to be calm.

Andrew's hands tightened upon her slender shoulders until he saw the pain fill her eyes. "Elizabeth, be still!"

"May I refuse his kind offer since it is a husband I want and not a brother? Can you take me back to my home? I will not stay here as your sister. I will not. You must know I can never agree to that travesty. If that is his only offer, I must refuse it and return home immediately," although that thought appalled her.

"No, you may not leave the village."

Elizabeth's perceptive gaze swept the curious crowd which still surrounded them. "Is there no other family who would adopt me so that we might marry? No woman who would call me her daughter and let us live with her? Is there no one here who will help us, Andrew?"

Andrew sighed wearily. "It matters not at all to him where you reside, Elizabeth. He would not allow our marriage no matter what family took you in, so none would be inclined to do so knowing how unhappy you would be with them."

Elizabeth took a deep breath and let it out slowly. "I am to have no say in what happens to me, no choice?"

"We must do as he says for now," Andrew cautioned firmly, and he slackened his hold upon her only slightly.

"For now? And how long will that be? If he will make me his daughter tonight, what will keep him from marrying me off to another brave tomorrow?"

Andrew shuddered, the horror of her question too great for him to deny. "He would not dare to do that to me. He wouldn't dare."

"Andrew, think! I am a prisoner here after all, no more than a slave your father may give away to whomever he chooses!" She tried to pull free of his grasp, to run away as fast and as far as she could run but he drew her to his side, his strength more than she could successfully fight.

"Elizabeth, stop it! Now tell him thank you. That is all. Just thank him for his kindness for now."

"I am not good enough to marry his son and you expect me to thank him for that insult? I will not. I will not be a daughter to that hateful man. I am your wife no matter what he says." Elizabeth turned to face the dark-eyed man, her hatred for him clear in her hostile stare. He looked strong, capable of snapping her neck for such insolence, yet she dared him to try and punish her with her defiant gaze and he looked away, as if bored by her presence.

"For now you will be my sister, Elizabeth. Accept his offer and be quick about it!" Andrew insisted in a hoarse whisper.

Elizabeth stared up at her husband, unable to hide her despair. "You will be content to call me your sister?"

"Yes, for you will be alive."

"Oh, I see. I do have a choice then. If I don't agree will he kill me?" Elizabeth's lips trembled as she asked that horrifying question.

"He may do whatever he wishes. You must be grateful he wants to take you in as his daughter rather than a slave."

"I came here as your wife. I will not be a slave!"

"Good. I'm glad you at last see reason. Now you will be his daughter. Smile and that will settle it." Andrew increased the pressure on her arms, ready to shake the words out of her if need be.

"Where will I sleep tonight? Not with my brother, I don't suppose?"

"No, incest is not permitted here either. You will sleep in your own bed, alone, but with my sisters."

"Andrew, if you do this to me, I will no longer be your wife. It will be finished between us forever."

"No, only for the present, Elizabeth. You will be my wife for eternity. We both know that."

Elizabeth relaxed against him. His voice sounded hollow, his anguish as deep as her own even if he would not show it and she realized arguing was futile, but his vow broke her heart.

"I will change his mind soon. My mother will help me do it. Please believe me, Elizabeth. We must let Six Bears have his way tonight, but this issue is not settled and he knows it."

"I would rather you slit my throat right now than live one day of my life without you, Andrew. It will be too difficult for me to survive here without you," Elizabeth replied bitterly.

"You are still more of a child than a woman or you would understand that we have no choice. I must agree tonight, but I will never accept my father's decision. I will never give you up. I think he can see that already."

"Then why has he done this to us? Just to test you? To make you choose to be an Indian all over again?"

Andrew nodded slowly. "Yes, I think that might well be his purpose."

"Then he can never agree to let you have a white wife. You will never change his mind if that is his

165

reason. He will force you to marry a woman from this tribe and you know it. He will never let you have me and none of our beautiful dreams will ever come true. Oh, Andrew, how am I to live here without you?"

Andrew looked down at his distraught bride and folded her tenderly in his arms to comfort her as best he could. He stroked her hair softly but could not dispute her words. He had never anticipated his father would object so violently to her and knew he would need more time to decide what to do than they had been given that night. "Please, do this for me just for tonight, Elizabeth. I will not fail you. You must trust me now for I promise you, I will make everything right as swiftly as I can."

Elizabeth met his level gaze with eyes filled with pain too deep to express. "I have no choice, do I? I am a prisoner here just as I feared I would be." Elizabeth turned back toward the chief and smiled as sweetly as she could when she felt as if her heart had been wrenched from her breast and cast at his moccasin-clad feet.

Nine

The three sisters led Elizabeth farther and farther away from their village, talking and giggling as they moved slowly through the trees gathering firewood. One minute they were by her side and in the next instant they were gone. Elizabeth stood still and listened for their high-pitched voices, but there were no sounds except the noisy chatter of the birds and the soft purr of the wind which rustled the leaves of the birch and maple trees which surrounded her. She was all alone in the forest with no idea how to return to the Seneca village and no incentive to even try and find her way back alone. What was the point in going back? She slumped down beneath the closest tree and sat hugging her knees dejectedly. She'd sit there forever unless someone came to find her. The sun began to set and still she remained by the tree, cold, alone and utterly abandoned by the three young women who were now supposedly her "sisters."

Andrew was furious with them, madder than he had ever been and yet the girls pretended not to understand. "She didn't run away. Don't lie to me. You deliberately left her out there alone, didn't you?" He shook his eldest sister until she began to cry and told him where they'd last seen Elizabeth. "If she has been harmed in any way, you three will suffer! She is my wife and I will not have her mistreated by my own sisters!"

Summer Moon stared up at him, her gaze defiant despite her tears. "She is only a sister too, Rising Eagle, no more to you than we are."

Andrew swore as he released the girl abruptly. "She is indeed my wife and you will treat her as such and you will not play tricks on her again, do you understand?" He towered over the dark-haired girls, his anger obvious in the wicked gleam which filled his light eyes. "You should have known better than to provoke me by being so mean to my wife!"

"You are different now, Rising Eagle, different since you came home. Are you now white, again, like her?" Fawn and Blossom hid behind Summer Moon but insulted him as viciously.

Andrew ignored their taunts and strode off to find Lady. At least Elizabeth would not have to walk all the way back home. He could not forget his sisters' insults as he rode through the forest. Even Red Tail had commented upon the difference in him, but to call him a white man was ridiculous!

By the time Elizabeth heard Andrew calling her name she was beside herself with anxiety, certain she had been left out in the woods to be eaten alive by some hideous bear or wolf. She leapt to her feet as she answered him and ran toward her horse, her fear forgotten in her delight in seeing her husband once again.

Andrew jumped down from Lady's back and lifted Elizabeth into the air. "I am so sorry, my love. Were you very frightened?" Andrew smoothed back her lovely fair hair and kissed her forehead tenderly.

Elizabeth was thrilled to see him. She hugged him tightly, clasping her hands around his waist, loving the softness of his buckskin shirt. "I am no coward, truly I am not, but I did not think your sisters could be so mean as to leave me here all alone to die in the forest. They hate me, Andrew, and I have tried so hard to make them like me."

"They are foolish children, Elizabeth. You must not be offended by their thoughtlessness. I am their only brother and they are simply jealous. I dealt with them harshly and they will not trick you so cruelly ever again."

Elizabeth stepped back from his embrace and her expression grew serious as she spoke. "Have you convinced your father to let us live as man and wife? If not, I want to go home. I must, Andrew. If you cannot accompany me yourself, would you please tell me which way to go, give me the directions? I think I can find the way. I watched carefully on the way here, but I am not certain I know the way through the deepest part of the forest. I want to take Lady and go home, Andrew. I will take her now, tonight, and you can say you could not find me. I cannot live here as a stepsister nobody wants. I came here to be with you, to be your wife, but we have been here nearly a week and this is the first time I've seen you."

Andrew pulled Elizabeth back into his arms and began to kiss her slowly as his hands pressed her hips to his. He wanted only to make love, to forget the problems they had found in the ecstasy they always enjoyed together. When Elizabeth pushed him away angrily, he was both shocked and hurt.

"Stop it! How dare you kiss me? Do you think if you kiss me like that I will forget how I have been treated? What will happen to us if your father finds out you are not treating me as a sister as he insists I be? He needs warriors, doesn't he? But not me. Would he kill only me for disobeying him? Perhaps give me away to some other chief as an amusing present?"

"No! Nothing is going to happen to you, Elizabeth, but you must be more patient. I was away for months. My parents feared me dead. Give me a little more time and I will change my father's mind. Please trust me."

"No, I cannot bear it, Andrew. I will not stay here where no one wants me. I came only to be with you, to be your wife." She wanted so desperately to make him feel her anguish, to see her plight. "Can you not remember what it was like when you first came to the Seneca? I do not understand anything anyone says to me, and they all stare so. I try to smile and be pleasant but I feel so lost and alone. I can't bear not to see you, not to be with you as you promised me I would always be. I would rather run away tonight than stay."

"No! You must not ever try to go by yourself. It is far too dangerous a journey and you would never reach home safely. Are you forgetting that I want you here. Believe me, I want you here with me most desperately," Andrew vowed in a hoarse whisper.

Elizabeth clenched her fists at her sides. "Why can't you understand me? I cannot live like this one moment longer! I will run away tonight before I'll return to your mother's longhouse and be called your sister!"

"Damn it, you are not my sister, but my wife! Now come back here to me right now!" Seeing her anguish

Andrew spoke again in a far softer tone, but his words were still a command. "Come here to me." He extended his hand and when Elizabeth reached her fingertips out to touch his, he pulled her back into his arms.

"Oh, Andrew, I miss you so terribly. I can neither sleep nor eat. All I can do is think of being with you and I am so frightened of what will happen should we be caught."

"My love, I will let no one harm you. Please do not worry."

"Had you been gone today, Andrew, away from the village on a hunting party, would anyone else have come to look for me?"

Andrew frowned as he held her tiny waist easily between his hands. He could not promise with any certainty that anyone else would have conducted a search. "But I was not away, and I came for you as soon as I saw you were not with my sisters. You may not have seen me all week, but I have kept my eye on you, my love. You have not been alone at all."

Elizabeth clutched his arms tightly. "Andrew, promise me, if you are ever away and come home to find your pretty, blond 'sister' has gone, do not believe what they tell you. I will not leave without saying good-bye to you. Should they tell you I ran away you will know they are lying and I have come to some terrible harm."

"Elizabeth, nothing will happen to you. They would not lie to me."

Elizabeth made another attempt to make her husband see the obvious. "What did your sisters tell you today?"

Andrew's expression held both surprise and alarm. How had she guessed what his sisters had said? He sighed sadly. "You are right, but they are just children."

"Andrew, how could you have forgotten that all of your sisters are older than I?"

It had not occurred to him to fear for her safety and yet he had never foreseen she would not be welcomed as his wife. "I will tell my friend, Red Tail, to watch out for you also, Elizabeth. He knows some English. I taught him my tongue as he taught me his. Please do not worry. I cannot bear to see you so unhappy. I wanted only to give you joy as my wife when I brought you to my home. I did not know we would face such awful problems."

Elizabeth put her small hands upon his soft shirt, her fingers lightly rubbing across his broad chest. "Andrew, do you not feel as I do any more? Do you not need me as I need you? I cannot live without your love when the very beat of my heart calls your name." When her soft cool lips touched his, he moaned softly and sank to his knees, pulling her down on the thick blanket of grass which covered the forest floor. He held her tightly in his embrace and proved with his strong young body that his need for her more than matched her need for him.

Andrew wrapped Elizabeth in the warm fur robe he had brought for just such a purpose and leaned back against the tree with her still snug in his arms. "I am sorry, Elizabeth, but do not ever believe because I am a man I have no heart. I love you so dearly and ache to make you my wife in my people's eyes. I never thought my father would refuse my choice, never even considered that possibility and whenever you pointed out our differences I never appreciated your fears were valid ones." Andrew paused then, his next question a most serious one. "Elizabeth, can you see our future? I have heard of Indians with great widsom who have that gift, but you seem to know what is to come, to sense things. Can you see the future in your dreams? I remember the day we saw the Algonquin in the forest. You heard them before I did. You heard them before their calls could be heard, Elizabeth, just as you gave me all my father's arguments against our marriage before you had even met the man."

Elizabeth hugged him more tightly, unwilling to let him go again now that they were so close. "I know only that I am frightened, more frightened than I have ever been. Perhaps I can see our future, Andrew. I know I can see my own fate whenever I look up into your eyes."

"And what do you see?" Andrew asked softly.

"Strength, power, a force which bound me to you although I fought it, a force which binds me still. When I look into your eyes I see a soul the very mirror image of my own. I gave up my father, my home, all I have ever known and loved to come here with you. I did it all willingly, Andrew, but now your father will demand that you make the same choice. He will demand it. You will have to choose between the Seneca and me." Elizabeth paused no more than a second before continuing. "If your choice is them I will understand. I ask only that you will help me to return home for I cannot remain here without you."

Andrew did not reply but sat quietly considering her words for a long while before he turned to kiss her lips softly. When she came into his arms he began to take her mouth with a brutal affection, his kisses so demanding he left her lips bruised and this time when he made love to her, his passion was so close to violence he found her weeping in his embrace, exhausted by his strength until she could no longer hold back her tears. Andrew had been so angry, furious with the fates which continued to torment them, to tear them apart, but he had never meant to hurt his beloved Elizabeth and was devastated by the power of his own lust which had for the first time brought her pain. She had never cried when they made love, not even the first time and her tears shocked him to his senses.

"Elizabeth, my father cannot demand such a choice. It would be impossible for me to make. I am Seneca but you are my very soul and I will never give you up. Forgive me, I did not mean to harm you. I meant only to show you how greatly you are loved. Never did I mean to cause you such grief." He buried his face in her silken curls until she ceased sobbing. "I did not mean to hurt you."

Elizabeth wound her arms around his neck and held him tenderly in her embrace. "It is all right, Andrew. I understand and you have not hurt me. You never would." She covered his face with light kisses, her touch as sweet as her words.

"But I have hurt you. I have brought you to my home where your life has become hell and I will not let it continue as it has this last week. My father wishes me to accompany him on a visit he must make, a gathering of chiefs of the six Iroquois tribes. If he has not willingly agreed to allow me to take you as my wife by the time we return, then I will take whatever action I must to force him to accept you!"

"No! No, you must not, Andrew. You must not threaten him in any way or even let him suspect you might for he will simply kill me to remove the cause of your dissatisfaction. No, my love, you must trick him as you tricked my father or we will never be allowed to marry. Now you must take me back. It is dark, quite late, and your father will be furious we've been together."

Andrew sat back, gazing at his bride's determined expression in the moonlight and knew she was right, but her insight could be used to their advantage rather than accepted as a curse. "Elizabeth, if I could convince Six Bears you are of no consequence to me, perhaps he would agree more easily to our marriage."

Elizabeth nodded in agreement. "Yes, I understand. If you wanted me, but only because I am a woman you've stolen, some sort of prize, not because you love me, he would not see my presence as such a threat. But how can you do that now? What can you say? If only we had known before we arrived we could have made him think I was your prisoner and a most unwilling one."

"Yes, we could have done that easily." Andrew helped her to mount Lady but remained silent, lost in thought until they reached his mother's longhouse. Then he pulled Elizabeth quite rudely from her horse's back and shoved her through the blanket draped doorway. His voice was angry as he spoke to his father, but his rage was all directed at his wife. Finally he released her arm and spoke hurriedly in English. "I told him I beat you for running off and you won't try it

175

again. Now try and look frightened and please forgive me." With those words he struck her across the face with the back of his hand, the force of his blow knocking her to her knees and the pain and shock which filled her eyes as she watched him turn away was every bit as convincing as he'd hoped they would be.

Elizabeth got to her feet slowly but no one came to help her as she made her way to her bed. As she staggered by Summer Moon the girl's smirk was all too smug. Elizabeth knew she could not expect sympathy from her new sisters after what they'd done to her that day but they didn't have to gloat. She made no attempt to hide her tears. She understood why Andrew had hit her but that made the pain of his blow no less real.

The next morning Elizabeth found herself being herded along by Fawn and Blossom to see Six Bears depart on his journey. Her heart sank as she watched Andrew bid his mother good-bye. He could hardly search her out now after the performance he'd given the evening before so she had expected no tender farewell, but to make matters all the worse, he was riding Lady. Elizabeth was afraid she understood why. He did not trust her to remain in his village when she had the means to make her way home. Well, she would show him. She would be there when he returned. She'd be cautious now, on her guard and if Moon tried to be mean again, she'd make the haughty girl sorry.

Andrew's eyes swept the crowd of faces and found Elizabeth's easily. Her blond hair made her stand out like no other, but he was appalled by her battered appearance. The right side of her lovely face was so badly bruised her eye was nearly swollen shut. Her words came back to him in an instant. She was fair, not only a white woman but a very fair one, her skin delicate, so easily bruised. He had only meant to prove something to his father, not to abuse her so brutally and he felt sick as he turned Lady to join the riders who had already begun to make their way toward the gate in the stockade. There was neither time nor means now to apologize to her and he hoped with all his heart she had understood his shockingly harsh action had been motivated solely by love.

Ten

Elizabeth found life in the Seneca village impossible to bear without even the hope of seeing Andrew. His mother and sisters now dropped what slight pretense they'd offered of welcoming her into their family and assigned her tasks filled with endless drudgery. She was sent out alone to gather firewood and given far more than her share of the weeding in the fields, but she gave no thought to complaining had she even had the language enabling her to do so. The more time she could spend by herself the better she liked it. Anything was preferable to remaining in the village or in the longhouse where all the women laughed and talked among themselves with never a word or glance in her direction. She was totally ignored as if she did not even exist, as if she were invisible unless there were some work to be done and then Rainbow would swiftly find her. She was given the most menial of chores when it came time to prepare the meals but she watched the woman who was now her "mother" and tried to remember how to fix the dishes she liked best. The little dark-eyed woman seemed to know a countless variety of ways to prepare corn, and Elizabeth found the food tasted good but she had no appetite and never finished even the scant portion they left for her. It pained her that she could not converse or understand the words for the most common of items she used everyday and feared she would never learn to speak Andrew's language when he was not there himself to teach her. He had been tutored with kindness and affection and had promised her the same tender care and instruction, but sadly that promise had not come to pass.

The days swept by with one blurring mercifully into the next as Elizabeth grew accustomed to the women's household routine. She learned how to sew garments from buckskin by watching the few women who did not complain when she sat and studied their hands while they worked. There were rolls and rolls of the soft skins under the beds in the longhouse. Andrew had not been boasting when he had called his tribe rich. Food and other goods were plentiful. The men were skillful hunters, the women talented farmers, and their village was prosperous as a result. No one was ever idle, least of all Elizabeth, but she never felt that she belonged. Not for one minute did she truly feel welcomed by the Seneca.

When the nausea which had plagued her on their journey to her new home returned more and more frequently in the mornings, Elizabeth knew the cause and got up before the others in the longhouse stirred in order to hide her sickness from their prying eyes. She felt trapped by the reality that had so swiftly overtaken her. She had been a fool to think it would not happen when she slept so often with Andrew. It had been inevitable, but she'd not dreamed their marriage would be forbidden or that she'd be left in a strange city where she could understand no one's conversation and nothing of their sacred customs. She could imagine how Six Bears would take the news that his adopted daughter was carrying her brother's child. He would doubtless force her to marry but he would never give her to Andrew and no matter how many prayers she said before dawn nothing was changed. The only part of the day which was agreeable was the late afternoon when she would slip away by herself to bathe and wash her hair in the nearby lake. Being an only child, she could not adjust to the constant company which surrounded her. She sought out every available opportunity for solitude and thought the time she spent at the lake the best, but her new sisters soon spoiled even that simple pleasure with their spiteful games.

Elizabeth could not believe they had stolen her dress. It was just too mean a trick for even them to do. But she had left the soft, buckskin garment where she always did, folded over the lowest branch of the old oak tree and it was gone. She sank down in the grass and waited, hoping they would return to remedy her sorry situation. She had far too much pride to walk home naked yet could see no other alternative and the horror of that embarrassment was too great for her to contemplate in a rational fashion. She didn't hear Red Tail approaching until he called out her name softly. He didn't use her Indian name. Andrew had told her it was a nickname for little sister and she despised that lie. But Red Tail called her Elizabeth as Andrew did and tossed his shirt to her while he stood waiting behind the tree. His kindess touched her for it was so unexpected and she slipped the worn buckskin shirt over her head. When she stood up she had to laugh for the shirt was much too large, but it did cover her so she would be able to return to Rainbow's longhouse with her dignity intact.

"Thank you. You're Red Tail, aren't you?" She thought he was for she'd seen him watching her more than once as she'd walked out to work in the fields with the other women.

"Yes, I am a friend." The brave's smile was wide as he realized the young woman knew him.

Encouraged by his grin, Elizabeth spoke quickly. "Red Tail, when will Rising Eagle come home? Do you know? He has been gone more than a month and—" She stopped when she saw he did not understand her question. He was as well built as Andrew, although not so tall. He was a handsome young man too, and he stood shaking his head slowly while his eyes raked over her slender figure which was barely concealed by his shirt. His garment clung to her damp curves seductively and he could not listen and look at her, too.

Elizabeth saw his expression change and froze, alarm rising in her throat with astounding swiftness. "Red Tail, I am Rising Eagle's wife. You understand me. I am your best friend's wife."

Red Tail nodded, her point obvious to him. "Yes, you are wife, not sister. I understand."

"Oh, Red Tail, when will my husband come home?" Elizabeth stepped closer, forgetting her anxiety for the moment.

"The sachems talk for many weeks. All must agree. Rising Eagle will come when Six Bears does."

A sachem was a chief. Elizabeth recognized that word as one of the pitifully few she knew. She thought quickly. She might have become pregnant the first time she'd been with Andrew. Two months had gone by and if Andrew were delayed many weeks she was afraid her condition would begin to show and he would not be there to help her avoid what was surely going to be a nightmare of a scandal. "Red Tail, I must speak with my husband. Could you go and bring him home?"

"No!" the young man replied impatiently. "He will come when Six Bears comes, not before."

Elizabeth did not know where else to turn. If Andrew did not come home before her so-called mother discovered her condition, then she was certain he would return home to find her another brave's wife. But what brave would take her? Children were born into their mother's clan. Andrew belonged to Rainbow's, that of the wolf. The animal's image decorated her longhouse, but what symbol would he have put on the house he promised to build for her? She had not the strength nor cunning of any animal to aid her and her children. When she did not speak again, the confused Indian by her side threw up his hands in disgust and walked off, but the next afternoon he was back, his grin wide as he watched her bathe. He did not let her see him until she had gotten out of the lake and put on her dress, but then he stepped out of the trees and called her name.

"Oh, Red Tail, you startled me!" Then she noticed his ready smile. "And how long have you been standing there watching me?" She had kept an eye on her dress but had not thought to look for him as well.

"I watch, you will have your clothes." He stood with his arms folded across his chest, his confidence apparent in his level gaze and proud stance.

182

"Thank you, but I do not think Rising Eagle meant for you to watch me so closely. What will he say?"

"He will say thank you." Red Tail's smile widened into a mischievous grin.

"Oh, will he? I think not. Here is your shirt though. I had hoped I'd see you this afternoon so I might return it to you."

"No one bothered you today?" Red Tail asked sympathetically.

"No, not today, although had you not been here it might have been a different story. Thank you for your company. Will you walk me home again?"

"Yes. I will come." Red Tail walked beside her as they returned to the village, but it was not until they neared the gate of the massive stockade that he spoke. "You love Rising Eagle, Elizabeth?"

"Yes, so very much. Thank you for walking me home. I will tell my husband how kind you have been to me. You are my only friend here, Red Tail."

"Wait." The Indian stopped at the edge of the clearing just outside the tall gate and looked about quickly to be certain they were still unobserved. "Your sisters are mean to you? Make you do their work?"

Elizabeth was surprised he understood her plight so well but relieved someone did. Andrew would not be pleased when he heard how she'd been treated, but at least there would be someone else to tell him. "Yes, Rising Eagle says they are only jealous children and I have tried to be patient and understanding, but it is so difficult for me to live here when no one likes me."

Red Tail's grin was immediate. "I like you."

"Yes, I can see that you do." Elizabeth returned his

183

warm smile. His teeth were even and white, his smile a charming one, but she was careful not to flirt with him.

"I saw Blossom with your dress yesterday, so I came. I will watch out for you as Rising Eagle asked."

"I was certain it was one of them. My dress was on my bed when I returned home yesterday afternoon, as if I would leave the longhouse without it!" She laughed at the incident which had seemed so tragic the day before, and he laughed with her, his sense of humor apparently as keen as Andrew's.

"Elizabeth, when you need me, I will come," Red Tail vowed seriously, his smile giving way to a stern promise.

"Thank you. It is so nice to have a good friend once again." Elizabeth stepped forward and kissed him lightly upon the cheek before turning to go. Her step was light, with the easy grace of a young doe as she moved away from him. Her expression was happy for the first time since Andrew had left. Surely he would be home soon and then things would be different. She moved her hand lightly over her flat stomach. Things would be far different, and she prayed they would be infinitely better.

The afternoon Six Bears returned home, Elizabeth had just walked up the trail from the corn fields. She was hot and dirty but her spirits soared as she saw the horses tethered near Rainbow's longhouse. Her eyes swept over the animals swiftly but her heart fell as she realized the one she knew was absent. Lady was not among them. She dashed into the longhouse where she found Six Bears speaking with his family, but he only shook his head and frowned when he saw her, as if he had hoped she would be gone and was exasperated to find her still underfoot. Elizabeth turned and ran back outside to find Red Tail, thinking he might know what had happened to her husband.

The returning braves had brought presents and everyone was milling about talking excitedly as they greeted their family and friends. At last Elizabeth found Red Tail standing with a group of young braves. She had already touched his elbow before she heard the men laugh. Red Tail gave her a murderous glance, then took her arm and drew her aside.

"You must never do this! Never come to me. I will come to you!" He snarled at her viciously, then pushed her away before rejoining his friends where he was greeted with loud calls and jeers.

Stunned by her friend's rebuff, Elizabeth ran from the crowds of happy people out through the open gate of the stockade before she stopped to catch her breath. Where was Andrew? Why had Six Bears come home without his son? If something horrible had happened to him then everyone would not be celebrating so happily, so she knew he must be safe, but where was he? She slumped down beneath a maple tree whose thick leaves shaded her from the late afternoon sun and hugged her knees tightly. She was exhausted, too tired to stand and sat alone for hours while the party continued to grow louder within the fortified walls of the village. It was very dark before she went into Rainbow's longhouse. She refused to call that place home. It had never been her home, never for a minute held the promise of welcome or love as a true home should. She lay down upon her narrow bed, not sleeping. Nothing had gone as they had dreamed it

185

would. None of Andrew's wonderful promises had come true. He had returned to the life he loved, but she was as out of place among his tribe as she had feared she would be. Had Andrew been as unhappy on her father's farm as she was now? Had he been simply miserable and never told her so? That would be like him, she realized. He would not let physical pain torment him so . . . purely, mental anguish meant little. But not to her. She felt as though she were dying inside. Little by little everyday there was less of her and if he did not come home soon, there would be nothing left at all for him to love. She was nearly asleep when she heard Red Tail's low voice calling her name softly as he bent down to touch her tangled hair.

"Elizabeth, forgive me. I did not want to hurt you."

Elizabeth sat up quickly and swung her feet to the floor. The longhouse had no chairs. The sleeping platforms which lined the walls served as such, but she felt as though she were entertaining a young man in her bedroom and was terribly embarrassed by that thought. She wanted only to get up and run away, but there was no place for her to go, no escape possible. "I am sorry I bothered you, Red Tail. I didn't know you were ashamed to know me, or that your friends would laugh at you for speaking with me."

Red Tail sighed impatiently. "They were not laughing at me."

"At me then? They think I am so pathetic they laughed at me?" Elizabeth saw by his puzzled expression that he did not understand her words. "I mean, they feel sorry for me, pity me?"

"No, Elizabeth, the men laughed because they like you. All the men want what Rising Eagle has."

Now Elizabeth grew even more frightened. Dear God, what if one of the braves asked Six Bears for her? She reached out to clutch his hand. "Red Tail, if Rising Eagle does not come home soon I must leave. Do you understand me? I cannot wait for him here much longer. I will have to go back to my home and wait for him there. Can you help me get away?"

"No, you must stay here," the young man replied forcefully, the matter settled, for he'd given his promise to Rising Eagle and would not go back on it now.

"But I can't! Don't you see? I am so worried Six Bears will give me to one of your friends and I have no way to stop him!"

Red Tail considered her words thoughtfully for a long moment, then shook his head. "No, Six Bears will soon leave to fight with the King's soldiers. He will not care about you."

Elizabeth sank back upon her bed and tried not to let Red Tail see how badly his insult had hurt her. She was not at all certain they were communicating well and forgave him his rudeness. "Is Rising Eagle fighting now? Is that why he didn't come home? I know he has killed many men in the past. Is that what he's doing now?" She could scarcely force her mind to accept such a terrifying possibility.

"No, he only speaks to the Iroquois for the soldiers."

"He's acting as an interpreter, you mean?"

"Is that a man who speaks many tongues?"

"Yes, that is the word. Interpreter."

"He is that, an interpreter, not a warrior."

Elizabeth rubbed her eyes and pushed back her hair.

187

Her head was splitting after hours of attempting to find some solution to her problems where none existed. She was glad the light was too dim for him to see her clearly. "I want to go home, Red Tail. I have no choice really. I must return to my home. Won't you please help me to leave?"

"No! You belong to Rising Eagle and he says you must stay!"

"How can I belong to him when he has left me so all alone? He has abandoned me, left me with strangers who despise me and I hate it here! I won't stay. I'm going home whether you help me or not!" Elizabeth screamed at her only friend, but no one overheard her angry words over the laughter coming from outside. Her rage spent, she threw herself upon her bed, filled with longing for the man who had not returned when she needed him so desperately and when she glanced up again, Red Tail was gone. The festivities were in full swing from all the noise she could hear. The whole village was celebrating, every last person ecstatically happy except her. Elizabeth listened for several minutes, then wondered if perhaps she weren't wasting the best opportunity she might have to slip away unnoticed. Maybe she should simply go, run as fast as she could and pray she could find her way home unescorted. She had promised Andrew not to try it, but would he never come back? Not ever? She was too tired now though, she knew that, far too tired to plan a successful escape and collapsed again upon her bed in a careless heap, Andrew's name coming softly from her lips in a melancholy call he'd never hear.

The next morning Elizabeth walked through the stockade gate with a proud graceful step as she joined the other women going out to work in the fields. She never let any of them see her sorrow, never gave in to her fears in front of them. She was the only white woman many of them would ever know and she wanted to appear as brave as possible for that reason if for no other. She thought of herself as an example of a womankind which deserved the greatest in dignity and would never disgrace herself or her heritage by letting the despair which filled her soul show in her manner.

The stifling August heat grew unbearably warm that day and she worked languidly, stooping to pull weeds from near the stalks of ripening corn in Rainbow's plot of earth. By early afternoon she could do no more and went through the woods to the lake where she tossed her dress carelessly aside and dove into the cold, clear waters of the lake to wash away the sadness as well as the soil. She floated in the cool liquid for nearly an hour before getting out, then pulled her dress hastily over her head as she heard the voices of people approaching. It was her sisters. She recognized the sound of their high-pitched laughter but she was horrified when she saw they were not alone.

The British officer was tall, lean with sharply defined features which gave him a menacing expression even when his face was in repose. His dark eyes swept over her shapely form with an insolent slowness, then came to rest on the soft swell of her breast which her close-fitting dress did not disguise. A reckless grin crossed his unlined face for his years were not many but his thick, black hair was streaked with gray. Elizabeth shuddered, a sudden chill shooting up her spine for everything about the man displeased her. He looked evil, through and through and she did not know how she could escape him with the lake at her back. She waited for him to greet her, but when he gave what she recognized as an Iroquois salutation she shook her head. "You must speak to me in English if you wish me to reply."

The lanky man was puzzled, his expression quizzical as he asked, "How do you live here among these savages if you do not know their language?"

Elizabeth glanced over her shoulder, gauging the distance to the lake. Surely the officer would not pursue her through the water for his uniform was immaculate, without a trace of dirt or grime and she was certain he was too proud of his appearance to risk going for a swim in full dress. Remembering his question, she replied proudly, "My husband speaks to me in English and to his people in their tongue. We have no difficulties communicating."

"Your husband?" The officer appeared astonished by that revelation. "You are married to a Seneca brave?"

"Yes, this is my husband's home." Elizabeth spoke with a calm conviction but the man was not deterred.

"Do you wish to remain here? My men and I will be happy to escort you to the nearest settlement if you would like to leave this village when we do."

Elizabeth licked her lips nervously. Her worst fear had been soldiers would catch Andrew and hang him for kidnapping her, but that possibility seemed extremely remote now. She wanted so desperately to return home, but something in the man's manner warned her he could not be trusted to see her safely back to Rainbow's longhouse, let alone to a white man's city. The lust which shone in his dark eyes was too obvious to be ignored. "No, I am most content here. This is my home now for it is my husband's and therefore mine."

"Where is this husband of yours?" The man glanced about them cautiously, scanning the trees and shrubs surrounding the water's edge with close scrutiny.

"He is nearby, waiting for me to join him." She spoke the lies easily. They rolled off her tongue with the innocent ring of truth. Then she noticed the girls were gone. They'd slipped away so silently she'd not seen them go. They did that so frequently she was no longer surprised.

"Your husband is close at hand? He is not away hunting, or on some other mission perhaps?"

"No, General, my husband is probably watching us now. He does not leave me unguarded for he is a very jealous man."

"Is he now? With good reason, no doubt. I am a colonel, but thank you for the compliment, if you feel I seem so important as to deserve a general's rank." His smile was a slow smirk.

"Your rank means nothing to me, sir."

The man's evil leer widened as he unfastened his belt and began to remove his bright red coat. "I understand that, but if you have a brave for a husband then surely you'll not say no to me."

"What is your question?" Elizabeth continued to step back each time the officer took a step forward. Despite her innocent demeanor she knew exactly what it was he wanted from her.

The dark-eyed man scoffed at her query. "How many of these savages have you had? All of them?"

"You misunderstand the Seneca, Colonel. They will not fight your battles if you abuse their women!" Elizabeth waited no longer to turn and run, but the man was too quick for her. He leapt across the low grass which separated them, knocking her to her knees. He then grabbed her around the waist and hauled her up to her feet with a forceful lift. She had never imagined him to be so strong and ceased to struggle, frightened he might injure her unborn babe.

"Ah, you know better than to fight me. I didn't want to have to waste my time in the effort to teach you such defiance is futile."

"Let me go, Colonel, before my husband arrives to slit your throat for handling me so rudely!" Elizabeth hissed through clenched teeth with what little breath she had left.

"I'll risk it. I have fought many an Indian brave and never lost." The officer spit out his boast as he turned her around but as he lowered his head to kiss her she slapped his face smartly.

"If my husband does not kill you for this then I will! Now leave me be!" Elizabeth ducked as he swung his fist at her face and his blow missed her cheek, striking only her flying hair. As she struggled to get away, she saw Red Tail step from the trees and called to him for help.

"What that—" The colonel released Elizabeth with a rough shove. "So you were not lying, girl. Your husband does indeed guard you jealously as well he should!"

Elizabeth ran to the startled Indian and pleaded in a voice too low for the British officer to overhear, "Please, please do not let him take me!"

Red Tail stepped in front of Elizabeth as he drew his knife slowly from the sheath at his belt. He stood proudly, his feet apart ready to spring should the Englishman not understand his warning. He stared intently at the tall, splendidly dressed officer daring him to approach. He said not a word, but his hostile gaze left little doubt that he would be both a terrible and fierce opponent in any battle.

The Englishman swore as he picked up his jacket. "Good day, madame. I was told there was a beautiful young woman with yellow hair living here. A woman I would find amusing. I was misinformed."

Elizabeth made no response as the man strode off down the trail. She waited until he had gone before she put her arms around Red Tail's waist to hug him warmly. "Thank you, my friend. You have saved me again from my sisters' mischief. When did the soldiers come?"

Red Tail slipped his knife back into its beaded sheath and shrugged. "Today, but they are not many."

"Thank God for that, but what shall I do, Red Tail? If they report I am here my father will be able to find me." Elizabeth's thinking was far from logical. She wanted desperately to return to the safety of her home, but did not want to be taken there by force.

"They have come seeking warriors, not women!" Red Tail laughed at her fears.

"I hope you are right. If they are gathering allies for their cause they'll have no time to report seeing me."

Red Tail looked down at Elizabeth a moment, then as his gaze softened he reached out to touch her cheek. "He did not hit you?"

"No, but he soon would have had you not come to

my aid."

"You must not come here alone, Elizabeth."

"No, you're right. I will wait for you to escort me."
Elizabeth shivered in spite of the warmth of the
afternoon. She took Red Tail's arm and held on tightly
as they returned to the village. "Red Tail, why is it
people are fooled so easily into thinking a man in a fine
uniform is a gentleman and you men in your
buckskins are savages? I have never known finer men
than you and Andrew and that colonel is a beast!"

Red Tail chuckled at her words of praise. "I am a
gentleman, Elizabeth?"

"Yes, you have taken such good care of me. If my
husband ever comes home I will tell him what a good
friend you are." Elizabeth hesitated a moment. It
wasn't right for her to consider leaving without telling
him good-bye, but she knew he would stop her, tie her
up at the very least so she said no more about wanting
to go home. When they reached the village she stayed
in the longhouse doing whatever she could find to
keep busy and in that way managed to stay out of sight
for the remainder of the time the British soldiers
were camped nearby. With an officer such as the one
they had, she had no desire to risk a chance meeting
with any of the enlisted troops!

Eleven

Elizabeth lay nestled in her soft bed of furs, and attempted to make her plans in a cool, logical manner. She had no more time to waste waiting for Andrew to return. He'd be too late. It had been over three weeks since the small British patrol had moved on but she knew if one such group of soldiers were roaming that far west they were probably not alone but part of a larger force. The next group to visit the village might possibly have her name and description. Even if they did not come looking specifically for her, as a white woman she was bound to attract considerable notice. She had absolutely no value as an interpreter, only as a pretty young woman and there was obviously only one response she could expect from a British officer!

At least she had been warned to anticipate their presence. Her task was a simple one. All she need do was travel unobserved for more than a week's time through a forest teeming with Iroquois, Algonquin, and British! Not one of whom would be likely to treat her in a pleasant fashion should they sight her. There might be rebel bands also, she thought suddenly, men on their way to join the Continental Army. She had not even considered them! It would be impossible to get home safely when she did not even know the way, but she had to try. She would follow the river which flowed from the nearby lake, follow it south for several days then turn toward the rising sun. Any effort was preferable to waiting meekly for what would surely be the most disagreeable of fates to overtake her. At the very worst, Six Bears might kill her, or trade her away to another tribe. The best she could hope for was to become Red Tail's wife, but that would be agony for him as well as for her to say nothing of Andrew's rage when he returned. No, she had to try and reach home no matter how slim the odds were she would make it.

She placed her palms over the slight swell of her abdomen. She could feel the babe move now, the tiniest of kicks, little elbows and knees. She couldn't tell which but she knew Andrew should be there beside her to share in the wonder as their first child grew within her body. Time was running out, the days speeding by so rapidly and she could not wait much longer for him to come home before she'd be forced to leave. The prospect of more British soldiers passing through the village was as terrifying now as having her pregnancy discovered would be. Neither eventuality could be avoided indefinitely. It was only a matter of time before one or the other occurred. It had been nearly four months since she'd left home. Her pregnancy was that far along. She had no real choice at all. She would have to leave, soon and alone since Red Tail had refused to help her.

It would be difficult to save food for the journey for she was certain her meddlesome sisters would steal any cache she hid in the longhouse. It was impossible to leave food in the forest, for the squirrels and other beasts would consume it greedily. She would have to hide what she could in the rolls of skins beneath her bed and pray she could find berries and nuts on the way home. Fish would be plentiful in the river. She could take hooks with her but she could not risk smoke from a fire signaling her location, so she'd have to try and eat the slippery creatures raw. That prospect was revolting in the extreme and she'd not attempt it if she had any choice. She was not at all pleased with her plan, or the fact she had given her word to Andrew that she'd not try and reach home alone, but she had not known how long she was to be left alone, or how difficult the secret she carried would be to keep.

In the days that followed she began to implement her plan carefully. She would have to steal a horse but since Andrew had taken Lady without asking, she felt the Seneca owed her a mare to replace her. That made sense to her and she hoped they would see things as logically, rather than considering her a thief. Six Bears had horses, several pretty mares that were gentle and she took them treats, got to know the temperament of each one and the animals became accustomed to her scent so they would cause her no problems when she took one from the camp. A woman on horseback would be easier to track, she knew that, but she had to move as swiftly as possible and that left her no other option.

She became intentionally forgetful, left her basket at the longhouse and would have to return from the fields to fetch it, went out early, came home late, followed a pattern so erratic none could predict it until her travels about the village went unnoticed. Andrew had told her of the harvest festival, and as soon as everyone went into the fields to gather the crops she would go. She'd not be missed until nightfall and since she had avoided the last of the tribe's celebrations, she hoped they would not notice her absence again. If luck was with her, she'd be able to travel one full day and night before anyone discovered she was gone. That would have to be enough time to get away. It would just have to be.

When the heat grew oppressive, Elizabeth sat down beneath a tree at the edge of the field to rest. When the others started back for the village, none came to fetch her and she cared little that they did not trouble her. The preparations for the harvest had already begun, and she was too anxious to leave to think of anything else that lazy afternoon. She closed her eyes and tried again to be calm, to go over in her mind the items she must take since she'd made the mistake of not doing so when she'd left her home so suddenly with Andrew. She had lost track of the days, but the autumn was full upon them, the heat different than the summer's but no less annoying. She shooed a fly away from her face and sat half dozing, half plotting her impending escape when the neigh of an approaching horse disturbed her reverie. It was a sound she knew too well not to recognize immediately and as she leapt to her feet she saw Lady coming up the path with Andrew by her side.

Andrew was walking slowly, his step weary and as he came near, Elizabeth saw the dark stains on his shirt and knew they were dried blood. An interpreter only? Why had she ever believed that lie? It was plain to her what he had really been doing and she was appalled she'd not known it all along. She stepped back, afraid now after all her plans had been made that he would be angry with her but when he began to smile she saw only the man she loved and ran to him, laughing and crying all at the same time. "Oh, Andrew, I thought you would never come home!" She clung to him, held him so tightly he could not pry her arms from around his neck and stood hugging her until at last she released him.

Andrew covered Elizabeth's wet cheeks with tender kisses, then really looked at her, saw the scratches on her arms from the bushes, the dirt under her broken fingernails, the sad state of her tattered dress and tangled hair. He looked up then, out over the deserted fields and asked, "Why are you here working all alone, Elizabeth? Where are my sisters? Why are they not with you?"

"Those three have not bothered to work a full day since I came to live in your mother's house, Andrew, but I am still here today because I prefer to be alone rather than to be with them." She stepped back into his arms and hugged him again. "I thought you would never return. When you were not with Six Bears I did not know what to think, but you have been fighting, haven't you? You could have been killed and I would not have known."

Andrew patted her hair lightly as he replied calmly, "No, I was in no battles of any kind, my love, but when I wished to come home a newly arrived British colonel made the mistake of refusing me permission to go. He underestimated my determination to leave."

Elizabeth's eyes widened in fear as she looked up at him. "Andrew, will they call you a deserter now, come after you here and hang you as an example to your people?"

Andrew laughed at her terror-filled expression.

"No, the matter was settled fully before I left. There are no soldiers pursuing me."

Elizabeth touched the stains on his shirt. "Settled? How, with your knife? My God, Andrew, what happened? You must tell me everything."

"You have not lost your curiosity, have you? So much has happened, Elizabeth, and you have heard of none of it." Andrew took her hand and led her over beside the tree where she'd been resting. He dropped Lady's reins so the mare could graze while they talked. Once Elizabeth was seated he squatted down beside her and, picking up a stick, began to draw a diagram in the dirt. "The revolution has begun in earnest, Elizabeth, and it has not gone well for the Colonists despite the fact George Washington was appointed commander of the Continental Army in June. The British soldiers are well-trained fighting men. Washington has recruits who have shot at no more than deer all their lives."

Elizabeth brushed his news aside with an anxious gesture. "But what of you? What have you been doing these many months?"

With a few deft strokes Andrew completed his drawing. "The tribes of the Six Nations were originally only five. The Seneca are here in the West, then the Cayuga, Onondaga, Oneida and last the Mohawk in the East. The Tuscarora joined us in my grandfather's time. They came up from the South to join our league. The Six nations are a union which has lasted two hundred years. We are strong, united against common enemies. We have never been defeated. You know we were the British allies against the French." He looked up at her, his brow creased by a deep frown. "Each summer the fifty sachems meet in an Onondaga village. Their tribe occupies the center of our lands. Their strength is considerable and with fourteen sachems they can sway the council to their point of view. Agreement must be unanimous on any issue but this summer the only subject discussed was war."

"The British have already been here, Andrew. They have come gathering men for war parties and I know they will come again." Elizabeth's large green eyes were still filled with fright as she looked up into his.

"Did they see you?" Andrew asked suspiciously.

"Yes, but they did not ask who I was, only if I wanted to leave with them."

"And you refused to go?" A slow grin lifted the corner of Andrew's mouth. He was not surprised by her decision, but pleased all the same.

Elizabeth looked down, pretending an interest in his map. She'd no desire to tell Andrew how close she'd come to being raped. "Yes, I said this was my home. Now finish your story. What did you have to do to come home?"

Andrew nodded, then continued to make lines in the dirt. "All is in confusion, Elizabeth. The Seneca, Cayuga and Mohawk will fight for the king as they did before. It is a matter of honor you see, an ally once befriended cannot be denied. The Oneida and Tuscarora say they will be neutral, give aid to neither side but I do not believe them. That is what they wished me to say to the British, but they will fight and it will be for the Colonies. I can see the truth in their eyes even though it is not in their words. The Onondaga can be expected to do both. They will fight, some for one side, some for the other." He scratched out the drawing with a vicious wipe. "The Six Nations have been split. We'll never again achieve the accord of the past and our enemies will surely destroy us."

"But Andrew, if the Seneca fight for the British and the Colonies win?" She reached out to touch his hand, unable to put her fears in words.

"Then we will lose our lands. If we are fortunate enough to escape with our lives we may be able to find new homes somewhere farther north, but the Six Nations will be finished after two hundred years and for what? For loyalty to a king whose wars should not even concern us!"

Elizabeth saw the anger fill his eyes and could not help but be frightened still. "Red Tail said you were working as an interpreter. Was that just a lie to save me worry?"

"No, it was the truth but I have said all I will. I have no wish to aid the British king. He can fight this war without me to assist him. I will defend my home, as we are sure to be attacked at some time, but I will not go out looking for men to kill when they have done no harm to me. I will not kill for sport!"

"So that is what you told the British colonel?" Elizabeth licked her lips thoughtfully, intent upon hearing this part of Andrew's tale.

"Yes, but St. James refused to believe me. He called me a coward, which was his first mistake." Andrew's eyes were cold as they swept over Elizabeth's smudged cheeks. "I said I would prove my courage then leave and that is what I did. He was arrogant enough to challenge me, but he did not fight well. It was an uneven match although he was my size. He had no cunning, no great skill with a knife."

"So you killed him?" Elizabeth felt sick with the awfulness of that question. "You have killed a British officer and you think they'll not come after you?"

"No, Elizabeth, I did not kill the man, merely disarmed him quickly then held my knife to his throat and asked which it would be. He traded my freedom for his life but none could have called me a deserter for I was never one of the king's troops. I began by helping my father. When he told me to stay with the British I did so, but I never meant to remain for as many months or years as it will take them to end this war."

"You have come home to stay then?" Elizabeth asked with delighted relief, happiness at last lighting her pretty features.

"Yes, and I am tired of waiting for my father to agree to our marriage. I cannot abide by his decision to aid the British cause and I will no longer allow him to forbid me to have you as my wife."

Elizabeth could see so many changes in her husband. Their separation had been no easier for him than for her. She could appreciate that fact now that she saw the bitterness in his eyes, the pain which filled his whole expression. But that he would now defy the man who was not only his father but also chief of the village was alarming, yet he seemed vehement. She swallowed slowly before she spoke. "Andrew, I have been so frightened that you would not come home, that you would never come back for me."

"I am home." Andrew tossed the stick aside and pulled Elizabeth into his arms, kissing her with a desperate passion. They were alone in the soft grass beneath the tree and he had no intention of wasting a moment of their reunion. As his hand moved down her slender body in a warm caress he froze, stunned by the change in her figure. "Elizabeth!"

The lovely girl scrambled away from him, knowing he'd be angry. "Yell at me all you wish, Andrew. Call me whatever names you please, but my child is yours."

Andrew went to her quickly and drew her trembling body back into his arms. "I would never be angry with you, Elizabeth, never. I am only proud that we have made a child together. My father must give you to me now. You are too obviously mine for him to continue to deny it any longer." He held her tightly in his arms then let his hand move slowly down her figure once again. "When did this happen? Do you know?"

"Perhaps the first time we were together but I was not certain when you left with Six Bears. I should have been I suppose, but I had so much to worry about. Everything had gone wrong and I didn't think this could possibly have happened to me too, but it had."

Andrew's fingertips lifted her chin gently. "I am sorry to have left you alone for so long, Elizabeth, but I thought I could change things, make a difference for my people. Make them see what is so obvious to me, that our unity is our strength, but the sachems closed their eyes to that simple fact. They have sold our future by siding with the British and do not even know it."

Elizabeth lay her head upon Andrew's broad chest and sighed wistfully. "No matter what the future brings, Andrew, I will not fear it if I am with you. I will never be frightened again if we are together." She lifted her lips to his and her kiss was too sweet for him to react calmly, but he held her carefully, his touch gentle in spite of his need as he drew her down upon the grass. He cradled her slender body in his arms tenderly, letting her feel none of his weight as his mouth continued to savor hers. Her kiss was delicious, the taste of her as delightful as he had remembered for so many agonizing nights when his loneliness had been more than he could bear.

Elizabeth tugged impatiently at his shirt and when he slipped it off over his head she trailed her lips across his bronze skin until she was satisfied he had not been injured by his adversary's knife, that none of the blood on his clothing had been his own. Her tongue teased him playfully and he began to laugh as he was forced to wind his fingers in her long blond hair to hold her still. He kissed her face hungrily, his lips brushing her eyelids and cheeks before he began to nuzzle her delicate ears softly. "I love you, Andrew. I love you with all my heart." Elizabeth surrendered herself completely to the passion he aroused with his enticing lips and soft touch. His hands knew her body so well, could draw forth desire she could not deny and she did not know how she had survived without his love for so very long. Her whole body cried out for his and he came to her eagerly, enfolding her in his loving embrace. The grass tickled her back and she wondered what he'd done with her dress, then ceased to care. Her husband was home at last and she was his, would be his wife forever. For as long as she lived she would always be his.

Andrew drew Elizabeth's dress over her head then smoothed it back into place and gave her an affectionate squeeze as he helped her to her feet. "Let me reach the village first. I will speak with my father and make things as they should have been months ago when first I brought you here. We have never doubted we are husband and wife, and you will now be treated as you should have been. I promise you that."

Elizabeth waved as Andrew swung himself up upon Lady's back. He returned her wave then turned toward the village at a brisk canter, his impatience clear in his haste to reach his home. She stood smiling until he'd disappeared from view. Then, looking down at her dirty dress, she grimaced. "At least I can be clean for my husband tonight and I am most fortunate he has never cared for my clothes!" She picked up her basket and ran through the forest, skirting the edge of the stockade as she made her way toward the lake. She hummed happily to herself as she bathed and washed her long hair in the sparkling water. She scrubbed her skin until it was a bright pink, then sat down and carefully combed out her damp hair with her fingers. It was foolish to hurry she reminded herself, for regardless of Andrew's enthusiastic optimism she feared Six Bears would give him a long and fierce argument. There was another hour or two of sunlight and she sat by the lake, dreamily contemplating the evening ahead, an evening she was certain she'd spend in her husband's strong arms.

Summer Moon's soft whisper carried over the breeze as she and her two sisters approached Elizabeth. The older girl smiled shyly and held out a small basket of deep purple berries.

"Why Summer, what are these?" Elizabeth looked at the girls' smiling faces and wondered if they had been present when Andrew had spoken to Six Bears about their baby. Their expressions were innocent and sweet for once, and she reached out to take a handful of the berries they offered, but the fruit was so bitter she made a face as she swallowed it. When the Indian girls giggled with glee she knew she'd been tricked again. "I should have known better than to trust you three to be kind! Have you come for me? I am ready to go back if it is time."

Elizabeth followed the graceful trio up the path for several yards but suddenly grew dizzy. She hesitated, stopped to lean against a tree in an attempt to catch her breath, but her companions went on ahead. She tried to continue up the path, to catch up with them but she couldn't seem to see clearly and had to sit down upon a fallen log to rest. She felt so strange. Her dizziness worsened and she gripped the old wood tightly, afraid she might slip to the ground. What could be wrong with her? she wondered. The heat perhaps? The excitement of seeing Andrew again? Whatever the cause she felt increasingly ill until she could scarcely draw a breath. The neckline of her dress was suddenly too snug, and she tugged at the soft buckskin trying to get the freedom she needed to take a deep breath and clear her head. When the foul taste of the berries filled her throat with a choking wave of nausea, she knew in an instant what had happened to her. That had been no silly prank. She'd been poisoned and Andrew's sisters had done it with wide smiles. She fainted then, horrified by what had befallen her when she'd thought her problems had finally come to an end. She slumped to the ground, unconscious, her breathing shallow, her fair skin tinged with blue.

Red Tail saw Rising Eagle enter his mother's longhouse and nearly cried out for joy. He was finally relieved of the responsibility for the beautiful Elizabeth and could not have been more glad to see his best friend returning home. He had not seen the pretty blond girl that afternoon and wondered if she might have gone to bathe. He went out the gate and ran easily to the lake but the shore was deserted. If she had come there she had already gone. As he started to turn away, his gaze fell upon a small purple berry and he knelt to pick it up. He was not mistaken. He knew the fruit well. Every child in the village was taught from the time he could walk which berries could be eaten and which could kill. Why would anyone have picked these evil berries and brought them to the water's edge? He looked around carefully. The grass was still damp in the spot Elizabeth usually dressed so he knew she had been there after all. There were many paths to the lake. He had come on one but she often used another and he started up that trail still holding the poison fruit in his hand. He had not gone far when he saw more of the berries scattered across the path where someone had tossed them and he dashed on, frightened by what he might find.

Elizabeth still lay where she had fallen, her skin clammy with perspiration and her breathing so faint Red Tail had to kneel down beside her face to be certain she was still alive. He shook her shoulder but she did no more than moan softly, without opening her eyes. He wanted to take no chances. If she had eaten the deadly fruit then he had no time to lose. He held her head, then forced her mouth open so he could put his fingers down her throat to make her vomit. She gagged and coughed, retching repeatedly but the foamy liquid which passed her lips was tinged with blood. Terrified, Red Tail lifted her limp form into his arms and carried her swiftly back to the village, but he did not hesitate before carrying his precious burden into his mother's home rather than Rainbow's. His mother came running, but when he held out the berry he had found she did no more than shake her head.

"Summon Rising Eagle to bid her farewell. She will not live the night," the small woman predicted sadly.

"No!" Red Tail shrieked his refusal. "No, I have kept her safe all this time. She must not die now, not when she has waited so long for her husband to come home!"

The dark-eyed woman shrugged helplessly. "The woman will die. Nothing can be done. She will be dead long before the moon is high tonight."

"No!" Red Tail motioned to one of the many youngsters who stood gaping at their unconscious visitor and yelled, "Run and bring Rising Eagle. Run!" He carried Elizabeth to his own bed and lay her down gently, carefully smoothing out her ragged dress before he sat down beside her. His mother touched Elizabeth's cheek and clucked her tongue. "So you wanted her, too. You are no better than any of the others. None of you will have this woman now."

Red Tail gripped Elizabeth's fingers firmly in his. "You are jealous of her, too? As jealous as the women who did this evil thing?"

"What are you saying?" The puzzled woman bent down beside her son. "Are you accusing one of us of killing her?"

"She will not die!" Red Tail responded angrily.

209

The woman turned away, confused by her son's words as well as his obstinate hope that would not change the outcome of a death that was so certain. When Rising Eagle ran past her she had to leap out of his way and missed being trampled under the brave's flying feet by mere inches.

"What has happened to Elizabeth, Red Tail?" Andrew questioned his close friend in the Iroquois tongue he spoke so well. He knelt down beside his wife and tried to imagine what could have happened to her. Her long hair was damp, her skin too cool. "You found her in the lake?"

"No." Red Tail shook his head then forced himself to tell where he'd found Elizabeth and what his mother had said. She knew more about healing and how to prepare medicines than anyone else in their village. If she said death was near and offered no hope, what could they do?

Andrew slumped back on his heels as he began to scream. He screamed again and again, shrieking hysterically that his wife would not die. He gathered her up in his arms and held her tightly, and would not let anyone else come near. His tears dampened her face but he could not contain his sorrow and Red Tail did not expect him to either. The curious occupants of the longhouse fled in fright when they at last understood the two braves' plight for none wanted to be near when the white woman died as the depth of the men's grief would be too terrible to witness.

Andrew pressed Elizabeth's face to his chest and kissed the top of her head lightly. "Why has this awful thing happened to her, Red Tail? She was so happy when I left her this afternoon."

"She did not go gathering the berries by herself, Eagle. I never saw her do that and if she knew you had returned she would have gone to bathe to be pretty for you. She wanted only to be your wife, to be with you. That's all she ever asked me, 'When will Rising Eagle come home?' That was her only concern. She did not pick the fruit by herself. Someone has tried to kill her."

Andrew's eyes narrowed to vicious slits. "My sisters?"

Red Tail nodded dumbly. "I can think of no others who would want her gone. This beautiful woman was a threat only to those jealous girls and no others."

"Then I understand why you did not take her to my mother for care. We must save her ourselves, Red Tail, but is there nothing we can do, no herbs that will help us ease her pain?"

The brave shook his head sadly. "There is nothing. All she wanted was to be with you, now—"

As Andrew stared at his friend's mournful expression, his features grew hard, his glance cold. "Think! What must we do?"

Red Tail sat for a moment, then offered the only advice he could. "She could not have eaten many berries. Their taste must be bad. Perhaps I reached her in time to save her. She feels so cold. If we keep her warm it will surely help."

"It is too hot in here already!" But Andrew took the fur robe Red Tail handed him and drew it up snugly around Elizabeth's throat. "Elizabeth, I will take such good care of you, just as you cared for me, but you must help me. You must try and help me." He talked on and on in a soft low voice, calling her name and telling her how dearly she was loved although he could see no sign she heard or understood his words of encouragement.

Elizabeth felt only the searing pain. Wave after wave of excruciating pain tore through her chest leaving her too exhausted to do more than attempt to breathe. She tried only to make her lungs work, to breathe in and out in a calm, easy rhythm, but her mind rebelled at such a strenuous task when it wanted only to escape the horror of the unending pain. The agony moved down her spine, through the long muscles of her legs, rolled down her arms and made her fingers tremble with the awful ache. She did not understand how she could still be alive with such torment tearing at every inch of her body, but she was not even certain that she was still alive.

Andrew held Elizabeth enfolded in his embrace. He could not bear to think she might die. She was the loveliest of women, his woman, and he could not live without her, did not want to spend even one day on the earth without her shining presence to light his way. He moved his hand over her stomach and felt the contractions clearly. The muscles tensed into knots then relaxed only to tighten once again. "Give me your hand, friend. Do you feel this too?"

Red Tail leaned forward then drew his hand away quickly. "There is a child, your child?"

Andrew cursed bitterly. "He is too small. He cannot survive this. He will be born dead but we must do all we can to help Elizabeth live."

"She does not deserve this. This is too horrible a fate for any woman to bear. I must call my mother, Rising Eagle. We do not know how to deliver a child.

Alive or dead we lack such skill."

As Red Tail rose Andrew reached out to stop him, taking his wrist in a forceful grip. "No! I want no one to touch her. You may stay, but no others! I want none of the women who were so cruel to her to come near her now. Where were they all for the months I was gone? Was even one of them kind to my wife, her friend?" He drew her fingertips to his lips and as he kissed them, he felt a tremor of pain surge through her whole body with a sudden shudder. "I thought that since this is my home, she would be loved as I have always been, that she would be welcomed here, greeted with the happiness I received. How could I have been so stupid!"

Red Tail sat down again at Elizabeth's feet. "She begged me to take her home, but I did not understand her haste to leave. She was thinking only of the child. I see that now. If only I had taken her home, she would be safe tonight instead of lying here dying."

"She is not dying!" Andrew screamed with a rage he'd once felt only in the midst of battle. That fury could be released, vented in the passion required to slay an enemy, but this anguish could not be quelled in the recklessness heroic deeds required. He was exhausted. He'd traveled far that day but the happiness he'd found had turned all too swiftly to the most agonizing pain. "I will not permit my wife to die, not tonight, and not like this." As he glanced down at her he saw she had brought her hand to her mouth. She bit her knuckle savagely and he pulled her hand away and shook her. "Stop that. This torment is nearly over, Elizabeth. By dawn the pain will cease. You must be as brave as you have been. You have always been a brave girl, Elizabeth. Try to be so just a little while longer."

Elizabeth opened her eyes slowly and looked up at her husband. He was close, just inches away and yet she could not make out his face clearly. Her voice was no more than a hoarse rasp. "Kill me now, Andrew. Please kill me now."

Andrew's tears splashed upon her cheeks as he answered with a solemn vow. "Never! I promised you that. Never!"

Elizabeth felt his anguish as deeply as her own and tried to smile. "You are my heart, Indian, my very heart. I love you so. I am sorry I have brought you only sorrow." Her eyes closed when she could no longer stand the pain. It pushed down upon her, strangling her in its ceaseless grip and she tried to hold on to her husband's hand, to remember the joy they'd always shared for she wanted her last thoughts to be of him. She had had the best of all lives. She had known Andrew and no woman had ever had more love than he had given to her and now she would leave him with nothing.

Twelve

At first light Andrew left his friend's longhouse and went to confront Six Bears. The chief had spent a sleepless night, but rose quickly and came forward, unable to read the message in his tall son's light eyes.

Andrew stood in a defiant pose as he greeted his father. "My wife will live. If she has survived this many hours she will not die from the poison berries no matter what you had hoped."

"I had no part in this, my son. I was here with you when she fell ill. You cannot lay this deed at my feet."

"My sisters are no more than your puppets. If they did not have your orders to kill Elizabeth then they were no doubt confident they would have your praise when they had done so!" Andrew replied in a hostile sneer. "We have lost our first child, a son, and nothing you say will convince me it is not your fault he is dead. Every Seneca man goes to live with his wife. Her people become his, yet I brought my wife here to you where you refused to make her welcome in your home. She has been treated no better than a slave while I was away. Since I have lost my son, you have also lost yours. I will take my wife to her home as soon as she is able to travel and I will remain with her there. We will not live where our children are murdered before they can be born!"

"No! You may not leave. I forbid it!" Six Bears' face filled with rage as he issued his stern command.

"I have obeyed you since the day you found me, a frightened child, lost and half dead from hunger, but I will not obey you now. I am a grown man, no longer your son, no longer Rising Eagle of the Seneca. Do not try and force me to stay here for I will gladly kill any man you send against me, even if you come yourself." Andrew made no attempt to hide the contempt he felt for the older man. "Tell your wife to gather up Elizabeth's belongings, every single item she brought with her, for I want none of her possessions left behind with you." He turned then and moved through the low doorway of Rainbow's longhouse out into the morning sun to return to his beloved wife and the new life he had been forced to choose.

Elizabeth wondered what Andrew could be doing. He was dripping water down her body so slowly it tickled terribly yet when she tried to call out to him, to make him stop, no sound came from her lips. The intense pain was gone. Now she felt only a dull ache throughout her limbs as if she'd been thrown from a horse. That had happened to her more than once, but she knew she'd not been riding. She lay very still, afraid to move as she watched her husband bathe her body with such tender care. She could see clearly again and was surprised to see Andrew had begun to grow a beard. He could not have shaved for many days, yet she had seen him only the afternoon before, hadn't she?

Andrew squeezed out the wet cloth and lay it aside as he began to cover Elizabeth's frail body with the light buckskin robe. When he saw her pretty smile he jumped in surprise, startled to find her watching him with such amusement. "Elizabeth, I have been so worried. I thought you would never awaken. Can you recall what happened? Who gave you the fruit? Can you tell me who it was?" He knelt beside her and took her small hands in his.

Elizabeth closed her eyes while she tried to remember. She could still feel her delight in seeing him walk up the path, the joy they'd shared making love in the warmth of the afternoon, the cool, sweetness of the water as she'd bathed in the lake, but then nothing else. She took a deep breath, forcing her mind past the barrier of darkness until she again saw Summer Moon's smile. "Your sisters came for me. Summer Moon had the berries. They were all smiling so sweetly at me, Andrew. They were smiling as if they were finally glad to know me, as if they were my friends." Elizabeth began to weep softly then, his image again blurred by her tears. "They wished me dead, didn't they? They wanted to see me dead."

Andrew choked back the tears which burned his own eyes. "My love, do not cry. I am taking you home to your father's farm where I hope he will allow us to stay until we can build a home of our own. I will learn how to live as a white man does. I am Indian no more, Elizabeth. I will be a white man for the rest of my life."

Elizabeth gripped his fingers weakly. "You would leave your home when you love it so dearly? You would leave the Seneca for me?"

Andrew's deep voice was filled with bitterness as he rushed to explain. "How can we live where my own sisters wish you dead, where our child—" He could

217

not bring himself to tell her what had happened. She was too weak, surely far too delicate to stand such tragic news.

Elizabeth waited patiently for Andrew to continue but when he looked away to hide his tears she slipped her hands from his and placed them upon her stomach. Her abdomen was flat now, more than merely flat, sunken, empty and she understood his sorrow immediately. Their dear little baby was gone. The torment which had nearly taken her life had claimed his. She reached up to caress Andrew's damp cheek. "At least I am alive. They did not kill me with their treachery, and they could never kill my love for you."

Andrew sat back as he saw the anger in his own eyes reflected in hers. "You will be well soon and we will go. Six Bears will not dare to stop us. As soon as you can comfortably ride Lady we will go. That very minute we will leave here. I will have everything ready so that we may depart at our first opportunity."

Elizabeth nodded slowly. "Yes, we must go. Can you find me something to eat, some soup perhaps? I will never grow strong unless I try and eat."

"Yes, this village has plenty of food, Elizabeth. If it has no love I care not, for it has food in abundance and that's all we need take."

Rainbow herself carried Elizabeth's possessions to her son. She stood at the door of the longhouse and waited for him to come outside. "The woman had many things, Rising Eagle, fish hooks, a rope, bags of nuts. I do not understand why she would have wanted such things, but I have brought them with the others."

218

Andrew took the things from the woman who had been his mother for twenty years and turned back into the bark-covered dwelling without speaking. He took the small bundle that was all Elizabeth owned in the world and placed it next to her bed.

"You were preparing to leave. Had I not come home when I did then you would have gone, wouldn't you? You promised me you would never try to reach home alone but you were going to do it!" He stared down at her, his green eyes blazing with anger as he waited for her to deny his accusation.

Elizabeth looked away. "I am too tired to fight with you. Please let me rest." She wanted only to sleep, to rest quietly where no one would try and hurt her so badly ever again.

Andrew refused to let her ignore him. "You know what would have happened to you? You would have died all alone. You would surely have died but you would never have reached your home safely!" Andrew's tone was hostile as he ridiculed her foolishness but the thought of what she'd been ready to risk appalled him.

Elizabeth's luminous green eyes were filled with sadness as she looked back toward him. "I nearly died here, Andrew. I might have reached home safely. I had that hope. Nothing that could have happened to me on the way home could have been any worse then what happened to me right here." Elizabeth pulled the light robe up around her shoulders and tried to go back to sleep. What difference did her plans make now? Everything had changed.

"I have your things. Your dress is clean. You can wear that when you are able to dress, but I don't want

219

to see you in an Indian woman's clothes ever again." He left her side for only a moment, then returned to sit nearby as she slept. He would trust no one now and so never let his beautiful young wife out of his sight.

It saddened Red Tail to see Rising Eagle sit so still for hours on end but he understood his friend's fears well. He came each afternoon to talk, to recall good times they had shared when they were still too young to understand the deadly sport for which their boyhood games prepared them. "Elizabeth is nearly well. She can get up from her bed, walk about. Soon you will be able to take her home."

Andrew nodded slowly. "Perhaps next week she will be strong enough to go. I do not want to leave before I am certain she can make the journey without falling ill."

"I will go part way with you. Then if you need help—"

Andrew interrupted firmly. "No, we will go alone, as we came."

"Are we no longer friends?" Red Tail was troubled. "I will always blame myself for not watching over Elizabeth more closely. Do you blame me too?"

"No. She would have surely died had you not found her when you did. You will always be my best friend, though I will see you no more once we are gone. I will not come back to the land of the Seneca. We will never meet again, Red Tail."

"In the next life then," the young man offered philosophically for he could not accept his friend's words as true.

Andrew chuckled. "No, not even then, for God would not expect white men and Indians to spend eternity together. Paradise would soon be destroyed by their senseless wars!"

Red Tail smiled at that prediction. "Your soul is Seneca, Rising Eagle, no matter how you deny it. We will meet again."

Andrew slapped his friend on the shoulder and ceased to argue over a matter that could not be settled. "I know I will never have another friend so fine as you, Red Tail." He got up then and went outside to see to Lady, hiding his sorrow in the routine of the animal's daily care. She was a fine mare, lively and strong as well as beautiful and he gave her his full attention. "I owe you my life, Lady. Were you not so pretty and John Cummins not so greedy, who knows what might have happened to me." He patted her glossy flank playfully as he brushed her silken coat. "We have traveled far together, my Lady, but somehow I do not think our journey has even begun." That sudden thought startled him. It sounded so much like something Elizabeth would say he wondered if he were learning her gift for prophecy, and if so, what did it mean?

In two more weeks' time, Elizabeth felt well enough to travel. The harvest festival had come and gone. There was plenty of food stored for the winter, corn, squash and beans in generous supply, and she saw no reason not to take some of their share for their journey but Andrew disagreed.

"I want to leave here with nothing, Elizabeth. I can hunt, fish. I can take care of us both very well."

The pain was still too clear in his eyes for her to dare and argue. "Yes, of course you can, Andrew. I thought it would be easier for us if we took provisions, but if you would rather not be burdened by the extra weight of the food then I will not mention it again." Elizabeth turned for him to fasten the last of her buttons.

"Your dress does not fit you well now. You are much too thin. Your father is going to say I starved you." Andrew put his hands on her waist to turn her around. She was so lovely he would never tire of looking at her but she was far more slender than she had been the previous spring.

"I will make new dresses when I get home if the ones I left behind don't fit me. Clothes mean little to me, Andrew. This dress will be fine until I get home." Elizabeth held out the skirt. The soft folds of the fabric fell into gentle pleats, hiding her narrow hips but her thinness showed plainly in her face and hands. "I always liked this dress best. That's why I wore it, but I can make another in a smaller size later if I must."

"You are a clever girl, Elizabeth. You know how to sew and cook, how to raise crops as well as how to read and write. You are a fine wife." Andrew tried to smile, but the teasing sparkle was missing from his eyes.

"Well thank you, but somehow I thought there were other talents you valued more." Elizabeth smiled seductively, her meaning clear. When Andrew frowned as he turned away quickly she didn't understand why he was angry and reached out to catch his arm. "Andrew, what is wrong?"

"Nothing. I have a lot to do to get ready to leave. That is all. Now I must go." He strode off then, hurried off to attend to his unnamed errands, and Elizabeth sat back down on her bed and tried to think what she'd done to offend him. Nothing she said seemed to please him although she was careful never to argue with him nor cause him problems when she knew he had given up everything he loved because of her. She saw only sadness in his deep green eyes. He had grown thinner too, she had noticed, past merely trim or lean to thin and she worried he might be the one to become ill on their way home rather than she. To not take food was lunacy. Surely it was, but she would not argue. If he was too proud to take rations from the people he was leaving, then she would hold her tongue. She had at least learned that from the Seneca, she thought bitterly. She now knew how to sit for hours thinking by herself without ever feeling the need to share those thoughts with another person.

Andrew waited until the sun was high in the sky before he told Elizabeth they were leaving. His reason was clear to her. He wanted to walk out of the Seneca village in full view of everyone. He would not sneak away at dawn like some frightened outcast. He was far too proud for subterfuge, too fine a warrior not to know he could defeat any challenge Six Bears might make and Elizabeth understood his plan although he had said nothing to her of why he wished to leave when he did. He brought Lady to the front of the longhouse where they'd been living and helped his delicate blond wife to mount her mare's back.

"You have everything?" Andrew surveyed their bedrolls with little interest. They were leaving with no more than they had brought. No, he realized sadly, they were leaving with far less.

"Yes, I think so." Elizabeth reached out to touch his shoulder. "Wait, Andrew, you needn't do this for me. Please, tell your parents you will come home to see them soon." He had cut his hair and tied it back as her father wore his and his beard had changed his appearance completely, detracting not at all from his even features but she had never seen another Indian man wearing a beard and knew that was why he'd grown his. He was Indian no more and his appearance that day plainly declared it.

"I have already said good-bye. I will not see those two again for they are no longer my parents, Elizabeth. Let us go." He took hold of Lady's bridle to lead the horse through the village and did not turn again to speak.

Elizabeth straightened her shoulders proudly, her posture as regal as his as she looked for the last time at the Seneca village she had thought she'd never leave. Their parting was attracting considerable notice as she had known it would. Every eye in the tribe seemed to be focused upon them and when they neared Rainbow's longhouse, Six Bears came through the door but he did no more than stare, his eyes dark, hidden beneath his thick brows as he frowned. No one spoke or called out, but at last Red Tail came from the silent crowd and walked up to Andrew's side. He did not speak but kept pace with his friend until they had reached the stockade gate.

Elizabeth whispered softly, "Andrew, please stop for a moment so I may tell Red Tail good-bye." She slipped from her horse's back and hugged the Indian brave warmly. "Thank you. You have been as wonderful a friend to me as you are to Andrew. I will never forget your kindess and someday I will repay it."

Red Tail lifted his right hand to smooth her shiny hair lightly and returned her smile. "Good-bye, Elizabeth." He hesitated briefly as if he wished to say so much more to her but dared not. He helped her to remount Lady, then turned and walked away, his moccasins making no sound upon the soft dirt of the path as he left his two dear friends to continue their journey alone.

Elizabeth wound her fingers in Lady's dark mane and held on tightly, expecting one of Six Bears' arrows to pierce her back at any second, yet none came and as they traveled farther from the village she began to relax. The chief had apparently decided to let them go, yet she knew in her own heart even if her husband did not, that he could never truly leave the part of himself that was Seneca.

Andrew headed west toward the lake, then followed its shore south. Elizabeth watched closely for landmarks, carefully observing their progress so she would know the way home should she ever again need to travel by herself. When he stopped in the late afternoon to fish, she was more tired than she'd thought possible, but did not want to let him see her fatigue. She sat and watched him. His expression was serious. He had promised to provide their food and intended to do so obviously and she did not disturb his concentration with idle chatter. They were safe here, still well within the Seneca lands. There were many villages similar to the one he had called home and she wondered if they might see hunting parties as they traveled, but they had seen none that day. She yawned and tried to stay awake but it was difficult. She ached all over and hoped Andrew would not notice how slowly she moved as she gathered wood for their fire. By the time she had enough stacked up ready to cook the fish, he'd caught three and lit the dry wood quickly to roast his catch.

The fish were delicious and Elizabeth smiled happily as she finished hers. "How far will we follow the lake, Andrew?"

Andrew frowned as he looked up at her. "You had hooks to fish. Did you plan to come this way, too?"

"Yes. I was not certain this lake ended in a river which flowed into the Susquehanna, but I thought the chances it did were good. I hoped there would be settlements where I could get help to find my way home. I thought the way we came through the mountains would be too dangerous for me to attempt alone, although it was the shortest route to my father's farm."

Andrew nodded as she spoke. "We will begin following the river tomorrow. There is a fork ahead. We must follow the branch to the left. That will then flow into the Susquehanna. Had you gone that way, it would have taken you home eventually, if you did not meet anyone who wished to stop you." His tone was suspicious, as if he thought that possibility unlikely.

Elizabeth ignored his taunting gaze in hopes of lifting his dark mood. "Andrew, would you teach me things as we go? I want to learn how to find my way by the stars, how to hunt for game and—"

"Why? You will not ever travel alone, Elizabeth." Andrew gave his attention to his dinner as if the subject were closed.

"I do not want to remain so helpless all my life, Andrew. I want to learn all that you know so I may take care of myself should I ever need to do so."

"Elizabeth, what I know has taken me a lifetime to learn. I cannot teach you how to survive in the wilderness in the brief time it will take us to reach your home. You are bright, but there is too much to learn for you to master it all so quickly. Do not worry so. I will take good care of you. You will not lack for food, nor be lost."

Elizabeth started to restate her request then thought better of it. She would just keep her eyes open and watch what he did carefully and he would teach her without being aware of it. That would be the best way since he seemed to regard her interest as a challenge to his ability to provide and it wasn't that at all. "Andrew, what shall we tell my father? What shall we say happened and what reason shall we give for coming home?"

Andrew sighed impatiently as he glanced up. "You do not want to tell him the truth? Is it too ugly to repeat?"

"No, but there are many ways to tell the truth, Andrew. Many possible explanations for what happened. We can simply say things were not as we expected them to be and we left. That would be the truth, would it not? But it would tell my father none of what actually happened to us."

"I understand, but he will hate me no matter what you tell him, Elizabeth. Make it as ugly as you wish. It is your story more than mine."

"Not our story, our life, what happened to us." Elizabeth leaned forward, eager to hear his answer. They had had little opportunity to talk while she was getting well. The longhouse was crowded. There was always someone nearby and although she knew no one could understand her words, she had not wanted to discuss their private plans for the future.

"You were alone, Elizabeth." Andrew shrugged noncommittally. "I was gone for so long and you were left all alone. You can relate what happened far better than I can."

Elizabeth sat quietly thinking while she watched him eat. He was solemn. None of her queries seemed to matter to him now. "I want to tell him nothing, Andrew. I want to give him no reason to hate either you or your people."

"They are no longer my people. I don't care what you say about them. The truth is damning enough, but say whatever you will."

"No! It is pointless to waste our emotions in hatred!" Elizabeth gestured emphatically. "I will never understand why your family was so afraid of me, so certain I would take you away for it was their own actions which forced you to leave them, not mine. I would have stayed forever, Andrew, even if no one had ever spoken to me or was kind. I would have stayed if we could have been together. That's all I ever wanted, just to make a home there with you."

"It is finished now. I will not go back. We will have to make our home elsewhere. There is plenty of land near your father's farm I can clear to make room for our house. I do not want to depend on him for food. I can hunt this winter, sell furs, buy whatever we need. Then next spring we can plant our own crops."

"Andrew, there is a possibility your family has responded to our letters which appeared in the newspapers by now. How long have we been gone? More than four months, closer to five? Someone may have answered who knew your family."

"They will not want me now, Elizabeth, not after so

many years with the Seneca. Who would want to introduce a savage as his son?" Andrew asked cynically.

"Stop that! You are no savage and never were! Perhaps your men are fierce in battle, but I never saw any of them do anything mean in the village and, thank God, no one ever brought home any captives. That was my greatest fear."

"The British do not adopt prisoners as their own. They do not permit it, Elizabeth. They like their enemies dead, not captured, but I have no interest in their war." Andrew got up to add more wood to the fire then came back and spread out their blankets. "Go to sleep now. We have talked long enough for tonight. You go to sleep and I will watch awhile."

"Keep watch? For what? Are we not safe here?" Elizabeth looked around hurriedly, surveying their surroundings with alarm.

"It is always better to be on guard. I do not want to be surprised by anyone tonight." Andrew's voice was calm, but his tension barely concealed.

"Will you wake me later so I may keep watch while you rest?"

"No, of what value would you be as a sentry?"

"I could wake you if nothing else! But if you would only teach me how to shoot with your bow, I could kill a man as readily as you if we were threatened!"

"Elizabeth, go to sleep." Andrew laughed at her defiant expression. "I do not need you to defend me. Just go to sleep."

"How can you expect to walk all day and then stay awake all night, Andrew? You are too thin as it is. We will never reach home safely if you exhaust yourself this way!"

"I am strong. Do not worry." Andrew moved away from the fire. He sat down where he could lean back against a tree to be comfortable and rested his arms across his knees.

Elizabeth cleaned up the remains of their dinner, then rinsed her hands in the lake before coming back to her blanket. Tired as she was, she could not get to sleep and lay tossing and turning every few minutes. The ground seemed much too hard to permit rest. She could not find a space where one pebble or several did not jab her body painfully in one spot or another, yet she knew the real cause of her torment was simply unhappiness. Andrew was so different now. He never smiled at her and she could not remember the last time he had kissed her or held her in his arms. When she could stand her loneliness no longer, she picked up her blanket and moved to his side. "Andrew, I am so sorry for what happened, but must it ruin everything for us? Won't you please tell me how you feel about me now? You have not even kissed me and—"

"Elizabeth," Andrew sighed impatiently. "Go to sleep. I don't want to talk any more tonight." He stood up and walked to the lake's edge where he bent down to gather small stones which he began to toss into the dark water. He did not turn around or come back to sit with her, and Elizabeth felt so terribly alone, so unwanted she carried her blanket to where Lady stood and hugged the mare's neck tightly as she tried to think. Everything had gone wrong, every single thing, and she couldn't understand why Andrew thought it was her fault. She had never done anything wrong. She'd done nothing but fall in love with him and that had ruined both their lives. It truly had. Discouraged by his aloofness, she took her blanket and lay down near the fire, this time too exhausted by sorrow to feel uncomfortable on the cold, hard ground and went right to sleep.

Andrew woke Elizabeth at dawn when he had breakfast ready for her to eat. She washed quickly in the lake then came to sit with him, but when he made no attempt at conversation, neither did she. She was hungry in spite of her somber mood and ate all that he had prepared, then rolled up her blanket and was ready to go. They followed the shoreline of the lake for the morning, but by afternoon had come to its south end where it narrowed and continued as a river which they followed until nightfall.

Elizabeth tried not to worry as she gathered up wood for a fire. Andrew had said not one word to her all day, not one. They had seen no one and she was glad of it, although she was tired of watching for signs that others were nearby. Each time a bird called she was certain someone was coming and she was glad to be stopping for the night. If Andrew were tired he didn't show it. He showed no emotion, she realized, none, as if he could walk forever and not even notice where he'd been but she was certain he was always alert for signs of danger. When he handed her her blanket again she stared up at him, her eyes filled with sorrow. "You aren't going to sleep?"

"Yes, I will rest, but I can see you are tired. Go to sleep now, Elizabeth, and I will see you in the morning."

Elizabeth twisted the edge of the blanket nervously in her fingers as she looked up at her husband. She had tried to be patient, to wait for him to come to her but she could no longer bear the ache which filled her heart in silence. "Andrew, you have always been so loving, so affectionate with me. What is wrong?"

"It has been no more than a month since you lost the child, and while I am glad you do not remember that night, I do. I will never forget it. Now please leave me alone and go to sleep."

"If you do not want to make love I understand, but could you not hold me in your arms, kiss me? Could you not give me even that?" She wanted to be reasonable, but she had never expected to have to beg a man so loving as he for attention. He had always wanted to make love to her. No matter where they were or what time of day it was, he had always wanted her and she had thought that was the way he would always be. Now she did not even know him, for the stranger who stood staring at her so coldly could not possibly be the Andrew she loved.

"Elizabeth, it is best not to begin something we would only have to stop. Surely it is too soon for you, far too soon. Now good night."

Elizabeth turned away quickly before he saw her face. She could not live this way, not when he made her feel she was not worth his trouble to kiss. She curled up in a snug ball and bit her knuckles to keep from crying as she lay wide awake long into the night. Why was he bothering to take her home if he would not want her when he got there? He would never make love to her in her father's house, she knew that. He would want to build his own house for her first. The people of Oak Grove often helped each other to build houses, but no one would come to help an Indian.

Maybe her father would let them borrow Jed for a while, at least until they had a roof over their heads. She looked up at the stars and remembered how different their journey to his village had been. He had made love to her under the stars each night and told her such beautiful stories. They may have been hungry and tired, but they had been so happy then, so much in love they had not minded the discomfort when it meant they would be together for always. That always was never going to come, she knew that now. Andrew didn't love her any more. He couldn't still love her and treat her with such indifference. It was over and he was too proud to admit it, too proud to admit he had lost everything for a woman he no longer loved.

Elizabeth forgot all about her efforts to memorize the way home. She sat daydreaming sadly of happier times as they traveled along each day and night. She slept huddled alone near Lady, close to the only friend she felt she had. She did not speak unless Andrew asked her a direct question, which he seldom did. He was so handsome she could not take her eyes from him and the longing within her grew more intense with each hour until she thought she might simply die from a broken heart long before they reached her home.

Andrew scanned the stars intently before he sat down beside the small fire. "We should reach your father's farm tomorrow, Elizabeth, tomorrow or early the following day. Perhaps I should bring him a deer, some gift to make our arrival less disagreeable."

"My father loves me dearly, Andrew. I am all that he has. He will not be sorry to see I have returned home. I promised him that I would come back when I could and we do not need to bring him presents. He'll be happy to see us. I know he will."

"He will be overjoyed to see you, but I will not be welcome." Andrew raked his thumbnail across his chin thoughtfully, his new beard providing a distraction for the moment.

"He will make you feel welcome or I will leave him again!" Elizabeth vowed angrily, then seeing the light in Andrew's eyes did not change, tried to be more reasonable. "I wonder what day it is, if it is still October, or perhaps November now."

"What does it matter? Surely the exact date isn't important."

"No, not really. I would have liked to have known when my birthday came though. I was sixteen in September and I didn't even know when that was. The day just came and went like all the others, without any special notice wherever I was."

Andrew looked up, as if seeing her dear face for the first time. "I'm sorry, Elizabeth. I had no present for you then and I still don't. I have less now than when I met you, nothing for you to share but the hours of the day."

Elizabeth replied in a throaty whisper as she rose to her feet, "I would be delighted to share your life, Andrew, but you've made it plain you no longer want me to share in anything that is yours." She gathered up her blanket to get ready to go to sleep and he did not stop her, did not follow or ask her to explain what she had meant. There had been a time he would have grabbed her and kissed her until she could not even think let alone argue, but now he did nothing but continue to sit and stare into the flames of their campfire.

Jed threw down his hoe and ran yelling for Olaf. He had recognized Elizabeth's fair hair in the afternoon light and was certain it was she who was riding slowly up the path from the forest. He knew it was Elizabeth, Elizabeth and that damn Indian brave, Silver Hawk. "Olaf, Elizabeth's come home. She's home!"

Olaf bolted through the front door of his home then tore down the narrow road at a dead run. He pulled his daughter from her horse and hugged her again and again as he exclaimed at how much he'd missed her. She looked so beautiful to him he could not let her go, but kissed her cheeks until she pushed him away with a sweet lilting laugh.

"Papa, I'm glad you're so happy to see me but please, let me breathe for a moment or I shall faint!" Elizabeth glanced past her father then and saw Margaret Nelson and her two little children standing upon the front porch of her home. "Papa, why is Margaret here today?"

Olaf blushed as he hurried to explain. "We are married, Elizabeth. I married Margaret two months ago." He turned his gaze upon Andrew then. "I am too happy to see Elizabeth to give you the beating you deserve, Andrew. Let Jed take Lady and come into the house. We have found out exactly who you are and it is a long story I'm sure you'll want to hear."

Elizabeth grabbed her father's arm in a frantic clutch. "What? You've found Andrew's family? You have found them!"

"Yes. Do you want to come inside and sit down while we talk or shall we stand out here in the middle of the road while I tell you?" Olaf chuckled at his daughter's dismay.

Elizabeth turned to her husband but he hung back, hesitated as if he had not understood and she reached out to take his hand. "I want to hear this even if you don't. Now please come with us."

Andrew frowned slightly as he looked at his father-in-law. "Olaf, I can understand why you would want to fight me. I thought you might try and kill me. I expected that, but why does the fact you have found my family make any difference to you today? Aren't you still angry with me for taking your daughter away?" His confusion was clear in his puzzled expression.

"Not as long as you have returned her to me unharmed. I had no idea she loved you enough to want to take up the life of an Indian. What is the point in my being furious now?" Olaf asked.

"I hoped you would welcome us, Papa." Elizabeth held Andrew's hand tightly, not daring to think how he might have greeted her should she have returned home alone, and pregnant.

Margaret came walking up to them then, no longer able to contain her curiosity. She had grown tired of waiting to hear what was being said. "Welcome home, Elizabeth, and you must be Andrew." She smiled prettily, but she held her two children securely by the hand so they could not approach the stranger.

Andrew's eyes lingered a moment too long on the

little boy, then he took a step toward the house. "I am happy to meet you, Mrs. Peterson. Well, Elizabeth, we have been invited to come in."

Elizabeth was tired. She wanted simply to take a bath and change her clothes, but she was too curious about Andrew's family to wait another minute to hear the story, so followed her husband eagerly into the house.

"A Mr. Haywood came to see us, a Stephen Haywood, your uncle's attorney, Andrew, but let me begin at the beginning." Olaf scanned the letter he had been saving, then found the place where he wanted to begin. "Your father was a man named Phillip Jordan, but I am sorry to say both he and your mother are dead. His brother, Matthew, is the one who sent Mr. Haywood to us. He brought several small paintings, a test I suppose, and asked me to tell which most resembled you. You look enough like your father to have been his twin and I could have identified the man out of a hundred miniatures. The few he sent were no challenge. Mr. Haywood was disappointed to find you had gone. He left money should you return, so that you may go immediately to Philadelphia. Your uncle is most anxious to have you come to live with him."

Andrew listened closely and when Olaf paused asked quickly, "That's kindly of him, but did his attorney tell you what had happened to my parents, how they died?"

"Yes, it's all right here in this letter. It is close to the story we imagined. Your mother was worried about her younger sister, afraid the woman would come to some harm because she lived with her husband on a

237

small farm in New York which was close to the area seeing constant fighting during the war with the French. She wrote letters but could not convince her sister to come to Philadelphia where she would be safe. Apparently your mother was so distraught over this she took you with her, Andrew, and went to get her sister herself. Unfortunately, she never reached your aunt's farm. Her carriage was set upon by bandits or French soldiers, it's not known which, but the two drivers were killed in the ambush and your mother apparently died instantly when the carriage over-turned. Her body was found in the vehicle but there was no trace of you. You had simply vanished and your father was heartbroken, quite naturally. He never gave up hope that you would be found alive someday, but he never recovered from his tragic loss. He let his brother run their family enterprise alone. His health failed and he died three years after your mother. Seventeen years ago it would have been now. When your uncle saw the inquiry in the Philadelphia paper he was understandably shocked, but elated to think you might be alive. There is no doubt that you are Andrew Jordan, none at all, and I am happy to say your uncle is an extremely wealthy man who has never married and considers you his only heir. I could wish no finer man for my daughter, Andrew. I am only sorry that Mr. Haywood did not arrive before you had left as we were unable to locate anyone who had ever heard of a Seneca chief by the name of Flaming Sky and had no way to find you."

Elizabeth turned to look at her husband and found him deep in thought, trying to remember his parents, she guessed from the troubled frown which creased his brow. She reached out for his hand and he squeezed her fingers warmly, the first gesture of love she could recall in a long while and it brought tears to her eyes.

"Do you have my mother's name there, too?"

"Yes, her name was Catherine," Olaf responded softly.

Andrew shook his head. "I still can't remember her, nor my father. What became of my aunt, the one my mother wanted so badly to save?"

"I asked the same question, Andrew. It seems she and her husband returned to England after your mother was killed. Your aunt blamed herself for the death of her sister and your disappearance and decided life here in the Colonies was not worth the risk. Apparently Matthew Jordan has not kept in touch with her since your father's death, so while you have relatives living in England, he can supply only their names, not their addresses."

"There is just my uncle then, this man who lives in Philadelphia?"

"Yes, but as I said, he is quite a wealthy merchant and expects you to come live with him in his home." Olaf folded the letter carefully and returned it to its envelope before handing it to Andrew to keep. "You'll want to go of course, but I think Elizabeth should stay here with us for the time being."

"What?" Elizabeth was shocked by that suggestion. "No, if Andrew wants to go to Phildelphia then I will go with him. Andrew, you'll want me to go, won't you?" She looked at her husband and prayed he would insist that she did.

Andrew tapped the letter lightly on his knee. "I am tired and you must be too, Elizabeth. Could we not bathe and change our clothes before we discuss this?"

Elizabeth was frightened by the aloofness of his manner but dared say nothing in front of her father. "Are the children using my room? If you have my dresses somewhere I would like to change."

"Of course, we have all your things, Elizabeth. I would not have thrown them out. Margaret packed them in a trunk, but they are still in your room. Come with me and I'll show you."

"Andrew?" Elizabeth waited for him to rise. "You left your clothes here, too."

Olaf spoke up quickly. "Your things are still where you left them, in Jed's quarters."

Nodding slightly, Andrew went out the front door, skirted the spot where Margaret stood playing with her children then headed toward the barn. The letter from his uncle was still tightly clutched in his hand, but his pace was slow, as if he were more tired than he would admit.

Olaf's expression changed radically once Andrew had left them. "He was right. Had we not found his family I would have killed him for taking you away!" He grabbed his daughter by the shoulders and shook her soundly. "Was five months time with the Seneca enough for you?"

Elizabeth stared up at her father, stunned by his angry outburst. "Stop it! I won't listen to you threaten my husband. I won't!"

"Husband? That is not what I'd call him. If he beat you, hurt you in any way, I'll see he suffers for it now!"

240

Elizabeth could not recall ever seeing her parent so angry. His blue eyes were nearly purple with rage and she rushed to reassure him she was well. "Andrew would never harm me, Papa, never. You can see with your own eyes that I am fine."

"At least he did not bring you home with your belly swollen with his bastard!" Olaf dropped his hands to his sides, still thoroughly disgusted with the young man.

Elizabeth drew in her breath sharply, for indeed his words had the force of a blow. "No, I lost our child a month ago. That is when Andrew decided to bring me home."

"What? This is awful, Elizabeth, just awful. That you ran off with that savage is bad enough, that you nearly had his child would have only added to the disgrace!"

"Disgrace? That Andrew and I love each other is no disgrace, Papa, none at all. Now if you'll let me go I will heat water for a bath and clean up before supper." Elizabeth went to her room for her clothes but found she hardly recognized it now that it was filled with the children's possessions. Her bed had been replaced by two small ones so she and Andrew had not even a place to sleep, she thought sadly. She had come home but it was home no longer for her. Forcing away the grimness of that reality she opened the small trunk, found something to wear, then went to prepare a bath while she tried to think of some compelling reason to make Andrew want to take her with him to his uncle's home.

The children's bright voices and sweet smiles provided a welcome distraction at the supper table, but the minute Margaret rose to clear the table Andrew asked to be excused and, taking Elizabeth's hand, led her outside. "Margaret is nice, isn't she? It will be good for you to have a mother again."

"I have no need for a mother, Andrew, and Margaret can't be as old as you are. She will be more like a sister to me than a mother surely." That thought made her stomach lurch. She had had enough of sisters to last her a lifetime.

Andrew shrugged, brushing away her comment as unimportant. "I read the letter several times, Elizabeth. I had not expected an uncle. Philadelphia is a long way off. Even if I did live there as a child, I can't remember the city. It was too long ago for me to recall."

Elizabeth waited patiently for him to continue but when he did not she asked hesitantly, "What have you decided to do, Andrew? Do you want to go and meet your uncle or not?"

Andrew pulled Elizabeth close, lacing his fingers behind her back to hold her near. "Yes, I do want to go and meet him. I'm sorry my father is dead. That my mother is not alive pains me too, for I have not forgotten them deliberately. I would like to speak to my uncle, to hear more of my parents and their lives, but I think your father is right, Elizabeth. I must go alone."

"Oh, Andrew, please!" Elizabeth could not abide by his decision and demanded angrily, "You must take me with you!"

"It will be a long trip and I don't want to take you to my uncle's home until I am certain you will be welcome there."

"Well, why wouldn't I be welcome, Andrew? I am your wife!" His comment made no sense to her, none at all.

Andrew gazed down at his bride, his glance as well as his words very stern. "I made a terrible mistake in taking you home with me to the Seneca. It was a mistake that cost us dearly and I'll not risk your life so needlessly ever again. The Colonies are at war, Elizabeth. Surely the roads are not safe and I will let no harm come to you now that you are again at home where you will be in no danger while I am gone. I will go to Philadelphia alone, get to know my uncle, learn how he makes his living and how I might earn mine. I want to be positive his house will be my home too before I come back for you."

"I could come with you and stay at your uncle's house, with your father's brother. That makes far more sense, Andrew. I belong with you, not here. Please don't leave me alone again."

Andrew hugged Elizabeth more tightly, then brushed her smooth forehead with his lips. "You are my wife, Elizabeth, and you will do as I say. It will be winter soon. Each day grows more cool and I know you will be safe here with your father. In a few months time I will return to stay here with you, or to take you back to Philadelphia with me. One way or the other I will come back for you as soon as I can. By the spring time I will know what is best for us and where we will make our home."

Elizabeth stepped out of his embrace and backed away. She was not stupid. She knew he didn't want her any more. She'd not make him say it to her face, nor would she beg to be his wife when it was clear he had made up his mind about that, too. "I will wait here then, for as long as it takes for you to come back for me. I will wait here in my father's house." She turned and walked back into the small farm house without shedding a tear. She would wait forever and he'd never return, but she would wait faithfully all the same.

Thirteen

Spring 1776

Olaf saw the handsome new carriage approaching and walked from the barn to meet it, but he would not have recognized Andrew had the young man not called to him as he climbed out of the shiny black coach. His appearance had not been altered so much as it had been enhanced. He seemed to be in the best of humor and the elegant fabric and cut of his clothes was a sharp contrast to the simple buckskins he had been wearing the morning he had left the farm in the fall.

"I have come back for Elizabeth as I promised I would. Where is she?" He nodded toward Margaret as she stepped out onto the porch and tried not to appear surprised by her obvious pregnancy. He smiled warmly at her two children then reached out to take his father-in-law's hand. "Well, where is my wife?"

Olaf turned to Margaret, his eyes pleading for help with the explanation he could not bring himself to begin. "I don't know how to tell you this, Andrew, but Elizabeth no longer lives here with us."

"What? Where is she? Didn't you receive my letters? Why didn't she let me know where she was going?" Andrew had waited too long to see Elizabeth to tolerate any further delay. He had expected her to run from the house to meet him as soon as he had arrived and could not hide his disappointment.

"I will call Jed to help your driver with his horses, Andrew. You must come inside. This will take some time to tell." Olaf led the way into his home after summoning the hired man and motioned for Andrew to take a chair. "I cannot look at you without thinking how greatly our situations have changed since we last spoke together."

"Yes, that is true, but where is Elizabeth? She hasn't fallen ill?" Andrew sat forward on the edge of his chair, not able to contain his impatience.

"We received your letters, but you did not say you would be coming so soon, Andrew. Perhaps if I had known you were coming I would have been able to do something, although I do not know what."

Margaret came to her husband's side and took his hand. She could offer comfort if not much in the way of tangible help. "Please try and be understanding, Andrew. We will tell you all we can."

Andrew opened his mouth to protest but did not when Olaf raised his hand. "Elizabeth did not think you would ever come back for her, Andrew. I know that you promised her that you would, but still she did not believe you truly meant it. You know what had happened between you but I do not, only that she thought she was no longer loved."

Andrew leapt to his feet. "She has not married another!"

"No, not that. Sit down. I am trying to explain." Olaf frowned, then tried once more to make his story clear. "When she read your letters, you spoke only of how wealthy a man your uncle was, how immense his holdings, how fine his home was and how elegant his life. She did not think you would ever want to take her there."

"Why not? Why would she have thought that? She is such a beautiful young woman, and so bright, she would be accepted anywhere I took her!"

Olaf's voice was low. "Have you forgotten so swiftly how badly she was treated by the Seneca?"

Andrew's handsome features hardened immediately into a mask of pure hatred. He knew not what Elizabeth might have told her father, but was certain it had been the truth. "Do not ever mention them to me. They no longer exist!"

Olaf glanced up at Margaret. He had no wish to anger Andrew, but could see no way to avoid it. "We are simple people. Our life here so plain. Elizabeth had been no farther than Oak Grove until she met you, Andrew. Although her mother and I met in Philadelphia, she could scarcely imagine the life you described, the fancy parties, the dancing and music. She felt you would be ashamed to introduce her to your new friends as your wife."

"Olaf, enough!" Andrew cried out in frustrated anguish. "Will you simply tell me where I might find Elizabeth?"

"That is what I am attempting to do. Just let me finish." Olaf sighed softly then continued. "When the last snow melted, she began to spend more and more time in the forest. She would take Lady out at first light and not return home until sundown. I know it was difficult for her to live here with Margaret and the children for she seemed so uncomfortable, so lost,

247

although this has always been her home. She just became more and more quiet until days would go by that we would not hear her speak."

"Elizabeth? You cannot mean it!" Andrew was astonished. "She was always so lively, so spirited. What could have happened?"

Olaf shrugged helplessly. "One thing just seemed to lead to another. She couldn't read any more. She would sit for hours with a book at the same page, just staring at it. When we got your letters she would give them to me to read to her. She carried them all around with her in the pocket of her apron but she would bring them to me to read." Olaf put his hand over his eyes but he could not hide his tears. "I love my daughter very much, Andrew, and I know that you loved her too, but she has never been the same since you brought her home. Margaret and I are going to have a child." Olaf paused to smile at his wife. "When we told her she did not say anything, nothing at all. She just took Lady and went to live in the forest and she has not come home since. I know where she is and I take her food and I have taken her your letters but she has not spoken to me since the day she left our home."

"Why didn't you send for me at once? I could not understand why Elizabeth did not answer my letters, but if she were too ill to reply why didn't you write to me?" Andrew rose to his full height, his gesture a menacing one, but Olaf seemed to have no energy to rise.

Margaret stepped quickly to Andrew's side. "Please do not fault us. Elizabeth tried to write to you, but she couldn't hold a pen, nor make the words she wanted to write. I asked her to let me write to you but she would not tell me what she wished to say. We didn't know what to tell you, and truly, we did not think you would ever return either, and now that you have, you must understand that you cannot take Elizabeth back to Philadelphia with you. We watch her closely, see that she has food to eat and she will be all right here, but in the city she would only be laughed at and that would be horrible for her."

Andrew stared at the pretty young woman, his eyes filled with disbelief. "Are you saying Elizabeth is crazy? Is that what you mean? She is only sixteen years old, and she is my wife. I came to take her home with me and I mean to do it!"

"Andrew, you never married Elizabeth. You never did, and I think it is a blessing now that you didn't. She would only be a burden to you now in your new life. Go back to Philadelphia and try to forget her. It is all you can do. She will never be well again," Olaf advised solemnly.

"How do you know if she'll be well or not? I'll be damned if I'll let my wife live in the forest like some deranged hermit! Now you tell me where I might find her or I'll go out and track her down myself!" Andrew was furious. He could not imagine anyone being so heartless as to let his beloved Elizabeth wander the forest alone. He was nearly shaking with rage that her father had permitted such an injustice to occur.

Olaf rose slowly to his feet. "Andrew, she is not really your wife, not really, and you have no right to take her away."

"What must I do? Take your preacher with me out there to find her? The woman is my wife, damn it, and she always will be!"

"Andrew, I know this has been a great shock to you to come here today and hear this sad accounting of what's happened, but please try and consider what is best for Elizabeth. Leave her alone. It is all she wants, to be left to live in peace."

"Olaf, I am leaving here with Elizabeth or I will not leave here at all. We are wasting valuable time. There are several hours of daylight remaining and I want to see Elizabeth this very afternoon!" Andrew insisted upon having his way. He had not expected to have to fight with Olaf on that day but he would do it if need be to see his wife.

"You will not even know her," Margaret offered sadly. "She is completely wild, Andrew, a creature of the forest, not Elizabeth at all. It would be so much better if you did not see her, just remembered her as she was when first you met her. She was so beautiful then."

"When I first came here I was the one who needed help and she saved my life. I would probably have been hanged for some crime I did not even know of, let alone commit, and I will not turn my back on her now."

Margaret implored him, "If Olaf takes you to see her, will you wait until then to decide what is best? Will you promise not to decide until after you have seen her for yourself?"

"Yes, I will promise," Andrew agreed quickly, but only because he wanted to see Elizabeth, not because he had any intention of following Margaret's advice.

With a knowing glance toward his wife, Olaf started for the door. "Do you want to ride, or we can walk. It is not far."

"I will walk. If Elizabeth has Lady then we can ride her home." Andrew slipped off his coat and tossed it over his chair. "I am hardly dressed for a trek through the woods but I have more than enough clothes now and only one wife. Let's go."

Not even the wildest of his imaginings had prepared Andrew to see Elizabeth that afternoon. She was exactly where Olaf had said she would be, living beside the stream in a house built of branches and leaves. There was a wall of stones surrounding the shabby structure, stones she had brought from all parts of the woods and stacked in heaps, the way shepherds build walls or mounds to pass the time as they tend their sheep. She was sitting by the water's edge, holding a stick and singing some children's song in a high, squeaky voice. Over and over again she sang the same line as if she could not remember the rest. Her dress was dirty, the hem ragged, her hair wild and unkempt but when she turned to look at them Andrew gasped with horror for her eyes were like those of a mountain cat, totally wild and fierce. He expected her to snarl and spit, but instead she leapt to her feet and dashed across the stones which spanned the stream to disappear into the thick stand of trees on the opposite side.

Olaf choked back his tears as he turned to Andrew. "Do you want to introduce her in Philadelphia as your wife? Do you want to take that lunatic with you to Philadelphia now that you are so fine a gentleman?"

Andrew was too shocked to speak for several seconds but then turned toward the older man, determined to see his mission through to completion.

"Please go on back to your home, Olaf. I will stay here with Elizabeth until she is ready to come home with me. I will take care of her for as long as it takes."

"Andrew, it may take forever."

"Then I will wait that long." Andrew took the bag of food they had brought, placed it beside the shack and sat down to wait. "If it takes the rest of my life, I will gladly remain for I will never leave Elizabeth as she is."

Olaf gave up in frustration. "She did not even know you!"

"She will. I want you to bring me some clean clothes for her, her hair brush, her perfume if you have any more. I'd like one of her nightgowns, too. The few things I left here will do for me. Will you bring those things out here tomorrow?"

"It is the least I can do, Andrew. I will see you tomorrow morning, early. Good-bye."

Suddenly remembering his driver Andrew added one more request. "Henry is a capable man. Will you give him my bed in Jed's shed and tell him I wish him to work for you until Elizabeth and I are ready to return to Philadelphia?"

Olaf readily agreed but he shook his head as he walked back toward his farm. It would take so much love and patience to help Elizabeth and he doubted Andrew would have enough of either to do it. He turned once and nearly went back but then pushed on for home. Perhaps after a day or two Andrew would see reason.

Andrew sat and waited for Elizabeth to return to her home. He could only hope that she would want to come back that night to sleep where she usually did, to

252

eat if she got hungry and he would be there waiting for her. It was all he could do not to break down in tears himself when he thought of how she must have suffered. He should never have left her alone after all she'd been through. It had been too difficult for her to be all alone and he should have known that. When he had gone, his intentions had been to protect her. He had enjoyed himself in Philadelphia, though, he had to admit that. He had been something of a celebrity, with plenty of attention from pretty young women and all the while the lovely girl he called his wife had been losing her mind all alone in the cold, dark forest. The blame belonged to him. He knew it did, but she was so young. Surely she could recover her health with him there to help her. She just had to. He would not accept another fate for her. He refused.

Andrew began to relax as the shadows lengthened beneath the trees. He had forgotten how peaceful the forest was, how quiet and calm yet full of life. After only six months of the harsh sounds of the city he had forgotten it all. There must be fish in the stream, he thought, and moved closer to look for the gleaming silver flashes fishes make. He picked up the stick Elizabeth had dropped and held it lightly. Perhaps it was precious to her and he lay it down again by the water's edge. He would need a longer stick and after a brief search found one which he fashioned into a spear by sharpening one end into a point. So intent was he upon spearing a fish for their dinner he did not see Elizabeth had returned to watch him.

Elizabeth peered through the leaves at the tall man. What was he doing? she wondered. She couldn't tell and moved closer to get a better view. He was pleasant to look at, dark, not light like Papa, but she couldn't remember his name. She frowned as she tried to recall what it might be but she could not. She could remember so little any more. That worried her greatly. What was the handsome man's name?

Andrew got the fish on the third try and tossed it up on the bank with a shout of triumph. As he glanced up he saw Elizabeth watching him and smiled. "Do you want to come help me, Elizabeth?" He bent down again to watch the fish dart among the rocks. He speared another, more easily than the first and tossed it up beside the other. "Come and help me, Elizabeth. Can you help?" He made his voice low, soft and inviting, trying to lure her back across the stream to his side, but she did not move. He caught two more fish then stopped to talk with her again. "I'll cook these for our supper, Elizabeth. Aren't you hungry? Don't you want to come eat these fish with me? I know they will be delicious." He cleaned the fish in the stream and continued to chat easily with her but she did not come forward. The coals of her fire were warm and Andrew added twigs and dry leaves then wood to build up the blaze, then waited for the fire to die down leaving the coals sufficiently hot to cook the fish.

As the fish roasted, Andrew gestured toward the makeshift house. "I'll ask your father to bring me an axe. We can build a larger house. There is plenty of wood here and I promised once to build you a home. Do you remember that, Elizabeth?" It all came back to him then, the memory oppressing him with unbearable pain and he turned away to hide his tears. He had not meant to cry in front of her but he had promised so much, so much love and happiness and

254

she'd had only loneliness too horrible to bear. He leaned against the small shabby hut and wept for all their beautiful dreams which had never come true.

Elizabeth watched the man weep and was puzzled. What was wrong with him? He had caught the fish so why was he so sad? She stepped across the slippery stones which bridged the narrow stream and walked cautiously up to his side. When he looked at her she reached out to wipe the tears from his cheeks. She remembered him then and smiled sweetly, her expression so innocent and dear. "Is that you, Indian? Have you come home to me at last?"

Andrew pulled her into his arms and held on to her as if he would never let go. She was too thin still, her figure much too delicate, and he pressed her body closer to his heart for he could not bear to release her. He wound his fingers in her hair and began to kiss her with a passion so desperate she had to cling to his arms in order to stand. He laughed then and hugged her warmly, kissing her dirt-smudged cheeks and stroking her tangled hair with a loving caress.

"Yes, Elizabeth, I am your Indian, and I've come home to you."

"I think your fish are burning." Elizabeth looked down at the four blackened fish and shook her head sadly.

"My fish? Oh, no, they are ruined. Well, let's catch some more. You help me this time, Elizabeth." Andrew held her hand tightly, afraid to let her go, but she seemed quite content by his side. They soon had more fish roasting over the coals and watched them more carefully this time.

Andrew could not stop smiling. At least Elizabeth

had spoken to him, remembered him and if he discounted her disheveled appearance, she didn't seem all that confused. She was sitting opposite him as they ate their supper, their catch supplemented with the food he'd brought along. The fish were good, delicious in his opinion, and he could not recall ever being so hungry.

"Do you like to fish, Elizabeth? Have you caught fish here in the stream before today?"

"Fish?" Elizabeth's eyes were more beautiful than ever, larger now that her face was so thin, but the bright sparkle he had loved was gone. Her gaze was blank as she stared back at him.

"Yes, you helped me to catch these fish, Elizabeth. Have you fished here in the stream by yourself?"

"No, not here."

"Is there somewhere else we can fish tomorrow? Do you know another place?" Andrew persisted in his attempts to draw her out into some kind of a conversation.

"Yes, but it is far." Elizabeth licked her fingers as she finished one piece of cornbread and reached for another.

"Will you take me there tomorrow, Elizabeth? May I go with you in the morning?"

Elizabeth looked up at him then glanced away. "Tomorrow you will still be here?"

"Yes, I'll be here tomorrow, Elizabeth. I'll be here with you for a long time. I like it here in the forest and want to stay. Is that all right? May I stay here with you?"

"This is Margaret's cornbread. It is good, better than mine ever was." Elizabeth frowned sullenly as she examined the texture of the bread closely.

"What? Oh, yes, it tastes good, but I always liked your cooking, Elizabeth. You are a very fine cook. I used to tell you that. Do you remember? I even liked your soup, the soup you fed me when I was sick and you took care of me. I made you think I didn't like it, just to be stubborn I suppose, but I did think it was very good. Can you remember taking care of me? You were a wonderful nurse, Elizabeth."

Elizabeth cocked her head as she listened to him, but she seemed not to have understood. "Do you know Margaret?" Her eyes swept over his face briefly, then returned to the cornbread she held in her fingers. Her nails were all broken and none too clean, but apparently that did not concern her.

"Yes, Margaret is your stepmother now, your father's second wife. I know her. She is pretty, but not nearly so lovely as you."

"Margaret has little children." Elizabeth began to break the cornbread into tiny bits and stack them on the side of her pewter plate. She had eaten her whole meal with her fingers, although Andrew had given her a fork.

"She has a boy and a little girl, John and Claire. They have blond hair like you do. They are as fair as you." Andrew struggled to think of something to say. Since Elizabeth seemed to want to talk about Margaret, he tried to help her stay on that subject.

Elizabeth looked up again, her eyes dark. "And a baby now, too?"

"No, not yet but soon I think. She'll have her baby before summer." Instantly Andrew could see what Elizabeth was thinking. Her thoughts were so clear to him, as if he could see into her mind. Fear tightened his throat into a painful knot for he could not bear to feel her anguish so intensely, but feel it he did.

"I think I had a baby once." Elizabeth's tears fell on her plate and she wiped her eyes on the torn hem of her filthy dress. "I think that I did, but I don't know where he is. I've looked for him everywhere, but I can't find him. I never hear him cry so I do not know where to look."

Andrew watched as Elizabeth's tears continued to fall, making tiny pinging sounds as they hit her plate. She had not shed one tear when he'd told her about their baby. Was that what had happened to her? She had been able to hide her grief as they made their preparation to come home, but once left alone her spirit had been far too fragile to bear such a terrible loss? He moved very slowly so as not to frighten her. He came to her side and put his arms around her thin shoulders to hold her gently in his embrace. He recalled then, she had asked him once to simply hold her in his arms and he had refused. He was so ashamed now as he remembered their journey back to her home. Why had he said no when she wanted his love so badly? Why had he been so lost in his own grief he'd had no time to see hers?

"Our baby died, Elizabeth. He died before he was born so we never heard him cry." Our son was murdered, he thought bitterly, murdered, and the same terrible anger he'd felt that night swept through him again and he leaned his head against hers as she wept. There seemed to be no way for him to comfort her now. She cried pitifully until he could not believe her tiny body could have held so many unshed tears. It

258

grew dark as he held her in his arms. He smoothed her hair back from her forehead and kissed her face lightly but still she sobbed on and on, her thin shoulders shaking in endless tremors of despair.

"It is all right, Elizabeth. Please do not weep so. Everything will be all right now. I am so sorry I left you all alone with such sorrow. I never meant to do this to you." He pulled her across his lap and hugged her as he whispered softly. He had not understood her need for him, nor the depth of her grief and it had overwhelmed her. He had felt only rage, anger he'd expressed by leaving his tribe forever, but she had kept all her tears to herself. When finally she fell into an exhausted sleep, he carried her into her little house and placed her upon her blanket, then lay down beside her and held her close. She would get better now, he was sure of it, and kissed her lips softly as he cradled her in his arms. He would take good care of her until she was well and strong again, for he would never allow her to spend another day alone.

Fourteen

When Andrew awoke the next morning, he found Elizabeth still sleeping soundly in his arms. She looked exhausted still, spent, dark circles marred the creamy skin beneath her eyes and her breathing was slow and deep. He decided he would let her sleep all day if she wished, and after kissing her forehead lightly, slipped out of the leaf-covered house noiselessly and went to wash in the stream. As the sun began to rise, he paced anxiously up and down the small clearing waiting for Olaf to arrive, his mind filled with useful items he'd not thought to request but now knew he would need. When his father-in-law called out a greeting, he rushed quickly to meet him.

"I have brought the things you wanted, her dress, nightgown, even perfume. Did Elizabeth speak to you? I did not sleep all night. I was so worried about her. If you frighten her she may run away and I won't be able to keep watch for her, provide for her as I have been."

"You needn't have worried. She remembers me, spoke with me. She is still sleeping, poor dear. I think she was exhausted long before I came. I hope she'll recover swiftly now that I am here to care for her. It is my fault this happened to her. I should never have left her here alone when she wanted so desperately to come to Philadelphia with me."

Olaf straightened up as he spoke. "She was not alone, Andrew. Margaret and I were here. We tried our best to help her, but it was too much for us. Nothing we did seemed to reach her."

"No, do not misunderstand me. I do not fault you for her illness. She is my responsibility and I was wrong to leave her here as I did. That mistake was mine, not yours."

Olaf handed the bundle he had carried to Andrew, then stepped back. He hesitated a moment, then spoke quickly. "You must think me a great fool for trusting you with my daughter again after what she has already suffered because of you."

"A fool?" Andrew was surprised by the man's sudden change of mood. "I don't understand what you mean."

"I should have thrown you off my farm that afternoon you returned with the deer. It was plain to me what you were when first we met. Perhaps it was too late even then. I doubt she was still a virgin after spending two weeks in the company of a man like you."

Andrew exhaled slowly in a valiant attempt to contain his fiery temper. "I will never speak of the things which happened between Elizabeth and me. They are private, our own precious memories and none of your concern."

"No, you are wrong, Andrew. Elizabeth would defend you even now if she could, but she is no longer able to do it. I want you to understand if you leave that girl here in the forest, leave her because you cannot make her well, but leave her carrying your bastard child again, I will hunt you down and kill you for it's what you deserve." Olaf's voice was low and cold. "I swear I will do it. You can go to Philadelphia, London for all I care, but you won't be safe from me. No matter how rich you are or how many men you hire for protection. I should kill you right now for what you've done to my daughter, for not respecting the sweet child she was, for breaking her heart and ruining her mind!"

Andrew appraised his father-in-law accurately. They were of almost equal size. He was slightly taller, more lean and muscular, but Olaf was very strong. They were nearly an equal match. But he knew he had the advantage of youth and his skill as a warrior to aid him, and the gaze he turned upon the man held no hint of fear. "I will never leave Elizabeth as she is. She has spent her last hour alone in these woods, Olaf. If you wish to try and kill me then do so now and we will be finished with your threats at once. If not, then mention it no more. When you go to your church on Sunday tell your preacher I plan to marry Elizabeth as soon as she is able to repeat her vows. She has always been my wife and I am her husband, but as you pointed out yesterday, I am not legally responsible for her since our marriage is not recorded in any book. You see I do not plan to leave her ever again and since you now know my family's name I do believe I have your consent for our marriage, do I not?"

Olaf was astounded by Andrew's determination. "You wish to marry Elizabeth as she is now?"

"Perhaps I should threaten to kill you for thinking I could love your daughter and abandon her to so cruel a fate as this. You have insulted us both with that question."

Olaf stared into Andrew's icy green eyes and shuddered at the controlled terror he saw mirrored in their depths. From their first meeting it had been Andrew's eyes he could not abide. The same bright gaze he loved in his beautiful daughter filled him with dread now. "I will speak with the Reverend Williams of your plans."

"Then you have decided not to challenge me after all? Not to try and avenge your daughter's honor, which for some reason you seem to think I have abused?"

"I do not merely think it, Andrew. I know it! You seduced my little girl, took her away from her home with promises which were all lies! You cannot deny that!"

Andrew's defiant expression did not change. "Seduced? I do not believe it is possible to accuse a man of seducing his own wife and Elizabeth has always been mine!"

A red curtain of anger descended upon Olaf's mind, turning all before him to the vivid color of blood as he screamed, "I forbid the marriage and so did your father. Isn't the fact your child is dead and Elizabeth mad not proof enough that indeed God himself opposes your marriage!"

Andrew dropped the parcel containing Elizabeth's things and sprang forward with the speed and strength of a mountain cat. His hands closed over the front of Olaf's shirt and he lifted the heavier man clear off the ground as he snarled in his face. "Yours is a God of love and he knows Elizabeth is mine even if you do not!"

Olaf struggled to get free and backed away in terror. "You are as mad as she is, aren't you? She is an obsession with you as you are with her! Why didn't I see that from the beginning? Your love is evil, Andrew, evil, and you will never live to marry my daughter!" Olaf turned and ran away through the trees, ran as fast as he could as if the very devil himself were pursuing him.

Andrew stood his ground, his whole body shaking with rage until he could bear no more and slammed his fist into the nearest tree. He did not even feel the pain in his fury. He felt only outrage at the fates which kept him from his beautiful wife.

Elizabeth heard the men's angry shouts and was badly frightened, terrified by their hostile voices and shrank back into the farthest corner of her makeshift house to hide. She covered her head with her arms and wept again, too scared to run away.

Andrew held his throbbing hand under the cool water of the stream and cursed with every filthy expression he knew in two languages. Love was not evil, not ever bad. How could Olaf have said such a vile thing? All he wanted was to love Elizabeth, love her and live with her in a home where they could find happiness at last. Why was that always such an impossibility? Why? He cursed his fate bitterly and vowed to marry Elizabeth the first day she could say the words, the very first day.

When she heard no sounds other than those of the forest, Elizabeth began to grow calm once again. Where was her Indian? Had he left her again after all? She crawled out of her house and saw him at once. He was kneeling at the water's edge. He was sad again. She could feel that from the set of his broad shoulders and her eyes filled with tears as she approached him slowly. "Indian?" She reached for his bloody hand and brought it to her lips, kissing the torn knuckles tenderly. "You were fighting, Indian?"

"Yes, Elizabeth, but only with myself." Andrew left his hand in hers for a moment then pulled it free. "I am all right."

"No, you are hurt, as badly as I am, but my blood does not show." Elizabeth picked up the stick she'd played with the day before and trailed it through the water slowly, lost in her own thoughts once more.

"Where are you hurt, Elizabeth? What do you mean?" Andrew wrapped his handkerchief around his hand and tied the ends with his teeth. He was certain he'd broken the bones in his hand but he had no one to blame but himself for such folly.

Elizabeth rocked back and forth on her heels as she swished the small branch through the cool stream. "Inside, I am hurt inside. The pain is terrible, but it does not show."

"Elizabeth!" Andrew put his hands on her shoulders, then winced as the agonizing pain shot up his right arm. "Elizabeth, are you really ill? Truly?"

Elizabeth got to her feet and began to step across the stones which filled the shallow stream bed. "You were my heart, Indian. Did you think I could live with no heart?"

Andrew rose quickly and followed closely behind her as she entered the trees. "Elizabeth, wait for me. I want to come with you. Where are we going?" He knew then her pain was as real as his own for he had missed her terribly. There would never be another

265

woman like her for him and he hurried to keep her in sight.

Elizabeth led him on through the forest in a winding, twisting path. She doubled back more than once, but then finally reached her destination. The stream was wide there, a deep, clear pool surrounded by elm and maple trees and drenched with the morning sun. Lady stood grazing in the tall grass at the small lake's edge but lifted her head to call to her mistress when she caught Elizabeth's scent upon the gentle breeze.

Elizabeth turned to Andrew. "There are big fish here, Indian. This is where I fish."

"Yes, this looks like a good place. How do you catch them? Do you have traps or a line? How?"

"With a line and hook. I leave them hanging there on the low branch of that tree for I cannot remember to bring them with me," Elizabeth apologized sadly.

"No, that is clever of you, Elizabeth, to keep your line and hook where they are needed." Andrew pulled off his shirt and tossed it upon the grass. It was warm enough to swim and then maybe he could convince Elizabeth to put on the clean dress her father had brought and he could brush out her long hair himself if she would let him. It was worth a try. He hated to just tell her to bathe when her appearance seemed to have escaped her notice so completely.

"Can you swim, Elizabeth? I like to swim. Will you come swimming with me?" Andrew flashed his most charming grin, hoping to entice her into joining him.

Elizabeth looked down at her ragged dress. "I will get all wet." She seemed confused by his invitation.

"Yes, of course. That's the fun. Take off your dress

and come into the water with me." Andrew slipped off the rest of his clothes and dove into the deep pool. The water was cool but not bone chilling, and he called to her from the center. "Come in with me. This is very nice, but I do not want to swim alone."

Elizabeth watched him swim for only a few minutes before she began to unbutton her tattered dress. Her clothes mattered so little to her she did not bother to fold them, but let them lie where they fell in the grass. She dove into the water, then swam to where Andrew was treading water.

"You swim as well as a fish, Elizabeth. You really do." He grabbed for her then but she slid from his grasp and darted across the pond with smooth even strokes. She was indeed an excellent swimmer and seemed to enjoy his game. Andrew laughed as she splashed him then tried to reach her again, but she was gone, disappearing from his view as she dove to the bottom of the small lake. He moved to where he could stand on the moss-covered rocks and shook the water from his hair. Where had she gone?

Elizabeth came up behind him and slipped her slender arms around his waist. She stood close and hugged him tightly with her head pressed to his shoulder blades in a loving embrace. His body felt so good next to hers, his strong muscles rippling under her touch and she smiled warmly. "I love you, Indian."

Andrew took her small hands in his and turned to face her, but she slipped from his embrace and was gone, her pale pink skin a blur as she sped away. They played for a long time, until both grew weary of their sport and she let him catch her. He ran his hands down her smooth back and hugged her hips to his. When he leaned down she lifted her lips to meet his and kissed him with such love and sweetness he could not bear to draw away and waited for her to end their kiss. When at last she did, he smiled. "Can you remember my name, Elizabeth?" Andrew had only wondered if she could but as he looked down at her she seemed to simply wither, to shrink, all her beauty fading in an instant, as that of a wild flower does when it is picked. She simply wilted before his eyes, her disappointment plain in her tear-filled gaze.

"Indian is not enough?" She was confused and frowned as she pulled away from his grasp. He tried to hold on and that only frightened her all the more. "Let me go, let me go!" She struggled so violently he released her and watched as she dashed from the pool. She grabbed her dirty garments and ran on without stopping to dress, too frightened apparently to pause long enough to don her clothes.

Andrew's happiness of only moments before vanished. He had not meant to hurt her, to force her clouded mind to remember what it could not. That had been mean and he hadn't wanted to hurt her again, only to inquire if she did recall. His hand felt better. Perhaps it was only bruised, the bones not broken after all. He pulled on his clothes and called to Lady. The horse should not be left so far from their house. He laughed as he thought of their shack. Well, he could not ask Olaf to bring an axe now, for the man would probably never return!

Elizabeth ran until her chest ached so badly she fell to her knees gasping for breath. With shaking fingers she buttoned her dress and wiped her eyes. Was he not her Indian after all? Not the man she had always loved? She could not stop crying and sank down in the grass where she lay for more than an hour sobbing pathetically, pulling tuffs of the long green grass from the earth as she wept.

When Andrew reached the little house there was no sign of Elizabeth. He had hoped she'd gone home, but there was no evidence she had returned since they'd left together. He patted Lady's flank and pulled himself up on the mare's back. He had no idea where to look, but perhaps the horse could help him locate her mistress. He had no real plan for a search. She could have gone in any direction, but he hoped she would be hiding close by. He rode in widening circles through the trees, straining for a glimpse of his wife to guide him. When at last he found her she was sound asleep in the tall grass where she had fallen, and he slid from Lady' back and walked soundlessly to where she lay. Her pretty face looked so sweet as she slept and he was dreadfully sorry he had made her so unhappy again. He wouldn't force her to remember ever again. He'd make no demands at all upon her and see how much she could do. However little that was, it would be enough.

He knelt beside her, then leaned down to kiss her lips. Despite Olaf's ranting, he could not imagine making love to her now. Her kiss at the pond had been delicious, but even if she had stayed they would not have made love. She was too fragile, too afraid of him still to make love willingly and he would not force her. He did not worry over the possibility of a child. After what she had suffered losing their baby he did not believe she could ever have another.

269

Elizabeth blinked as his kiss awoke her, and this time she did not pull away. "I am so sorry, Indian. I do not know your name, only that I love you. Is that not enough?"

"Yes, it is enough, my love. You will recall my name soon. It is not so important to me as the fact you love me still. You are all that matters to me. Come let me lift you upon Lady's back and when we get home, I'll help you change your dress and brush out your pretty hair. Your hair is so beautiful you should let it grow forever, until it trails behind you as you walk."

When Andrew leapt upon Lady's back behind her, Elizabeth leaned against him as they rode home. Her back fit perfectly next to the line of his chest and he encircled her waist with his arm. The day was warm still and they felt lazy, relaxed, as they reached the small clearing where she made her home. When he helped her from the mare's back, she reached up to kiss him and it seemed most natural for him to respond.

Elizabeth wound her arms around his neck and clung to him, her only thought of him, of his strong lean body and how dearly she loved him. He was truly her heart, exactly as she had told him. He was her very heart, she loved him so.

Andrew tried to catch his breath as he took her hands in his. "Let me help you to put on your clean clothes, Elizabeth." He had only meant to help her with the buttons but his hand brushed against her soft, cool breast and he froze instantly, shocked by the surge of passion which rushed through his loins. As he looked down, her luminous green eyes held such love, such a glow of trust and affection he reached out to

270

stroke her cheek lightly with his fingertips, but she pulled his hand to her lips, kissing his palm tenderly before placing his hand again at her bare breast.

"Elizabeth—" Andrew's words caught in his throat as she moved his hand over her soft, smooth skin. When she stepped closer and began to kiss his face, he could not draw away but folded her gently into a warm embrace as he tried to recall why he had thought only moments before they would not make love.

As Elizabeth felt Andrew's kiss grow more ardent she leaned against him, pressing her whole body along the length of his. She gave herself up to the intoxicating sensation his warm mouth brought. His lips were soft, yet insistent, and she clung to him, drawing in the love she could feel coursing so rapidly through his veins. She wanted only to know his delicious taste and tantalizing touch once more, to enjoy his loving and return it. Her fingers moved through his thick curls, combing his hair lightly as her arms hugged his neck. She loved every inch of him for surely he was as perfect a man as had ever lived and he was hers. When he slipped her dress from her shoulders, she let it fall without protest, then helped him to ease off his shirt. She loved the way his warm flesh felt against her own and shuddered with the delight of his touch. She had no thought then, no painful memories, no broken heart which would never mend. Her love was home, holding her, kissing her, loving her once more and she smiled with pleasure as he carried her onto her blanket.

Andrew had not made love to Elizabeth for so long, for so very long, and he wanted to savor the touch of her delicate body, to enjoy the same passionate response they had always shared but she was so changed he seemed not to have the same woman in his arms. Her thinness only made her beauty more exquisite, but her whole being was different. She was no longer the playful creature he had adored. She was shy now, hesitant, unsure of how to please him as if she had never lain with him before. He tried to reassure her, to make love to her as he always had, but she could not hide her tears and he grew alarmed.

"Elizabeth, have I hurt you? I did not mean to cause you any pain. Tell me what is wrong?" He cradled her gently in his arms, sparing her the burden of his weight.

"Oh, Andrew, it is not the same. I want you as I always have, but it is not the same." Elizabeth turned away from him and sobbed as pitifully as she had the night before, her despair too great for him to console.

"Elizabeth, you do know my name, you do!" Andrew was so excited by her casual use of his name his enthusiastic shout startled her out of her sorrow.

"What?" She turned back toward him, lifting her long hair away from her eyes. She looked puzzled for a moment, then her whole face lit up with a delighted smile. "Your name is Andrew. Andrew Jordan, isn't it?"

"Yes, my love. Now come back here to me." Andrew drew her into his arms and whispered as he kissed her lovely pink ears, "It is not the same, Elizabeth. It is so much better." When he kissed her again, she was no longer crying but relaxed in his embrace and he found her shyness enchanting and smiled to himself as he recalled Olaf's words. Truly she had been the one to seduce him in the beginning for he had never been able to resist her sweet smile and gentle touch and could not do so now. He buried his face in her long golden hair, drinking in the joy of its softness before his lips sought hers, too hungry for her warm body to delay a moment more when she was so willingly his wife.

Elizabeth lay quietly in Andrew's arms, filled with the rapture she'd thought lost to her forever. She felt safe in his embrace and snuggled against him as she fell asleep, this time exhausted by pleasure rather than sorrow and her smile was a contented one as she dreamed only of him and what their life would be.

Andrew held Elizabeth in his arms as she slept but his thoughts were far different from hers. While her features were graced with an angelic smile, his were set in the determined frown his uncle had so often found unsettling. He could not forget the long, bleak winter months of their separation. His world had changed completely in the short space of the one year he had known Elizabeth, turned upside down, yet he could not imagine not loving her as deeply as he did. He might be dead had she not taken him in so readily, but never had he expected his love for her to change his fate so completely. It had been his own arrogance perhaps, his pride in the destiny he had chosen for himself which had blinded him to the problems she had foreseen. She could see the future. He had no doubt she did possess that gift, but a future seen could not be changed. The gods were both blind and deaf to his pleas, neither saw nor heard his constant entreaties for the simple joy of being allowed to love the delicate beauty in his arms. Her hand lay upon his chest. She was still so fair in spite of her days spent outdoors in the sunlight that they appeared to be two entirely different creatures, one pale, one dark, one slight, one strong, one woman, one man. He smiled at that comparison for all they had ever wanted to be was a man and a woman, husband and wife.

Elizabeth stirred restlessly and drew closer. "Andrew, will you stay with me this time?"

"Yes, I will stay until you are bored of our life in the forest and wish to see my home in Philadelphia, then I will take you there with me, my love."

"You will take me with you?" Elizabeth sat up to look into his eyes more directly for she did not believe his words. She frowned slightly as she searched his expression for another meaning not so easily heard nor seen. "Do you mean it? I may go with you this time?"

"Yes, and you will be the most beautiful woman in the city, Elizabeth, far more lovely than any of the others will ever be."

"How can that be true?" the pretty girl asked skeptically.

"Do you not know how precious you are? Your eyes are the most unusual shade of green, as brilliant as emeralds and your hair like the finest yellow silk. Your fair complexion has the perfection of pearls and your figure is exquisite. I will hire a maid for you. She'll care for all the beautiful clothes I'll buy and see to your every need. I am very rich now, Elizabeth. I can take such wonderfully good care of you now."

Elizabeth looked away, the light in her pretty eyes changed, darkened as did her mood. "Are you happier now as a rich white man than you were as a rich Indian? I remember all that you told me of your people, how pleasant our lives were going to be but none of it came true."

Andrew felt sick. Had she kicked him she could not have hurt him more but he knew the pain he felt was slight compared to what she had suffered. "I thought my words were true. I believed them, Elizabeth. I would never have taken you home to the Seneca had I known what a hell we would find. That's why I went to Philadelphia alone, to be certain you would find a happy life before I took you there." If only he had not remained away so long, he thought sadly. If only he had returned immediately to claim her, but he wanted her to find perfection when she came and that had been his mistake.

"No, I do not want to ever leave this place, Andrew. I am content to be here with you. Do not ask me to leave."

Andrew drew her back down into his arms and began to kiss her slender white throat as he caressed her smooth, supple back. She was a woman now, no longer a loving child. She had grown up far too painfully, far too soon and if he could make her happy in a shack in the forest then that was what he would do. They needed nothing his uncle's fortune could provide. They needed only each other. His lips moved over the soft swell of her breast, then down across her flat stomach and he could still smell the same fragrance of wild flowers her lovely body had always held, even without perfume. He thought only of giving her pleasure as he made love to her again, to the exquisite woman she was, but in his heart he wept for the delightfully loving girl she had been for he knew that dear Elizabeth was lost to him forever.

The mild spring days came and went, one blurring into the next, until Andrew lost all track of the time. He neither counted nor cared how many days they had spent together in the peace of the woods. He had made a bow and arrows to hunt and found the game plentiful, his eye sure, his hand still so steady and quick he could kill the fleetest of creatures before it knew it was being hunted. He had not thought it possible he could be content living so quietly, but their days seemed full though they might do nothing more than sit quietly beside the stream from dawn to dusk holding hands and delighting in each other's company. Elizabeth would stay with him for hours, leaning against his shoulder as he sat hugging her and Andrew could think of no reason to ever leave. Elizabeth was thoughtful, but smiled at him more and more frequently as the days passed. Sometimes he would look up to find her watching him and her eyes would gleam with the bright sparkle he remembered so well and he would laugh with the joy of truly having her with him again.

"Andrew, what has happened to Papa? Why doesn't he come to see us?" They were fishing at the small lake in the early morning sun, catching their breakfast as they often did.

"I am afraid he is still angry with me for taking you away as I did, my love. He will never forgive me for that."

Elizabeth moved with a slow, graceful step as she threw out her line. "You did not take me, Andrew. I went with you most gladly, if you'll recall. All you had to do was ask and I went without the slightest bit of argument."

"Yes, I know, but he blames me for all that happened, for not protecting you from the harm I should have foreseen."

"You have been the best of husbands, Andrew, so loving. If I am content, why should he still be angry? This is my life to live, not his, and I want to spend it with you."

Andrew shaded his eyes with his hand and looked at her more closely. Since he had come to stay with her she had been as pretty and well groomed as when they'd first met. They washed their clothes in the stream, swam nearly every day. Her flaxen hair glistened in the bright sunlight with the sheen of health and although her figure was still slender, it had once again taken on the gentle curves he found so attractive. She was lovely, always calm and spoke with him on any subject he cared to discuss. She was changed, that was true, no longer the headstrong, defiant girl she had been, but anyone who had not known her would find no fault in her behavior or manners. She was very charming in all that she did, pleasant and sweet, a delightful companion in all respects.

"Elizabeth, perhaps we should go to see him. I need tools to enlarge our house and he must want to see you. I'm certain that he does. It is only his anger at me that keeps him away. Maybe Margaret has had their baby by now. You may have a little brother or sister. Wouldn't you like to go for a visit?"

"No. Please go alone, Andrew. I will stay here." Elizabeth gave her full attention to her line although she had had no bite.

"Tell me why I must go alone, for they are your

family, not mine." Andrew held his breath. He was pushing her. He knew that and waited anxiously for her reply.

"When I have given you no son, you cannot understand?"

"Elizabeth, you are very young. We may have another child one day. We may have a dozen, but if we do not we have each other. You are all I will ever need to be content." Andrew moved behind her and pulled her into his arms. "I want to marry you in your church. Do you think you would like that? I asked your father to speak with Reverend Williams, but I do not know if he gave the preacher my message or how the man might have replied."

Elizabeth turned to face him. "You wish to marry me in church? But why? Am I not your wife as you have always told me I am?" She was teasing him now, using his own words playfully as she smiled mischievously.

"Yes, you are most definitely my wife and as long as we remain together here in the woods it matters little, but should we return to Philadelphia I would like the marriage to be a legal one. I want no question that we are wed."

Elizabeth grew wistful when she saw how serious he was. "Were we to be married in a church I would feel no differently, no more your wife. I don't want to go to Philadelphia, Andrew, not ever."

"We must go one day, but not until you wish to accompany me. You are so lovely, Elizabeth, such a beauty. I am so proud of you and I'd like everyone to meet you. You will be the prettiest woman there."

Elizabeth reached up to touch his cheek, caressing

his face softly. "Are the people of Philadelphia so foolish that they will see no more than my face? Will they not be able to see what is in my heart? Beauty is of no importance in a woman if she has no heart."

Andrew's lips brushed hers gently but he did not touch her. He waited patiently and the fishing line slipped from her fingers as she wrapped her arms around his neck. He had discovered quite by accident that she would make love to him if he but waited, controlled his own passion to wait for hers. He brought his arms up slowly to encircle her waist as she kissed him more deeply. She was enticingly affectionate now and they made love often, wherever they wished for the forest was theirs to claim. Her lips moved down his neck to the hollow of his throat as her hands slipped down his shirt to enjoy his warmth. Her touch was easy, yet sure. She knew his body well and as her fingertips traced over the muscles of his back he pulled her down into the soft grass. She laughed at him then. He could stand only so much of her slow loving before he had to have her, to make her his own at his own far more demanding pace.

Andrew could not remember as he surrendered himself totally to his passion if she had agreed to marry him in her church or not, but frankly no longer cared. "Elizabeth, am I not your heart?" He gave her no chance to respond as his mouth covered hers. He wanted her too desperately to argue, and she seemed not to mind. He felt her tremble as her passion increased to match his own and they were lost in the delights of the love they shared with such innocent enjoyment. Andrew had found a strength in Elizabeth now which amazed him. She took all he could give but returned it, never tiring of his kiss or unquenchable hunger for her. She could make love with him forever, yet never be the same woman twice. He had no idea how she did it, but she constantly grew with his love. She grew stronger, more confident, more secure, until he could abandon himself to his passion for her without fear she would not respond. She was love itself and he prayed to every god he could think of that he could give her another child. He had never consciously thought of a baby until that very hour and the effort stunned him. It was a magical thing to realize what his loving could do and he hoped with all his heart she would conceive his child again, and soon.

Fifteen

Elizabeth's long silken hair draped gently across Andrew's bare chest as she leaned down to kiss him. "I would like to marry you in my church, Andrew. Perhaps it is time now after all."

Andrew's hand wound through her shimmering tresses as he pulled her mouth back down to his. He kissed her slowly, sealing their bargain with affection before he replied. "I will go speak to your father and the preacher. You'll need a dress. Do you have one at home?"

"This is my home, here with you and you know how little I have. This one dress and no other." Elizabeth smiled happily, her lack of wardrobe no real concern to her.

"When we reach Philadelphia, I will buy you the most exquisite gowns which can be made. I do not want to wait for a new dress to be sewn for our wedding though. I will see what can be found in Oak Grove."

"Are you so impatient after more than a year as my husband to make me your wife in the church?" Elizabeth's fingertips traced the curve of his cheek. She still thought him the handsomest of men. His skin was tanned as dark as it had been when they'd met for he seldom wore a shirt. His glossy hair was long, thick and shiny. She loved to feel its softness when she kissed him, but he had continued to shave for she had convinced him he was far too handsome a man to hide his face behind a beard. When he had worn one he couldn't tell if he were smiling and that bothered her. She loved all his expressions, his sly smiles as well as his wide grins, and since he was always ready to please her, he readily consented to being clean shaven. He had been back to her father's house to get some of his things. Henry was still there, ready to drive their carriage home whenever they wanted to go. Word had been sent to Matthew Jordan giving Elizabeth's frail health as the reason for Andrew's delay in returning to his home. Margaret had a baby boy and Olaf seemed so enraptured with his new family he ceased to complain about Andrew's presence with his daughter.

"Yes, I want to marry you today, if possible. If not, then tomorrow." He raised up on one elbow and smiled broadly. "I think you are ready to come home with me, Elizabeth, to come to Philadelphia and be my wife."

Elizabeth sighed softly as he looked about their small home. "You must return and I will go with you, my love, but truly I know we will never again be so happy as we are today."

"I do believe you can see the future. I honestly do. I will buy you a book to write down your thoughts and then I will take great pleasure in proving you wrong! I will make you happy wherever we go. I know I will."

"You always have, Andrew, but we have escaped the war here. Surely in Philadelphia we will be caught up in it. The world consists of so much more than you and me, dearest, and that is what presents all our

problems. Here in the forest, we are all that exists."
Elizabeth paused a moment then continued more
seriously. "There is no way to escape the future. It
simply comes, no matter what thoughts I might wish
to transcribe and how desperately you try to change
them."

Andrew observed the determined set of her chin and
shrugged. "I will make no attempt to influence the
outcome of this cursed war. There were reports of
fighting between British soldiers and the rebel army
around Boston before I left Philadelphia. It must have
spread in the last months."

Elizabeth agreed thoughtfully. "Yes. Once begun I
am certain we will pursue our cause to the end."

"We? And just who is this we of whom you speak? I
refuse to take sides in this conflict. I did no more than
act as an interpreter for the British, but my uncle was
greatly encouraged by that fact for he is a Loyalist as
are all his friends. I know your choice is clear, but for
myself I was a warrior too long. I do not relish the sight
of battle as those who have never fought do."

"Andrew, will it be possible for us to live in
Philadelphia and for you to remain neutral? To take
neither side? The Seneca are fighting with the British.
If the Indians have chosen a side, how can you not do
so as well?"

Andrew scowled angrily. "I will not fight, Elizabeth.
The Colonies mean nothing to me and the Crown less.
I care not what the outcome of this rebellion might be
and I do not want to fight only for the glory of the kill.
When I was no more than your age I had killed many,
and not with a musket from afar as these British in
their fancy red uniforms do, up close with my knife

and tomahawk where my enemy's blood splattered my own skin as well as his."

Elizabeth shuddered at that gory image and shut her eyes tightly for a few seconds, but when she looked up at him again she tried to smile. "Yet God kept you safe for me, Andrew. I pray he will continue to watch over you so carefully forever."

Andrew did not know how to reply, for as he looked into his beloved's eyes he thought only that God took very little notice of Elizabeth, left her alone when she needed protection and he knew he had done the same. It was not just for so lovely a creature not to be kept safe and well. "I will go now and speak to your father. Do you wish to come with me this time?"

"No, I am content to rest here." Elizabeth glanced away. She did not want to return to the house that had been her home. The memories were all too sad there.

"Elizabeth, you will come for the wedding, won't you?" Andrew teased her with a light kiss as he stood.

"I shall have to, won't I?" Elizabeth teased him as well.

"Yes. Let us get married tomorrow morning and leave for Philadelphia as soon as we have bid everyone farewell."

"Is that to be my honeymoon?" Elizabeth inquired coyly. She was well now, a woman of grace and wit, as strong emotionally as she had ever been due to his loving care.

"Your honeymoon? My love, I do believe we began our honeymoon a long while ago and I never intend for it to end. Do you?"

"I shall have to wait and see. If you grow bald and fat it will be difficult for me to pretend much passion."

"Pretend! When have you ever pretended with me, Elizabeth?" Andrew pulled his shirt on over his head, then gave her his hand to help her rise.

"I'll not reveal my secrets. You shall have to catch me at it, Andrew." Elizabeth slipped her arms around his waist and kissed his lips lightly, her passion for him obviously very real.

"That will be quite a challenge. You needn't worry. I shall grow neither bald nor fat, I promise you." His kiss was a teasing one until she made it her own. She could do that so easily, turn his affectionate play to passion with a caress or seductive glance and she did so now as her slender body melted smoothly against his lean frame, her grace complementing his strength beautifully.

Andrew took her hands from around his neck and laughed as he pushed her gently away. "Elizabeth! I will be home soon. Do not tease me now for I have no time to finish your game. Catch us some fish for supper since I will have no time to hunt. I'll hurry so I can return before dark." He hugged her warmly, then left for the short journey to the Peterson farm.

Olaf's greeting was polite if not warm as he welcomed Andrew to his home. "Elizabeth did not come with you, yet she will marry you tomorrow? Are you certain she is able to make such a promise?"

"Yes, she is fine now, has been for weeks. It was only that somehow we decided to marry when we went to Philadelphia that has delayed the ceremony." Andrew stood at a cautious distance from the older man. He didn't trust Olaf now since he knew the man's true feelings, but he hoped they could continue to live in peace when Elizabeth was so dear to them both.

"You cannot be serious about taking her there!" Olaf was aghast at Andrew's plans. "I have not seen her since the first day of your stay, but I cannot believe she could be well enough to accompany you to Philadelphia, nor to live there happily when I know how distracted she was."

Andrew sighed impatiently. He had no interest in arguing with the man since the decision had already been made. "You will see for yourself tomorrow, Olaf. She is quite well. You will notice a difference for she has grown up to be a lovely young woman, but she is no longer ill, not in any way. Now I am going into Oak Grove to see the Reverend Williams and try to find a dress for Elizabeth to wear."

"Is she close enough to Margaret's size to wear one of hers? Margaret has a lovely dress—"

"Olaf, I appreciate your gesture, but no thank you. Unless, do you by any chance have her mother's wedding dress?"

Olaf shook his head sadly. "No. We buried her dear mother in that dress, Andrew. She was so lovely, I could not bear for her to spend eternity in anything other than the finest of lace." He turned away to hide the tears which had filled his eyes. "I am sorry, Andrew. Margaret has made me so happy, but still it is not the same."

Andrew felt a sudden kinship for the blond man and reached out to touch his shoulder gently. He understood his father-in-law's unexpected display of emotion well for he knew no woman could ever replace Elizabeth in his heart. Her mother must have been very special as well. "Well, then, I will find her something new. Now did you ever tell Reverend Williams of my intention to marry Elizabeth in his church?"

Olaf regained his composure and hurriedly wiped his eyes on his sleeve. "Yes, I did approach the subject with him once. He was not receptive, Andrew. He is a good man but follows his Bible to the letter."

"What does that mean? I know I should be used to problems as often as Elizabeth and I must overcome them, but what can his objection be?" Andrew forced himself to remain calm but he was furious all the same.

"He merely told me he doubted you were Christian, Andrew, and said he would marry no heathens in his church."

"Then I will convince the man I am most devout! Is Margaret well enough to come to the church tomorrow for the ceremony?"

"Yes, both she and the boy are fine. They are napping now, but both are well and we will want to bring the other two children also."

"Of course. It is settled then. We will stop by so Elizabeth may dress here in the morning and then we'll all go into town together." The two men chatted only briefly before Andrew changed his clothes and summoning Henry, took his carriage into Oak Grove. If the Reverend Williams would marry only fine Christian gentlemen in his church, then that was what he would see.

Lewis Williams was a portly man. He peered at Andrew over his gold-rimmed spectacles and shook his head emphatically, making the loose skin of his cheeks quiver frantically. "Impossible. What you ask is simply impossible. First of all, the bans must be read prior to the marriage. I cannot simply marry whomever comes to my door, Mr. Jordan. Secondly, I want to marry only God fearing Christians here in my parish. Elizabeth was always one of my favorites, that I will freely admit, such a dear girl. At least she used to be before she—" The minister suddenly realized the cold gleam in Andrew's eyes was a most hostile and challenging stare. He found himself unable to complete his sentence in any diplomatic way.

"Before she ran off with an Indian? Is that what you really want to say? As you can easily see, I am no Indian, Reverend Williams."

The embarrassed man nodded "no." The young man before him was dressed in a splendid suit, far finer material than any he'd ever owned. If Andrew Jordan had once lived as an Indian brave, there was no trace of that experience in either his manner or his dress.

Andrew leaned forwardly slightly, his tone conciliatory. "Since you have such a fond feeling for my, my intended bride, let me explain what I have in mind. I would like to make a donation to your church in Elizabeth's name. Shall we say one hundred pounds to be used to further your work, to be spent as you see fit."

The overweight man's pale blue eyes widened in surprise. "One hundred pounds?"

"Yes, for your own personal use, you understand. It must be difficult for you to feed and clothe your own family on your salary. I want the money to be used for your private needs, to enable you to better spread the gospel, of course."

"Of course. That is a most generous contribution, Mr. Jordan, but there is still the matter of the bans. They have not been read and—"

Andrew inquired softly, "Perhaps you have heard that Elizabeth has not been well?"

"Yes, poor child. I did hear that she was not herself, was unable to attend services here with her family as she always has. I was sorry to learn of it."

"Yet you did not once go to visit her?"

"Ah, well, no, I am sorry to say I did not." The man stuttered nervously, uncertain as to where the conversation was leading.

"You seem to be able to adhere only to some of the Christian principles, sir. I am sorry you would insist upon the reading of the bans prior to a marriage while you neglect so vital a mission as visiting one of your flock who has fallen ill. Perhaps we should wait until we arrive in Philadelphia to marry, although I did so want to please Elizabeth. It was her fondest hope that we be married here in your church." Andrew stood up and casually brushed a speck of lint from his coat sleeve, then turned toward the door of the vicar's small office.

"No, wait!" the minister spoke up quickly. "Do not be so hasty, Mr. Jordan. Perhaps since Elizabeth has been ill no one could leave her to come and ask me to read the bans?"

Andrew smiled slightly. He had known the man's greed would not permit him to let so large a contribution slip through his fingers. "Yes, that is correct. I did not want to leave her alone today even for the few hours I need to arrange for our wedding,

289

but she did so want to be married tomorrow and I would do anything to please her."

The heavy-set man rose slowly to his feet. "I will tell all of the Peterson's friends whom I can reach. They will want to attend."

"It is agreed then. You will perform the ceremony for us tomorrow morning?" Andrew could suppress his smile only with a great deal of effort.

"Yes, I will be ready whenever you arrive."

Andrew shook the man's pudgy hand and said good-bye to begin his search for a wedding gown. Surely he could find something pretty or he'd hire women to sit up all night and sew one!

Elizabeth hugged her knees as she sat watching her fishing line. She had found the small lake teeming with life once she had learned to be still and look for it. Waterbugs and dragonflies flitted across the surface. Delicious silver fish swam in its depths. Speckled frogs hopped along the banks and song birds filled the surrounding trees with their lilting melodies. She knew the precise names of none of the creatures, but recognized and loved each one nevertheless. The noises of the forest were varied and although she listened attentively, they did not distract her from the enjoyment of the calm of that peaceful afternoon. She had begun to miss Andrew the moment he was gone and longed for him to return.

Elizabeth was so attuned to the tranquil mood of the woods, she felt the strangers' presence long before they could be seen. They were hiding behind the

clump of trees near the boulders to her left. The birds'
cries had warned her but she sat as though unaware of
the newcomers' arrival, waiting patiently to see what
they would do before she chose any action of her own.

After a few moments she could perceive their scent.
They were not Indian but white men and that
frightened her more. She would have been able to
greet Indians with a few words at least, had they been
hunting or passing by, but white men would hide and
watch her for no good purpose. What could they
want? She obviously had no money to steal. Andrew
had ridden Lady so she had no horse to take either.
That left only herself. She knew she was attractive.
Andrew told her that often enough, but what could the
men want? To kidnap her, rape her, perhaps even
murder her? With a slow graceful motion she got to
her feet and moved her line. If they had not attacked
her yet, were they merely curious? She edged her way
around to the right putting more distance between
herself and the strangers and when she reached the
farthest point of the lake she dropped her line and
dashed into the woods. She heard the men shout and
ran on, intent upon reaching the cabin to get Andrew's
bow and arrows to defend herself before she could
come to any harm at their hands. She ran in an erratic
path leading them through a maze in and out of the
trees until at last she darted into her house, grabbed up
the weapons then sped on, moving again in a wide arc
toward the small lake.

The two men were confused by her actions. She ran
like no frightened woman but like a cunning fox
eluding hounds. They could glimpse only a flash of

291

color as she ran ahead of them and then disappeared again. When they came to the humble house, they stopped in amazement, taking time to sort through the meager possessions. When they found nothing worth stealing, they took fallen branches and lit them from the coals of the fire to make torches which they tossed upon the roof. The small dwelling burned quickly, sending up a cloud of gray smoke and the men howled with delight at the results of their mischief.

Elizabeth watched them as she fit the notch of the long arrow into the bowstring. Andrew had taught her how to hunt simply to amuse her, never expecting men to be her quarry, but as she took careful aim she recognized one of them as John Cummins, the trapper who had sold her Andrew and knew the other man must be the partner who had helped to torture her husband so cruelly. Andrew's arrows were perfectly made, and this one flew with unerring precision to its target. The trapper's laughter changed instantly to a hoarse gargling gasp as the arrow pierced his chest. He stared down at the bright red blood spurting from the wound, then fell over backward, amazement clear in his wide eyes as he died. His companion shrieked in horror but as he turned to flee, Elizabeth's second arrow went deep into his back and he fell only a few yards from his friend. His hands clawed at the ground, then went limp and she knew he was dead, too.

Elizabeth leaned her head against the tree behind which she'd been hiding and tried to think what to do next. She had no desire to look at the dead men but she knew she had to remove Andrew's arrows or he would be blamed for their deaths should their bodies ever be

292

found. She walked cautiously up to Cummins' side, put her bare foot on his chest and withdrew the bloody arrow with a sharp twist. She removed the other arrow from the stranger's back and tossed both weapons on the burning remains of her home. She knew the men must have had a wagon of some sort and made her way back to the lake to find it. The mules could not be left in their harness to die.

Andrew declined Margaret's offer of refreshments in favor of returning more quickly to Elizabeth, but as he stepped out onto the Peterson's porch he sighted the smoke curling up toward the heavens and gave a terrified shout. He leapt upon Lady's back and sped through the forest, dreading what he would find. He called Elizabeth's name as he neared the clearing, but heard no reply. The ruins of their house were still smoldering, sending tendrils of smoke high into the air and as he tied Lady's reins to a low branch he spotted the men's bodies and Elizabeth's name escaped his lips in a panic-filled scream.

He recognized the dead men at once even after more than a year's time. He knew their unshaven faces instantly. They were still warm and the holes in their bodies unmistakably made by arrows. He slumped down to his knees, knelt beside them in the dirt and tried to think how to deal with such horror as he had found. What in God's name had happened? Could Elizabeth have killed the two men all by herself? He found no answers to his questions in the gruesome scene before him, and as he stared at John Cummins he swore angrily, "You deserved this, you bastard. You both did!"

He got to his feet and called Elizabeth's name again and again, but only the silence of the trees greeted his calls. Surely this grim deed must have snapped her mind in two. Had she wandered off, too dazed to wait for his return? The smoke might attract someone, but that possibility was remote. There was a chance someone might come to investigate and the bodies must not be found. Two wandering trappers would not be missed, but he knew they'd have to be buried before he could search for his wife.

Andrew had just trampled down the earth over the second grave when he heard the creaking sound of the old wagon approaching. He knew that sound as well as the beat of his own heart and darted behind the closest tree to await whomever might appear. He drew his knife, ready to spring should the trappers have had a companion.

Elizabeth drew the mules to a halt and seeing Lady, called out for her husband. When he stepped out from behind a tree with his knife drawn, she shook her head. "I have already killed your enemies, Andrew. Now what shall we do with this wagonload of furs?"

Andrew walked toward her as he replaced his knife at his belt. "Elizabeth, thank God you are safe. What happened here? I have been with you all these many months and leave you for only one afternoon to return to this?" He was amazed to find her explanation lucid. She knew what the two men were after. Burning their makeshift house had been only a momentary diversion from their pursuit of her.

"Should we report this deed, Andrew? Tell the authorities in Oak Grove what happened?"

"No, never. I've buried their bodies and now let's unhitch this wagon and burn it up with all it contains, until there is no trace of those evil men's existence."

"The furs are not very good, but it seems a shame to waste them, Andrew."

"There must be no way to tie us to the men's disappearance. If we sold the furs it would be obvious we had done away with the trappers." Andrew reached up to help Elizabeth down from her seat and gave her a loving hug. "That you were unharmed is all that matters. Now let us hurry."

Elizabeth nodded and unhitched the team. They could live loose in the forest until someone caught them. She understood why they could not simply be given to her father. "Andrew, is this not an unusual time of the year to be out trapping?"

The tall man's eyes widened a moment as he realized she was correct. "Indeed it is. Animals have too light a coat this early in the fall to be worth much. Perhaps they were up to something else and only took a few pelts to cover their true purpose."

"But what purpose could two men such as these have had?"

Andrew spoke quickly as they unloaded the wagon. "It is possible they were sent to find something other than furs. Information perhaps, or simply to make accurate maps. Let us not worry over their mission. It is finished now."

Elizabeth was astonished. "You mean they were spies?"

Andrew chuckled at her innocence. "Yes, they could have been. If so, the rebellion has overtaken us already."

"I am frightened, Andrew. If someone sent these men, won't they be suspicious when they do not return?"

"Do you think Cummins could have been relied upon to complete any task?" Andrew moved swiftly to toss the stack of pelts upon the coals of their home. The dry skins caught fire quickly, again igniting a bright blaze.

"No, of course not."

"We will be gone tomorrow, Elizabeth. Now toss the last of the furs into the flames and hush."

The wagon and furs burned to ashes under Andrew's watchful eye. He wanted no trees lost and was cautious to keep the fire under control as it destroyed all evidence of the crime. In the light of dawn they raked the coals with sticks and buried the metal parts of the wagon and harness many yards away from the graves, then covered the heap of ashes that was all that remained of their forest home with dirt until there was no sign of the night's grim business.

"This is our wedding day and we have not slept one hour. I should not have left you alone, Elizabeth. When I think of what those two would have done had they caught you, I cannot help but shudder."

"Yet it was the trappers who were caught, wasn't it? I thought only of what they had done to you, Andrew, never of the danger to me." Elizabeth's beautiful green eyes held only love as she looked up at him.

Andrew pulled Elizabeth into his arms and held her

pressed tightly against his chest as he smoothed her smoke-scented hair. "My dearest, I will never ever leave you alone again. I promise." He kissed her lips lightly and smiled, glad that the long night was over. "I found a beautiful dress for you, my love. A seamstress had just bought it as a sample hoping one day to sell it and I believe it is exactly your size. If not, Margaret said she will alter it quickly. Let's go. We can bathe and dress at your father's house and go into town when we are ready."

Elizabeth looked around the small clearing. Andrew had done such a proficient job of camouflaging their campsite, the scene was a completely natural one, as if no human foot had ever stepped across the terrain. Their months together there had been erased as if they'd never occurred, and she smiled wistfully. "I have loved living here with you, Andrew, but there must be an end to all things and our time here is over."

"You are wrong, Elizabeth, for there will never be an end to our love, nor the days we spend together." Andrew chuckled as he pulled her near, ready to prove exactly what he meant in the way he knew best.

Elizabeth and Andrew were married that morning with several dozen guests filling the small church. Olaf's friends had been anxious to attend, eager for another opportunity to see Elizabeth's Indian but they found it impossible to believe the tall, handsome man at her side could ever have been called a savage. His velvet suit was elegantly cut, his carriage expensive and his driver dressed in the finest livery. It was Elizabeth herself, however, they most wanted to see. She was so lovely, her fair hair shimmering in the sunlight as she left the church on her husband's arm. Her dress was exquisite, made of silk and lace of the palest pink. It set off her fair beauty to perfection. She was a stunning bride, and if her father's eyes were filled with tears as she rode away, his friends were all too tactful to tease him for it.

Sixteen

Andrew cradled Elizabeth lovingly in his arms as they rode in his luxurious carriage. Before that day she had never ridden in any conveyance other than her father's wagon, and she touched the leather seats fondly. "Andrew, what will they think of me in Philadelphia? You will have to teach me so much, or I am dreadfully afraid I will embarrass you with my ignorance."

"Elizabeth, ignorant you are not. The ladies in Philadelphia will be as jealous of you as my sisters; I have no doubt. But you are my wife and shall have no reason to be concerned with their petty rivalries."

Elizabeth sat up straight and smiled broadly at her husband, her deep green eyes sparkling with delight as she teased him. "Why, Andrew, were they all fighting over you? You would be worth it, of course, but I never worried about other women. Should I have?"

Andrew's smile spread to a rakish grin. "Do you really think I'd ever give you cause?"

"I know you like pretty women, and if Philadelphia has many then I wonder if you would be able to resist their charms or even want to try," Elizabeth replied thoughtfully, her smile wistful.

"Elizabeth." Andrew's fingers separated her long

golden hair into silken strands, then he leaned forward and kissed her with a slow, smooth passion which made all doubts vanish from her mind. When he spoke his tone was serious, his expression as thoughtful as hers. "I told everyone I met I was married and although some seem to regard that as no reason not to have affairs, I was not among them. I should warn you now my uncle was not pleased to learn I had a wife for as soon as he learned of my existence he began plotting alliances which would strengthen his business ties."

"Yet he is a bachelor himself? Why didn't he marry if he wished to enhance his business interests in such a fashion?" Elizabeth was astonished by the man's lack of logic.

Andrew shrugged. "That I do not know, but he is now a man in his sixties and from what I could tell he has devoted all his energies to business and cared nothing for women. My father was the younger of the two sons, a rake from all I hear. At least my uncle has no kind word for his memory but he has high hopes for me to be able to follow in his footsteps when I inherit the Jordan fortune."

"Had I known you were a millionaire, Andrew, I might have offered two horses for you." Seeing his startled expression, Elizabeth apologized hurriedly. "I'm sorry. I shouldn't have said that, but John Cummins is much on my mind. I had no idea it would be so easy for me to kill a man. I never even suspected I could be so vicious and yet it was as simple as shooting a pheasant. They were laughing, making rude jokes and never for a second considered I might harm them."

"Elizabeth, I have no doubt in my mind what they

would have done had they caught you. They would most likely have kidnapped you to rape as often as they pleased, then sold you to some other trapper or traded you to Indians for furs. Failing that, they would have killed you to keep you from revealing their deeds. Had I even seen them passing through the forest I would have killed them for what they did to me. I would have done it gladly for revenge. You merely saved me the effort."

Elizabeth stared into the cold gleam in her husband's eyes and believed him. "Yes, better that the sin be on my conscience rather than yours."

"Sin? There is no sin in killing vermin, Elizabeth. You have done a great service to mankind by ridding the world of those pests. Let us speak of this no more. The matter is closed forever. It need never be a concern to us again."

Elizabeth frowned, but thought better of pursuing their discussion. For some reason she knew they had not heard the last of John Cummins—his ghost would haunt them, of that she was certain. She felt a shiver along her spine but suppressed it quickly and changed the subject to their original one. "Your uncle is unlikely to welcome me then, is he? Did he have any idea when you said you were married that your marriage was not a legal one?"

"No. I told him we were married and gave no details. He did not press me for them either. We have been married for one year as far as he knows."

"Shall we give today's date, only move back the year? If he should ask when we celebrate our anniversary, we must agree upon the date."

Andrew chuckled at her reasoning. "You amaze me,

301

Elizabeth. I swear you are more devious than I ever am. I love the way you think."

"Only the way I think?" Elizabeth's teasing kiss delighted him as always and he pulled her back down into his embrace, savoring her taste with a newfound delight for now she was truly his and no one could ever take her away. They soon fell asleep in each other's arms, too exhausted from the previous night's work to resist the gentle rocking motion of the carriage for long.

At nightfall they stopped at an inn Andrew had visited on his way to the Peterson farm. The innkeeper remembered him as being a pleasant young man who tipped well and gave them the best of his accommodations. When the man departed from their room to prepare their supper, Andrew turned to his bride. "My one thought while I was in Philadelphia was how wonderful it would be to make love to you in my father's four poster bed. It is my bed now, of course, but I will probably always think of it as his. This one will do for tonight, however." He pulled his wife into his arms and hugged her warmly. "I shall always remember the first time we made love, when I was Silver Hawk and you were no more than a beautiful child."

"A child? Oh, no, Andrew. Once I'd fallen in love with you I was no longer a child. I wanted only to be a woman. It has been more than a year since we were first together. It was in the springtime, and now it is almost fall."

"The months I spent without you were the loneliest of my life, Elizabeth." Andrew's lingering kiss was interrupted by the innkeeper's wife and daughter who brought in a surprisingly delicious meal of roast beef, vegetables from their garden and freshly baked bread. The women giggled as they left the room and Andrew exclaimed as he realized the reason why. "Oh, my God, I forgot to tell Henry not to mention our wedding! He must have told those two this is our wedding night. Damn!"

"Will he also tell your uncle the truth? That we have only just married?"

"No, not if I make it worth his while to keep silent, which I will do first thing in the morning. Let's not worry about him now. I am famished. When did we last eat? Do you recall?"

"No, in truth I cannot." Elizabeth was as hungry as her husband and helped him to finish all of their ample meal as well as the small pitcher of wine. "I have never tasted wine before, Andrew. I have had ale and rum in tiny amounts, but never this and I don't think I like it." She found her vision blurred as she smiled impishly at him. His teasing grin seemed to float in the air and she covered her mouth as she began to giggle. "If the ladies in Philadelphia drink this often, I am sadly afraid I am going to be in real trouble."

Andrew's words were soft and loving, but Elizabeth couldn't quite follow his conversation as he helped her from her chair and began to unbutton the tiny row of pearl buttons which fastened her bodice. "This dress is lovely, my dearest, but no garment is as superb as you are with none." His lips trailed down her throat, caressing her flushed skin lightly as he swung her up into his arms and carried her to the bed. The clean white sheets smelled of sunshine, but it was her fragrance he loved. The soft subtle aroma of spring flowers teased his senses anew as she moved to undress him swiftly. She knew how to please him with both her passion and imagination, and as he joined her upon the bed, he wrapped his arms around her narrow waist and whispered in her ear.

"It is difficult to believe this is your wedding night, Mrs. Jordan, for you seem to be no innocent bride."

"If it is innocence you want, sir, I fear you are far too late." Her sensuous kiss silenced his teasing and he moved quickly to caress her more intimately, his tantalizing touch driving the thought of play from her mind as passion overtook her reason again. Her body flowed perfectly with the rhythm of his, returning the joy he gave so expertly. He was lost in her fascinating embrace, captivated by her spell of love. He adored her, and said so again and again as he made love to her that night, but now he spoke only in English, only in the sweet words he knew she would understand and remember always.

Elizabeth lay back against the pillows as she held Andrew locked in her embrace. She loved the feel of his warm, lean body against her own and pressed him more tightly to her breast. She ran her fingertips down his back, tracing the muscles as they tensed and relaxed. He had such grace in spite of his strength, such tenderness in his caress. His fiery kisses moved across her cool flesh with a promise of undying devotion and she surrendered all thought, giving herself up to her senses which delighted in being his wife. Andrew was love to her, the sweetness of longing, the joy of coming together as one, the peace of lying contentedly in each other's arms. The words love and Andrew were the same in her heart.

As they readied to leave the next morning, Elizabeth took her husband's hand and turned to look back at the comfortable room. "Truly the bed makes no difference to me, Andrew. When I am with you I can think of naught but giving you pleasure. I fear your four poster bed, no matter how magnificent, will never hold any greater charm than the straw of my father's barn."

Andrew laughed, and after hugging her warmly, kissed her once again. "You are truly well, Elizabeth, as charming and bright as the day I first saw you open your front door to come out and rescue me. Yet you are a woman, mature and thoughtful. I can imagine how you will be greeted in Philadelphia for you are such a beauty but barely seventeen. I am afraid I will be regarded as the same sort of rake my father was reputed to be."

"Surely a rake is not married, is he? Nor faithful to his wife if he were? I would never fault your father for his behavior. From what we were told he never recovered from losing you and your mother so tragically. That he wished to find love wherever he could is understandable to me."

Andrew smiled at his bride. She had such a unique perspective on life, he had learned. She could accept all except cruelty in others. She saw goodness everywhere and in everyone, and he hoped she never lost her innocent belief in mankind as he had. "Elizabeth, I will always be faithful to you, always. I trust no one on earth save you. I know you would never lie to me and you must know I will always tell you the truth."

Elizabeth reached up to touch his deeply tanned

cheek with a soft brush of her fingertips before standing on her tiptoes to kiss him. "Oh, Andrew, I would never lie to you, never. You will always be able to trust me."

"Come, let us hurry. We still have a long journey before us and we can continue this discussion in the carriage." Andrew winked slyly as he swept her along toward the door and she laughed as she took his arm to go down the stairs. It was plain talking was the last thing he wanted to do, and she had never been able to resist him.

As their arrival was unexpected when at last they did reach Philadelphia, Matthew Jordan was still at his warehouse, a stroke of luck for which Andrew was grateful. He had bribed Henry and instructed him to forget he had attended his master's wedding under the threat of a penalty so severe Andrew had only to hint at what he'd suffer and the frightened man swore never to divulge the truth. The driver hurried into the stately brick home to summon the surprised staff to come immediately to extend a welcome to Andrew's wife. Mrs. Blackstone, the housekeeper, took charge efficiently, offering Elizabeth every type of service possible to provide for her comfort. Andrew asked only to have their luggage taken to his room, but as they reached the second floor landing, Mrs. Blackstone separated Elizabeth's belongings.

"Mrs. Jordan, your suite adjoins your husband's. It was redecorated last spring prior to your anticipated arrival and I hope you find everything prepared to your satisfaction. If not, tell me immediately and I will arrange for whatever you require."

"I am to have my own room?" Elizabeth was

shocked by that announcement. She had no idea how the people of Philadelphia lived for she had never even seen so magnificent a house let alone been inside one, but she knew without a moment's hesitation she did not want her own room.

Andrew saw his wife's reluctance to follow the well organized housekeeper and reached out for her hand. "Mrs. Blackstone, my wife will share my room. Please see her things are brought in with mine."

The primly dressed woman was aghast at the young man's suggestion. "Surely you do not mean it, Mr. Jordan. A wife must always have her own room."

Andrew drew his bride closer to his side. "Why is that, Mrs. Blackstone? Is it possible the servants here do not know that a husband and wife enjoy sleeping together?"

The housekeeper blushed a deep crimson and stepped so near none could overhear her comment. "We are extremely discreet here, I can assure you, Mr. Jordan, and how often you choose to visit your wife's room will never be a topic of gossip."

Andrew laughed heartily at that promise. "You may call the room next to mine my wife's if that will satisfy your requirements for propriety, but she will in fact share my room and most especially my bed. Is that clear, Mrs. Blackstone?"

The woman was too incensed to argue. She nodded curtly, agreeing to his demands, but as she turned toward the beautiful young woman at his side, she stared in surprise. "Please forgive my rudeness, Mrs. Jordan, but you remind me so much of a young Swedish girl who once worked here. I don't know why I didn't notice the resemblance immediately, but it is

307

astonishing. Now, I will send Meg up to help you unpack, wherever you wish your wardrobe to be kept." With a disapproving frown, the feisty servant took her leave.

Elizabeth followed her husband into his spacious room and rushed to thank him for his thoughtfulness. "Thank you, Andrew. I hesitated to contradict the woman's directions, but I want to share a bedroom with you. I don't want a room of my own. Is that how married couples live here? Must wives lie alone in these enormous beds each night and pray their husbands will come to see them? I could not bear such loneliness ever again."

"Elizabeth, do you really think I could leave you alone for even one hour, let alone an entire night? Now if you would really like to have your own room, and you will certainly need it for all the pretty clothes I'll buy for you, you may move your things next door and I will simply sleep with you in your bed each night."

Elizabeth shook her head, her pretty lips set in a determined line. "No, I'll always want to be with you, Andrew. It matters not where they hang my clothes."

"My love?" Andrew put his hands upon her waist to draw her near, then gently lifted her chin with his fingertips. "Do not fret, Elizabeth. It will take some time for you to grow accustomed to this house as your home, but you will. I'll always be here and we need never be separated ever again. I've promised you that and I meant it."

Elizabeth would never grow weary of her husband's delightful company. "How many servants are there here, Andrew? I have never given orders to anyone

308

except you and Jed, and that was so different."

"You already know Henry, and there are two other men who tend the horses and act as drivers. Mrs. Blackstone manages the house, and there is a cook who has two helpers since my uncle entertains so frequently. Meg will be your maid and there are two other young women who help with the cleaning and washing. Not so many people really since this is such a large home. From what I saw while I was here, my uncle's staff is no larger than most of his friends have."

"But Andrew, that's more people than I saw in a week back home!" Elizabeth realized suddenly that Matthew Jordan's house was as different from her father's home as Rainbow's had been, but she dared not point out that comparison to Andrew.

"They are all here to help you, Elizabeth. Just ask them for whatever you need. You heard Mrs. Blackstone. Everyone is most anxious to please you. I am certain they are happy to have a woman here again and will do their best to see you like them."

"I'm sure I will like them, Andrew. I will get used to your home in time, but it is all so new to me now." Elizabeth stepped into her husband's arms to hug him and lay her head upon his chest as he drew her close. "I wonder who it was Mrs. Blackstone knew. Have you ever met anyone who looked like me?"

"No, you are so exquisitely beautiful I cannot imagine any other woman having either your sweet features or lively charm."

Elizabeth snuggled against him, reassured by his calmness and strength as always. She looked exactly like her mother. She had the same delicate bone structure, smooth creamy skin and glossy blond hair. Only their eyes were different. Hers were as green as Andrew's while her mother's had been a bright clear blue. Could Mrs. Blackstone have known her mother? She knew her parents had met in Philadelphia. Could the Jordan home possibly have been where her mother had worked before her marriage? No, she thought, for surely that would have been too great a coincidence. She yawned sleepily then and mentioned nothing to Andrew. It had most likely been someone else anyway. There were so many lovely blond girls from Sweden. It must have been another young woman the housekeeper had known.

"I have a surprise for you. Come with me." Andrew took Elizabeth's hands from around his waist and led her into the adjoining room and opened the wardrobe. "I bought only three dresses because I wanted you to be able to choose your own garments, but I wanted you to have something to wear while your other gowns are being made. I will take you to the dressmaker's tomorrow and you may pick out whatever you like."

Elizabeth was astonished by his selections for the gowns were exquisite, as lovely as her wedding gown. "Oh, Andrew, how beautiful these clothes are. Thank you so much. I never realized how unfashionable my dresses were. At least you will not be ashamed of me in these."

"Elizabeth, your dresses are very sweet, exactly what the young girls wear on the farms, but here in the city you will need a more sophisticated wardrobe. That is all, and I would never be ashamed of you!"

"Be honest. My dresses are really a fright, aren't they? I can imagine what Mrs. Blackstone will say when she sees them. I was surprised Margaret had kept them."

Andrew frowned impatiently. "You need not concern yourself with the servants' opinions, Elizabeth. You are my wife and you may do as you please here in your own home." Realizing he'd been too stern Andrew leaned down to kiss her and Elizabeth forgot all her worries in an instant as his warm mouth met hers. She loved him far too much to think of anything other than his delicious taste when he kissed her.

Mrs. Blackstone was in the kitchen giving the cook the revised instructions for dinner when Meg rushed into the room and interrupted her. "Mrs. Blackstone, Mr. Andrew wants me to bring him some whiskey and a needle. He says he's going to pierce his wife's ears! Whatever shall I do?"

The housekeeper shook her head incredulously. "So it's to be whiskey after all is it. Looks just like his father but I had prayed he had none of his sire's vices. Well, we will do as he requests, Meg. How much whiskey does he require? A full bottle or merely one glass?"

"Only one glass, ma'am. He wants his wife to drink it before he does it." The frightened girl wrung her hands nervously, then wiped them on her long white apron.

"His wife! Well, really, Meg, come with me!" Mrs. Blackstone fetched the bottle of whiskey, one crystal glass and an assortment of sewing needles before she knocked at the young man's bedroom door.

"Ah, there you are. Come in, Mrs. Blackstone. Perhaps you can assist me. I have my mother's jewelry and would like for Elizabeth to be able to wear it, but as you can see she will need pierced ears to wear the earrings."

"Mr. Jordan, please. Your mother was a very beautiful woman and her jewels worth a fortune, so I can see why you would wish your wife to wear them, but you must rely on us to see to her needs. The jeweler can change the earrings. It is not necessary for your wife to have her ears pierced like some gypsy."

"Why, Mrs. Blackstone, are you calling my mother a gypsy?" Andrew's smile was teasing as he leaned down to hug Elizabeth. She sat at his side where they'd been examining his mother's jewels and smiled at his humor, for she thought his joke amusing.

"No, of course not, but she was a completely different type of woman. Mrs. Jordan is a lovely young woman, but your mother was a far more sophisticated one. I meant her memory no disrespect, sir," the housekeeper apologized in an embarrassed rush.

"I understand. I had not intended that my wife wear the larger pieces as they would indeed overpower her, but there are many exquisite jewels here that would become her."

Seeing the housekeeper's disapproval, Elizabeth attempted to put her mind at ease. "I don't mind Andrew doing it, Mrs. Blackstone. You see my husband and I are very close, have been inseparable these past few months and perhaps we should ask your assistance, but it will take us awhile to remember we are no longer alone. Please excuse us. Now, can you help Andrew?"

Mrs. Blackstone's expression softened as she nodded, for she was impressed by the intelligence of Elizabeth's request. "Of course, I will be happy to help, Mrs. Jordan, but it is very near the time your uncle will return home and I doubt the wisdom of your drinking this whiskey just prior to meeting him for the first time."

Andrew had to agree. "A good point, although it might help Elizabeth considerably if he were no more than a blur. Well, what do you suggest? How shall we proceed?"

"I am afraid I have no idea how to do this other than to get it over with quickly. Those small gold hoops should be good to wear first. I doubt there will be much bleeding but, Meg, bring us a towel and some water just in case."

Andrew held Elizabeth's head in his hands and smiled. "Are you sure you trust me to do this?"

"Yes, just hurry. We don't want to be late for our first dinner here with your Uncle Matthew. Your hands are steady. I know you can do this. I'm not afraid."

Andrew talked to his wife as he worked with swift, sure motions. His voice was calm, his manner reassuring as he explained what he was doing as he went along. Mrs. Blackstone looked at their faces with intense interest. That the green of their eyes was the same vivid hue was remarkable, but other than that there was no similarity between them. The line of Andrew's jaw was firm, determined, his coloring dark while his wife's fair beauty was of such a delicate sort. But when he took her hand and led her to the mirror the housekeeper began to frown. It wasn't so much their appearance as their posture, their proud carriage, the way they moved together that attracted her notice. They each moved with the same sure step and graceful turn, but perhaps that was only because they were so close and so much in love. When Andrew spoke to her, the daydreaming woman jumped in surprise.

"I'll drink that whiskey myself, Mrs. Blackstone. That was far worse on me than Elizabeth, I'm certain. Now if Meg will help my wife to bathe and dress for the evening, I will wait for my uncle downstairs." Andrew finished the fiery liquid in one gulp, then kissed Elizabeth's lips lightly before turning to go.

Mrs. Blackstone left with him but watched him closely as he descended the stairs, her glance a critical one. "I hope, sir, that whiskey will not become the habit with you that it was with your father."

Andrew was surprised by the woman's insolence, but held his temper as he considered her age and the time she'd served his family. "You needn't worry, Mrs. Blackstone. I have my dear Elizabeth, and sadly my father lost everyone he loved."

Seventeen

Matthew Jordan's suit was a somber gray, well tailored in the finest wool, but very modest in style. He was of medium build with an unruly thatch of white hair that seemed to have defeated his lifelong efforts to tame it. His eyes were identical to Andrew's, a rich deep green giving his stern features an animation he would otherwise have lacked. In his youth he had been as handsome a man as his brother, but his far more serious nature had not permitted him to take advantage of that asset as Phillip had. He had spent his life amassing a fortune he jealously guarded and although he seldom smiled, the glance he turned upon his nephew was filled with affection. As they returned to the parlor after dinner, he took Elizabeth's hand lightly in his. "My dear, I am sorry I wasn't at home when first you arrived. I hope I have made you feel welcome now. I had despaired of my nephew ever returning he was gone so long to fetch you, but I see now why he was so set upon bringing you here to live." Matthew had observed Elizabeth closely as they dined and had found no flaw in her manners, conversation or appearance. She was an exceptionally pretty girl, all blond and pink with such enormous green eyes whose long thick lashes fascinated him, but her startling resemblance to Marie Larson disturbed him greatly. Was it only his imagination, or was this beautiful young woman that girl's exact duplicate? How long had it been? he wondered. Seventeen years, or eighteen? "Excuse my rudeness, Elizabeth. I don't mean to stare. It's only that you remind me so much of a girl who was once employed here."

Elizabeth pretended to take a sip of her sherry then set the tiny glass aside. After learning the effect wine had upon her senses, she didn't want to risk embarrassing Andrew that night. "Uncle Matthew, Mrs. Blackstone mentioned the same thing. I am most curious as to who this girl might have been. Please tell me something about her."

"That is not all that easy to do, but I will try." Matthew pursed his lips thoughtfully as he tried to recall the details of the story he wished to relate. "Andrew's father was quite ill, had been for many weeks and—"

"Tell her the truth, Uncle. My father was drunk, wasn't he, not ill?" Andrew stood beside the fireplace, clad in one of his new suits. He looked very much a part of the tastefully and expensively furnished room. He was a dashing figure of a man no matter what he wore. Velvet or buckskin, he was exceedingly handsome, and Elizabeth smiled up at him as he spoke.

"This is your uncle's story, Andrew. Please let him tell it."

"Thank you, my dear. As you can see, I fear Andrew is exactly like his father. Phillip was less than easy to handle also. Now where was I. Oh, yes, Phillip was ill, regardless of the cause, Andrew. He had been out late one night and caught a chill. He was demanding, obnoxious to our servants, but the doctor insisted he have constant care. The only solution seemed to be to hire someone new which I immediately did, a lovely Swedish girl, only recently arrived in the city from her parents' farm. She was as beautiful as you are, Elizabeth, and quite serious for so young a woman. She had a wonderful effect upon Phillip, calmed him down with her sweet companionship and turned his thoughts again to life and happiness after so many years of depression. Alas, she came too late. Phillip did not regain his health although he tried so hard to get well. He was never strong enough to get out of his bed again for more than an occasional stroll around his room. He died quite suddenly one night. It was his heart, the doctor said. He was just worn out from his years of grief and yes, Andrew, you're right, his drinking. The girl was with him when he died but left immediately, left the house that very night and was never seen again. Had Phillip known how ill he was, I have no doubt he would have left her well provided for in his will. As it was she received nothing, unless, of course, the gossip was true."

Andrew stepped forward, intrigued by the tale. "What gossip was that, Uncle?"

"More than one of the servants told me the girl was pregnant, carrying your father's child when he died."

"Oh, I see, he might have been too ill to get out of his bed for long, but she could have been in it with him. Is that it?" Andrew scoffed at the idea. "He must have had far more stamina than anyone thought."

"Yes, I considered the story preposterous myself, yet the rumors persisted. I can't help but think if you had a half-brother or sister somewhere the girl would have brought the child to me, asked for some money to help her raise the babe. I would have paid her gladly, for she did make my brother's last days happy and I will always be grateful to her for that."

Elizabeth's expression was thoughtful as she considered his words. "Perhaps she was too proud, Uncle Matthew. Maybe she truly loved Phillip and was too proud to ask for charity to raise his child."

Matthew Jordan was also in a pensive mood. "You know the whole episode was remarkable in many respects. The doctor had suggested a nurse and the girl just appeared at the door looking for work that very afternoon. Her disappearance was as mysterious as her arrival. She came to tell me Phillip was dead and when I went to look for her later, she had already gone, vanished. No one ever saw or heard from her ever again, as far as I know."

"She sounds like an angel of mercy, Uncle, a magical being who appeared to care for a dying man and then returned to heaven with his spirit in tow."

"Andrew, really, you seem hardly the sort of man to believe in angels!" The older man laughed at his nephew's fanciful imagery.

"Oh, but I do. I have one right here. Elizabeth rescued me from a fate as desperate as the one from which this girl tried to save my father. What was her name. Perhaps someday I'll have the good fortune to meet her and find out if I really do have a brother. He'd be seventeen now, wouldn't he?"

"You could have a sister, Andrew. The child could just as easily have been female if it did exist. The young woman's name was Marie Larson and she looked exactly like your wife."

318

As the two men turned to smile at her, Elizabeth felt her whole world explode within her heart. She could not hide her panic and quickly lowered her eyes before they saw her fright. It couldn't be true, none of it could be the truth. Surely the story was no more than the most imaginative gossip. If her mother had worked in the Jordan household, why hadn't her father told her when he learned Andrew's family name? The answer was obvious. He didn't know anything about Phillip Jordan because her mother hadn't told him. Could the reason have been she wanted him to believe her child was his? Dear God, no!

"Elizabeth, are you ill, my love?" Andrew moved swiftly to her side and took her hand.

"I am afraid I'm rather tired, Andrew. You must have things you'd like to discuss with your uncle. Will you excuse me, please?"

"Of course, my dear. I should have considered the demands of your travel and not talked at such length tonight. Forgive me, I am an old man and tend to enjoy reminiscing too much, I'm afraid. It was most inconsiderate of me," Matthew offered quickly.

"Please do not apologize. It was a charming story, Uncle. Thank you for telling us. I'll just go on upstairs to bed now though, if I may."

Andrew saw something more than fatigue in his wife's expression and persisted. "Are you certain you are not ill?"

"Yes, I am fine. Only tired. Now good night." Elizabeth stood on her tiptoes to brush her husband's cheek lightly with her lips then slipped out of the room and hurried up the stairs.

Matthew Jordan waited until he heard the bedroom

door close on the second floor before he turned to Andrew and spoke in a harsh whisper, "Just how old is your wife?"

"Her age is the least of the things I thought you'd notice about Elizabeth." Andrew sighed sadly. He could see what was coming and dreaded it, although he knew it could not be avoided.

"Andrew, I want to know that young woman's age immediately!" Matthew demanded crossly.

"She is seventeen, Uncle, just seventeen." Andrew turned back to his place by the fire. "I am twelve years her senior, but truly she has never seemed the child to me others seem to see. She has always been only Elizabeth to me, my Elizabeth."

"We will simply not reveal her age to anyone, but my God, Andrew, why did you never tell me she was so very young? She is a beauty, I'll agree, and seems very bright, but when I think of the young ladies here in Philadelphia who would gladly have become your wife, I could weep. You could have had your pick, a girl with real breeding, with family and reputation to say nothing of wealth, instead of that lovely child from some insignificant wheat farm!" Matthew was beside himself with frustration for he could see all his dreams for Andrew coming to naught.

Andrew's gaze grew as sharp as Toledo steel as he stared at his aggravated relative. "Had I not met Elizabeth when I did, I would not be here today. I love her more dearly than you will ever understand, and I never want to hear this subject discussed ever again. She is my wife, the only woman I will ever marry, and I care nothing of how little her family can add to your financial empire. I plan to take her to the dressmaker's tomorrow morning and then I'll come down to your warehouse to work for the rest of the day."

"Work? After all these months? How kind of you. Can you even recall what it was I taught you last winter? You were gone so long to bring Elizabeth I doubt you will remember anything of any value to me now. She looks very healthy, by the way. What was this illness that kept her from traveling for so many months?"

Andrew poured himself a drink from the crystal decanter on the desk, then downed the whiskey in one quick toss before pouring another. He stared defiantly at his uncle apparently unwilling to respond to his question.

"Do you know something? You are so much like your father it is frightening! Not only do you look like him, but you seem to have the same devotion to your wife and to drink that he had. For you to love your wife is very touching, for you to have grown so fond of whiskey quite another matter altogether!"

"Do not worry, Uncle. I have no compulsion to drink, no tragedy to forget, at least none now Elizabeth is here with me. I told you how we lost our child. It affected her far more deeply than I had realized. I should have brought her with me when I first came here to meet you. Her illness was entirely my fault."

"Andrew, I don't understand at all. You mean she was still ill, weak from the miscarriage?" Matthew inquired curiously.

"No, physically she was strong, well. It was her emotions I didn't understand. I felt only my own sorrow, my own anger, and understood none of hers. I gave her no comfort at all when she needed it most desperately. I even made her endure the humiliation of begging me for my affection." Andrew turned away momentarily to hide his own shame. He had been a great fool and it had nearly cost Elizabeth her life, not once, but twice. "When I left her alone, she simply withdrew from the world to forget so many things which should never have happened to her. My leaving her alone to come here included."

"Your marriage is the only thing which should never have happened! Why did you bring her back here if she is so likely to become unbalanced? We could have paid her family, arranged for an annulment. We still can! I'll speak with my attorney in the morning, in fact. It isn't too late!" Greatly encouraged, Matthew leapt upon the small chance he saw to have his own way.

Andrew shook his head emphatically. "No, Uncle. Elizabeth is fine, completely well and she'll never be ill again."

"She is very young though. She is so delicate, slender of build. She could easily suffer another miscarriage. Then what will happen to her? Could she bear another such heartbreak and still keep her sanity? You dare not take that risk!"

Andrew's determination was clear in the set of his jaw. Had his uncle been a younger man, he would have struck him for what he was suggesting. "She will have no more children. I'm certain the contractions caused by the poison must have torn her insides to shreds. We have been together as man and wife for nearly five months and she has not conceived. I don't believe she can."

"What?" Matthew gasped in horror. "If the woman is barren and you know it, then I insist you divorce her. You must have an heir, Andrew. This is tragic for Elizabeth, I realize that, but if you state it in those terms, she will understand you need a wife who can give you children."

Andrew gazed into the flames, their brightness taunting him with the reminder of the warmth he found only in his beloved's arms and his voice was sure as he replied, "No, I need only Elizabeth. No other woman will ever take her place. I need her too badly to ever give her up. I would not even consider it for so ridiculous a reason as having a child."

Matthew persisted in his argument. "But if she can never give you a child, Andrew, it would be better to leave her now!"

"I don't know for certain that she cannot conceive, only that she has not. She may give me ten sons, who knows. Five months is not long." Andrew showed little interest in his uncle's concern. He knew the man understood nothing of love and made no attempt to teach him that night.

"A barren woman of no family cannot be allowed to remain as your wife, Andrew. It is as simple as that." Matthew frowned suddenly when his nephew did not respond. "What do you really know of her people, her mother especially?"

"Her mother died several years ago. I never met the woman. Her father has remarried. He is a hardworking man, doesn't approve of me since I ran off with his daughter but I don't care about his opinion."

"He would not oppose a divorce then?"

Andrew slammed his now empty glass down upon the desk. "There will never be any divorce. Forget that possibility now. I will stay here and work for you as long as you are kind and polite to my wife. If ever you mention the word divorce to Elizabeth, I will take her and leave! Do not try and separate us, Uncle. Don't even try it. Six Bears made that mistake and learned too late how dearly I prize that woman's love."

Matthew nearly choked on his own frustration, but he nodded in agreement and changed the subject to a pressing business matter. Still, as they talked he could not forget Elizabeth's remarkable resemblance to Marie Larson. Was it only coincidence that she was the right age to be Phillip's daughter? The man smiled as they talked on about nothing more important than business, but his doubts would give him no peace until he learned the truth.

Elizabeth lay across Phillip's four poster bed, her gaze red with fury. It couldn't be true. She refused to believe the tale Uncle Matthew had spun held one particle of the truth. She tried frantically to recall what her parents had told her of how they had met. Some friend had introduced them. Her mother had been working in Philadelphia, her father only visiting his older brother. They had fallen madly in love and had married after only a brief courtship. Was it possible there had been more than one young woman named Marie Larson living in Philadelphia then? She grasped for any hope as she lay in the darkness of Phillip's room. Andrew had teased her about making love in the bed where he himself had been conceived, but had she been conceived there also? No! She refused to accept it. It was all a horrid lie, just gossip and nothing more. She undressed hurriedly and put on the soft white nightgown which lay at the foot of the bed. It was lovely, trimmed with delicate lace, but she felt no joy as she climbed into the high bed, only dread at what new problems the future would bring.

As she waited for Andrew, she tried to imagine what they could do if it were proven they were brother and sister. She knew what she wanted. She wanted to leave with him, to go away as far as they had to go where no one would ever suspect their secret. She loved him too deeply to give him up no matter what the reason and she knew in her heart he would feel exactly the same. They were too close now, closer than any tie of blood. No matter what they found to be the truth, brother or not, Andrew Jordan would always be her husband and she his wife.

When Andrew came up to his room he undressed quietly, slipped into the large bed beside Elizabeth and was pleasantly surprised to find her still awake. He pulled her into his arms and she amazed him as always with her spontaneous display of affection. She kissed him while her small hands caressed him with the most tantalizing of touches, her fingertips traveling down his lean body, drawing his passion to a peak from which he could not retreat. She never simply teased him with her playful kisses and easy touch for she gave all the love he could ever want without hesitation. She simply loved him with all her heart and let him know it, made him feel it through every inch of his strong, bronze body and filled his heart to overflowing.

Andrew was nearly asleep when he remembered

their afternoon and sat up abruptly. "Did I hurt your ears? Do they bother you now?"

"No, not at all and I have never complained that making love hurts my ears!" Elizabeth giggled as she pulled him back down beside her and snuggled close to his chest. "You did a fine job. My ears will heal promptly. I have no doubt."

"I'll buy you some diamond earrings tomorrow after we go shopping for your new wardrobe." Andrew hugged her affectionately and kissed her soft curls.

"Diamonds? Andrew, are you so very rich? I will always think of you as my Indian so it is difficult for me to remember you are heir to a fortune."

Andrew thought for a moment, then replied matter-of-factly, "I believe there are one or two men in the Colonies with more money than we possess, but Uncle Matthew says they are of no particular importance."

"But you are?" Elizabeth teased impishly.

"In his view I am," Andrew responded with a low chuckle, amused by his own importance.

Elizabeth lifted her lips to his, then complimented him softly. "In my view also, Andrew, you are the most important person in the world to me. Tell me honestly now, did your uncle like me? I couldn't really tell. He was polite, but even though he apologized for staring, I got the impression he was disappointed in me for some reason."

"Nonsense. He loves you already. Now come back here." Andrew wound his fingers in her golden tresses to hold her mouth captive beneath his as he moved to take her again. He would tell any lie to save her from the sorrow his uncle's true feelings would bring. "Elizabeth, you are the only woman I have ever loved, or ever will, only you." He gave her no opportunity to respond to his deeply felt promise but carried her spirit aloft with his in the glorious passion they shared. He would never leave her again, never leave her for a moment to believe she was not adored for she was love itself to him. All that love could ever be, that was Elizabeth to him.

Eighteen

When Elizabeth awakened first the next morning
she propped her head on her elbow and observed her
sleeping husband closely. In the clear light of dawn
she knew her fears had been groundless. Had the
Marie Larson who cared for Andrew's father been her
mother, then the stories of a baby were no more than
gossip. It was possible her mother could have fallen in
love with a dying man, especially one so handsome as
Phillip must have been, but she had been far too sweet
and honest a woman to have wed one man while
carrying another's child.

Her eyes swept her husband's features slowly.
Other than the color of their eyes, none of their
features were in the least bit similar. They were as
different as could be except for the startling bright
green of their eyes. It was not all that uncommon for
Swedish girls to be green-eyed. Their eyes were always
blue or green, their hair blond, their skin fair. No, she
and Andrew were two separate and distinct people
with no blood tie between them, none whatsoever. As
long as Uncle Matthew liked her she wouldn't worry.
No one was likely to ask for her mother's maiden name
and if they did she would lie. That thought startled
her. She had never told anyone lies, but she wanted

nothing to spoil her happiness now. If there were only some way to prove Phillip was not her father. But how could that be done with him so long dead and her dear mother gone, too? Her mother had told her such wonderful stories of the time she'd spent in Philadelphia, but she'd mentioned no man named Phillip, no men at all other than her father. Perhaps she'd considered her daughter too young to share such a secret since she'd not trusted her husband with such a confidence. Yet, if Phillip had been anything like Andrew, how could her mother have resisted his charms? But even had they known each other and been deeply in love, that was no proof that she was in fact Phillip's daughter. Every fiber of her youthful being rejected that possibility. She was Olaf Peterson's child and no other man's, of that she was positive.

Andrew lay watching his wife's serious expression for several minutes before he let her know he was awake. "Elizabeth, what is wrong? Tell me."

"You know me too well now, Andrew. I cannot hide even my thoughts from you, can I?" Elizabeth smiled brightly, happy to see his charming grin.

"I hope you would never wish to do so. I want to know all your thoughts, your dreams, all there is to know of you, all that I might share."

Elizabeth leaned down to kiss him softly. "There is something I must do, something I must prove to myself before I discuss it with you. I won't trouble you with it until I learn the truth." She left their bed quickly and Andrew was too puzzled by her remark to stop her.

Elizabeth found the sight of British soldiers on the

329

street unnerving. They were lounging everywhere she looked, their uniforms new and their expressions cocky. "Andrew, why are there so many soldiers about?" Her last encounter with a British officer was still clear in her mind, and she shuddered at how close she'd come to being ravaged by that hateful man.

"King George has no wish to lose these colonies, my love. He has sent thousands of his best troops here to defend his claims to these lands."

"I am well aware that there is a rebellion in full sway, Andrew, but I did not think the men were fighting in the cities." Elizabeth's eyes filled with alarm as she looked up at her tall handsome spouse.

"Would you like to discuss the war battle by battle, Elizabeth? My uncle is a staunch Tory as I told you and he has kept close records of British victories. He will be happy to tell you about them by the hour if you but show some interest in the subject."

"No! The less said about the war the better. It no longer fascinates me as it once did," the pretty blonde replied with a determined tilt to her chin. The subject was not one she'd pursue with anyone.

"At last, I do believe you are finally becoming neutral as I have chosen to be. Now here is Madame Depré's shop. Smile as though you had no cares save buying beautiful dresses on this fine morning." Andrew winked as he opened the door to the elegant establishment and ushered his wife inside.

The petite dressmaker was delighted to make suggestions for Elizabeth's wardrobe. "Your wife's figure is exquisite, Mr. Jordan. She will look lovely no matter what she selects. Leave everything to me and I will dress her like a princess." The lively woman's dark eyes sparkled as she smiled at the young couple.

"It is not that I do not trust your judgment, Madame Dupré, but I would like a certain look for my wife, a simplicity of line in very fine fabrics. I don't want her in so much lace she looks more like a doll than a woman." Andrew gestured impatiently at the drawings the woman had displayed for his approval.

"But Mr. Jordan, Elizabeth is as perfect as a porcelain doll. Lace and ruffles are the correct choice for her!"

"No, she is slight of build but no empty-headed doll and I'll not have anyone mistake her for such. Do you understand what I mean, Elizabeth?" Andrew turned to her for assistance.

"Yes, I do." Elizabeth squeezed her husband's hand then began to explain to the seamstress, "Madame Dupré, I am just seventeen years old and my husband would appreciate it if you did not make my youth all that obvious. Age means nothing to us, but it seems to cause constant comment among our relatives, so I am certain anyone we meet will speak of my youth, too. I have never worn lace and ruffles and have no wish to adopt such frivolous styles now. Indeed, with the country in such a state of confusion, ostentation seems most inappropriate. I would like nice dresses, pretty ones, but the most tasteful you can create."

The charming woman smiled warmly. "Ah, now my dear, I understand. We will confine the lace to your lingerie. I know exactly what would become you. We will chose fabrics of vibrant hues and I insist you never hide that beautiful hair of yours under wigs or powders. It is simply glorious as it is and you will be the envy of the entire city I can assure you. If these

331

sketches do not suit you, they can be easily adapted so that they will, but you are mistaken, dear, if you think this is not the time for parties. The Loyalists amongst us entertain the British officers constantly. Not a week does pass without a lavish ball of some sort being given. I am sure you will attend many and I will see to it that you are beautifully gowned for such an occasion." Madame Dupré found the young couple enchanting. She knew the Jordan name well and what he could afford and suggested only the best in satins and silks to which Andrew readily agreed. Price was no object to him. He wanted his wife to have a wardrobe which would suit her personality and station and was more than willing to pay any price for it.

As they were leaving the dressmaker's shop, Andrew drew Elizabeth to his side and whispered, "Here comes the young woman my uncle wished me to marry. I'll introduce her to you now."

Elizabeth tried not to stare as the tall brunette approached. She was lovely, fair, but with ebony hair and eyes of the deepest blue. As she looked at Elizabeth her gaze became positively venomous.

"Why Andrew, I had no idea you were back in the city, and this is your wife?" She extended her small gloved hand and Elizabeth took it, but only for the briefest of clasps as they were introduced.

"Esther Nolan was kind enough to try and civilize me, Elizabeth. I am sorry to say her teachings had little effect, however." Andrew smiled at the young woman, but the light in his eyes wasn't warm. He had considered her meddling in his life a bothersome nuisance he'd been barely able to tolerate and his memories of her were not in the least bit fond.

"But that's not true, Andrew!" the young woman argued coyly. "You are a well mannered gentleman now instead of the buckskin-clad savage your uncle was afraid to have sleep in his house."

Elizabeth was disgusted by the haughty brunette's taunt and spoke up promptly to defend her husband. "You are mistaken, Miss Nolan, if you think Andrew could ever have been described as a savage for no finer gentleman has ever walked the earth, regardless of how he chooses to dress!"

"Well, my goodness, Andrew, the little thing has spirit, doesn't she? You lived with the Indians, too, did you not, Mrs. Jordan? Perhaps I might call and give you lessons on our society as well," Esther offered sarcastically.

Andrew's laugh broke the tension, but his expression was not a pleasant one. "My wife needs no tutor other than me and I am a most willing one. Now good day, Esther. We have other errands to attend to and are late."

Esther reached out to lay her hand upon his sleeve. "Had I known you were in town, I would have sent you an invitation to my party this Saturday. I will have one delivered to you as soon as possible. Good day."

Elizabeth took her husband's arm and waited to be certain Miss Nolan had entered Madame Dupré's shop and could not overhear her remarks. "What a horrid woman! Why on earth would your uncle have wanted you to marry her?"

Andrew smiled at his bride's innocence. "She is from a wealthy family who are as loyal to the Crown as

333

he is. You'll meet the entire lot on Saturday."

"You mean we'll attend her party?" Elizabeth asked incredulously.

"Of course. There will be no end of gossip about us if we do not. Besides, a few of her acquaintances are pleasant, and I'd like you to make some friends here."

"I don't need other friends, Andrew, not when I have you." Elizabeth smiled sweetly, but she was not being coy, only telling him what was truly in her heart.

Andrew squeezed her hand affectionately. "I know how you feel, for I have no need for others in my life either, but perhaps they have need of us."

As they strolled down the crowded sidewalk, Elizabeth grew worried. "Oh, Andrew, I am so afraid we'll lose the wonderful closeness we share. It will be difficult to enjoy the same solitude we knew in the forest for here we are constantly surrounded by strangers."

"Do not fret, my love. I will never be far from your side." But Andrew was concerned as he slipped his arm around her narrow waist. His uncle would expect long hours of work from him and Elizabeth would too often be alone. If only they could have a child, just one healthy baby, he knew she would be content. He smiled to himself as he thought of his father's bed. Perhaps it would bring good luck and their marriage would be blessed with many fine babies. As he glanced down at his lovely wife, he hoped there would be girls as pretty as she as well as sons.

As soon as Andrew left for his uncle's place of business that afternoon, Elizabeth searched their bedroom carefully. If Phillip had kept a diary or journal it might provide a clue as to what his relationship to Marie Larson had actually been. Her mother had kept no such book, of that she was certain, but perhaps Phillip Jordan had. Still, even if he had, would he have confided anything so intimate to a book that might not remain private? If he had died suddenly, he would have had no time to see the book was safeguarded or destroyed. When she found nothing of Phillip's in their bedroom, she didn't give up, just redirected her efforts to other rooms. Was it possible Uncle Matthew would have his brother's things in his room?

She found the door to Matthew's room securely locked. She stared down at the gilt doorknob and wondered why he felt it necessary to lock the door to his room, but he certainly had. The other rooms of the large house were all open, light, well furnished rooms used for guests, she supposed, and the books on the shelves were well worn classics of English literature, not of a personal sort. The library on the first floor contained hundreds of volumes and she read the titles for over an hour as she scanned the crowded shelves, but if Phillip had kept a journal, it was not on display for anyone to read. The desk held only writing paper, pens, ink, nothing unusual, and she gave up her search in frustration. Finally selecting two books, she took them upstairs to read. She had never seen so many books as her new uncle owned. Perhaps Andrew would read with her that night. They had never done that but it would be such fun to read together and surely he and his uncle could not have business to discuss every evening. She could not even remember when she'd last held a book in her hands, but opened the smaller of the two, eager to begin. She stretched out on the large bed to read, but soon the slender volume of poetry slipped from her fingers and her eyes closed in sleep.

Her dreams were strange images that afternoon, vague memories of Summer Moon and the others staring at her as they whispered and then she saw the basket of purple berries and was filled with the same terror which had clutched her chest that afternoon. Summer Moon's smile had been so sweet but the fruit deadly, and the pain which tore through her loins had the same frightful intensity it had that fateful day and she awoke shaking with fear as a high-pitched scream escaped her lips. Dear God, would she never forget? But the sudden burst of pain had been real and when she tried to rise she fell back, exhausted by the attempt.

Meg came running into Andrew's bedroom, her eyes wide with excitement. "Mrs. Jordan, are you all right?" Seeing her mistress was far from well she rushed away, hurrying down the back stairs to summon Mrs. Blackstone immediately.

Elizabeth tried to catch her breath as she looked up into the servants' anxious faces. "I am fine. Please don't worry. It was only a dream, but the pain seemed so real I was quite startled by it. I am feeling fine now though, truly I am."

"My dear, you are so pale. I insist you remain in bed until your husband can be called. He may wish to send for Mr. Jordan's physician, Dr. McCauley, to attend you."

Elizabeth shook her head emphatically. "No, do not bother Andrew for no more than a bad dream. Please don't. It would only worry him needlessly, upset him without cause and I forbid it. You will not disturb him,

Mrs. Blackstone. You will not."

The housekeeper nodded reluctantly. "Mrs. Jordan, you are still shaking with fright. I need not tell Mr. Andrew anything for he will soon notice your discomfort himself when he returns this evening."

"I will rest a little while longer and I'll be fine. Now promise me you won't mention this to my husband. I'm embarrassed to have disturbed you all. I won't have him upset by my foolish dreams."

"As you wish," the efficient woman agreed. "You are the mistress of this house, Mrs. Jordan. We are here only to serve you and will not go against your wishes. I have never seen a more devoted husband than Mr. Andrew is to you and I will trust him to observe what must be seen. I beg you not to try and fool him should you really be ill."

"No, of course not. I would never deceive my husband about anything, Mrs. Blackstone. You may go now and cease to concern yourself with my health." Elizabeth lay very still as the two women left the room. Soon the fluttering beat of her heart returned to its normal steady pace and she knew she had only imagined the pain for now she felt none. There was no reason for her to experience such pains ever again, unless, but no, she was not pregnant, she knew that for certain, but as she tried to recall when her time was due she could not. She had not bothered to count the days while they'd lived in the forest and had no idea how long it had been. Three weeks, four, perhaps longer. Could she have conceived a child at last? As she lay quietly listening to the busy household preparing for dinner, she tried to think how she would tell Andrew if ever she were to find herself pregnant

337

again. She would wait several months, be certain she could carry the babe to full term. She'd not tell him until she could no longer keep the secret. That would be the best way. He had been as heartbroken as she when she'd lost his son. She'd not allow him to suffer such pain again if she could spare him the sorrow by keeping quiet about her condition until he discovered it for himself as he held her in his arms. She would simply wait patiently and pray her hopes proved to be true before telling him of her suspicions. That matter settled to her satisfaction, she pushed herself up to a sitting position slowly, but felt no recurrence of the shattering pain. It had been only a dream after all, as doubtless a new baby would be too. Another child was no more than a dream, but one she carried close to her heart.

Elizabeth summoned Meg to prepare her bath and then dressed for dinner. It was difficult to remain busy in a house with so many servants, she thought, but there were so many interesting books to read and a wonderful garden filled with fall flowers, surely she would be happy there in the Jordan home. She had been happy with Andrew when they'd had nothing, so why should his wealth present problems when poverty had not? She laughed to herself as she brushed her hair. Meg had offered to style her curls but she had been reluctant to accept such service and coiled her hair upon her head and secured it herself. Certain her appearance was pleasing, she descended the stairs to be ready to greet her husband and his uncle when they returned.

Elizabeth was surprised the following afternoon when Esther Nolan came to pay a call as she'd not expected the young woman to seek her friendship. Mrs. Blackstone ushered Esther and a young woman, who was introduced as her cousin, Stephanie MacFadden, into the parlor.

"It is so kind of you to receive us, Elizabeth. I wanted to bring your invitation to my party over personally and be certain I placed it directly into your hands."

"Why, thank you, Miss Nolan, how thoughtful of you." Elizabeth accepted the large white envelope and gestured to a grouping of chairs near the fireplace. "Won't you please stay a while? Andrew said we would attend your party, but there's no reason for you to rush off, is there?"

Esther and Stephanie sat down as the pretty brunette replied excitedly, "Oh, good. Everyone will want to meet you. You must find Philadelphia very exciting after living all your life on a small farm." Esther's smile did not extend to her blue eyes. They were cold, filled with disdain as she removed her gloves and folded her hands in her lap, apparently ready for a lengthy visit.

"The routine is far different here, that is true, but my life has always been most exciting." Elizabeth's smile was as insipid as her guest's. She would play along if that was what the girl expected. Was this what city women liked to do, say one thing when they meant quite another? "I find the presence of British troops here surprising. I thought all the soldiers would be fighting in the countryside rather than remaining here in the city where there is no enemy to confront."

"Personally, I find the British a welcome sight. It serves to remind those who are disloyal to our king of the consequences of this foolhardy rebellion. I hope it will be over swiftly, and our lives can return to a more normal pattern. There will be several British officers at my home on Saturday night, very dashing men I'm certain you will enjoy meeting."

Elizabeth was appalled by that thought, but was saved from commenting as Meg entered with a silver tray bearing a tea service and small cakes. It took all her concentration to serve her guests with what she hoped was proper etiquette and that gave her time to think of something to say. "I believe Andrew knows many of your friends already. I shall look forward to meeting them, too."

"Yes, I introduced Andrew to everyone here in Philadelphia that he should know. My cousin, Stephanie, met your husband only once, soon after he had arrived here last fall. I dare say she will hardly recognize him Saturday evening, he has changed so greatly."

Stephanie appeared to be as shy as Esther was bold, and Elizabeth felt drawn to the hesitant young woman immediately. Her hair was a hazy shade of brown, not dark and rich like her cousin's nor light enough to be considered blond. Her eyes were a pale blue and while she resembled Esther somewhat, she seemed to have none of her livelier relative's confidence or shrewish disposition. "Yes, I know my husband's appearance has changed since he adopted more fashionable attire and no longer wears a beard. He is the same man, however. Do you live here in Philadelphia too, Miss MacFadden?" Elizabeth smiled warmly as she attempted to draw the young woman into the conversation.

"No, my home is in Boston, but my father sent me here to live for the time being. He is not in sympathy with the Patriots and feared for my safety at home." Stephanie glanced up quickly as she answered, then returned her gaze to her teacup which shook precariously in her fingertips.

"I have never been to Boston. Is it like this city with so many shops and people milling about the streets?" Elizabeth inquired curiously.

Stephanie ventured a quick peek at her hostess as she replied, "Yes, it is a busy place, not so large as Philadelphia, but a bustling city all the same."

Esther leaned forward and touched Elizabeth's knee as if she were a close confidant. "Tell us something of your life with the Seneca. What was it like for a white woman to live among those savages?"

Elizabeth gasped at the impertinence of that question and replied coolly, "I prefer not to recall those months. I am far happier now and have no desire to relive my memories."

"Oh, I see. It must have been dreadful for you then. Did all the men, the braves, take advantage of you?" Esther licked her lips at such a thought. Obviously she had no regard for Elizabeth's feelings.

"Miss Nolan, I was then, as I am now, Andrew's wife. The Seneca respect marriage as we do here." That was not exactly the truth of her situation, but she saw no harm in withholding the details of her ordeal during her months with Andrew's tribe. "May I serve you more tea, another cake perhaps?"

Esther declined the offer of more refreshments but persisted in her blatant prying. "What is it like to be with an Indian man, Elizabeth? Is it different from being with one of our own kind?"

Elizabeth simply stared at her guest. Red Tail had held her hand, hugged her. That had felt no different than a white man's embrace. What a silly question, she thought. "Miss Nolan, I can imagine no experience more pleasant than being in my husband's arms, whether he calls himself Seneca or white. He is a wonderful man and a delightful husband."

"Well, yes, of course, but surely—"

"Men are men, Miss Nolan. Some are kind and some are heartless beasts. Somehow I got the impression you knew that rather well."

Esther sat back and frowned, finally realizing Elizabeth had gotten the better of her. Stephanie, however, put her hand to her lips to stifle her giggles and looked up at Elizabeth with her light eyes filled with a bright warm glow of admiration. The pretty blush her laughter had brought to her cheeks made her plain features come alive and suddenly she was far more attractive.

"Stephanie, really, stop that snickering. It's most unbecoming!" Esther was infuriated with her cousin's show of humor. "We must be going, Elizabeth. I hope you will come to call on us some afternoon soon."

"Thank you." Elizabeth stood as the two young women left the room and shook her head. It would be a long while before she called at Esther's home! The woman's nerve was extraordinary. Was that what she could expect from the ladies of Philadelphia; an insatiable curiosity about what it was like to make love with an Indian brave?

Andrew laughed when she described her visitors and the subject of their conversation. "The next time someone has the audacity to ask you how Indian men make love, tell them our feathers tickle terribly!" He caught her in his arms and swung her down upon his bed where he began to kiss her throat with exaggerated hunger.

"Andrew, stop it! We'll be late for dinner!" Elizabeth put her hands upon his chest, but her playful push hardly discouraged his ardor, nor did she want to succeed.

"Do you really care?" Andrew's lips caressed her cheek, then moved down her throat as he unfastened the tiny hooks which secured her bodice.

"Not a bit, but what will your uncle have to say?" She touched his hair fondly with her fingertips, releasing his thick curls from the ribbon which had confined them at his nape. Her lips found his and all thought of propriety left her mind. The only food she required was the rich, delicious taste of his kiss. His loving filled her senses so completely she hungered for nothing save more of him.

Nineteen

Andrew hugged his wife and exclaimed proudly, "You will be the loveliest woman at the Nolan's tonight, Elizabeth, and Esther will no doubt despise you for it, too!"

"And you will easily be the handsomest man, Andrew." Elizabeth smiled prettily at their reflection in the mirror. "We look very civilized, don't we, almost as if we belonged here in this city. It is truly amazing what a difference beautiful clothes make, but I feel no different inside, not one bit." Elizabeth had thanked Andrew repeatedly for his generosity. He had provided not only a new gown of gorgeous lavender satin, but silk lingerie, stockings and delicate slippers along with a cloak of the softest velvet. She looked every inch a fine lady, but was far more proud of being Andrew's wife than of having such a splendid wardrobe.

"As long as you love me still I will be content. Now come along. Henry is waiting with the carriage. The Nolan's home isn't far, but we must leave now." He held her cloak, then reached for her hand and paused for one final word of advice. "No matter how curious the people are tonight, do not let them upset you. Fine manners are much more than beautiful clothes. That

344

is only an elegant facade. You are as perfect a lady as was ever born and anyone of real quality of character will see that instantly."

Elizabeth was pleased by her husband's easy praise and sweet advice. She decided to simply relax and enjoy the party. He had taught her all the latest dances. They were more complex than the ones she had learned in Oak Grove, but no more difficult. She loved to dance and looked forward to the evening. She would just ignore Esther, and anyone else who was rude enough to ask about her life with the Seneca.

They had been at the Nolan home for nearly an hour when Elizabeth turned to meet the latest arrivals. The tall British colonel stopped abruptly as he came through the door, apparently as astonished to see her as she was to see him, but when Esther took his arm he had no choice but to come forward to be introduced. Elizabeth looked up into the Englishman's cold, dark eyes and made no attempt to smile as he was presented, but Andrew's curt greeting surprised her. She found his defiant smile unsettling and wondered what could be wrong.

"Colonel St. James and I have already met, Esther. Perhaps you will recall when last we spoke together." Andrew nodded slightly, his statement a clear challenge rather than friendly conversation.

"Indeed, I do." The splendidly clad officer bowed slightly, then turned his attention to Elizabeth. His glance raked over her with an insolent stare, as if she had been standing naked rather than so beautifully clothed. "I believe we have also met, Mrs. Jordan. It appears you have a preference for marrying Indians."

Elizabeth replied calmly, "I prefer to marry

345

gentlemen, be they Indian or white, Colonel."

Esther stared at the hostile looks passing between her guests and was completely mystified as to the cause. As she wanted no unseemly conduct to spoil her party, she reached for Andrew's arm. "Please come and dance with me. Perhaps you would be so kind as to invite Mrs. Jordan to be your partner, Clayton."

"It would be a pleasure. Mrs. Jordan?" The tall man extended his arm and Elizabeth placed her hand lightly upon his sleeve. The musicians had just begun to play but she hoped the number would not be a lengthy one. The man was light on his feet, but he had none of her husband's grace and style and she found his possessive touch utterly revolting and longed to escape his company.

"I did not realize your husband was Matthew Jordan's nephew until tonight. The last time we met he was another man entirely." Clayton glanced over toward Andrew, then confided sarcastically, "Don't you find it difficult to trust a man who can change his identity so completely?"

Elizabeth returned his stare, intrigued by his comment. "I assure you my husband is always the same man. He plays no one false by his manner of dress."

"There is also the matter of his name, Mrs. Jordan. I've forgotten just what he called himself. He was working for me as an interpreter and we had a disagreement over the length of his enlistment." As the man moved across the dance floor, his hand slipped far too low upon her slender hip, a breach of etiquette he seemed to totally disregard.

Elizabeth didn't miss a step as they moved in time

with the music. She was still a graceful dancer even if her partner was not. She had realized instantly he must be the man Andrew had fought to win his freedom to return to her. She'd not known his name, St. James. She'd not forget it now and avoid meeting the hateful man ever again. "A disagreement, Colonel? I believe it was a rather bloody knife fight, wasn't it? With all the blood spilled being yours?"

The colonel released Elizabeth immediately, then grabbed her wrist and dragged her across the dance floor to her husband's side. "Mr. Jordan, your wife would prefer to dance with you instead. Miss Nolan?" He reached for Esther and swept her across the room in perfect time to the strains of the orchestra while Andrew was left staring down at his beautiful bride.

"Whatever did you say to that bastard?" Andrew led her off the floor as he whispered his question, but his delighted grin let her know he approved of her insult no matter what it might have been.

"Only what he deserved," Elizabeth replied sweetly.

"What did he mean about your husbands? Am I not the first?" Andrew handed her a cup of punch from a passing tray and quickly finished his own.

"He was with the group of soldiers I told you about, the ones who came to your village. I didn't know his name. He didn't bother to introduce himself to me, but I let him think I was Red Tail's wife so he would leave me alone."

"I see." Andrew's eyes narrowed as he watched the man dance with their hostess. "Tell me exactly what happened, Elizabeth. If he insulted you in any way I will kill him right here, tonight."

"You have your knife?" Elizabeth looked up at his

determined expression and knew he meant it. All she had to do was tell the truth and the despicable Colonel St. James would be no more. Andrew would not waste time in dueling. He'd simply challenge the man to a fight and swiftly slit his throat. She could see it all in her mind's eye, even to the blood pouring down the man's snow white shirt. It was a sight she had no desire to witness, on that night, or any other.

Andrew opened his coat slightly to reveal his weapon. "I will be happy to challenge him. It would be an amusing spectacle for Esther's guests, wouldn't it? So many think me still a savage. It will be a pleasure to show off my skill."

"Yes, it would, but what is the penalty for an attack upon one of the King's officers? I don't believe that price would be worth your trouble in killing the swine."

"Swine? Then I do have reason to do it?" Andrew turned his attention to her then, his green eyes laughing at the danger he'd gladly face if she so chose.

"No, Red Tail defended my honor admirably and I suffered no harm at the man's hands. Let us simply ignore him, Andrew. He knows you can beat him. You've done it before and need not prove anything to him a second time. He has obviously not forgotten that humiliation," Elizabeth spoke calmly, unwilling to risk so precious a life as her husband's over a matter long decided.

Andrew inclined his head thoughtfully for a moment as he considered her words. "As you wish, but you know I will kill him if you but give the command. Tonight, or any other time you need my protection, you will always have it."

Elizabeth tried to smile, but the threat in his words was unmistakable and she was apprehensive still. "May we go home now, please. This party has proved far more tiresome than I had thought possible. While I enjoy dancing with you, I find the company here less than agreeable."

"No, we will stay for a while longer at least." Andrew turned back toward the dancers and stared straight at Clayton St. James until the man turned away, leading Esther outdoors for some fresh air. "You see, we have gotten the better of that coward again, Elizabeth. Let's dance once more and then perhaps it will be time to depart for home."

As they joined the other couples, Elizabeth smiled up at him, her eyes sparkling with mischief. "How did you learn to dance so beautifully, Andrew? You are the best dancer here and I know it has been many months since you have had any practice."

"My uncle asked Esther to teach me. His purpose was an obvious one, but I find that young woman's charms extremely easy to resist. All I did was learn to dance." Andrew winked slyly, his grin charmingly wicked.

"Andrew, you are awful!" Elizabeth laughed at his remark, yet she knew he was sincere. She was the only woman he loved and he had made that very clear. She'd never be jealous of Esther Nolan, nor of anyone else. She leaned close to his ear as she whispered a suggestion so enticing he led her from the dance floor and took her straight home to bed.

To her absolute horror, Elizabeth found Matthew Jordan had invited Clayton St. James to dinner at their home the very next evening. The officer arrived on time, looking immaculate as always, but the sight of him simply turned her stomach and she was certain she'd not be able to swallow a single bite with him seated at the same table. As it was, he surpassed even her worst fears that evening.

"I have been entertained here frequently, Mrs. Jordan. Now that you have taken up residence here, we shall have the pleasure of seeing each other often." The man bowed slightly as Matthew welcomed him to their home.

"I'll look forward to it, Colonel." Elizabeth stayed beside Andrew but he seemed unconcerned by their unexpected guest. He did no more than nod or reply with a word or two when he could not avoid being drawn into the conversation. The subject turned quickly to the rebellion and he made no statements which could be interpreted as opposition to the British cause, and yet his manner was never friendly.

As the meal drew to a close the Englishman changed the subject suddenly. "Mrs. Jordan, I believe your home is in Oak Grove. Is it not?"

"Philadelphia is my home now, Colonel." Elizabeth forced herself to be civil as she replied, but it was a great effort. The man had tried to rape her, and now sat chatting as if they were old friends rather than the bitterest of enemies as she felt they truly were.

"Of course," he agreed impatiently. "But you were living in Oak Grove quite recently though, were you not?"

"My father's farm is near Oak Grove, Colonel, and until a few weeks ago I was living close to his home."

"A trapper I know once told me an incredible tale about a young woman he'd met on the way to Oak

Grove. Perhaps you might know her."

"Yes, I may." Elizabeth did not like the turn of the conversation in the least. She wanted only to bid the arrogant dandy a terse good-night.

"It seems he and his partner had managed to capture a notorious felon, an Indian by the way, Andrew, a man who had been terrorizing the countryside for many months. He was approaching Oak Grove with the man in custody when he stopped at a farm to water his mules. A beautiful young girl there offered to trade her horse for the captive and being a practical man, the trapper agreed to the bargain. I wonder if you know who the girl might have been?"

Elizabeth returned the hateful man's cool stare without flinching. Surely Uncle Matthew had repeated that story to him and he was only testing her, attempting to see if she would lie or speak the truth. "That sounds remarkably like the way I met my husband, sir, only Andrew was never a felon. It was the trappers who were the villains in my view."

"Ah, I was hoping that story was about you, Mrs. Jordan. You should be able to help me then."

Andrew eyed the man for a long moment, then shook his head. "I doubt we would be inclined to assist you in any matter, Colonel."

"That remains to be seen. As it so happens, these two trappers were in my employ. They were to contact several people, relay messages as it were while they wandered about, provide information that might prove useful to me in the future."

"Spies you mean, Colonel?" Elizabeth felt Andrew's knee brush hers but she could not resist making that taunt.

"Subjects loyal to his majesty can hardly be referred to as spies, Mrs. Jordan," Clayton scoffed at her use of the term.

"That is a matter of opinion," Elizabeth responded calmly.

"We need not debate the issue, Mrs. Jordan. It has come to my attention that John Cummins and his partner, a man by the name of Robert Runess, have disappeared, simply vanished. They were due in Bloomsberg two weeks ago at the latest. They should have passed through Oak Grove sometime before that but were not seen in that town either. I wondered if perhaps they had stopped by your farm once again to water their mules if that was their habit."

"I saw Mr. Cummins only once, Colonel. He stopped by our home in the spring of 1775, when he had Andrew with him. He said his partner had gone on ahead that day so I did not ever meet him. I'm sorry to hear you must resort to employing men of his type as he was most disreputable in his appearance and I have no doubt his partner is no more honest. They probably received a better offer from the rebels and have gone over to your enemies to sell whatever information they had gathered."

Clayton frowned, his dissatisfaction clear. "You did not see them recently then?"

"No, I did not, but I had not seen John Cummins before that day in 1775 either. If he traversed our part of Pennsylvania frequently, he must have used a variety of routes for he was a complete stranger to me."

"I will continue to search for the two men

nevertheless. I fear they have become victims of foul play and if so, I will see their murderers hanged promptly."

Andrew continued to appear quite bored as he listened to the colonel's remarks. "If they are dead, please let me know. It will save me the trouble of looking for them myself. I have been far too busy of late to give the matter any thought, but I have a score to settle with John Cummins and Robert Runess and I hate to think someone has beaten me to it."

Colonel St. James responded curtly, "I hope you will wait until this rebellion is suppressed before you go looking for revenge, Andrew. I would hate to have to hang you when your uncle has been so loyal to King George."

Matthew Jordan had no idea what was going on at his table, but talk of hanging appalled him. "Gentlemen, please! Such talk is most inappropriate in front of Elizabeth. I am inclined to agree with her, that men who have treated Andrew with such contempt could not be expected to be loyal to either side. I'll wager they are talking with General Washington this very night, plotting some further bit of mischief. Now let us go into the parlor and think of more pleasant topics to discuss."

Elizabeth excused herself immediately, having no wish to spend an additional second in St. James' wretched company but she paced their bedroom nervously as she waited for Andrew to join her. When he at last came through the door, she rushed to his side. "If you think I'll let that fiend hang you for two murders I committed, you are mistaken!"

Andrew laughed at her hoarsely whispered vow and

drew her into his arms. "Elizabeth, I have no intention of allowing either of us to be hanged for any reason."

"Did you tell your uncle the truth?" Elizabeth turned so Andrew might help her unhook her dress, her pose a coquettish one even if her mood was not.

"No, I will never speak of that day to anyone and neither will you. It would only confuse the old man to know what happened. He doesn't possess your considerable talent for lying, my dear, and I will not trust him with any of my secrets which might endanger our lives."

Elizabeth slipped out of the satin gown and tossed it over a chair, the lovely garment of little concern to her now. "I would not put it past Colonel St. James to produce two bodies he'll swear are those men. He mentioned them only to see what our reactions would be."

Andrew undressed with the same speed as his wife, littering their spacious room with his discarded apparel. "Yes, I believe you're right, but the man undoubtedly prefers making threats to taking any action. He lacks the courage to follow through and he'll not risk losing my uncle's support by arresting me, no matter how much he'd like to do it."

Elizabeth climbed into bed and watched her husband's face closely as she explained. "I have no talent for lying to anyone other than St. James, Andrew. There's something about that snake that simply inspires deceit in my heart."

"Perhaps I should convince my uncle to find some other source of current information about the war's progress. The less we see of the colonel, the better."

"Oh, no, Andrew, absolutely not," Elizabeth hastened to caution her husband. "We mustn't arouse his suspicions. We must insist Uncle Matthew invite him here as frequently as he always has. That should confuse him completely as he'll expect us to try and avoid him."

Andrew was amazed by her wisdom. "You're a crafty wench, Elizabeth. I am fortunate not to have you for an enemy." He snuffed out the candle at their bedside and joined her beneath the covers with only one thought on his mind.

"How could we ever be enemies when we love each other so?" Elizabeth clung to him so tightly Andrew pulled away, shocked by the strength of her passion.

"Elizabeth," Andrew spoke her name in a soft, mellow tone, stilling her fears as he took her hands in his. "My love, I will never allow any harm to befall you. Never again. You will always be safe with me and I have eluded far more cunning enemies than St. James will ever be, so you need have no fears for my sake either."

"I love you so much, Andrew, I couldn't bear to lose you." Elizabeth's lips were so enticing he responded eagerly to her plea for affection. They were too finely matched a pair, too deeply in love to worry for long over any problem when they had the beauty of an unending passion to share. Warm and sweet, lean and lithe, they were a couple too lost in each other to fear even the threat of death when they were together.

The next week Elizabeth returned to Madame Dupré's for the first of her fittings. Henry drove her there in the carriage as Andrew had gone with his uncle for the day and Elizabeth had assured him she could go to the dressmaker's without need of an escort. As she entered the exclusive shop, Stephanie MacFadden greeted her shyly.

"Mrs. Jordan, how are you? I didn't have an opportunity to speak with you at Esther's Saturday night. I was hoping we might talk." The young woman's voice was a soft, hesitant whisper.

Elizabeth smiled warmly. "We were sorry to have to leave so early, but it was unavoidable. I'd hoped to see you again, too. Can you wait while I have my fittings and then perhaps you could come home with me or my driver will take you home if you'd prefer."

Stephanie bit her lower lip nervously as she tried to decide what to do. "Esther expects me home soon, but I could wait a few minutes, I suppose."

"Good." Elizabeth took the shy girl's hand as they went back to the small fitting rooms where Madame Dupré greeted her enthusiastically.

"Ah, Mrs. Jordan, you are right on time. I have the first of your garments ready. Please slip on the dress and I will adjust the fit to perfection."

Elizabeth found the fitting tedious. She had made her own dresses with no help at all and it seemed silly to make such a fuss over clothes, even such fine ones. "How much longer must I stand here, Madame Dupré?"

"Only a few moments and no more, my dear. I want this bodice to fit correctly. I must consider my own reputation as well as your beauty," the gracious woman offered with a charming smile.

Elizabeth laughed at the friendly woman's good-natured rebuke. "The dresses Andrew ordered for me fit so perfectly. How did you make those?"

"He simply described you, and most accurately too

but it was obvious he adored you and had your image well implanted in his mind."

Stephanie spoke up softly, "I danced with your husband one time at the party, only briefly. We had to change partners and I moved on but he is a very fine dancer, and his touch is so gentle."

"For a savage you mean?" Elizabeth's impish grin made Stephanie break into a lilting giggle she tried unsuccessfully to stifle behind her glove.

"My cousin embarrassed me terribly that afternoon. Your husband's manners are very fine, and he is very handsome. His eyes are so unusual, so clear a green that . . . Why, Elizabeth, your eyes are exactly like his, aren't they?" Stephanie exclaimed in surprise.

Elizabeth averted her gaze quickly, not wanting to draw any further comparisons. "Yes, the color of our eyes is identical. It is a coincidence only." At least she was convinced it was even if she still had no proof to support her beliefs. She stood quietly for the remainder of the fitting, then chatted happily as Henry drove Stephanie to her cousin's home.

"Would you like to come in? Esther will wonder why I'm so late," Stephanie offered nervously.

"Thank you, Stephanie, but no, I—" Elizabeth halted in mid-sentence as she saw Esther step through her front door followed closely by Clayton St. James. He nodded toward the carriage as he recognized the occupants, but the gleam in his dark eyes was one of pure lust, not friendship, and Elizabeth drew back instantly.

Stephanie frowned as she observed her new friend's suddenly subdued expression, then whispered, "Esther thinks him most handsome and charming, but I don't. He frightens me. He seems, well, so ruthless."

"Yes, he is that," Elizabeth agreed with her companion, then changed the topic to a far more pleasant one. "Please come to see me sometime soon, Stephanie, perhaps some afternoon when Esther is busy so we might have an opportunity for a long visit."

Stephanie's pale eyes brightened with a pleasing sparkle as she readily understood the invitation was for her alone. "Yes, she has many friends. It shouldn't be too difficult for me to slip away. I will come visit you soon. Good-bye."

Elizabeth tried to signal Henry as Stephanie stepped from the carriage, but she was not swift enough and the British officer approached her vehicle with a broad smile.

"Mrs. Jordan, how nice it is to see you once again."

Elizabeth saw no reason for such exaggerated politeness and said so. "Thank you, but there is no need for us to play games with words, Colonel."

"Mrs. Jordan?" The tall man's eyes swept her pretty features with an intense gaze. He was puzzled by her remark and could discern no hidden meaning in her expression.

Elizabeth's deep green eyes flashed angrily. "We need not pretend a regard for each other we do not feel, Colonel St. James. You are my uncle's friend and he values your friendship, but you and I have no such relationship."

"I disagree, Elizabeth. I'd say we are extremely old and dear friends. How does Andrew like being your second husband? Tell me what happened to the brave who was your first? Did he give you up willingly or did Andrew simply murder the man?"

Elizabeth saw no point in admitting she had tricked him at their first meeting since it would only put him on his guard in future encounters, so she ignored his question entirely. "That is no business of yours, Colonel, now good day. Henry, let us hurry home." Elizabeth was grateful when the elegant carriage lurched into motion, leaving the immaculately groomed officer no choice but to leap aside.

Elizabeth tried valiantly to hold her temper, but once she'd reached her uncle's home she closed her bedroom door and shrieked with frustration. Clayton St. James was a despicable villain, a hateful brute. That she had to pretend to be civil was impossible! Yet she knew she had no real choice. He'd go for Andrew. Wasn't that what he'd threatened? To get him for her "first" husband's murder?

Twenty

At his first opportunity Andrew escorted Elizabeth to her Uncle William's home where she was enthusiastically welcomed, greeted as though she were his own dearly loved daughter rather than merely a niece paying a social call. The excited man exclaimed upon her fair beauty, his blue eyes sparkling with delight. While he resembled his younger brother to a great degree, his blond hair now had a silver glow and the trim build of his youth had assumed stocky proportions. His wife was petite, dark-haired with twinkling brown eyes and seemed to be as pleased as her husband to meet the pretty young woman who was their niece.

William Peterson shook Andrew's hand warmly as he ushered the strikingly handsome couple into his parlor. "Rebecca, let us offer our guests some refreshments. We have no tea, of course, but perhaps some ale would be more fitting for this fine occasion."

"Ale, William? I doubt Elizabeth is accustomed to drinking ale." Rebecca Peterson laughed at his suggestion, but made no haste to serve any other sort of liquid refreshment.

"Would you like to have some tea? Had I known I would have brought some." Andrew took a seat on the small sofa and drew his lovely bride down by his side. "My uncle's stores are vast and I see no reason not to share them with our relatives, if I may consider you as such." He smiled easily, comfortable already in the charming couple's friendly company.

William's eyes scanned the finely dressed young man with renewed interest. "My brother told me only that you had relatives living here, Mr. Jordan, but you are not Matthew Jordan's kin, are you?"

"Yes, he is my uncle. We live in his home," Andrew responded rapidly, seeing no reason to be ashamed of his wealthy relative.

Rebecca sank down into the nearest chair and covered her mouth with her hand as she gave a sharp gasp. "Oh, dear, we had no idea who you were, sir."

"I am Elizabeth's husband, no more. Why are you so alarmed, Mrs. Peterson?" Andrew kept Elizabeth's hand clasped tightly in his, but he could not imagine the reason for her relatives' suddenly startled expressions. "Do you know the man?"

William drew up a chair close to his wife's and sighed sadly. "Indeed we do. Our eldest son worked in his warehouse until his politics became known."

Andrew nodded with sudden insight. "Now I see. Elizabeth has mentioned you support the Rebellion but let me assure you, I do not have any political leanings one way or the other. While my uncle may be a staunch Loyalist, I am not. You need have no fear of me."

William glanced nervously at his wife, then turned to his niece. "Does my brother still persist in his neutrality?"

Elizabeth honestly did not know and said so. "It has

been so long since I discussed politics with my father, I can't report his present views, but since he was opposed to all war as senseless violence, this one can be no different in his view." She was sorry the conversation had turned so swiftly to the war and wished she could think of some more appealing topic to discuss. "Are any of my cousins at home? I would love to meet them."

Rebecca apologized immediately. "Why no, dear. Martha is married now and lives in Virginia, while our two boys are . . ." The woman looked toward her husband for guidance and seeing his warning glance completed her explanation in vague terms. "They are away."

Elizabeth saw no reason for such subterfuge. "They are fighting with the Continental Army. Is that what you mean?"

Rebecca blushed deeply, not knowing how to respond and William came to her rescue promptly. "They are away from the city. That is explanation enough, Elizabeth. When they are next at home I will see that you meet them. They are handsome young men and you will like them as much as they are sure to like you."

Andrew noted accurately that the Petersons' comments were directed solely toward his wife. "Would you rather Elizabeth came here to visit you alone? If my uncle's politics upset you so greatly, I will stay away."

William Peterson nodded coolly. "You must see our side of this, Mr. Jordan. Elizabeth is our kin. We can trust her to be discreet, but you—"

"What is it you think I'll do? Ask my uncle's British

friends to search your home for propaganda and munitions?" When William paled noticeably, Andrew rose to his feet. "I'll wait outside, Elizabeth. Chat as long as you wish, but I can see my presence here is upsetting your aunt and uncle needlessly."

Elizabeth reached out to take her husband's hand. "Wait, Andrew, please. Uncle William, Aunt Rebecca, you need have no fear of my husband. He is the best of men and will never bring any harm to your household or family."

William eyed the young man before him with a more earnest regard. The fine cut of his coat and britches hid none of his powerful build and the pride in his bearing was unmistakably that of a gentleman. "Yes, I can see you are telling me the truth. Andrew, please sit down with us. Now, Rebecca, where is that ale?"

The lively little woman hurried to see to her husband's request, and Andrew sat down again at his wife's side. He let his gaze travel around the humbly furnished room. The Petersons' house was located in a modest section of town, but the small dwelling was comfortable, cluttered with treasured possessions, and it was obviously filled with love. He could not help but remember the home he'd so recently shared with Elizabeth. No better than the most meager of shacks, it had served them well and they had never thought it inadequate for their needs had been so few. When Rebecca returned with the pitcher of ale and four tankards, she poured generous amounts for the men but only a small sip for herself and Elizabeth. "I meant what I said. If you'd like tea, or any other commodity which is becoming scarce, I can get it for you. I'm sorry about your son's job. Perhaps I can help him to find another if he returns to Philadelphia anytime soon."

"That is unlikely, Andrew, but thank you. As for your uncle's goods, I would sooner do without than take what he owns. I am sorry, but I am committed to this rebellion as are my friends, as committed as your uncle is to his mistaken allegiance."

Andrew chuckled at William's outburst. "Tea is tea, sir. It has no opinion in this matter and might as well fill your cup as his."

Rebecca spoke up eagerly. "Oh, William, do you think we might—"

"Silence, woman! The answer is no. I'd rather die of thirst than drink that traitor's blasted tea!" William slammed his tankard down upon the small table beside his chair to emphasize his point.

"But Uncle, Matthew Jordan is no traitor. He is loyal to the king who has ruled the Colonies for years. If any are traitors, it is the Patriots, no matter how just their cause might be." Elizabeth smiled sweetly, knowing her logic would be immediately open to question.

William cocked his head quizzically as he observed his beautiful niece with an amused glance. "I recall my brother saying you were far too liberal in your views to suit him. You have not changed, have you, lass? You do not want to see your cousins fail in their fight to free this land from the tyranny of King George, do you?"

Elizabeth laced her fingers firmly in her husband's as she responded. "I don't want to see any men killed, least of all my own cousins, but Andrew and I do not wish to take sides. What difference will our support do for either side? We are but two people, not an army."

"Don't you believe it, Elizabeth. We all matter in this, each one of us." William turned his glance back to Andrew and asked casually, "My brother mentioned your past in his letters. You were not raised as a pacifist, were you?"

"No, indeed, I was not. But that is another story all together and not one I'll relate here," Andrew replied firmly.

"You should not encourage him, Uncle. The Seneca have chosen the British side rather than ours, yours." Elizabeth caught herself quickly, but not before everyone had noticed her slip and joined in the laughter.

William leaned forward in his chair, intent upon winning Andrew to his point of view. "A man skilled in the art of war is valuable to our side too, Andrew. Would you like to speak to others, men more eloquent and persuasive than I on this subject? Your talents are needed and I would not like to see them go to waste when your help may shorten this war and bring all our sons home more swiftly."

Andrew drained his tankard of ale and replaced the pewter mug upon the tray. "You are a surprising man, William. First you did not trust me because of my uncle's politics and now you wish to recruit me for the Continental Army? I have no desire to put on a blue coat and fire a cannon at the British."

"No? Perhaps buckskin would suit you more. A man such as you leading a band of Indian warriors could do far more damage to the British forces than any cannon."

Andrew rose swiftly and lifted his wife gracefully to her feet. "You are mistaken. I am Andrew Jordan, a merchant, sir, not a Seneca sachem ready to lead braves on raids and I'll not fight in any battles of this war or any other. We must be on our way. I hope you will be kind enough to receive my wife here in your home should she wish to call again, but I think it would be better for all of us if I do not."

"Andrew!" Elizabeth was shocked by her husband's curt good-bye and turned toward her startled relatives without any hope they understood his feelings. "I am so happy to have met you and hope to meet the rest of your family soon."

William gave his niece a warm hug and his wife squeezed her hands tightly. "Yes, do come to see us again, Elizabeth. You and I have much to discuss even if the men do not."

Elizabeth sat lost in thought as the carriage made its way through the narrow cobblestone streets toward their home. "I'm sorry, Andrew. I should have known what my uncle would say to you. I read enough of his letters to know politics has great appeal to him. I hope you were not too terribly offended by his rudeness."

Andrew took her hand and brought it to his lips. "I was far more rude than he, for after all, a man should be able to say what he thinks in his own home. He is sincere in his beliefs and I cannot fault him for recognizing me for what I am."

Elizabeth's perceptive gaze swept her husband's expression slowly, caressing the contours of his handsome face with her adoring gaze. "I see only a strong and handsome man, a very intelligent man, too. What is it you think he saw?"

"What was it your father called me once? A mercenary? That's what I think he saw, a man who could be convinced to join the Patriots' cause for the pure glory of battle."

Elizabeth tried to swallow the painful lump which filled her throat. "Is battle all that glorious? Are men truly drawn to the thrill alone, not repelled by the horror of death?"

Andrew directed his gaze out the window at his side, surveying the passing scene as they neared his uncle's neighborhood. "I never gave any thought to my own death, Elizabeth, only to that of my enemies. I was highly respected too, strong, cunning, fearless, all that a Seneca warrior is expected to be, but I am no longer that man, and that's what your uncle didn't understand. War interests me not at all now. I find the prospect of combat thoroughly disgusting for I can no longer summon the rage which makes killing the ultimate joy."

Seeing the set line of his jaw, Elizabeth readily believed her husband and spoke no more about the rebellion. She rested her head upon his shoulder and yawned sleepily. "Who is coming for dinner tonight, Andrew? I've quite forgotten the guest list. All of your uncle's friends are important so these must be also, but just who are they?"

Andrew chuckled as he wrapped his arm around her tightly and drew her near. "Their names are unimportant, as are their faces. They're wealthy Loyalists who will be eager to discuss the latest British victory and I will not even listen. I will simply look at you and think how happy we will be when all the guests have gone home and we may be alone."

"Must we wait until the last one says good-bye, Andrew?" Elizabeth lifted her lips to his and as always his mouth promised the endless delights of his love and she knew she would not see or hear much of the dinner party conversation either for she had no interest in anything save her husband.

As Elizabeth scanned the smiling faces at the long dining table that night, she suddenly realized something she had completely overlooked. Phillip must have had some friends, perhaps close ones who might have known the extent of his regard for Marie Larson. She'd already decided against arousing Mrs. Blackstone's curiosity by asking her about the young woman, for she would undoubtedly only repeat the household gossip Matthew had already related. Excited by her inspiration, Elizabeth looked more closely at the men present. There were several of the right age, younger men than Matthew but apparently lifelong friends from the conversations she could overhear. She turned to whisper to Andrew, "Have any of your uncle's friends ever told you they were good friends of your father?"

Andrew seemed surprised for a moment by her unexpected query, then shook his head sadly. "If my father still had any friends left at the time of his death, I've not met them. What made you think of him tonight?"

Elizabeth smiled warmly at her spouse. He had never looked more handsome and her love shone brightly in her pretty eyes. "I think of him often, Andrew. This was your parents' home too, and I wish I had known them, or someone who did. We know so little about them other than their names and I am

368

curious, that's all."

"As usual!" Andrew laughed at her comments then took her hand in his as he smiled again. "My father would have loved you, Elizabeth. Apparently he liked anything in a skirt and a young woman so beautiful as you would have enchanted him."

Elizabeth's heart lurched wildly as she thought of her mother. Had she adored Phillip as she loved his son? Somehow she hoped that she had for the man deserved to find happiness before his tragic death, yet she could not accept the possibility she herself might be the result of that love and shuddered with a sudden chill.

"Elizabeth, are you ill?" Andrew grew alarmed as he felt her shiver.

"No, not at all. I'm fine." Elizabeth winked slyly at her husband and finished her meal with no further thought of locating Phillip's friends. If they hadn't made themselves known to Andrew there was no way for her to locate them and most likely they did not exist. Every path led to a dead end and yet she knew the truth had to be found somewhere, if only she knew where to search or whom to ask.

Elizabeth was kept busy in the following days with additional trips to Madame Dupré's for fittings, afternoons spent chatting with Stephanie when the shy young woman could elude her inquisitive cousin and the more or less constant preparations for Uncle Matthew's many dinner parties. The man entertained constantly it seemed, using his spacious home to further both his political and business goals. As Elizabeth listened to her husband on such evenings, she marveled at the depth of his knowledge. He had quickly mastered the complexities of his uncle's business affairs and could give correct answers about any of the commodities the man imported and sold at handsome profits, but still took no part when the discussions turned to the progress of the war. He would simply withdraw into himself and let those around him carry on the vivid tales of the fierce fighting which raged throughout the eastern colonies before both armies prepared to withdraw to their winter quarters. Elizabeth would take his hand and he would smile, but she could see his pain and readily understood its cause.

As to her own quest, Elizabeth never gave up hope that she would soon discover some evidence, and no matter how unexpected the source, she kept her ears open and watched closely, hoping to find some shred of tangible proof to refute what she considered to be no more than vicious gossip, but still she dared not reveal her fears to Andrew. On her second visit to her aunt and uncle's home she found Rebecca alone and presented her with a canister of tea which the appreciative lady hid quickly before her husband returned to refuse it. As soon as she possibly could, Elizabeth directed the conversation to her consuming interest. "My mother was so dear to me, Aunt Rebecca. Did you know her well?"

"No, I'm sorry to say I did not. Olaf brought her here so we could meet her and both William and I were impressed by her sweetness as well as her beauty, but after he took her home to Oak Grove I never saw the lovely young woman again." At that thought Rebecca's eyes filled with tears which she brushed away with an embarrassed dab of her handkerchief. "I'm sorry. I hope I haven't upset you, but my memories of your mother are so few. Your father visited us occasionally, but Marie always stayed at home to care for you."

Elizabeth tried to hide her disappointment for she'd hoped her aunt would have more to relate. "I thought perhaps you might have been acquainted with her before she and my father were married, might have been the friend who introduced them."

"No, I met her after Olaf did. I'm sure she must have had many friends for she was so very pretty, but I knew none of them. As I recall, she had no family still living to attend the wedding and that's why Olaf wanted the ceremony to be in Oak Grove, so he could give a proper party for her in celebration. How is your father, Elizabeth? He is happy with his second wife, isn't he? I know he must be delighted to have so fine a son and—"

Elizabeth pulled on her gloves as she rose to her feet. "Yes, every man should have a son. I'm certain my father is delighted to have one at long last. Please excuse me, my uncle has invited company for dinner again this evening and I must return home." She moved gracefully toward the door, forcing her mind to focus on the details of the evening's festivities rather than on her own heartbreak.

"Elizabeth?" Rebecca followed her attractive niece, fearful she had said something to offend her.

Elizabeth turned to kiss the dark-eyed woman's cheek lightly. "Good-bye, Aunt Rebecca. I'll try and come to see you again soon." She waved as she climbed into the carriage and asked Henry to hurry home, knowing she was no wiser than when she had come but infinitely more depressed. The child she had hoped had been conceived in the forest had proved to be no more than a dream after all. She had kept a careful tally of the days since then so as not to be disappointed again without reason. Now she was positive her time was overdo and her anxiety grew with each passing day for she wanted so desperately to give Andrew another son but greatly feared she could not. Her mother had borne only one child and no others. Would that also be her fate?

Andrew bent his head to kiss the soft curve of Elizabeth's pretty, pink shoulder as he began to help her undress late that night. "Elizabeth, are you happy here, content with our life? You seem so restless of late, and I cannot help but worry as to the cause."

Elizabeth turned slowly, her expression as serious as his. She had so many reasons to be unhappy but chose only the most obvious to relate. "I have little to do here, Andrew. The life is pleasant, but it doesn't seem real."

Andrew lifted an eyebrow quizzically. "Not real? How can our life be otherwise?"

Elizabeth kept her deepest fears hidden in her heart as she attempted to explain. "The clothes you have bought for me are exquisite, but I used to weave the cloth and sew my own garments. The food we are served is delicious, but how can I take any pride in our meals when I neither grow our food nor prepare it? Uncle Matthew's acquaintances are pleasant, but I agree with none of their views and keeping still gives me a terrible headache nearly every night they are here. Most of the women seem to care little for what is happening in the world. They are concerned only with news of the latest in fashions from Europe as if we must copy their styles endlessly with no creative thoughts of our own. While the finest of our country men are dying each day, these people pay the British officers lavish compliments as if they were sent to the colonies to do no more than attend our uncle's parties. And then—"

Andrew smiled widely as he drew his wife into his arms. "Yes, you see this city exactly as I do, Elizabeth, but I'm certain all its residents are not so silly as those we are forced to entertain."

Elizabeth licked her lips thoughtfully, then spoke with deliberate slowness, "Andrew, my Uncle William mentioned men who held different views from your uncle's. Perhaps you would be wise to seek them out and hear what they have to say if you are as dissatisfied with our life as I am."

Andrew released her abruptly and sat down on the edge of his father's bed to pull off his boots. "That is not necessary. They have already found me. They came to the warehouse on one pretext or another and asked to speak with me. Sometimes we actually did transact some business, but usually they bargained for a few minutes in a vain attempt to lower our prices and then they casually asked questions like how I can stand to work in that airless building from dawn to dusk, adding endless columns of figures, when the winter weather is still mild and there is so much to be accomplished before the first snow falls." Andrew looked up, certain his wife would understand his callers' words.

"They are referring to the war, of course?" Elizabeth slipped out of her petticoats and camisole without the slightest blush of embarrassment touching her cheeks. She drew her lace trimmed nightgown over her head, then sat down beside her husband and laced her fingers in his. "What do you think of these strangers, Andrew? Do they seem sincere?"

"I have never met more serious and determined men. I have no doubt the rebellion will succeed with patriots such as your uncle knows working so hard for victory."

"They want you to join their cause, to fight as Uncle William suggested?" Elizabeth held her breath, not daring to predict his reply.

"Yes, my fame as a warrior seems to know no bounds. Although I deny all interest in fighting now, hardly a day goes by that someone does not appear at the warehouse to try and tempt me into joining one regiment or another."

Elizabeth reached up to kiss her husband's cheek sweetly. "Andrew, you are no happier here than I am, are you? Being with you is paradise for me. No matter where you wish to live I will be happy to go with you. I know you are a fine man, and a proud one. If you want to join the Continental Army I will never ask you not to do so."

Andrew drew his slender bride into his arms as he stretched out across their large bed. "If my father were alive, perhaps the family enterprise would mean more to me. As it is I grow more bored and restless each day. It does not seem right that our prices continue to increase when people are so desperate for our goods. You see none of the common man's suffering here, Elizabeth, but the shortages in consumer goods are becoming acute. My uncle manipulates the economy for his own gain and I am not proud to be a part of it." Obviously frustrated, Andrew continued, "That he would disown me for leaving his firm concerns me not at all, Elizabeth, and I have no loyalty to a king I've never met, but as I told you I no longer have any reason for the anger which makes an Indian brave so fierce in battle. I would be useless to either side."

Elizabeth's pretty eyes widened as she drew away. "Andrew, you would not consider helping the British again, being a translator with the Iroquois or whatever. You would not!"

Andrew chuckled at her indignation. "I have permission to join General Washington's forces, but not those of King George. Is that correct?"

Elizabeth threw her arms around her husband's neck and hugged him tightly. "Do not tease me for I cannot bear to think of your risking your life for either side."

Andrew clasped Elizabeth tightly to his chest as he kissed her golden curls. "My love, I will stay here for the duration of the hostilities, then when this blasted war ends, I will tell my uncle good-bye and take you away. We will go west, until we find the place where the sun sets if we must, but we will be together in our own land as we were in the forest and both of us will be far happier for it. I promise you that, my dearest. I promise, I will not leave you, not now, not ever."

Elizabeth's pink-tinged lips sought his with unmistakable passion. She wanted proof of his words, of his devotion and he supplied it readily, his need for her consuming him as always and they lost themselves in the delights of their love. They lay enveloped in the most exquisite of ecstasies until sleep overtook them like a powerful drug and they slept, exhausted by pleasure, content in the strength of their enduring love.

Knowing their lives would return to the tranquility they had enjoyed once the war drew to an end, Elizabeth ceased to worry over the possibility of their common heritage. She forced the prospect from her mind as being no more than vicious gossip and gave her energies to the management of her new home. For once she knew she would not have to spend all her life there in such frivolous pursuits, she could accept them as temporary and therefore bearable. She and Andrew were popular, young, intelligent and attractive. They were invited to all the Loyalists' homes and went without complaining until Elizabeth awoke in the early morning hours after one such party to find Andrew gone. She lay still, hardly daring to breathe as she tried to imagine where he might have gone. When he returned to their bedroom shortly before dawn, she greeted him with a hoarse whisper.

"You might have told me you were leaving so I would not have worried so. I know better than to accuse you of being with another woman, and you've no need to sneak out at night to discuss the rebellion with the British, so that leaves only one possibility as to your whereabouts!"

Andrew closed their door cautiously before he replied. "I am sorry. I hoped you would not wake while I was out, but I was gone longer than usual tonight."

"Andrew! You have gone out after midnight before this!" Elizabeth was aghast at his revelation.

"Yes, but I am plotting no intrigues, merely talking with men whose ideas interest me," he replied softly.

"Well then, let's invite these friends of yours to come for dinner where I might hear their thoughts too." Elizabeth was furious with her husband for not trusting her enough to tell her what he had been doing but she bit her tongue rather than accuse him of deceiving her when she had secrets of her own she wished to keep solely to herself.

"That would not be wise, Elizabeth. Their names are well known to my uncle's British companions, and I do not want to see these men arrested while they are in our home. No, it is not safe for them to come here."

"Then it cannot be safe for you to meet them elsewhere either!" Elizabeth pointed out with piercing logic.

"Probably not." Andrew joined her in bed and reached for her narrow waist, but she pushed him away angrily.

"Andrew, I mean it. Fight in this war if you must, but do not lie to me about what you are doing!"

Andrew sat up, forcing Elizabeth down among the pillows as he moved his hands to her delicate wrists. "I did not lie. Not ever. We will speak no more of this night, or of whom I wish to meet. I will not give you information which will place your life in jeopardy, Elizabeth. It is better if you know nothing."

Elizabeth peered up at her husband, straining to make out his expression in the darkness which veiled the bedroom. "Tell me no more than that you will be going out. If I am not to know where you have gone I can at least pray for your safe return."

Andrew leaned down, relaxing his hold upon her as his lips brushed hers softly. "I will tell you, dear wife, but the danger to me is slight and I do not want you to worry about me needlessly."

"You would not worry if you were to awaken and find me gone?" Elizabeth began to giggle, for that prospect was so unlikely she could scarcely imagine it.

"You have always been the rebel, Elizabeth. Perhaps I should suspect you are spying for your uncle already. These British officers are fools and tell us far more than we should know without even realizing it."

"Andrew!" Elizabeth was astounded by that comment. "I could never be a spy, never, and neither should you! Spies are hanged, aren't they, not considered to be soldiers although they most certainly are?"

Andrew lay down and drew Elizabeth's head upon his shoulder. "No, I have no talent for spying, none whatsoever. My talents lie in another direction altogether."

Elizabeth shivered despite the warmth of his embrace for she knew all too well just what talents he meant. She turned toward him then, covering his face with gentle kisses he could not resist. "You are a man of many extraordinary talents, but I wish we'd never come to Philadelphia. The life here is frought with too many perils."

Andrew laughed at her fears, drew her into a playful hug and swiftly banished all anxiety from her mind with loving too distracting to allow contemplation of anything other than the delicious taste of his kiss.

As the days passed, Elizabeth noticed the difference in her husband. He was often preoccupied but a slow mischievous smile would curve across his lips as if his thoughts were most amusing and although now he would warn her when he would be away, he slipped out more and more frequently to meet with men whose names he would never reveal. He seemed happier, more content than before, and she decided if he had been able to balance his dislike for his uncle's business with his keen interest in discussing the issues and strategies of the war, she would keep still. Whenever Colonel St. James visited their home, Andrew pretended such total ignorance of the war effort the man had ceased to speak to him at all, a fact which delighted both Elizabeth and her clever husband.

The days before Christmas were few when Matthew Jordan summoned Andrew and Elizabeth into his library before dinner. He seemed strangely silent as they took their seats and they were curious as to what he might wish to discuss in such secrecy. Andrew knew he had done nothing to arouse the older man's suspicions. His actions were all above reproach and he knew Elizabeth lived the most exemplary of lives as well. There was nothing for which they could be faulted and yet he saw something in the man's eyes that was new and grew wary. The sixth sense which had seen him through many a battle warned him to be on his guard and he sat up straight, anxious to hear his uncle's words.

Matthew Jordan took a brass handled poker and jabbed viciously at the log on the hearth. The small room was becoming too warm, but his efforts sent up a new flare of sparks and he replaced the poker in its stand and let well enough alone. He then unlocked his desk drawer and withdrew a stack of faded parchment which he held lightly as he looked up. "I hardly know where to begin, Andrew. I know you are blameless in this unfortunate set of circumstances, but I have no choice but to reveal the truth to you now, no matter how painful I find that duty."

"What are you talking about, Uncle? If there is something I have not completed to your satisfaction at the warehouse then tell me about it tomorrow. There is no need to involve Elizabeth in a business discussion," Andrew scowled angrily. Not understanding his uncle's comments, he had no wish to pursue them. That the man owned his time during daylight hours was bad enough. He would not give him his evenings, too.

"I wish this were only a business matter, but unfortunately it is not. I did not want to believe this," Matthew gestured with his handful of papers. "It was merely my suspicion, one I could not in good conscience ignore. My attorney, Stephen Haywood, is discreet. I assigned him the task of gathering this information and he was most thorough, diligent in his pursuit of the truth. He handed this proof to me only this afternoon. I am sorry to be the one to give you this news, Andrew, but Elizabeth is Marie Larson's daughter, her child and your father's as well. She is your half-sister and therefore no longer your wife."

Elizabeth's hands grew cold, like ice as she gripped them together tightly in her lap. She could scarcely believe what the man said, but he seemed to have it all, every scrap of paper, every document which could have been found to support his argument, and he waved them dramatically as he continued his story.

"It is all right here, and very plain as to what happened. Marie Larson left here the night Phillip died, and married a man named Olaf Peterson two weeks later. Approximately seven months later she gave birth to a baby girl whom they named Elizabeth. No other children were born to that marriage."

"Seven months doesn't prove anything, Uncle Matthew. My mother always said I was born early, premature. I am not Phillip Jordan's child. I know I am not." Elizabeth could barely whisper a denial of his horrible accusation. He had no proof after all, only more innuendoes.

"You have Phillip's eyes, Elizabeth, green eyes so unusual you recognized your own brother at first glance." Matthew Jordan threw down the faded parchment documents as irrefutable fact and stared coldly at her.

"I warned you, Uncle. God help me I warned you what would happen should you try and separate us!" Andrew leapt to his feet so quickly his chair toppled over backward with a loud clatter.

Matthew gestured innocently. "Your wife has known the truth all along, Andrew, from the very beginning, from the first night you brought her here and I told you about Marie Larson. She knew I was talking about her mother. You saw her face, the way she left us so hurriedly. Do you see the reason for her haste to flee now?"

Elizabeth forced herself to stand, willed herself to remain upright even though she was sick with fright. "It is a lie, no more than malicious gossip from servants who were probably just jealous of my mother

381

because Phillip liked her so much more than he liked them." The same evil jealousy she'd seen from Andrew's sisters, she thought with sudden insight. "Did you expect me to sit calmly and declare that fable you told us to be the truth?"

Matthew shook his head sadly. "I only wish it were a lie, to save us all the embarrassment of this terrible disgrace. The marriage has been annulled, erased from the Reverend William's church records so no reference to it will ever be found. That the ceremony was such a recent one was another rude shock to me, Andrew. Your whole marriage seems to have been founded on a web of lies." The weary man frowned as he turned to Elizabeth. "I'll give you a large dowry to attract another husband when you return to Oak Grove. You are exceptionally pretty. Surely some prosperous farmer will propose marriage, perhaps more than one."

Andrew's voice was bitter as he snarled, "Uncle, if Elizabeth is my sister then half of my inheritance is rightfully hers and I will gladly give her the portion which belongs to me also for I am leaving her tonight and I will never return!"

Matthew spoke calmly, his comments obviously well rehearsed. "Andrew, be sensible. Your marriage was a regrettable mistake, a tragic error, but it is fortunate I discovered the truth so promptly and that—"

Elizabeth shrieked her denial this time. "It is not the truth! You are the one who has woven the web of lies!" She turned toward her husband, pleading for his trust. "Andrew, you don't believe this wretched gossip could possibly be true!"

Andrew swore a bitter oath. The truth was plain in her eyes, her beautiful deep green eyes and the love which shone in their sparkling depths wrenched his heart in two. "Of course I believe it. Your own father, or rather that poor bastard who believes himself to be your father, told me our union was cursed and now I know the reason why happiness has eluded us so continually. We were never meant to be husband and wife. When you knew Marie Larson was your mother, why didn't you tell me that simple fact? It is obvious you've known what the truth is all along, so why are you denying it now? If you will lie to me after all we have shared, then our marriage is finished, for I do not want to be deceived by my own wife!"

"Andrew, I wouldn't lie to you. I didn't tell you about this because it's just not true and I didn't want you to worry over something which can never be proven one way or the other. That would have been cruel to taunt you with something which could have caused such needless pain."

"Cruel? To warn me of a possibility which is considered a sin everywhere?" Andrew's gaze filled with disgust at her treachery.

Elizabeth grasped frantically for the only knowledge she possessed which might convince him she had hidden nothing of any real value from him. "You never met my mother, Andrew, never saw my parents together. My mother simply adored my father, loved him as dearly as I love you, and she would never have lied to him, told him I was his child if truly I were not."

Andrew turned away to force the loveliness of her face from his view, but her image was as vivid as ever in his heart and he reached to put his hands upon her shoulders and looked her straight in the eye. "My dearest, when you have deceived me so readily to spare me pain, how can you still believe she would not have hidden such a secret from your father? It is obvious Olaf knows nothing of our blood tie or he would have given me that news swiftly to separate us for all time when we returned from the Seneca to his home. It is also plain you can't go home to him and destroy the beauty of your mother's memory with this story either. You must remain here. This is your rightful home. I am certain had my father lived only a few more weeks, days perhaps, he would have married your mother. I will be the one to leave, for we can no longer stay here together for you know full well I cannot regard you as a sister and to do otherwise now would bring disgrace upon both our families."

Alarmed, Matthew interrupted quickly. "She could still be your mistress, Andrew. Many gentlemen keep such a woman. It is possible to be discreet about such an alliance. There is no reason for you to give up your inheritance, or all I have built up to give to you!"

"Elizabeth is my very soul!" Andrew screamed at the frightened man, his fury exploding in a frantic cry. "If I cannot have her as my wife I must leave her! Can you understand nothing of love?"

"But where will you go?" Elizabeth's eyes were wide with terror. His clandestine meetings had already led him into the war. She knew they had. But that now he might plunge himself into the midst of the fighting horrified her. The rage which filled him that night would be more than sufficient to spur him into any battle, no matter how fierce or foolhardy the fight might be.

"I will go and do what I do best, sister dear. I will slaughter my fellow man as a warrior must. I will find the most savage band of rebels fighting this blasted war and join their number this very night."

Matthew Jordan's pale face grew ashen as he gasped, "No, dear God, no. Andrew, you must not go!"

Andrew scoffed at his uncle's plea. "Do not worry. I will not disgrace your name. I will again be Silver Hawk, blood thirsty savage, a renegade to the people who raised me as well as to your king!"

"I will come with you!" Elizabeth grabbed Andrew's sleeve, but he shoved her away.

"No! I cannot keep you, Elizabeth. I will not break your heart again and again and the secret we would share would destroy us both. We'd not dare have children, or any kind of home."

Elizabeth stepped back, shocked by his bitter rejection. Her soft voice was honey sweet, her words irresistibly inviting as she called to her husband. "Since Silver Hawk, son of Flaming Sky, has no father then neither do I. When will you see what I have always known? We belong together. I am your home."

Matthew's breath caught in his throat, his blood turning to ice in his veins and he shook with the chill. "The woman is a witch! She is a witch!" He tried to move away from her but his back was to the fireplace and he could not escape her hypnotic presence.

Andrew stood transfixed at the door, the light from the fire on the hearth blazing in his eyes as well as hers. "No, she's not a witch though she has enchanted me since the moment we met. Are you a prophet still, my beauty? Can you see my future even though you deny our common past?"

"Yes, and it is life I see, Indian, a long life you should spend with me," Elizabeth replied softly.

Andrew strode back to Elizabeth and swept her into his arms, kissing her with such brutal passion she staggered when he released her, but he grasped her narrow waist tightly to hold her fast. "Tell me the truth about this at least. If it can be proven beyond all doubt that our blood is the same, would you even care?"

"No. Were you my father himself I would still wish to be your wife I love you so," Elizabeth answered with a pride she couldn't hide. "There is no shame in our love, Andrew, no matter what you believe tonight. Look only into your own heart and you'll find the truth that must be seen."

A low moan of agony escaped Andrew's lips as he released her and sprinted from the room. The front door slammed shut with a crash which shook the entire house, but Elizabeth's words still rang in his ears. A curse, a blessing, he could not discern which and he ran on and on until his mind ceased to torment him with his loss and he felt only the agonizing pain which filled his lungs each time he gasped for breath.

Elizabeth fought the nausea which filled her throat and readily knew its cause. "You are too late, Uncle, too late to change what will be. I will prove your lies for the vile gossip they are. I swear I will. I will prove whatever I must to win Andrew back as my husband."

Matthew shrank away from the slender young woman who terrified him so and inched toward the safety of his own room, creeping along sideways as a crab goes scurrying through the rocks seeking the protection of his sea-drenched lair.

Elizabeth sank back down into her chair, stunned by the bitter rejection of the man she loved with all her heart. She prayed with unfailing conviction for God to protect him. She wanted him to feel the strength of her love surround him in spite of his doubts. She could not fault him, for it had been her own folly not to have told him Marie Larson was her mother. Surely if he had heard that first from her lips rather than his uncle's, he would have known whom to believe and would have kept her with him always.

Twenty=One

Elizabeth sat up in bed, her heart pounding wildly as the knocking at the door increased in both tempo and volume. "Just a moment, I'm coming!" Was it past dawn? Snow was falling steadily, obscuring the view from the window with a blanket of light gray and she had no idea how long she'd slept or what the hour might be as she rushed to open the door.

Mrs. Blackstone looked past Elizabeth into the room, her anxious gaze sweeping the unmade bed. "Mr. Andrew is not with you, Mrs. Jordan?"

"No. What is it? What's wrong?" The harried woman's question was urgent, but Elizabeth had no wish to explain why her husband could not be found by her side.

"It's his uncle, Mr. Matthew, he's taken ill. He's always downstairs before this. I had his breakfast ready to serve and when he didn't come for it as usual I went up to his room looking for him. He's still in his bed and he's so still, hardly breathing." The house-keeper's eyes filled with tears as she explained what she'd seen.

"What?" Elizabeth raced down the hall to the man's room and approached his bed hesitantly. "Uncle Matthew?" she whispered his name softly, but he did not turn toward her, just continued to stare up at the ceiling as if he were in the depths of a trance. "Mrs. Blackstone, you must send someone for Mr. Jordan's physician at once!" She waited, pacing anxiously up and down the lavishly furnished room until the housekeeper returned.

"Henry has gone for Dr. McCauley, Mrs. Jordan. Oh, dear, what shall we do?"

"We will wait patiently for him to arrive. That's all we can do. Now I want you to remain here while I go and dress. I'll be no more than a minute or two."

"Yes, Mrs. Jordan." The frightened woman pulled up a straight-backed chair and sat down at the foot of the bed, apparently not daring to go any closer to the ailing man.

Elizabeth could not imagine what could have happened to Matthew after he'd gone running from the library. He'd always been such a vigorous man, able to work long hours then talk half the night away with his friends. She'd slept in each morning, often taken brief afternoon naps or she could not have kept up with his social obligations and yet he never seemed to tire. Her thoughts spun about inside her mind as she pulled on her stockings and smoothed out her skirt. This was too much to bear, Andrew gone and now this terrible thing had happened to Matthew. She'd scarcely slept, wept more than rested all night and now there was this tragedy to face. When the doctor arrived, she was waiting at the front door to greet him.

"Dr. McCauley, I am Elizabeth Jordan. I believe we met once at a dinner party here. I thank you for coming so swiftly. Mr. Jordan seems to be dreadfully ill. I'll show you to his room."

The small dark-eyed man nodded slightly as he started up the staircase. "No need for that. I knew my way around this house before you were born, my dear." He went straight to Matthew's room and after sending Mrs. Blackstone to see to her other duties, examined his patient at length before coming out to discuss his diagnosis.

"Matthew seems to have suffered a stroke. It's too early to be certain, but the paralysis appears to be complete. Did he have some sort of shock? I think he is trying to say his nephew's name. I met the young man some months ago. Is he here?"

Elizabeth tried to reply calmly. "No, he is not. He left our home last night and I have no idea when he might return." If ever, she thought bitterly, but kept that to herself.

"What? Did they have some argument then? A quarrel which could have upset Matthew to this extent?"

Elizabeth saw Meg lingering at the end of the hall and took the physician's arm as she led him downstairs to the parlor. "Please, we need not discuss the circumstances in front of the household staff." She closed the door, knowing the servants would soon be gossiping no matter what she did or said. "The three of us had a long talk last night. We were all upset, my husband most of all. He has left Philadelphia and I have no idea where to reach him. How serious is this stroke of Mr. Jordan's? Won't he recover in time?" Yet as she remembered the rigid figure in the large bed, she already knew the answer.

"With the fine care I know you will provide for his comfort, he may improve somewhat, but he'll not be able to manage his business affairs or even leave his bed. You are a very young woman to be burdened with such responsibility. Are you certain your husband cannot be reached?"

"Positive. I don't even know where to begin a search for him." Then she recalled the many nights Andrew had gone out. If he had been meeting with men her Uncle William knew, she might be able to reach him through them. "I will try my best to let him know he is needed here."

"Good, I will leave detailed instructions for Matthew's care with his housekeeper. Hire extra help if you must, but don't try and care for him all by yourself, child."

As the man turned toward the door, Elizabeth reached out to touch his sleeve. "Dr. McCauley, did you mean what you said? Have you been Matthew's physician for many years?" Elizabeth moved in front of him, deftly blocking his way to the exit.

"I have known Matthew for more years than I care to count. Is that important for some reason? Do you doubt my qualifications? There are other physicians in the city. Do you wish to call another?"

Elizabeth hastened to reassure the man. "No, please don't misunderstand me. My only question is whether you might have known my husband's father. Were you Phillip's physician also?"

"Yes, but it saddens me to admit I was for I could do little for a man who sought death so eagerly as he, Mrs. Jordan. He was a wild one, a firebrand. I trust that while his son resembles him in appearance, his character is of a more admirable nature."

"Andrew is a fine man as I am certain his father was

also, despite your memories. I wonder though, if you might recall the young woman who was employed here as his nurse. Marie Larson was her name."

Dr. McCauley pursed his lips thoughtfully. "A nurse you say? That's not how I would have described Marie. She was far more to Phillip than that. More than a friend, too. She became his sole reason for existence, the very beat of his heart toward the end."

Elizabeth's knees grew weak and she leaned back against the solid oak door for support. "What a lovely compliment. You knew her well then?"

"No, she had time for no one but Phillip. I remember her for her devotion to him. It was a touching sight. The sweetness of her smile lit his entire room with happiness."

Elizabeth remembered the beauty of that smile fondly, too. "Marie was never a patient of yours herself, was she, Doctor?"

The slightly built man looked puzzled. "She was in perfect health, radiantly alive. Why would she have been a patient of mine?"

Elizabeth opened the door with a wide smile. "No reason. I thought perhaps she might have consulted you after Phillip's death."

"No. I've not seen her in all these years. You resemble her to a great degree, by the way. Have others remarked upon that also?"

Elizabeth lifted her chin proudly for there was no longer any reason to deny the truth. "Yes. Everyone here has noticed but it is not so remarkable. Marie Larson was my mother."

"Oh, my God!" Dr. McCauley's leather bag slipped from his grasp and he grabbed frantically to keep it from crashing to the floor.

"I see you have heard the gossip. Well, no matter. It was untrue." Elizabeth listened carefully as the man gave Mrs. Blackstone his instructions for Matthew, then walked him to the door. The ailing man's care would be exhausting, but she would see it was carried out precisely as the physician had prescribed.

It was late that afternoon before Elizabeth had a moment free and after summoning Henry to bring the carriage, she drew on her warmest cloak and opened the front door only to find Clayton St. James striding up the front steps. "Please excuse me, Colonel. I must be on my way and cannot invite you to come inside now."

The man frowned impatiently as he brushed aside her comment. "This is no social visit. What is this rumor I heard? Has Matthew really fallen seriously ill?"

Elizabeth shivered and pulled her cape closer to her throat. "How such sad news could have traveled so swiftly astounds me, sir, but it is true. Matthew has suffered a stroke and is gravely ill."

"Is he permitted visitors?" Clayton inquired solicitously.

While she found the man's concern surprising, Elizabeth had no time to waste in conversation and tried to slip past him to enter the waiting carriage. "No, not yet. Please excuse me. I have an errand to run and can tarry no longer."

The agile man barred her way rudely. "Does your husband permit you to travel about the city without an escort, Elizabeth?"

Elizabeth's eyes flashed angrily as she returned his

393

icy stare. "The street is filled with your troops, sir. Do you doubt they can protect me from harm?"

Clayton took Elizabeth's arm and led her down the steps, seeing that she was properly seated in the elegant carriage before he answered her taunt. "Your personal safety is not something I would trust to other men if I were Andrew."

"Which thank the good Lord you are not!" Elizabeth slammed her door shut and Henry called to the team, but to her great despair she found the egotistical officer following her carriage closely and frantically signaled Henry to change their destination to Madame Dupré's shop. She was not merely imagining she was being followed for the arrogant man made no attempt to be discreet in his pursuit but arrived at the dressmaker's at precisely the same moment as she.

"Why Elizabeth, you shock me. You have come to buy dresses when your husband's uncle is so dreadfully ill he cannot even see one of his dearest friends? Andrew will be ashamed to hear of this, of that I'm certain."

As Elizabeth paused at the door of the establishment she was outraged by the man's audacity. His dark eyes sparkled with mischief and she realized instantly he'd undoubtedly heard of Andrew's sudden departure from whomever had carried the news of Matthew's illness. She smiled innocently as she replied, "My husband is not in Philadelphia at the moment, sir, so if you wish to report my behavior you will have to wait until he returns."

Clayton nodded slightly, amazed by her candor. "And when will that be, madame?"

"I have no idea. Now good day. I cannot be late for my appointment." Elizabeth slipped through the door and waited several minutes before daring to peek through the curtains at the window to see if she were still being observed. To her horror she found Clayton St. James leaning against her carriage, nonchalantly awaiting her return. She jumped in fright then as the kindly Madame Dupré tapped her shoulder lightly.

"Mrs. Jordan, I did not mean to alarm you. Forgive me. What may I do for you today?"

Elizabeth asked for the first thing which entered her mind. "I need some new gloves. Do you have some nice ones I might see?"

"But of course. I have the loveliest gloves ever made. They are from France and as soft as an angel's wing. Come let me show you some."

Elizabeth cast a worried glance over her shoulder, but Clayton had not moved and she spent nearly an hour trying on pretty gloves before she selected three pairs and, carrying the small parcel, left the shop and exclaimed in surprise, "Why, Colonel St. James, have you been waiting for me all this time? I had no idea you were not busy with far more important duties."

Clayton smiled coldly, the curve of his lips not changing the dark light in his eyes. "As I said, your safety is a matter of great concern to me, Elizabeth. I will see you home but do not beg me to come in for tea for I have another appointment and cannot tarry."

Elizabeth did not even pretend to enjoy the verbal sparing St. James' words presented and quickly climbed into her carriage for the return to the Jordan house, but when she arrived she found the hostile officer nowhere near ready to depart. He again took her arm and escorted her to her front door.

"Since Matthew has taken ill and Andrew has left the city, I think it would be wise if I left one of my men here to safeguard your home. Do not trouble yourself on his behalf as I will see he is relieved by another guard shortly. Good day."

Elizabeth nodded briefly, then stepped through the door but once inside, she could no longer stifle her temper and yelled angrily, "That man knew! He knew Andrew had gone and I'll bet he knows exactly where he's gone, too!"

Meg came rushing in from the kitchen, and asked excitedly, "Did you call for me, Mrs. Jordan?"

"No, I'm sorry, Meg. I was only speaking to myself. How is my uncle? Has there been any change in the time I've been away?" She moved swiftly up the stairs to his room and glanced in the half open door.

"No, Mrs. Jordan. He is no better than he was this morning." Meg dried her eyes on her apron and sniffed loudly. "He is a good master, ma'am. He pays us well and is kinder than most. Whatever shall we do if he—"

"Meg, hush! The man can hear you!" Elizabeth shushed the foolish girl quickly. "I will stay with him for a while before it is time for his dinner. Now why don't you go and see if cook has it ready since Dr. McCauley requested something special for Mr. Jordan, and there will be no more talk of his not doing well. He is strong and may recover more swiftly than the physician thinks." But Elizabeth's optimism proved unfounded, for while Matthew hung onto life as the days passed, his improvement was slight and the change in his condition minimal. She went into his room frequently to encourage him in hopes the sound of her voice would give him some comfort but there was no sign that it did. If anything, her presence seemed to disturb him but still she continued to visit him as she felt she should.

While Matthew's many friends came frequently to inquire about him during the holidays, Stephanie MacFadden was the only woman among the many Elizabeth had met who continued to see her. She welcomed the sweet girl and taking her hand led her up the wide staircase to her room. "I hope you don't mind talking here, but the room is comfortable and I enjoy spending my time here." For it was that room, more than any other she'd shared with Andrew and her memories of him were sweetest there, but that was a secret she held too precious to reveal.

"What has happened, Elizabeth? I went home to Boston for Christmas and when I returned last night Esther told me about Matthew's illness and said Andrew had disappeared! I could not believe her gossip could have a grain of the truth. Please tell me what's happened." The sensitive girl was nearly in tears she was so worried about her friends.

"Andrew hasn't really disappeared. He's merely left the city, gone to do what he feels he must." Elizabeth sat down upon the window seat and curled up to get comfortable, then patted the cushion next to hers. "I can't possibly tell you why this has happened. Please don't ask me to explain, but our marriage has been annulled and my husband felt he had to leave. He took nothing with him in his haste to depart and I am desperately worried about him for Andrew is usually a coolly logical man and that was not his mood that night." Elizabeth paused to glance over at her friend. They were so completely different, had lived lives which would never have crossed paths had Andrew not brought her there to Philadelphia to live. She could easily tell she'd only confused Stephanie all the more by her brief explanation of her circumstances.

Stephanie's mouth fell agape as she sat down. "You mean Andrew has left you to join the Patriots? Is that what he's done? But how could he have turned his back on you, or on his uncle, and how could he have forsaken his loyalty to the king?"

Elizabeth tried not to laugh, but that question was truly ludicrous. "Stephanie, I'll say nothing about our marriage for that is a private matter, but you must remember Andrew has lived most of his life as an Indian brave, not as a loyal subject of the Crown. He cannot be faulted for what he is, nor can any of those who have sided with the Patriots."

Stephanie was hopelessly perplexed by Elizabeth's revelations and removed her gloves with nervous tugs while she tried to phrase her next statement in the most logical manner. "Clayton St. James was at our home this morning. I don't like him one bit, Elizabeth. I thought I heard him mention Andrew's name although I didn't overhear Esther's reply."

Elizabeth leaned back against the window sill. "Yes, I know that spider has already thrown out his web. He has a score to settle with my husband and probably thinks he'll gain the upper hand now, but he's mistaken. He'll never take Andrew alive."

"Elizabeth, what are you saying?" Stephanie squealed in horror. "How can you say such a dreadful thing? How can you even think it?"

398

Elizabeth smiled softly as she glanced out at the drifting snow, her mind's eye focusing upon another scene entirely, a day in early spring, drenched in sunlight and filled with promise. "When first I saw Andrew he was a sorry sight, Stephanie, cut and bleeding but so strong and proud, with a defiant light in those green eyes of his which turned my blood to fire. He is simply all a man should be, the very best of manhood and the likes of St. James will never touch him or even come close."

Stephanie waited a long moment and when Elizabeth said no more she spoke slowly, "I think I know how Andrew feels. I have questioned my father's position time and again. These last few days while I was home were no exception. It doesn't seem wrong for the Colonies to want to be free of a king who is so distant in both location and affection from us. What need have we of a sovereign here in this new land?"

"Why Stephanie, you sound exactly as I once did!" Elizabeth laughed in delighted surprise. "If Andrew is in fact fighting with the Continental Army, then the only thing which will keep me safe here is that St. James will not dare harm me when Matthew is so powerful an ally. While he lies ill, his future so uncertain, nothing will happen to me, but I am worried about your coming here. Perhaps it is too dangerous for us to be friends."

Stephanie rose to her feet and lifted her chin proudly. "I may be shy, but I'm no coward, Elizabeth. We can still be friends if you'll allow it."

Elizabeth stood and hugged the slender girl warmly. "Of course I want your friendship. You are my dearest friend, the only one I have now that Andrew is gone."

The young women parted company reluctantly, neither certain of what the future would bring.

Without Andrew's loving presence, Elizabeth felt lost and unwanted in the Jordan home. She wandered the rooms, sadly recalling the happy days she'd spent there with her husband and could not believe she would not know that joy again. She had decided against visiting her Uncle William for there was still a British soldier stationed in front of the house at all times and she knew the man was on duty to report on her activities rather than to offer assistance should Matthew's condition suddenly worsen. Her path to her uncle's would be followed. Perhaps then his activities would be monitored and he and his friends arrested. It was a possibility which worried her daily, and she had no desire to see harm come to her relatives and so stayed away. Then one late afternoon, when the sun had already begun to set, her aunt appeared at the front door.

"Aunt Rebecca!" Elizabeth greeted the tiny woman affectionately, ushered her into the parlor and shut the doors so their conversation could not be overheard. "I have thought of you so often and wanted very badly to come and see you but—"

"Yes, we know what has happened, all of it." The diminutive woman glanced about the room nervously as she perched on the edge of her chair. "I came because we knew your home was being watched and it was too dangerous for you to come to us."

Elizabeth stared at her aunt, surprised the woman was aware of her predicament. "Has William heard anything from Andrew? Does he know where he is or how I might reach him?"

Rebecca brought her fingertip to her lips in a gentle warning. "It is difficult to pass messages but it can be done. We do know Andrew was with Washington's men last week at Princeton, when the Patriots handed Cornwallis a sound thrashing."

"He was not injured?" Elizabeth whispered softly, afraid to hear the reply.

"No, he was not harmed. Both Armies will not retire for the winter as the weather is now too harsh. Washington will be in Morristown, but Andrew will most probably not remain with him for long."

Elizabeth nodded sadly. "Andrew wanted no part of the Continental Army, but I didn't think he would leave them so swiftly once he'd joined their forces."

Rebecca frowned impatiently. "No, you do not understand. Andrew will be sent on other missions and he will continue to do what he has been doing for us, passing information to the people who need it most."

Meetings he had said, discussions with men whose ideas had interested him. He'd said that merely to reassure her when he'd been spying all along. Suddenly Elizabeth gasped as everything became painfully clear. "Dear God, Andrew's always been a spy, hasn't he? Before John Cummins caught him, he was many days journey from his home and I never asked him why he was so far south all alone." Elizabeth was aghast she could have been so foolish that she had not even suspected her husband's activities had a hidden purpose.

Rebecca moved quickly to her niece's side. "You must not think of spying as evil, Elizabeth, for it is not. Andrew is clever, very wise. He merely told us what he could not help but observe. I don't know how long he has been on our side, perhaps no more than a few weeks, nor do I know this John Cummins of whom you speak, but you must not be ashamed of your husband's deeds when they are such brave ones."

Elizabeth took a deep breath to regain her composure and squared her shoulders. "No, I am not in the least bit ashamed of Andrew, no matter what he's done, but I have reason to believe the British suspected something even before he left for Colonel St. James was here the very next afternoon looking for him. He may have avoided capture by the slimmest of margins and surely Uncle William and all his friends are in terrible danger, too."

Rebecca smiled knowingly. "They are grown men, Elizabeth. They know the risks of their actions but had one of their meetings been raided, the British would have found no more than a friendly game of cards, no weapons, maps, propaganda, nothing which would have pointed to treason. It is the idea of freedom which cannot be contained now. We will win this war. We will. Washington's victory at Princeton has given us all renewed hope that the British can be defeated and no more lives lost in our cause."

As Elizabeth sat listening to her aunt speak of the rebellion, an idea slowly began to take shape in her mind. She could not beg Andrew to come home. She had no proof as yet to still his fears and once he'd left to join the army he could not return to his former life managing the Jordan enterprises. But even if he could not come home to her, there was something she could do to help him. "Aunt Rebecca, I can do so little here. I must care for Andrew's uncle, but it is obvious to me now he will never recover sufficiently to return to his business. Andrew was most distressed by his uncle's practice of asking increasingly higher prices for goods in short supply and I know what he would do were he to take over the running of the warehouse now."

Rebecca interrupted hesitantly. "But Elizabeth, what has that to do with us?"

"Just listen for a moment. I will send for Stephen Haywood, Mr. Jordan's attorney, and have him supervise the sale of all the goods remaining in the inventory at present. What we'll sell first will be the luxury items, silks, brocades, whatever will command a high price and then I'll take the profits from that and give it to you to give to my uncle's friends so they may pose as merchants and purchase from Mr. Haywood whatever the Army needs, blankets, foodstuffs, anything of value. Then when the money is again in my hands, I'll simply donate it to General Washington to use to purchase arms and ammunition."

Rebecca Peterson clapped her hands in delight. "Elizabeth! That is too wonderful to be true! But wait a moment. The British will be able to trace such a large contribution to its source. We cannot risk your being imprisoned, even for so worthy a cause as this."

Elizabeth leaned back in her chair, a thoughtful frown gracing her brow as she contemplated that dilemma. At last she leaned forward and smiled. "We will have to stage a robbery then, to make it look as though I had no part in helping the Patriots. I will merely sell everything off because I am not able to run the business by myself and then I'll be robbed of all I've earned. I will summon Mr. Haywood in the morning and we'll put the first part of this plan

403

into action."

As Rebecca rose to leave she took Elizabeth's hands in hers. "I think Andrew made a great mistake in not confiding in you, my dear. I will see that he learns of what you are doing to help him win this dreadful war."

"No, that is unnecessary, Aunt Rebecca. If any message can be sent, tell my husband only that I wish him well in all he undertakes and that I'll do my best to see he has a home to which to return at the war's end." She closed and bolted the front door before peeking through the curtains to observe her aunt's progress past the soldier who stood lounging against the steps. He didn't even turn to watch the small, ill-clothed lady pass by and Elizabeth smiled, certain her plan would succeed.

Stephen Haywood had come to the house several times to inquire about Matthew's health and did not think it odd when Elizabeth asked him to remain for a few moments to discuss a business matter, but when she explained what she wished him to do, he was astonished.

"But Mrs. Jordan, what you suggest is preposterous!"

"As I understand it, my name is again Miss Peterson, is it not?" Elizabeth sat with her hands firmly clasped in her lap, intent upon having her own way that morning.

"Well, yes, as a matter of fact, I suppose it is, but—"

"Then please address me as Miss Peterson, or if you prefer I use my natural father's name, call me Miss Jordan, but do not refer to me as Mrs. Jordan again unless my marriage is to be recognized for the legal one

404

it is."

The attorney took out his handkerchief and wiped his perspiring forehead in a vain attempt to regain his composure. "I did no more than check up on your mother's past, Mrs., ah, Miss Peterson, the date she married, the date you were born, the date of your own marriage to Andrew, matters of public record. You cannot blame me for the unfortunate result of my inquiries."

"Of course not. You are as innocent in this matter as I am, aren't you? That's beside the point now, however. I want that warehouse emptied as soon as possible. My uncle cannot manage it properly, Andrew had no wish to, and I simply refuse to devote any of my time to the business when my uncle is so ill and requires my constant care and attention. When the war is over, should Andrew wish to resume the activity of the company, he will have the capital I'll raise to reinvest. I have no intention of squandering the profits of this sale, Mr. Haywood. On the contrary, it is a fortune I'll guard very well."

Stephen Haywood did not doubt the seriousness of the young woman's words for a moment. One way or another she was a Jordan and for the time being obviously taking charge of the family affairs. "Matthew's business interests are extensive, Mrs., Miss Peterson. Disposing of the inventory of the warehouse will be tedious, but I will give it my immediate attention."

"Good. First I would like a full accounting of what is currently on hand and its present price. Can you bring that by to me this afternoon? I would like the items of higher quality to be sold off first, at slightly reduced prices, then the other items can be sold at bargain rates and we won't have to worry that any valuable commodities will be damaged if a large crowd assembles."

"That is a wise decision, Miss Peterson. That can be done easily and I'll return this afternoon, shall we say at three?"

Elizabeth smiled sweetly as she rose to bid him good day. "Thank you, Mr. Haywood. I knew I could trust you to help me. It is so difficult for me to have so much responsibility. Can I call upon you for further advice and assistance?" She batted her long eyelashes coyly as she'd seen Esther do and the man actually began to blush.

"Of course, your servant, miss." The attorney left to complete his assignment promptly as he tried to recall when he'd last met such an attractive young woman, and one with such incredible wealth.

Word traveled rapidly among the finer families of Philadelphia that all the imported items they'd longed to purchase as they'd done in years past were going on sale at reduced prices at the Jordan warehouse and they rushed to send representatives to bid on the items they wanted so as not to miss such a splendid opportunity. In less than a week's time, every bolt of silk and velvet was gone, along with all the delicate crystal from Italy, and the fine china from France. Exotic perfumes and exquisite lace, heavy silver cutlery and the finest in brilliant gemstones all made their way into the homes of the prominent Loyalists leaving the warehouse stocked with only the most mundane of stores in which they had no interest whatsoever.

That weekend, Rebecca Peterson again called at the Jordan home, bringing a wicker basket which was filled with ripe oranges when she left. At least the basket appeared to be laden with the tangy fruit but in fact held sufficient gold to purchase every item left in the warehouse which would be useful to the Continental Army.

Colonel St. James observed the activity at the Jordan loading docks with distinct boredom. Elizabeth had paid several visits to the establishment, but had stayed only briefly and he had lost interest in watching her activities when they were so routine. She went so few places, he could predict her destination from the direction she chose upon leaving her home and, finding no challenge in such a pursuit, soon delegated the job to one of his lieutenants. The young woman continued to fascinate him, however, and he made a point of stopping by her home nearly every day to offer some words of encouragement to Matthew even if he received slight response from the ailing man for it provided his only chance to speak to the lovely blonde.

Elizabeth made no pretense of enjoying St. James' incessant visits. The man seemed to be forever arriving or leaving, and he paid Mrs. Blackstone such outlandish compliments the woman allowed him free run of the large home. But to find him outside her bedroom door upon waking in the morning was too much for her to bear in silence. "Colonel, don't you think you might pay your calls to my uncle at a more reasonable hour? It is barely dawn." Elizabeth slammed her door shut for emphasis. She'd slept poorly and was fighting off the nausea which continued to plague her mornings.

"Forgive me. I was merely leaving Matthew's room and had no intention of disturbing you. He is always awake this early and does not seem to find my visits disagreeable." The tall man followed her down the stairs and stood waiting for an invitation to remain for breakfast and when none was offered, he suggested it himself. "I have been meaning to speak with you, Elizabeth. Perhaps over breakfast would be a good opportunity as neither of us has any time to waste."

"Breakfast, Colonel?" Elizabeth turned toward the dining room with no hope of discouraging the man. He simply ignored her obvious dislike of him and she lacked the energy to fight with him that day. "I am not fully awake before ten. I hope you will not find my lack of conversation rude." She slid into her chair without his assistance and rang the small silver bell for service.

Clayton chose the seat opposite hers and grinned wickedly. "Just listen to me then, my dear, for I have news of the most fascinating sort."

"I beg you to repeat your tales of the war to my uncle, as they do not interest me in the slightest." She placed her napkin in her lap and covered a yawn with no real haste.

"This story will amuse you, however. It seems there is an Indian brave with rather remarkable powers. He can appear in one location at dawn and at another many miles distant before noon. He is sometimes alone, more often with a band of his own kind, but wherever he steps, destruction follows in his wake."

"Is that a fact?" Elizabeth eyed the man coldly, certain he was about to announce some truly ghastly deed she knew she didn't want to hear. "Indians are cunning creatures, Colonel. Is this man of whom you speak one of your own forces?"

"He is a renegade, no more, a man who survives on his own lust for vengeance. He is responsible for a growing amount of unrest and, while the Continental Army as well as our own remain in their winter quarters, this outlaw roams the countryside searching out those who are loyal to King George and setting a torch to their property. Sometimes it is one house in a small village, ten homes in another."

"Why should I be interested in that tale? Keeping the peace is your job, isn't it, not mine?" Yet, a slow smile curved across her pretty lips. Set the sky in flames, Andrew, she thought proudly and was pleased he was causing such havoc for the British. "That you are unable to provide protection for Loyalists must cause considerable problems for you. These Indians are merely burning farmhouses, not taking any prisoners, though?"

The colonel shifted uncomfortably in his chair as Meg entered with their breakfast on a silver platter. He waited until they were again alone to complete his story. "At times they do take some captives, never women and children, men only, and those they release some miles away after confiscating their clothes."

Elizabeth tried to suppress her laughter but failed. "How perfectly dreadful. In the chill of winter that is severe punishment indeed."

"It will not seem so funny to you when I apprehend these men, Elizabeth, and I promise you that I will," he vowed in a hoarse snarl.

"Will it not be a challenge to find this band if they

are seen at such distant locations? Are you certain it is not many small bands, raiding parties using the confusion of the war to cover their own thievery?"

"What?" The man's dark eyes filled with puzzlement. "That is impossible. Such groups would attack indiscriminately. These savages prey only upon those loyal to our king."

Elizabeth nodded slowly. "I see. Well, do you think our home is in danger? Has anyone been attacked here in Philadelphia?"

"No, of course not. I said at the beginning that these felons were roaming the countryside, not preying upon city dwellers!" he snapped angrily.

"Oh, yes, so you did. Will you excuse me, sir? I have an appointment at the warehouse and will be late if I do not hurry." As Elizabeth left the room, Clayton stared after her only briefly, then picked up his fork and began to eat with a hearty appetite.

Elizabeth traversed her usual route to the Jordan building. Wagons were waiting to be loaded, merchants milling about as the final consignments were sold, and she made no attempt to recognize any of the men for to do so would bring danger to both herself and them. She walked into the small offices and found Stephen Haywood poring over a thick ledger. "I had hoped to see this all finished by now, Mr. Haywood, and yet the building still appears to be full to the rafters."

"That it does." The man chuckled as he stood to greet her. "Everything is sold, however. I am making out the receipts now. The drivers will present these and then pick up their goods. The warehouse will be emptied shortly, I can assure you, as most buyers are anxious to return home with their wares."

Elizabeth glanced down the list of merchants, but recognized none of the names. Some receipts were made out to men from towns many miles distant and she wondered how her uncle had managed to accomplish that trick. "You have the last of the money then? I will take it with me now."

"I doubt the wisdom of your having so much in your home, Miss Peterson. These are perilous times. If something should—"

"Nonsense, Mr. Haywood. Our home is well protected, as safe as any," Elizabeth reassured him quickly and, taking the sachel bearing the last of the money, left for the Jordan home. She had left a generous bonus for all the employees of the warehouse and gave her thoughts to the next phase of her plan. The robbery was to take place three days hence, at dawn. The men were to sneak in, pick up the money, then leave the house in a shambles as if they'd searched everywhere for more than they'd found. Rebecca had told her the names of none of the men who would pose as the thieves, but she certainly hoped no true villains would appear to steal the gold before the Patriots could seize it.

The grandfather clock on the landing had just struck two when the man's hand closed over Elizabeth's mouth, bringing her fully awake as she struggled frantically against his grasp until he whispered softly in her ear, "I am your cousin, Thomas. I'll not harm you. Let me bring the lantern and you'll see."

411

Elizabeth sat up, ready to scream for help should the need arise, yet as the young man released her and brought the light to her bedside, she recognized him instantly as her kin. "Why, Thomas, you are the image of your father!"

"Aye, that I am, except I have our Grandmother Peterson's green eyes, the same as you do."

"What? Come closer, Thomas. I can't see you well enough." Elizabeth peered up at her cousin, unmindful of the lovely figure she presented in her lace nightgown with her blond curls spilling about her shoulders in wild disarray. "Your eyes are green, aren't they, as green as mine!"

"Yes, and so are my sister's. Now, why does that please you so?" The handsome man gave her a hug, then stepped back to admire her from a more discreet distance.

"The color of my eyes has presented something of a riddle of late, that's all. There's no time to explain more than to say it is important to me to know my father's mother had eyes like mine. Now, why have you come tonight rather than waiting the three days as we'd planned? Has something gone amiss? Where are the others? Have you come all alone?" Elizabeth glanced furtively about the room, but saw to her great relief they were alone.

"My men are downstairs, tipping over the furnishings with the stealth of mice so your servants won't be awakened. Haywood was overheard criticizing you for keeping all he'd taken in these past few weeks and if he said it to one customer, he most likely said it to others, and not all those who bought supplies from the Jordan

412

warehouse were our men and therefore trustworthy. There is no end to the greed in this world, Elizabeth, and you are not safe here if anyone truly wishes to take your uncle's wealth by force."

"I'm certain you are right, but what of you and your companions? Will you be able to leave the city safely?"

"Yes. There are many of us. The plan will work well and the army will be better outfitted soon, thanks to your generosity. I must leave now, dear cousin, though I hope we'll meet again when the Colonies are free."

Elizabeth scampered out of the high bed and brought the sachel from its hiding place in the adjacent room. When Thomas took it from her, she leaned up to kiss his cheek softly. "If you see Andrew, my husband—"

"I have not met the man, Elizabeth, nor am I likely to either, although I have heard his name. He travels with the speed of the wind, undaunted by the snows of winter, and I doubt we will meet until spring, and only then if he returns to fight with the army. I'll see he learns of this though, as it will surely please him."

Elizabeth laid her small hands upon his. "I beg of you to find him, Thomas, and say only that you are my cousin and bring my love. I want so desperately for him to know I do not hate him."

Thomas blushed, embarrassed by the depth of her obvious devotion to her husband and smiled as he apologized, "I must bind your hands and feet, Elizabeth, then I'll throw most of your possessions about. Otherwise, it will be plain this was no theft."

"Do what you must, and be quick about it, for I want you safely away before dawn." Elizabeth returned to her bed and, although he bound her hands and feet snugly, she was not uncomfortable as she rested, too excited to sleep as she listened to the sounds of Thomas' exit from the house. She heard no cries of alarm and knew he and his friends had been successful in their escape. When Mrs. Blackstone came screaming into her bedroom the next morning, she had her statement of what had transpired during the night so well rehearsed, the hysterical woman never doubted for a second that the house had been vandalized by the meanest of bullies and went running to summon the authorities immediately.

While her servants were fooled, Clayton St. James was not. He paced up and down the parlor, his long stride never varying as he interrogated her with undisguised sarcasm. "This house seems to be alive with intrigues, Elizabeth. That it could have been robbed strikes me as doubtful."

Elizabeth's eyes grew enormous with bewilderment. "Why, Colonel, how can you call the series of tragic misfortunes which has befallen us intrigues?" She lifted her lace trimmed handkerchief to wipe away a nonexistent tear and turned her most innocent glance upon him.

"That Matthew is so severely stricken is indeed a misfortune, that Andrew showed his true colors by fleeing to the Colonists was not, nor was the fact that so large a sum has disappeared from your possession!"

Elizabeth gestured helplessly. "Do you wish to conduct your own search, sir? I will open the house to

414

your men should you wish to do so. Your own guard saw I did not leave my home from the time I returned from the warehouse with the money and the time of the robbery last night."

Clayton glared angrily, his temper beyond his power to restrain. "Do not presume that my affection for Matthew extends to you, Elizabeth! I intend to regard this so-called theft as a military matter and pursue it to its conclusion." He continued to stroll up and down in front of her for some minutes, not speaking, but his mood plain.

Elizabeth glanced down, trying to appear subdued when she wanted to scream. "Presume upon his affection" indeed! The man had no end of arrogance and she ceased to listen as he again began a bitter tirade until he reached out to lift her chin with a vicious snap.

"If you were not a party to this treachery, how do you explain the peculiar fact you were not raped by these men who pillaged your bedroom?"

Elizabeth's face flooded with color as she recoiled from his touch. "Not all men have such insatiable lusts as you, sir!" Instantly she regretted that outburst for Clayton's face grew dark with rage and she thought he would surely strike her a savage blow for such insolence, but he did not, although his next question had the same power to wound.

"Why did you not inform me Andrew is no longer your husband?"

"Andrew will always be my husband, always. I'll never say otherwise," Elizabeth forced herself to reply calmly, but she was shocked he had learned of the annulment and wondered what the source of that knowledge could be.

"Regardless of what you may state, your attorney informed me you are no longer Andrew's wife. It is a matter of public record. The annulment was filed through the courts and cannot be disputed, no matter what lies you tell."

Elizabeth sat quite still, uncertain as to what the man wanted of her now. She would offer no explanation, no confessions, no apologies, nothing, for she despised him most thoroughly and would give him no help willingly.

"Well?" Clayton stood directly in front of her, glaring fiercely, as if his mere presence were enough to command respect if his rank were not.

"I beg your pardon, did you ask me a question?" Elizabeth took a deep breath and let it out slowly. Perhaps she no longer had the protection she'd thought she did in Matthew's home and for the first time she felt afraid, truly afraid of the man's power and what he could so easily do to her life.

"Your situation in this city is a tenuous one, Miss Peterson, or do you plan to revert to your first husband's name? No matter, I will not allow you to reside in this house if your sympathies continue to lie so clearly with Andrew rather than his uncle! You will not syphon off any more of Matthew's wealth for the traitors to King George who have the audacity to call themselves 'Patriots'!"

"Are you ordering me to vacate this house? Is that what you're doing?" Elizabeth knew he had such authority, but wondered if he'd dare to use it.

416

"No, not at all, merely demanding that you place your loyalty where it rightfully belongs." Clayton paused a moment, then spoke in a far softer tone, his change of mood surprising her all the more. "You give Matthew the finest of care. I can see that, but you are a young and attractive woman, Elizabeth. Since you are no longer wed, and Matthew is unable to entertain and provide companionship for you, I will take it upon myself to see you're never left without an escort."

Elizabeth read the man's intention clearly in the devious shine of his dark eyes. They gleamed like obsidian and she could not suppress a shudder, yet replied sweetly, "I cannot allow you to do that, sir, for being seen with me can only damage your own reputation."

"I will worry over the quality attached to my name, you needn't!" he shouted hoarsely.

Elizabeth rose slowly to avoid his touch and stepped away as she replied, "I have a good reason for avoiding all social obligations, sir, as you were so swift to point out. My marriage is no longer a legal one, but I am carrying my husband's child, a condition I shall not be able to hide much longer, nor do I wish to deny the existence of a child created out of love. So you see, my circumstances do not allow me to accept your attentions, though I will always remember your kindness to me." Elizabeth nearly choked on that compliment but managed to say it in a convincing fashion.

Clayton St. James gave a furious gasp as he saw the woman he wanted so desperately snatched from his grasp. He turned and left the house and on his subsequent visits to see Matthew he did not once seek out Elizabeth's company, nor acknowledge her presence in the home in any way. That he would insult her so rudely did not offend her in the slightest, however, for the less she saw of the despicable Colonel St. James the better she liked it.

Twenty-Two

The sameness of her days made time pass slowly for Elizabeth, but the dreary winter of 1777 gradually turned to spring, then drifted on to early summer and she found facing the uncertainty which filled her life nearly impossible. Matthew improved somewhat, but he was not strong enough to care for himself and he spoke little, apparently embarrassed by the stumbling results of his attempts at communication and his mood was often sullen and withdrawn. She read to him daily, without fail. Although he offered no sign he was grateful, she considered it a duty she would not shirk regardless of how little she was appreciated. She was certain the memory of the ghastly scene they'd had the night Andrew had run from the house was still in his mind as it was in hers, but she did her best to ease the boredom of his days. While she made no effort to disguise her pregnancy, the man had never remarked upon the obvious change in her figure so neither did she. She saw no point in bringing up the subject since he could not demand she leave his home as he knew she had nowhere to go.

Andrew was never far from her thoughts. She slept only fitfully without his comforting presence and longed for his loving warmth. The night her cousin had entered her room now seemed to have only been a dream, not truly reality, but the faintest of memories which teased her mind like a forgotten name which must be remembered. If only Thomas had been home when she and Andrew had gone to call, if only she'd met her father's mother even once, but the dear lady had been dead for some years before she was born. Her deep green eyes peered back at her from every mirror, a taunting reminder of her beloved's face, and she could not forget for an instant the dreadful way they'd parted. Was he angry still or did he long to know her love again as she hoped for his? As she lay in bed each night, her sole company was the child who grew within her slender body and the many tiny kicks she felt were her only source of hope for the future. She would laugh softly and think of the son who would soon be born. He would be a boy Andrew would be proud to claim. She was certain of that.

As the day was a warm one, Stephanie had dressed in a new summer outfit and the deep blue of the sheer fabric made her light eyes sparkle with the reflected color. Whenever she visited she would bring whatever news she could, for the fighting was vigorous and bulletins were published daily. Indians were often listed among the combatants as well as the casualties but never by name. "I am sorry I can do no better than this, Elizabeth," the sweet girl apologized sadly. "I keep hoping we'll have some news of Andrew, but we never do. General Burgoyne's exploits are well documented. He's come down from Canada far too easily. If his forces cross the Hudson, I shudder to think how we'll stop them."

"I don't really expect to read Andrew's name in the headlines as though he were a general. Do not fret so for I am confident he is safe and well." Why she chose to believe that she didn't know, but believe it she did. "Perhaps it is this glorious weather that has lured me into complacency, but I feel Andrew is in no danger. I am not even certain what he is calling himself, whether he wears buckskins or the uniform of an officer, so I shall simply have to have faith in his considerable abilities to care for himself, as the war bulletins will never tell me what I truly wish to know." She read the brief description Stephanie had brought then tossed it aside, too restless to consider General Burgoyne's threat to the Continental Army.

Stephanie watched Elizabeth move slowly toward the window of her room and asked shyly, "Summer is already here. Isn't the baby due soon?"

Elizabeth laughed as she placed her hands over her swollen waistline. "Indeed he is. Andrew would be greatly amused if he could see me now. I can scarcely walk. Traversing the stairs is almost too much for me, so I don't think it will be many more days before the child is born."

"Yet, Andrew has no idea he will soon become a father? He did not even suspect the truth before he left?" When she knew how close the couple had been, she found that difficult to accept.

"No," Elizabeth responded softly. "It was a secret I wished to keep for a while and the weeks before he left were such busy ones for him I doubt he even considered I might be pregnant again. Then, suddenly he was gone and I had no opportunity to reveal we might have another son."

"How can you be so calm about this, Elizabeth? You seem so composed and yet—" Stephanie paused, unable to find a tactful way to express her thoughts.

"And yet I have no right to be?" Elizabeth smiled at her friend's innocence. "I can only trust in the love Andrew once had for me and pray he will come home. I want him to find both me and our child well and strong. I would have no hope at all, no reason to exist, if I truly thought he'd never return."

"I envy you so, Elizabeth, for you have known the true beauty of love and I'm sadly afraid I never will."

"You are very young to believe your future will be so bleak, Stephanie. Have you never had a beau?" Elizabeth teased her good friend with playful affection. "I find it impossible to believe you have not. If you have none here in Philadelphia, is there no man in Boston who is waiting for you to return?"

Stephanie fidgeted nervously with her handkerchief before she finally confessed. "There was a man, somewhat older than I, a friend of my father's, and I always thought he was rather fond of me, although he never did actually tell me so."

"Are you fond of him?" Elizabeth sat down on the window seat carefully, none too comfortable no matter what her pose.

"Well, I, I really don't know. Perhaps I was but it's too late now for he married a young widow last November." Stephanie blinked away her tears, obviously more deeply affected than she cared to admit.

Elizabeth was too close to such pain herself not to understand Stephanie's sorrow. "I'm sorry you were hurt, but had the man loved you he would have followed you here, at least sent letters. He would have let you know he was waiting for you to return to Boston, not simply married another young woman when you were no longer within easy reach. He sounds very fickle to me, and I think you're better off without him. Now don't let that experience trouble you for there must be a nice man just waiting to meet you who will adore you and let you know it, too."

Stephanie could not help but smile at Elizabeth's enthusiastic encouragement and her pale cheeks lit with a happy glow of pink. "You make me want to believe you, Elizabeth. When I see how dearly you love your husband, I mean, Andrew." She looked down quickly, embarrassed by that slip of the tongue.

"He is my husband still, Stephanie. He'll always be for I shall never want another." Elizabeth yawned noisily then giggled. "Forgive me, I'd like to lie down for a nap. Will you come to see me again soon?"

"Of course, if not tomorrow then the next day." Stephanie gave her friend a light kiss upon the cheek as she prepared to leave. "Will you send for me when your time comes? Since Andrew cannot be with you, I will come to help if I may."

Elizabeth turned away to hide her anxiety. "Thank you for your kindness, but if it is anything like the birth of my first child, I do not want you to have to witness it."

"Oh, Elizabeth, are you so very frightened? I thought Dr. McCauley knew an excellent midwife. Won't she be able to ease the birth with her skill?"

"The midwife has a fine reputation, but none can truly help, Stephanie. A woman must bear her child alone no matter how many stand by to assist her."

"I still want to come. Don't think I'll be afraid because I won't and if it's going to be awful for you, I'll not leave you with a stranger!" the shy girl insisted emphatically.

"If you must be here then I'll try and send for you. Now you should be on your way for the afternoon is nearly gone." Elizabeth stood at the window to wave as her friend left the house but despite her words of agreement, she had no intention of making the frail girl suffer along with her as she was certain she would and forced back her fears. "Oh, Andrew, I will need your courage as desperately as I did before, and where will you be?"

As chance would have it, Elizabeth and Stephanie were together, sitting in the garden drinking in the fragrance of the blossoming summer flowers when her labor began. She had been restless all day, but tried to appear interested in Stephanie's description of the latest of Esther's parties. Her mind was wandering though, returning again and again to the lovely days of the previous summer which she'd spent so happily with Andrew. She missed him more each day and no matter how much time she spent in the company of others, her deep need for him was undiminished. The perfume of the flowers was heavy upon the air, the day humid, and she thought perhaps the heat was the cause of the dull ache which throbbed in her back with annoying frequency.

"Elizabeth?" Stephanie leaned forward to tap her knee. "Are you ill? You've grown so pale. Perhaps we should go back inside now so you might lie down."

Nodding in agreement, Elizabeth began to rise, but the ground suddenly lurched beneath her feet. The bright colors of the flowers blurred before her eyes and she swayed, too dizzy to take a step and risk falling. When Stephanie rushed to ease her back into her chair, she was breathless. "It's the heat I'm afraid, though I'll be no more comfortable inside. I'll just rest a moment more and then go up to my room."

"You'll do no such thing. You stay right here where you are and I'll summon Henry or one of the other men to carry you. I'll not chance having you fall and hurt yourself or the baby." She wasn't fooled, for Elizabeth seemed far from well.

"No, Stephanie, please—" But the young woman was already halfway across the garden, rushing to bring help and didn't hear her feeble protests. Elizabeth took several deep breaths, but felt no better and grew frightened. What if she should faint before assistance arrived? She sat back in her chair and held on tightly, but that only made her dizziness worse. When next she looked up, she could recognize the man who stood before her only by the brilliant shade of his red coat.

"Are you ill?" Without waiting for a reply Clayton scooped up the young woman and carried her across the garden toward the house. "I was just leaving when Stephanie found me. She's gone to fetch the doctor as you apparently gave her quite a fright."

Elizabeth was appalled to be the subject of such unwanted attention from the Englishman, but had no choice other than to wrap her arms around his neck and rest her head upon his shoulder. "I'm sorry to be such a bother," she offered hesitantly, but she couldn't bring herself to thank him for carrying her.

"Shall I take you up to your room or into the parlor?" Clayton shifted her slight weight easily in his arms before taking her through the door.

"My room, please."

"It is a great pity you've not thought to invite me up to your bedroom before this, Elizabeth. Today seems most inopportune."

Elizabeth blushed deeply under that taunt but kept silent. Any conversation she began he would twist to his own purpose and she had no desire to prolong his stay in her room.

After Clayton had laid her gently upon the large bed, he stepped back to survey the room with a skeptical glance. "This is obviously no lady's bed chamber. Why do you call it yours?"

Elizabeth relaxed against the pillows and lifted her arm to cover her eyes. "It is the room Andrew and I share. Please forgive me, I'd like to be alone to rest now."

"I think I should remain with you until the doctor arrives for I have no wish to be blamed for any injury which might befall you while you are alone." Clayton turned away from the bed and strolled about the spacious room observing its furnishings closely. "We have not spoken to each other in months, Elizabeth. You have not left this house and I am seldom in it. You will understand, of course, why I thought it best if I did not come to call."

Elizabeth uttered a noncommittal reply and paid no further attention to his remarks until she heard him speak Andrew's name. "I beg your pardon. What did you say just then?"

Clayton stepped close to her side and stared down with an arrogant boldness which matched his words. "I said, only last week that murdering bandit you call

426

husband slipped through a trap which was laid specifically for him and escaped capture by the narrowest of margins. I had so hoped to bring him home to bid you farewell before the birth of your child. I thought that would make a rather touching scene before I had him hanged."

"You fiend!" Elizabeth sprang to her feet, provoked beyond the limits of her endurance. She lashed out to slap the mocking grin from his face but doubled over in agony as the ache in her back turned to a searing pain which tore down her spine then curled around her waist in a vicious cramp. The officer grabbed for her, catching her before she could slip to the floor and lay her again upon the bed before he ran to the door to summon whatever help he could muster.

Mrs. Blackstone and Meg dashed up the stairs, shoving the colonel aside as they rushed to Elizabeth but the young woman could not answer their solicitous questions coherently. She was curled up, drawing her knees to her chest but that brought no relief from the swift, forceful contractions which held her paralyzed in their grasp.

When Stephanie returned with Dr. McCauley a few minutes later, she took one look at her friend and turned to rebuke St. James. "What have you done to upset Elizabeth so badly? What have you done to her?"

Clayton shrugged innocently. "Why should I wish to torment the unfortunate woman? She is going to give birth. That should be obvious as the reason for her tears, not my presence here, I assure you."

Elizabeth looked up through the wall of pain which surrounded her and whispered a desperate command.

"Get him out of this house. Get him out!"

Dr. McCauley tore off his coat and flung it aside as he shouted, "You heard the lady, St. James. Be gone!"

"As you wish." The tall man gave a courtly bow and walked swiftly from the room, but his expression was one of disgust, as though he were greatly offended to have been banished so rudely.

The physician examined Elizabeth quickly, then shouted a series of terse commands, sending the servants scurrying for the supplies he required. "When did the contractions begin, Elizabeth?"

"Now, just now," Elizabeth answered through clenched teeth. She tried unsuccessfully to stifle a cry as the next wave of pain washed over her, nearly ripping her body in two with its blinding intensity. She had never expected her labor to begin so suddenly or to be so intense. This torment surpassed even the worst of her fears and she could not stop the huge tears which poured down her anguished face.

"There is no time to send for the midwife, my dear. The child is coming now. Forgive me if I have torn your stockings or slips, but I must undress you swiftly."

Elizabeth cared little what the man did. She only wanted the birth to progress with all possible haste and followed his directions as best she could. She breathed deeply in the short space between contractions and then pushed with all her strength until at last she heard the child's first tiny wail and lay back too exhausted to look as the doctor held the slippery babe aloft and exclaimed excitedly, "It is a girl, Elizabeth. You have a splendid daughter!"

Elizabeth could not believe her ears. How could the

child possibly be female when all along she had called the unborn babe son? "A girl? The baby is a little girl?"

"Yes, and a beauty. Just like her mother!" Dr. McCauley was ecstatic. He seldom had an opportunity to deliver a child and had found the experience as thrilling as he had remembered it.

Elizabeth stared up at the faces of those clustered around the bed. Everyone was smiling so happily, entranced by the birth of her daughter and yet she felt only the deepest of shocks. She had been so certain the babe she carried would be the son she'd longed to give Andrew that she'd not even considered her chances of having a baby girl were equally as good. When the physician placed the still squirming infant in her arms, she could think of no lucid comment to make upon the pretty child. Her daughter fit comfortably against her breast and peered up at her with eyes of a clear and luminous green, their vivid hue unmistakable. She'd expected green eyes, known all along the child would be green eyed as his parents, but this sweet baby was not at all what she'd envisioned during the long months Andrew had been gone. Even though she now had an explanation for the color of her eyes, she still had no tangible proof she was not Phillip Jordan's daughter and suddenly that sorrow overwhelmed her and her eyes filled with tears which spilled upon the new baby with slow, steady drops.

Dr. McCauley touched her shoulder with a comforting pat. "What is wrong, dear? The birth went so well. The child is perfect. There's no reason for such sadness, none at all." He turned then to motion to the others to leave them and all filed quietly through the

429

door except for Stephanie, who made no move to depart.

"I'll stay with her, Doctor. I'm certain a brief labor is no less tiring than a prolonged one. Elizabeth will need her rest and I'll stay to be certain she and the baby are fine."

"That would be very kind of you, Miss Mac-Fadden." The man hesitated only a moment, then gathered up his coat and bag. "I'll come by this evening to see you, Elizabeth. Rest quietly until then."

"Thank you, Dr. McCauley. I'm sorry I was such a poor patient."

The man laughed at her apology and came back to her side to give her hand a gentle squeeze. "First babies are not usually born with such rapidity, and you were an excellent patient, Elizabeth, a most cooperative and enjoyable one."

Elizabeth smoothed the wisps of pale blond hair which covered her daughter's scalp and explained softly, "This is my second child. Our son did not live."

"I'm sorry. I didn't realize you'd had another baby. That explains the ease with which this child entered the world, and you needn't fret for she's very healthy and will thrive."

When they were alone, Elizabeth glanced over at Stephanie as she dried her tears. "She is very pretty, don't you think? It is only that I wanted so badly to give Andrew another son to make up for the one we lost so tragically."

Stephanie sat down upon the edge of the bed and looked closely at the tiny girl. "She looks exactly like her mother, Elizabeth. She'll be lovely and Andrew will adore her, I'm sure of it." She looked away for a moment, collecting her thoughts and then continued. "I'm sure you will never forget your first baby, nor should you, as he was so precious to you, but I think a daughter will be ever so much easier for you to raise alone."

Elizabeth never thought of herself as being alone. She always considered Andrew to be her husband still, to be the best part of her life. She tried to believe that he loved her and wanted her as desperately as she wanted him, but what if that weren't true? What if he had forgotten the anguish she'd caused him by turning to another woman, an Indian maiden perhaps, who would understand him and accept his commands without question as she'd never been able to do. She kissed the little girl's forehead lightly and smiled. "I know our future seems uncertain, but I cannot believe I'll be alone forever. I just won't believe that. Please don't you think it, either."

"I'm sorry, but I do think you should be more practical now that you have a child to tend. What is her name? Do you have one already selected for her?"

"You are a wonderful friend. I could name her for you, or there's my mother's name, but I'd really like to name her for Andrew. I'd like to call her Andrea. That's as close as I can come to his name for a little girl." Elizabeth whispered the name softly and the baby turned to look up at her again, curious about her parent and eager to see what the world had to offer on that bright afternoon.

"Just look at her, Elizabeth!" Stephanie giggled with great amusement. "She seems to want to know who you are, too!"

431

The two young women found the pretty child delightful in every way. Her skin was fair, her delicate features exquisite. She was lovely and Elizabeth shed no more tears for she was not in the least bit disappointed in her daughter. The little girl was all any mother could hope to have and she hugged her tightly and tried to imagine how she would present the child to Andrew and hoped he would soon learn of their good fortune in becoming parents at last. Wouldn't the perfection of their tiny daughter prove their love was untarnished? Wouldn't Andrea herself be proof enough for him that God had blessed their union and looked upon their marriage as a true and valid one which should endure for all time? "Oh, Andrew," she whispered softly. "How I wish you would listen to your heart as I listen to mine."

Twenty-Three

Andrea had just fallen asleep when Elizabeth heard the bell at the door and she rushed to respond. General Howe had made the British occupation of Philadelphia official only two weeks prior, and she feared the visitors would be military men seeking quarters in the Jordan home, but she found Colonel St. James at the door, smiling with the evil leer she had grown to dread. He was surrounded by troops whose uniforms were dusty and disheveled from many days on the road, but he was as immaculately dressed as always, as perfect in his appearance as a toy soldier in a display case might be.

"Miss Peterson, how good of you to greet us yourself. You are just the person I wished to find at home this evening."

"Colonel, if this is a social call, I am afraid I cannot invite you to come in. The hour is dreadfully late and as you know, my uncle retires quite early." Elizabeth knew far better than to assume the man at her door was there without a good reason, but still she couldn't resist defying him in every way possible.

"I have brought you a present. May I bring it inside?" Clayton rocked back on his heels, ignoring her protests over the lateness of the hour.

"Why would you wish to bring me a gift, sir?" Elizabeth inquired skeptically.

The tall officer moved past her without waiting to be invited to enter, then motioned for his soldiers to follow. Four came in and moving to the side, made way for a similar group carrying a stretcher. "Look for yourself, Elizabeth. I believe I have found Andrew Jordan, but perhaps I am mistaken."

Elizabeth gasped sharply as the colonel raised a lantern to illuminate the face of the fallen man. It was Andrew lying upon the litter, his face ashen, his breathing a shallow rattle in his throat. "Who has done this to him? Was it you?" She cast the British officer a hostile glance, then knelt beside her husband. She brought his limp hand to her lips, kissing his cut and bruised knuckles tenderly as she moved her fingertips to grasp his wrist where she found his pulse surprisingly strong and was encouraged by that comforting beat.

"Unfortunately, I can take no credit for his condition. He was only one of those captured by Burgoyne's forces at Saratoga. He'd been shot through the leg and left for dead by those savages he commanded. The one heathen who remained behind was brought along as it was feared Andrew might not survive the journey without someone to attend him. He is alive tonight only because he was recognized and it was wildly known how greatly I would prize him as a prisoner. Where is the savage who was captured with him?" The colonel raised his voice and Red Tail was shoved forward from the shadows which enveloped the front porch. His hands were bound behind his back and he staggered, almost falling, but caught himself and stood proudly beside his friend.

Elizabeth recognized the Indian in spite of his bruised face and torn buckskins. He had obviously fared little better than Andrew and she stood gracefully and placed her hand upon his shoulder in a tender caress. "Bless you for not deserting Andrew when he needed you most."

Red Tail's tone was defiant as he responded, "None deserted him. He sent all the others away when he grew too weak to fight."

Clayton was astonished. "My God, this creature speaks English?" He stepped closer to peer at the Indian's face, then swore, "This is the man you introduced to me as your husband, is he not?"

"Yes, he is the same man. He is like a brother to Andrew and to me also. Now why have you brought them here, Colonel? What do you have planned for my husband and Red Tail? Did you bring them home only so that I might witness their suffering?" Elizabeth had no hope at all the man had acted out of mercy, or regard for her feelings. She knew he had some evil purpose in mind, but could not imagine what it might be.

"Hardly. I merely want Andrew Jordan alive and his friend has been useful to attend him. I plan to quarter them both here, under close guard of course, until Andrew is well enough to be useful. I will send my finest surgeon to attend him as his wound is a severe one, and I want him to recover completely." Clayton paused a moment, then continued in a low voice. "There is only one small thing you must do to repay me for my compassion and generosity, Elizabeth." His sardonic smile turned to a devilish grin as he waited for his words to register clearly in the lovely young woman's mind.

Elizabeth smiled sadly at Red Tail, then turned to face Clayton squarely. She dreaded what he might ask for she knew whatever favor he wanted would not be a small one. "What bargain must I make to safeguard my husband's life? Name it quickly and I will agree for he means all the world to me and I will refuse you nothing."

"Good. You understand me, girl. I knew you would." The finely uniformed officer drew Elizabeth into his arms and held her in a firm, hard grasp as he stared down into her bright green eyes. "You must consent, and most willingly, my dear, to become my mistress. You must leave here tonight with me and take up residence at my inn. It is a fine one and you'll be most comfortable. Don't trouble yourself worrying over that matter."

Elizabeth forced herself not to gag, not to become deathly ill from the horrid nature of his demand. "And my baby. She is too small to leave behind. Only three months old. Will you allow me to bring her with me?"

"The child must come with you, I insist. I did not intend for you to interrupt your duties as the babe's mother."

"That is all you want and Andrew will be safe? Will you give me your word you will not harm him?"

"As long as you continue to amuse me, keep me entertained as I am certain that savage taught you to do, he will be quite safe, although he will remain under arrest here in this house. We are arranging a simple exchange, your life for his. Is that acceptable to you?"

"Red Tail must not be harmed either. You must let

him stay here to tend my husband. I'm certain he knows the Seneca's methods for healing wounds such as the one Andrew has suffered and will do far better than your surgeon at making him well. You must promise to guarantee Red Tail's safety, too," Elizabeth requested bravely. She hated the tall, gray-haired man, despised him and seeing no way to escape his wretched bargain, pressed for every advantage.

"So you think you are worth the lives of two grown men? The Indian means nothing to me. He may stay here as long as he is useful, but if ever you cross me, girl, both men will hang, and I will see to it that you are there to see them swing from the gallows! Is that clear?" The colonel stepped back slightly, then placed his hands on Elizabeth's shoulders ready to shake her soundly should she argue. "Do you understand? The very first time you tell me no, or fight me in any manner, they will both die. They are traitors to their king and deserve no better fate than that, unless you choose now to save them by coming with me."

"I will come. May I bring some of my belongings?" Elizabeth held her breath while the hateful man considered her request.

"No, bring only the child's clothing and nothing more. I will buy a new wardrobe for you and whatever else you require. Pack your baby's things and get your cloak. You have five minutes, not a second more. Guards, take these two prisoners upstairs and find a room which can be easily guarded. They are never to be left alone. Not for one second of the day or night are they to be left unattended. These savages are crafty creatures, and I do not want them to elude my grasp now that we have them in custody at last."

437

The soldiers picked up the litter and carried it up the stairs as Elizabeth followed hurriedly to direct them to Andrew's room. "Take him in here and place him on the bed carefully. Can't you see how badly he is injured?" She watched as the men drew away the stained blanket. Andrew's leg had been bandaged but the once white linen had been dyed a dark red by his blood. "Dear God, Red Tail, will he live? Can you make him well again?"

"He will not die. The English doctor wanted to cut off his leg, but I would not let him do it."

Elizabeth sank down upon the edge of the bed, forcing the horror of that ghastly thought from her mind. She touched her husband's fevered cheek with a loving caress. "Thank you, my friend. I will not worry if you are with Andrew. Somehow we will all live. I know that we'll survive this wretched war to find happiness again, but please do not tell my husband what I have had to do to save you and he. Never tell him what I have had to do. Give me your promise."

Red Tail turned to one of the guards who released the captive's bound hands but stepped back hurriedly, obviously afraid of being so near the powerfully built Indian. Barely able to conceal his smile, Red Tail turned back toward the bed and pulled Elizabeth gently to her feet, then whispered, "He would gladly die for you, Elizabeth."

"Yes, I know, but I'll not let him die for me now, not like this when he is half dead already and cannot even fight. I must go with St. James and you must promise never to tell Andrew where I have gone!" Elizabeth insisted her friend give his word.

Red Tail nodded slightly, but his gaze was dark. He

438

did not want to see her go with the British officer, but knew he could not fight for her honor against all the soldiers who stood in the room waiting eagerly for him to make just such a foolhardy attempt so they'd have an excuse to kill him. "I will not tell him, yet." He emphasized the last word, certain she would understand they would come for her the minute Andrew was able to lead such a rescue.

"Thank you." Elizabeth reached up to kiss his cheek lightly, then ran from the room to get her daughter before the colonel had time to reconsider his decision and make her leave the precious baby behind.

After a brisk ride to the inn, Clayton escorted Elizabeth up the stairs and held the door open as the lovely blonde entered his rooms. They were light and warm, the best accommodations in the city at present, and as fine as he had boasted. She looked around, but saw no crib for her child. "Do you think the innkeeper might have a cradle for Andrea? She needs a place to sleep."

"There is one, in the next room. I have the two and do not want the brat to sleep in here with us."

"Andrea is a lovely baby, not a brat at all, Colonel. Please remember that." Elizabeth's eyes flashed angrily with a deep green brilliance as she looked up at him. He was nearly Andrew's equal in height, if nothing else. His whole appearance disgusted her from his silver gray hair to his dark brown eyes. She found nothing about him she liked. Although she knew other women found him handsome, she most assuredly did not.

"Put the brat to bed," St. James responded curtly, emphasizing his insulting term in defiance of her request. "Hurry up about it. I want to see what it is now own."

"Am I to be inspected as a slave is before she is sold?" Elizabeth inquired bitterly.

The colonel laughed heartily at her question, then nodded. "Exactly. I did not think you would ever have seen such a spectacle."

"I have not, only heard of how the wretched creatures are treated, and I didn't realize that was to be my lot."

"See to the child. I am growing weary of your chatter." St. James gestured impatiently as he removed his white leather gloves. He threw them aside, then began to remove his coat, eager to get on with the evening's amusements.

Elizabeth crossed to the adjoining room swiftly and lay Andrea down gently in the cradle. The cherry wood was old, but very finely carved and she was pleased at least her baby would be comfortable even if she were not. Assured her daughter was sound asleep, she untied her bonnet as she walked back into the other room. She unfastened her cape and draped it and the bonnet over the back of one of the chairs beside the round table which sat in the corner opposite his bed. Gathering all her courage she turned to confront the man who was now her master. "What is it you wish me to do?"

The dark-eyed man was sprawled across the room's only comfortable chair, lazily unbuttoning his shirt while his eyes racked over her figure. "Take off your dress, girl. I want to look at you."

Elizabeth's eyes never left his face as she began to disrobe. She felt sick with shame and her fingers

440

trembled badly, but he saw none of her fear in her glance. If she openly defied him, he would only beat her into submission and rape her. She knew that by just looking at him and that would buy no time at all for Andrew to grow strong enough to escape. No, she had to please him by being the most wanton of whores, convincing him she was no more than a slave to her own base desires. It was the only way to protect the man she loved and she would gladly submit to any humiliation to save him and Red Tail from the hangman's noose. She dropped her dress slowly upon her cape and stepped closer to him as she began to untie the ribbons which held her lace camisole in place. She pulled the pale pink ribbons undone, then reached down to loosen those which held her petticoats. When the hateful man's breathing quickened noticeably, she knew she was succeeding well in her purpose and stepped closer still.

"Hurry up, girl," Clayton whispered hoarsely.

"I am, but I do not want to risk tearing my clothes in my haste as they may be the only ones I'll have for some time." She fiddled nervously with the ties at her waist, concentrating upon her task, but as she glanced up, the lust which shone clearly on the man's sharp features sent a shiver down her spine she couldn't repress for the game she was playing did nothing to quell her fears.

"I will buy you more beautiful dresses than your savage ever did, if you please me, that is."

"I will try, Colonel." Elizabeth made a deliberate effort to reply in a sweet tone, disregarding the string of vile insults which churned through her nimble mind.

"Call me Clayton. My rank seems out of place between us." The man stood then, stretching to his full height before he grabbed for her silken undergarments, yanking them hurriedly from her slender body, not satisfied until she stood nude before him. He tossed the foamy lace to the floor and reached out to touch her high firm breasts with an insolent grasp. "You are every bit as pretty as I knew you would be that first time I saw you with the Seneca. That buckskin dress hid none of your beauty. Your figure is perfection. Motherhood has not flawed your looks at all."

Elizabeth forced herself to stand still even though the touch of the man's pale fingers revolted her completely. "Thank you, Clayton." She smiled shyly as his hands continued to travel down her soft flesh, exploring the contours of her shapely body with far more curiosity than she had thought possible. She felt strangely detached as his hands moved over her, as if she were a third person in the room watching him paw a stranger. Andrew's slightest touch had always flooded her body with pleasure, but this numbness she felt now helped sooth her ravaged feelings as the most erotic of sensations would not have, for that would have been a betrayal she could not have borne, but the tall man read none of her relief in his hunger to possess her.

"Yes, you will do. Get into my bed and be quick about it."

Elizabeth stepped lightly across the polished wooden floor to the high iron bed and pulled back the blanket. The linens were at least clean, freshly laundered and that comfort was the only one she had as she climbed into the bed. Andrew would kill her for what she was doing. She knew that plainly, but she didn't even care. She would not want to live after dishonoring her husband as she was about to do, but Andrew would be alive and that was all that truly mattered to her. When the officer joined her in the bed she made no move to resist him, nor did she lift her arms to hold him in her embrace. He was not overly rough with her, only crude as he satisfied his lust hurriedly then lay back, exhausted by his efforts to possess her completely. She had felt nothing, nor had she expected to and was glad it was over so quickly, the second time or the hundredth would be no worse than the first time surely. Once done, the deed would be endlessly the same with a man so arrogant as he.

Clayton St. James raised himself up on one elbow and grinned down wickedly at his beautiful captive. "How does a gentleman compare to that savage you call husband?"

Elizabeth answered truthfully. "There is no comparison between you, Colonel, I mean Clayton." She felt the nausea rise in her throat and coughed slightly to suppress it, regaining her composure as she attempted to pursue the ruse she had begun. "Do you enjoy games?"

"What sort of games?" Clayton lifted an eyebrow quizzically, then leaned forward, bending his head down to her breast so he could bite her playfully. "That kind of sport is what you mean?"

"Perhaps." Elizabeth also turned upon her side then reached under the sheet to caress him intimately, her touch a teasing promise of what was to come.

"My God, woman, you did not have enough?"

443

Clayton could barely speak as her tantalizing moves quickened his pulse and again filled his loins with heat which demanded a release.

Elizabeth licked her lips seductively, purring her question, "Do you mind if I mount you this time? Have you ever done this?" She moved upon him as she whispered, "Now we'll see who finds their pleasure first. How long can you wait, Clayton?" Her voice was enticing, her long fair curls covering the fullness of her breasts as she continued to hold him captive within her body.

Clayton responded with a hoarse rasp, "This is a challenge?"

"Yes, if you will accept," Elizabeth answered sweetly, all her concentration upon the discomfort in his eyes rather than the act she was performing so expertly upon his outstretched form.

"Continue then if you can."

Elizabeth was clever enough not to push her luck. When she sensed by his ragged breathing he could take no more, she lay down upon him and sighed as if he'd given her the most exquisite of pleasures. "You have won, for you are too strong a man to beat." He tossed her on her back then and took her swiftly, his haste even greater than before, although he believed he had won their bet.

"It is not late, Clayton. Do you want more?" Elizabeth placed her hand upon his heavily furred chest. That hair was as gray as his head's, yet she thought he was probably no more than a few years older than Andrew.

"No, if I do I will wake you later. I am going out for a while." He left the bed and after hastily donning his

444

uniform, strode from the room, locking the door after him as he went.

As soon as she was alone, Elizabeth sprang from the bed and went to the wash stand where she scrubbed herself repeatedly with the cold water from the porcelain pitcher, but she still didn't feel clean yet. She knew the warmest of baths would do no better. She would never feel truly clean ever again, no matter how much soap she used, for it was not dirt which stained her white skin, but the knowledge of what she'd had to do. She had managed to please him it seemed, but she had not thought it possible to feel such loathing for another of God's creatures and tried again to wash his scent from her body. She had only just begun to learn to hate the despicable man, however, for when he returned he was not alone.

Clayton St. James came through the door ahead of two of his junior officers. They had all been drinking heavily and from the sheepish grins on their faces, she could tell they'd been boasting of their prowess with women. Elizabeth pulled the sheets up close to her throat as Clayton turned up the lamp.

"Ah, you are still awake. That's good. You are so unique, Elizabeth, such a treasure, I didn't feel I could keep you all to myself tonight. Surely you will not object to my friends sharing in my good fortune." His comment was not a request, however, but a demand.

Elizabeth nodded her consent. "I am yours to do with as you please, Clayton, to keep for yourself or to give away. That was our bargain. However, I would prefer one man at a time. Decide among yourselves who will be first and the other two must wait outside." She held her breath, anxiously praying they would listen to her plea. She had thought she'd only have to tolerate one horrid man's attentions, not to be repeatedly raped by his entire garrison.

"She speaks like a lady who knows her own mind. Let us oblige her, gentlemen." Clayton stepped back to the door. "I have the whole night. Decide which of you will be first and which second."

The two young men hesitated slightly, then one withdrew a pack of cards and laid it upon the table. "Shall we cut for the privilege of being first to take her?"

The other agreed readily and drew an ace, thus ending their sport quickly. When his friend left, Elizabeth sat up and watched the man closely as he approached her bed. He reminded her of the farmers' sons she had known. She hoped he knew as little as they. "How old are you, Lieutenant?"

"Twenty, lass. How old are you?" He began to take off his coat, then pulled his shirt from his britches.

"I have just turned eighteen. Have you had many women?" She eyed him closely and her judgment was correct. He blushed under her stare, his manhood not that great a source of pride to him as yet.

"I have had women. How many is none of your concern. I hear you know of a game which is most entertaining."

"Yes, I know many such amusements. Since you were willing to draw cards, are you a betting man, Lieutenant? Would you care to make a small wager on our sport?"

"Why not? I think I can beat you if the colonel did. Shall we say all the gold I have here in my purse?" The young man tossed the leather pouch upon the table where it landed with a heavy thud.

"Agreed. If you win, I will match that amount. I have it also." Elizabeth had not one penny, but she knew the man was too anxious to have her to worry over her ability to cover her bets. She continued to watch him as he undressed. He was well built and undoubtedly strong so she had no intention of making him angry enough to beat her senseless with his fists. What she had in mind was far more subtle. "My husband is an Indian brave. His people taught me many erotic pastimes. The Indian men have great skill in pleasing women, but you probably already know that."

"Indians?" The young man appeared puzzled by her announcement as he sat down on the foot of the bed to pull off his boots.

"Yes, they are very strong. Why I have had braves ride astride me as they would a horse from sundown to sunrise and then only stop to go out hunting." Elizabeth managed to keep her face straight, but the affect of her words was exactly what she had hoped it would be.

"All night? Their men can make love to women all night?"

"Oh, much longer than that. In the winter, when there is no need to hunt and the men are at home, they do not stop for days."

"You don't mean continuously. They can stay—" The man hesitated to describe what he meant.

"Hard as granite. But they are grown men. You are still young so do not worry about yourself, yet." Her voice was calm, as if she were a mother offering advice to her son. "I have heard some white men can last no more than an hour or two. Hurry and show me what you can do."

"An hour!"

"Surely you can do better than that, can't you? Why, if I'd known you were no good at this sport, I never would have made the bet with you. That is unfair to offer you a challenge when you stand no chance of winning."

The red-faced lieutenant drew his boots back on and reached for his shirt. "Madam, I had no idea what you expected of me."

"You'll not stay? You'll not even try to beat me in a game or two?" Elizabeth asked forlornly.

"I think not. Keep the gold. Your tale is worth it, though I fear that is all it is, a tale."

"Lieutenant, dress more slowly. There is no need for you to be embarrassed in front of your friend by your lack of stamina. You are too young to worry yet about endurance. Surely it grows like strength, comes with age. I will promise not to tell you did not have me if you will remain silent as to what happened while you were with me."

"I will gladly keep silent!" The young man nearly flew out the door, so great was his haste to leave her. Elizabeth sprang from her bed and picked up the purse of gold. She hid it in the pocket of her cape and leapt back into bed when she heard footsteps approaching in the hall.

The next man was not so well built, nor so bright as the first. He seemed hesitant and Elizabeth moved gracefully from her perch atop the high bed and walked toward him boldly displaying all her charms to

448

his full view. "Surely you have seen a woman nude before tonight, haven't you?"

The man swallowed nervously and nodded, but his eyes grew large as he looked her pretty form up and down hungrily. "I, yes, I have seen women."

"Good. Let me help you undress. Do you like to play games, Lieutenant?"

"Yes, ma'am. I like the sort of games the colonel described."

"He told you? That wicked man. You should never tell, Lieutenant. A lady has to watch her reputation and she'll never allow you to return to her bed if you bandy her good name about all over town. Now, how much gold have you?"

"Gold? Some."

"Good. Put your purse on the table. I hope it will be enough to make this sport worth our while. I will match your bet. Now, undress quickly. I want to see what you have to offer me." She stood with her hands on her hips, her pose more wanton than the man could bear. He ripped off his uniform, tossed it aside and looked toward the bed eagerly.

"Oh, you poor man. I had no idea you were so small. Well, no matter. You're young yet. Doubtless you will grow."

The man's eyes widened as he looked down at himself. "Small! You think I am small? I am no smaller than any other man."

"Good heavens, you know more unfortunates like yourself? Forgive me for mentioning it, but had I known I would never have offered to bet with you. You have no chance of winning. I lived with the

Seneca for a while. Their men are quite different from the white race, but perhaps you knew that." Elizabeth moved her hands apart in a meaningful gesture.

"You don't mean they have . . ." The man was dumbstruck by the proportions she indicated.

"Every last one. They seldom wear clothes in the summer so I saw them all naked and they were all the same, all of them. It is a pity white men have so little in comparison. Enough of that, Lieutenant. Come show me what you can do, if anything, with what little you have." Elizabeth climbed back upon the bed and smiled invitingly.

"Look, lass, I don't think I want to do this after all. Keep my gold. Just don't tell anyone about my, well, my . . ." The man looked down, his whole expression woebegone.

"Never. I'll never tell a soul. Your secret is safe with me. If anyone asks, I'll say you were magnificent, but you must promise never to come back here, or tell anyone else about me."

"Yes. It's a promise! You'll never see my face again!" He grabbed his clothes and donned them rapidly as he had no desire to tarry and be humiliated any further. With a brief wave he was out the door and gone, thankful to be on his way so quickly.

When Clayton St. James returned nearly an hour later Elizabeth was huddled in the rumpled bed, her hair a tangled mess and her delicate body shaking with loud racking sobs. "Elizabeth, what is all this? What is the matter?"

"Your friends are beasts! Animals who have none of your grace. Must you treat me so meanly? I thought

450

should I become pregnant at least I would know the child's father was a fine English gentleman, but I shall have no such comfort now." Elizabeth continued to wail in loud, miserable sobs, all completely faked.

"A child? But your daughter is no more than a few months old. Surely you cannot conceive again so quickly!" Clayton responded with astonishment.

"I am only eighteen and have had two children already. I am afraid I do conceive very easily. You must know families who have a baby each year. Anything can happen when a man sleeps frequently with a woman. But now I will not even know whose child I may have, to say nothing of what might happen to your health."

"My health? What has my health got to do with this?" The colonel stood with his hands on his hips, totally confused by the beautiful young woman's words.

"Have you not heard of diseases which a man can get from whores? They are terrible. I know, and if you wish to pass me about among your friends, who knows what sicknesses they may have caught and I will then give them all to you!" Elizabeth hid her face in her hands, too fine an actress to stop playing her part now. "Do you know for certain one of those lieutenants is not already infected with some vile disease?"

"Good lord, I never even considered it!"

"Never? A man with your experience has not heard of such things?" Elizabeth wiped her eyes on the edge of the sheet and looked up at him, her gaze filled with innocence.

"Yes, of course I have, but I did not think that my

451

men would bring disease to my bed."

"You know so much more than I do, Clayton. How long will it take for me to know for certain I can sleep with you again without fear of contaminating you?"

"What? I don't know. I will have to ask our surgeon such a question."

"Can you ask him tonight? If I have already caught such an illness, I do not want to give it to you."

"Nor do I want it! I will go wake him and come back, or maybe I will sleep elsewhere!" Clayton strode out of the room, slamming the door loudly as he stepped out into the hall and this time he did not bother to lock her in.

Suppressing a gleeful giggle, Elizabeth got up from the bed and went in to the other room to nurse her daughter. She held the sweet child to her warm breast and forced herself to make plans for her next encounter with Clayton and his men. The ruse she'd used that night had worked only because the men were too young and inexperienced to recognize her blatant lies for what they were. Had the officer brought home men of his own age, she would have had to submit to them meekly. Dear God, she prayed, please help me. How many men must I bed to save Andrew?

She had just placed her daughter in the comfortable cradle when she heard the door close in the next room. Startled, she waited to see who had entered, but it was Clayton and she was relieved to see he was alone. "Did you find your surgeon so quickly?"

"Yes, I got the man from his bed and had him examine the men who were here. They swore they'd had no women for months before you and the

452

physician proclaimed them both healthy. You have no need to worry, girl."

Elizabeth had drawn her cape about her shoulders, but flung it aside as she approached him. "Good. Then come to bed with me, Clayton, and you must show me a game this time. Do you know some?"

The colonel swore as he turned back to the other room. "I am tired, Elizabeth. Leave me be."

"As you wish." Elizabeth lay back down in the bed and moved toward the wall. She cradled her head on her arms as she turned upon her stomach and hoped the man would indeed leave her alone. But when Clayton joined her he pulled her into his arms and lowered his mouth to her soft, pink tipped breasts. She put her hands on his shoulders and drew him close. "I fear my baby leaves little left for you, sir." She held her breath, waiting for his teeth to sink into her tender flesh, but he used only his lips and tongue upon her this time.

Clayton laughed as he raised his head. "Your milk is sweet, but I've no wish to starve your infant to please myself. The rest of you is more to my liking."

"I am happy I please you, but I beg you not to give me to others. Surely no true gentleman shares his mistress."

"Yes, that is the custom, quaint though it may be, but I will agree. You gave me a fright tonight with your talk of disease, and I'll not risk that scare again. I will keep you only for myself from now on. That is a promise."

"Thank you, Clayton. Those boys were a poor lot compared to you." Elizabeth was glad he could not see her expression as he lowered his head again to her breast. She would sooner suckle the devil himself than the man who held her so tightly, but she stroked his hair and called his name softly as though he had brought her the greatest of pleasures instead of the total revulsion which filled her whole body with pain.

Twenty=Four

The next afternoon, Clayton returned to the inn early in order to take Elizabeth shopping. "Did Madame Dupré make all your gowns?"

"Yes, she did, but her shop is expensive. Perhaps you'd rather we go elsewhere." Elizabeth smiled sweetly, as though the size of the Englishman's expenditures mattered greatly to her.

"You think King George does not pay his officers well?" Clayton asked caustically.

"I'm sure he must with all the taxes we've had to pay." When she responded playfully with a teasing sparkle in her eyes, the tall man grinned in return.

"You are witty, lass. That's good in a woman. I can afford Madame Dupré no matter what she charges to dress you for me."

"I will not require much, Clayton. Surely we will not leave here often, will we?" At least she hoped not. She had no desire to ever be seen in public with the man, but he had other plans.

"On the contrary. We will be entertained frequently. You undoubtedly know your uncle's friends. They are all loyal to the Crown and invite me to their homes often. I will take you with me from now on."

Elizabeth's astonishment was clear on her pretty

features. "You wish to parade me in public as your mistress? Surely Matthew's friends will be greatly offended. They are important men, not ones you British can afford to lose as allies to your cause. I beg you to reconsider. You would do better to court their daughters than to flaunt our liaison."

The colonel scowled angrily. "You are right, of course, but there is a purpose in what I do. I want the young men of this town to see what happens to their property when they abandon their rightful king to follow these so-called 'Patriots'!"

"Meaning they will lose their women, is that it?"

"Yes. It is a good lesson for them, don't you think? They will think twice about leaving their comely brides when they see how easily I have taken you."

Elizabeth shook her head. "I am a simple farm girl, of no consequence to anyone in Philadelphia, and are you forgetting my marriage was annulled? You have stolen no one's wife, Clayton."

The arrogant officer stepped closer, pulling Elizabeth into a forceful embrace. "Do you think I do not know the truth of that annulment, you incestuous bitch?"

Elizabeth gasped in surprise. She'd not thought either Matthew or Stephen Haywood would tell a soul of that scandal. "That is a lie, sir. Andrew is not my brother. I know he is not."

"Your uncle proved to the magistrate's satisfaction that he is indeed your blood relation, your half-brother. He is both father and uncle to your bastard child."

Elizabeth gathered her thoughts calmly in order to respond without angering the man further. "Is this

456

the real reason I am here, Clayton? So that you may punish Andrew by taking me as often as you like?"

"Of course. I will see that he knows about it, too. I would like nothing better than to take you right in front of him. I may just do that, too."

All color drained from Elizabeth's face at that hateful threat. "You promised. You gave your word my husband would not be harmed!"

"How will he be harmed if we perform in front of him? The damage will all be done to his spirit, not to his body you know so well. My word as a gentleman is still good, although I would rather see your brother hang, he will remain under my protection for as long as you please me. But let me warn you, Elizabeth. Should you try and run away, you will be caught and brought home to watch Andrew die the traitor's death he deserves. Then I will personally tie you to that bed and let every man who walks by in the street below come up here and have his fill of you. Then, my beauty, I will sell whatever is left to the filthiest whorehouse I can find! Now let us go buy some gowns and when I tell you to wear them you will come with me wherever I wish you to go. Do you understand me now?"

Elizabeth was nauseated by the man's vile threats. She felt dizzy and had he not been holding her so tightly she would surely have fallen. "Yes, Clayton. I did not mean for you to think I was arguing with you, refusing to go where you wish me to go. You must forgive me." When he lowered his mouth to hers, she forced herself to accept his kiss as she had welcomed his other advances, yet she could scarcely breathe, she was so disgusted.

Clayton drew away when he was satisfied he'd subdued her spirit for the present. "Come, let us hurry. We have no more time to argue if we are to arrive before the shop closes." The dressmaker's shop was in the next block and he walked with long brisk strides, pulling Elizabeth along beside him as if she were some naughty child. Madame Dupré welcomed them warmly, smiling graciously as she recognized Elizabeth.

"Why, Mrs. Jordan, how are you? I have not seen you in such a long time. I hope you have been well."

St. James spoke up quickly to correct her. "Miss Peterson is no longer married to that treacherous rogue, Madame. You will not address her by his name again."

The middle-aged woman's eyes widened in alarm at the man's angry tone. "I am sorry, Miss Peterson. I did not realize you were no longer married."

Elizabeth looked away, unable to give any coherent reply as Clayton described what he wanted made for her. The dresses were to be elegant and sophisticated, as beautiful as any she had ever created and he wanted them completed immediately.

"Very well, Colonel. My shop is well known for the beauty of our work. You will not be disappointed. Would you like to take a chair here or come back to the fitting room with us?"

"I have no interest in watching you take measurements. I will stay here, but do not be long."

"Of course, Colonel. I will not keep you waiting for more than a few minutes." Madame Dupré took Elizabeth's hand and led her back to one of the small fitting rooms. She drew the curtains closed and turned to stare again at her young customer. "I am greatly surprised to find you with such a man, Elizabeth. After knowing your husband, I cannot believe you would do this. Andrew was the most charming of men where this colonel is an arrogant oaf!"

Elizabeth unfastened her garments with cool detachment. "Please, you must hurry, Madame Dupré. Do not make him angry. I am with him by choice and you must not criticize him in any way. This city belongs to the British, regardless of our feelings, and I cannot defy him."

"Why have you left your husband? Surely it was not for this man?"

"The story is too long and sad to relate here. Do not judge me too harshly for I have bought my husband's life with the only thing I have to sell." She dropped her dress to the floor and again implored the seamstress to hurry.

"Oh, dear child, how may I help you? Is there no way to send a message to Andrew so he might save you this humiliation?"

"That is impossible. He is gravely ill and only alive today because it serves St. James' purpose. Now we must not speak of my plight any further. Just measure my waist and be quick about it."

When a few minutes later Clayton wisked back the draperies of the fitting room, he found Madame Dupré writing down the last of the measurements and Elizabeth was smoothing down the folds of her skirt, ready to depart. He scowled impatiently and reached for her hand. "I see you are finished. Good, we must go. When may Elizabeth return for the first fittings?"

"Shall we say in a week's time, Colonel? That will

give me enough time to prepare the first of the garments you have ordered."

"I will expect at least three of the dresses to be ready and no fewer. Miss Peterson cannot wear the same gown everywhere she goes!"

"I will do my best, Colonel, but fine fabrics cannot be sewn so hastily as muslin." She wrapped her measuring tape around her hand and jammed it back into her apron pocket with a savage shove. She heartily disapproved of the obnoxious man's manner and wanted no part of his business. "If you think we will be too slow, perhaps you should take your requests elsewhere."

Clayton St. James' dark eyes narrowed menacingly. "Do not push me, Madame. You will not enjoy the result. Now, good day. We will return at this time next week." He held Elizabeth's cape for her, then took her arm to lead her away.

It was quite late before Clayton returned to his quarters that night and he found Elizabeth in a somber mood. She was sitting in front of the small fireplace warming her feet and did not rise to meet him. She was wearing only her camisole which covered her shapely figure from neck to toe with its lace trimmed folds. Her hands were clasped in her lap, as still as a Gainsborough portrait. She had never been more lovely. He could not take his eyes from her but could not understand her subdued expression.

"What's got into you tonight, my dear? You are not in the mood for more sport? You have no interest in playing your games with me tonight?"

"No, Clayton. You see, I thought last night that you had seized my husband in order to take me for yourself, but you told me this afternoon that quite the opposite is true. You have taken me only to torture Andrew most cruelly. I thought you felt some affection for me. It has always seemed so to me, but I have always been married, or with child and unable to return your attentions," Elizabeth lied convincingly, her gaze holding his.

The Englishman struggled to pull off his black leather boots, then threw them across the floor with a loud clatter. "Do you expect me to believe now you wanted to return my affection when you have scorned me in every way possible for more than a year?"

Elizabeth nodded seductively. "Why, yes. I admire persistence in a man. I thought you would be willing to vie for my affection as a gentleman should, not simply wait until I could be bargained for as a prize of this wretched war."

"So now I must simply take you. You are no longer willing to be my mistress? You prefer the role of victim of rape perhaps?"

Elizabeth rose with deliberate slowness. She removed her camisole and let it fall to the floor where she let it lie as she moved toward the bed. "I will not fight you. I gave you my word. You need not rape me for I am willing to share your bed, but now that I know you do not care for me, it will not be the same." She pulled back the covers and lay down, stretched out gracefully as a sacrifice might be upon some pagan altar. "Take me as often as you wish, Clayton. Shall we keep count? It was three times last night, twice this morning, again this afternoon. How strong do you feel tonight?" Her voice was an enticing whisper, throaty and alluring, but taunting still.

Clayton was puzzled as he joined her in the bed. Her mood was far too perplexing for him to comprehend. "What has happened to your spirit, girl? Where is the woman who teased me so wantonly last night with her eager games? Perhaps I was wrong to promise to keep you for myself. Would you prefer I go find some more amusing company for you if you are so bored with me already?"

Elizabeth ran her hand down his lean back and purred softly. "I am heartbroken that you have no true affection for me, that your interest all these many months has been no more than revenge. That is too hard a thing for a woman so sensitive as I to bear lightly, Clayton. I had hoped you brought me here out of love." Elizabeth was continually surprised at how easily the lies sprang from her lips. She could not look him in the eye and tell him the truth of her anguish, her disgust at his touch, yet her insipid lies seemed to please him each time. He drew her into a gentle embrace and she hugged his neck warmly, her soft breasts brushing his chest with a tantalizing caress.

"If you want me to love you, then you must keep me happy, no more of your silly complaints. Now what other pleasures shall we have tonight? Come show me something different."

"It is warm by the fire. Have you ever made love in a chair?" When the man was eager to try what she suggested, she shut her mind to the experience. As she closed her eyes tightly, she tried to imagine what to suggest next. Surely there were only so many possibilities they could attempt each night and she hoped her natural curiosity would present an endless number of variations to the basic theme of making love. When he carried her back to the bed, he fell asleep quickly, but she lay in his arms, too unhappy to rest. When she heard Andrea's tiny cry she scrambled over the colonel's sleeping form to reach her infant before the girl's noise awoke him. It had been lunacy to bring the child with her. She should never have agreed to that. She knew that now, but where could she send the baby? The child was no safer than she with the British officer and she did not want her daughter to ever know the life her mother had been forced to lead, let alone share in it. No, she must not keep her daughter there at the inn any longer than necessary. As soon as she could be weaned, she'd send her back to Matthew's house. Then Andrew would be able to see her, to see his beautiful little girl and know their love had never been wrong, never incestuous or sinful, but as pure as the love in God's own heart. She tried to smile as she touched the little girl's head lightly. "I love you, Andrea. I love you so." She rocked the baby as she nursed her, then placed her in her crib for the rest of the night. She was a sweet and contented baby, and Elizabeth knew she would not awaken again before dawn. She was not so lucky with the colonel, however, for as she returned to his bed, he caught her around the waist and chuckled as he held her captive in his arms.

"I hope tending the child does not leave you too exhausted to entertain me."

"No, not at all," Elizabeth responded sweetly, yet the touch of his hands filled her with a loathing she could scarcely conceal. He was in no mood for play now it seemed. His deep kiss was filled with lust and she forced back the shriek which threatened to escape her throat with a piercing wail. She had been wrong. Each successive time was indeed more horrible than the first. It was all she could do not to become violently ill as she lay in the hateful man's arms. She could not bear much more of the colonel's affection, yet knew she would have to submit willingly. She had chosen her fate gladly and knew escape was impossible. He might take her a thousand times before Andrew grew strong enough to flee the city and she would have to survive for however long it took for her beloved to get away, then she would kill herself and gladly.

Madame Dupré attempted to explain the reason for the delay in the completion of Elizabeth's gowns but Colonel St. James was not in the least bit pleased.

"How could your measurements have been so inaccurate? Why should it take so much time to finish her gowns!"

Elizabeth sat down and folded her hands patiently in her lap while the two others in the small fitting room argued. She had learned rapidly not to dispute Clayton's word and knew better than to take the dressmaker's side against him.

"My measurements were accurate when I took them two weeks ago, Colonel, but the young woman has grown far more slender. I simply cannot keep up with her figure when it changes so quickly!"

Clayton turned to stare at the attractive blonde. "Stand up, my dear. How could you be any thinner. I watch you eat dinner every night. I am not starving you, am I?"

"The meals at your inn are delicious, Clayton. I have never tasted better." She could not complain about the quality of the food, only the company she was forced to keep. The dress she'd worn on the first night she'd gone with him now hung loosely from her shoulders, no longer a perfect fit, but baggy and unattractive.

St. James swore bitterly. "Madame Dupré, Elizabeth must, I repeat, must, have a gown to wear tonight!"

"Sir, I am doing my very best as it is. The pink gown is finished. It is merely too large. I will have a seamstress alter it immediately and deliver it to Mrs. Jordan, excuse me, Miss Peterson's home before six this evening."

"We are staying at the Hunted Stag. Do you know it?" Clayton had lost all patience with the woman. His tone was curt, nasty.

"Of course, it is nearby. The gown will be ready by this evening. As for the others, I hope to have them for you by next week at the latest."

"I would swear that is exactly what you told me last Tuesday, Madame!" he responded sarcastically.

"Miss Peterson's figure is exquisite. I want my gowns to fit superbly, to show off her beauty to every advantage. Surely you do not want her to look as though she's wearing hand-me-downs!"

"Of course not. She is easily the most beautiful young woman in this city, in perhaps all of the Colonies as well and I do not want her to be ill-clothed. Now please complete the fitting as rapidly as possible. I will wait in the front of the shop." Clayton closed the draperies with a vicious snap of his wrist and walked

465

off, at last leaving the French woman to complete her task in peace.

"Have you been ill, dear?" The seamstress pulled a straight pin from the cushion she wore on a band at her wrist and took a small tuck at the waist of the pink satin dress. "Your waist is more than an inch smaller now."

Elizabeth sighed wistfully. "I am quite well, Madame Dupré. Let us not keep Clayton waiting." She turned gradually as the woman placed the pins to adjust the fit of the bodice to her satisfaction.

"You have grown hard, Elizabeth. I am sorry to see what you have had to do to survive. I do not blame you, but oh, what a sweet child you were when first you came here with Andrew."

"If you please, Madame, let us not discuss anything other than my clothes. I cannot bear to remember what I have lost." Yet as she blinked back her tears, she knew Andrew would never be truly lost to her. He was the very blood which coursed through her veins. The last breath she took would whisper his name.

"Yes, I understand, child, forgive me. The gown will be ready for you to wear to the party tonight as promised."

Elizabeth slipped out of the lovely dress and reached for the blue wool she had worn to the fitting. "You are a true friend, Madame Dupré. I appreciate your fine work even if Clayton does not."

"Is he good to you? Does not abuse you?" The sympathetic woman reached out to push a stray blond curl back in place in her young companion's coiffure.

"What would you consider abuse? He does not beat

me and for that small kindness I am most grateful."
Elizabeth tied the ribbon of her bonnet under her chin
and swept her cape about her shoulders, then went to
find Clayton, knowing exactly what he'd want from
her when they returned to his inn.

The soft knock at the door startled Elizabeth badly.
Who could it be? Naomi, the innkeeper's daughter,
always rattled the door with a sharp kick when she
brought food up on a tray and it was not time for the
noon meal yet. She waited a moment longer and
convinced the light tapping had to be a woman, opened
the door slightly so she might peek out at her caller.
"Why Stephanie, you mustn't come here!"

"Why not?" Stephanie swept past the pretty blonde
and moved to the center of the sparsely furnished
room. "I wanted to see for myself that you were safe."

Elizabeth closed the door hurriedly and leaned back
against it. "Yes, I am safe. Andrea and I are both quite
safe."

"Your uncle's house is surrounded by soldiers. I
went to see you time and again but they stopped me
from approaching the front door. Finally, I saw Mrs.
Blackstone on the street this morning and she told me
where I might find you. Why are you here? I know you
despise St. James, so why are you staying here in his
rooms?" Stephanie was clearly upset by the circumstance she could not accept as true.

Elizabeth paused to collect her thoughts, to describe
what had happened in the best possible light. "I came
here willingly. Colonel St. James brought Andrew
home. The soldiers are at the Jordan house to guard

him. My husband is badly injured, but he is home and I pray he will recover his strength with proper care."

"Andrew has been captured!" Stephanie reached out to take her friend's hands. "Where? How did it happen? Do you know?"

"Yes, he was taken prisoner at Saratoga. The fighting was fierce, and although Burgoyne finally surrendered to General Gates, it was not before Clayton had discovered my husband was among those wounded. Andrew and I are both his prisoners and you must never come here again, Stephanie. I couldn't bear it if he got you, too."

"Me!" Stephanie's eyes widened with the shock of that possibility. "Why would he ever want me when he has you? Oh, I'm sorry, Elizabeth. That was a tactless thing for me to say."

"Yes, it was, but I do not trust him one bit. We'll just have to see each other elsewhere. He plans to take me out frequently. We were entertained only last night, in fact. We'll be able to see each other sometimes."

Stephanie nodded with understanding. "If Clayton will be hard on you, then I will not come back, but maybe I could get messages to Andrew for you. I could try to help you in that way."

"No!" Elizabeth spoke too sharply, then seeing the pain in her friend's expression, she tried to apologize. "I'm sorry, but Andrew must never know where I am. Somehow he'll have to escape. I know he'll try and get free just as soon as he's able to walk unassisted and I don't want him to have to deal with this disgrace, too. He is all that matters to me. I want him to escape. Red Tail is with him and they'll get away the first chance they have. I know they will."

"Who is Red Tail? Is he an Indian?" Stephanie's pale blue eyes lit with excitement.

"Yes, and he's Andrew's best friend. He'll not fail my husband and neither will I, but he must not know where I am. Please, Stephanie, don't torture Andrew by telling him what's happened to me."

Stephanie brushed away her tears, but she understood Elizabeth's determination to spare her husband undue anguish and readily agreed. "I promise. How does St. James treat you? Is he kind?"

"Kind? A man who would hold a man's wife ransom in exchange for his life? No, he is never kind, but I will survive this ordeal. If the Seneca couldn't kill me, then Clayton St. James never will." Elizabeth turned away with a swish of her skirt. "You must go now. I don't want Clayton to find you here with me."

Stephanie stammered her question in spite of her embarrassment. "What does he do to you? Just exactly what does he do?"

Elizabeth was surprised by so obvious a question. "I am his whore. What did you think? I cannot call it making love. It is never that. He knows the act, but not how to do it with affection and tenderness. Andrew taught me so much of love, Stephanie, so many of the beautiful expressions of the deepest of feelings, but Clayton knows nothing. Had I not known Andrew first, I would think all men hateful brutes and would never speak to one ever again!"

Stephanie was puzzled. "Yet Andrew was an Indian when you met."

"Yes, and he is Indian still. Through and through my husband will always be an Indian brave."

"Is his friend, Red Tail, as nice a man as Andrew?" the young woman asked shyly.

Elizabeth smiled as she went to open the door. "Yes, he is, and his life is well worth saving. I only hope I can do it. Now you must go. Hurry. Clayton comes and goes at all hours of the day and he mustn't find you here."

Stephanie hugged her good friend tightly, then looked both ways before stepping out the door and finding the hallway clear, she rushed away.

Elizabeth found Andrea sucking her fingers noisily and sat down in the rocking chair to nurse her hungry child. "I can scarcely hold you without crying, my precious daughter, but I want so much for your daddy to see you. He would love you so dearly. He is tall and strong, such a fine man and so handsome. You have his eyes, our eyes, my pet, and I want so much for my husband to see his child."

"Your brother!"

Elizabeth gasped in alarm as she looked up to find Clayton standing at the door. She'd been so lost in conversation she'd not heard the door open in the next room. He was obviously furious with her, his evil black eyes glaring angrily. He'd overheard her loving patter to her baby and was outraged.

"If ever I catch you within a block of your uncle's house, I'll hang that fine, handsome brother of yours! Just remember that. You take one step into that house to see Andrew and he and his red-skinned friend are dead men! Is that finally clear?"

Elizabeth continued to rock Andrea in a slow steady rhythm as the dear baby fell asleep, her stomach full. She was blissfully unaware of her mother's torment and felt safe and loved. "Yes, Clayton, I understand you. I am never to see Andrew again."

"Good! Now put the brat to bed in her cradle and come in here to me."

She could see the man was jealous, but thought the emotion misplaced. She removed her clothes casually, caring little what he thought of her. "You may possess my body as often as you wish, Clayton, but I'll never give you my heart. You know I love Andrew far too dearly to see him hang for no reason save your pride. I am here, yours. Why are you still so unhappy?" She had to grab for his right hand then as he took hold of her hair, drawing her close while his left hand moved down her hip in a now all too familiar caress.

"Go ahead and scream. You'd like to, wouldn't you?" the man snarled angrily.

"No. I have made a bargain with you and I'll keep my half. I will not cry out." As Elizabeth spoke, she suddenly felt faint and went limp against the colonel's forceful embrace, startling the man so badly he nearly dropped her.

"Elizabeth!"

"I am sorry." Elizabeth raised her hand to her eyes and rubbed them slowly. "I'm dizzy, that's all. Just let me catch my breath."

Clayton swept her slight form up into his arms and lay her trembling body upon his bed. He threw off his well tailored uniform quickly then joined her, pulling her into his arms but he did no more than draw her close to his side. He propped his head on his elbow and stared down at her. "Well, have you recovered sufficiently to earn your keep?"

"No." Elizabeth clenched her fists tightly at her

sides. To wait for a recovery sufficient to enable her to welcome his attentions was pointless. She turned on her side too, moved against him as she raised her hand to his cheek, luring him into a kiss whose desperation he would never understand, but he responded eagerly to her enticing gesture and made love to her with far more tenderness than he'd shown before. She feigned a contented sleep when he had satisfied himself, but as soon as she heard his boots thud down the stairs, she got up and retched, thoroughly nauseated by the disgusting nature of the life she'd been forced to lead.

Twenty-Five

Clayton St. James was never satisfied with his looks. He paused before the small shaving mirror and frowned, certain the war was taking its toll in his appearance. Disappointed, he turned to tell Elizabeth good-bye. "Did I remember to tell you I'll try to be home early today to take you to Madame Dupré's to order a riding habit?"

Elizabeth was certain she could not have understood him. "I beg your pardon, Clayton, did you say a riding habit?" She was still in bed, the sheet drawn up to cover her breasts. She'd been eating an apple and had nearly choked at his question.

"Yes. I want to take you out riding with me. We need to have her make you something stylish. Don't you like to ride?"

"Yes, I love to ride, but I've never owned a tailored habit. I don't even know how to ride side saddle. I always just pulled up my skirt and rode like a man."

Clayton scoffed at that notion. "You are such a child, Elizabeth, a very beautiful one, but I will not permit you to ride through Philadelphia at my side looking like some urchin from the farm lands!"

"Truly, sir, that is all that I am." Elizabeth's green eyes were calm and clear, her manner sweet, not

473

teasing as she munched the bright, red apple. It was juicy and sweet, simply delicious and she much preferred concentrating on it rather than her companion.

The Englishman strolled back to face her, a sardonic grin twisting the edge of his thin lips. "Not Phillip Jordan's bastard?"

Elizabeth shook her head emphatically. "No, I am not that."

"We will not dispute the matter since I know the truth even if you persist in your denials of it. I will make an effort to be back before her shop closes. If we start today, perhaps she will actually have the garment completed by spring!" He turned away, then remembering something more, paused at the door. "I have already found a fine mount for you, a gelding, by the way, a handsome horse who'll give you no trouble."

"My own mare is at my uncle's house. Couldn't I please ride her instead? I've never ridden sidesaddle. I'll have trouble no matter how gentle your horse might be."

"Impossible!" Clayton slammed the door as he gave his command, waking Andrea from a sound sleep in the next room.

Elizabeth ignored the baby's cry for a moment and after wrapping the sheet tightly around herself rushed after the tall British officer. "Clayton, since Madame Dupré's is just down the street, I could go alone this morning while Naomi watches Andrea. I know how you hate to sit and wait while I have fittings."

"If you think you can outsmart me, young lady, by telling me you'll be one place when you intend to go another, you'll be damned sorry!" Clayton snarled in his usual hostile tone of voice, as if he were addressing a garrison of raw recruits rather than a beautiful woman.

"Clayton, please, Andrea is crying. May I go alone or not?" Elizabeth had no more time to plead. She rested her hands lightly upon his sleeve and waited for him to reply.

"Oh, go ahead!"

Elizabeth ran back into his rooms to attend her baby. Where did he think she might go? She was forbidden to see Andrew, and where else was there to go? Was he simply jealous again, afraid she was interested in seeing someone else? Giving up her efforts to understand him, she played happily with her daughter until Naomi was finished with her morning chores and could care for the baby while she was out.

Madame Dupré nodded as she listened to Elizabeth's request. "Of course, something in velvet. Mrs. Jor—, excuse me, Miss Peterson, why is it I can never recall your proper name?"

Elizabeth tried to suppress a smile as she described what she needed. "I want something which will look hideous with a British officer's uniform, orange or purple, or—"

"Elizabeth, really!" The seamstress laughed heartily, although she readily understood the young woman's interest. "If we make the garment in a very simple but elegant style in beige or tan, only Colonel St. James will be seen. You will be invisible by his side."

"Yes, perfect! Thank you, Madame Dupré. I knew you would be able to provide exactly what I wanted." The pretty blonde hugged the woman warmly and

475

stood humming softly to herself as she waited patiently for her measurements to be taken again.

"Miss MacFadden asked me only yesterday if I had any appointments scheduled for you. Would it offend you if I sent her a message so she might come here at the same time?"

Elizabeth shook her head emphatically. "Please don't. She is my best friend, but I can't draw her into my problems. It is far too dangerous for her to be involved in my life now."

"As you wish then. Now if you'll just turn one last time I will be finished."

Elizabeth thought the matter settled, but when next she came to the dressmaker's shop, Stephanie was there waiting for her. "Please don't be angry, Elizabeth. I pestered Madame Dupré until she had to tell me when you'd be here. I hope you won't mind that I sent a message to Red Tail."

"You sent him a note? Oh no, if it falls into Clayton's hands—" Elizabeth cried out in horror.

"Do not worry so. It was a spoken message only. I told Henry and he told Red Tail we would be here today. I would not trust such a thing to paper, but we are wasting precious time. Red Tail will be missed soon."

"What!" Elizabeth wrenched free of her friend's warm embrace. "Red Tail is here? You fool! Clayton will kill him for this!"

Stephanie took Elizabeth's hand and led her into the storeroom where they found the Indian seated on a bolt of cloth but he leapt to his feet as they entered. He pulled Elizabeth into his arms and kissed her hungrily, as if she were his wife rather than Andrew's, yet she

476

did not feel his welcome overly familiar after all they'd shared and returned his affectionate greeting with the same joyous warmth he'd given it.

"How were you able to slip past the guards? I thought you were never to be left unguarded?" Elizabeth asked hurriedly.

"They let me go out for herbs to make medicines. I have been out many times before today." The Indian grew more serious as he continued, "Rising Eagle is no better, Elizabeth. My medicines are healing his leg, but it is his spirit that needs you. You must come to see him."

Elizabeth closed her eyes and lay her head upon his chest for a long moment before she looked up into his dark brown eyes. His gaze was warm, tender, but she had to make him understand the danger if he did not see it. "Red Tail, Clayton St. James will hang you both if he even suspects I've been in that house. I cannot go to see my husband when the risk is so great. I cannot."

Red Tail straightened up to his full height, then spoke slowly to also make his point clear. "Rising Eagle is dying, Elizabeth. He is dying and I cannot save him. Only you can do it."

"If he dies then it will not matter that I did not visit him, but if he lives I do not want to see you both hang. Can't you understand what a fiend St. James is? He despises Andrew and will hang you both and demand I watch!"

The Indian refused to give in. "You must come, Elizabeth."

"I know you are brave, but don't do this to me. I won't watch you die for nothing!" Elizabeth's eyes filled with tears and spilled over her thick lashes at the

477

anguish of that terrible possibility.

Red Tail reached out to touch her fair hair lightly. "For you, Elizabeth."

Elizabeth reached up to hug his neck tightly. "No, you can't throw your life away for me. I won't permit you to do that."

Stephanie stood quietly watching the well built Indian with growing interest. Elizabeth's trust seemed to be well placed for the man radiated a quiet strength, a calm born of confidence rather than bravado. Although he was dressed in buckskins, his manner was not in the least bit wild, but gentlemanly and polite. "Red Tail, if Andrew is so ill, is he conscious? Is he awake? Would he even know Elizabeth if she did go to see him?"

The brave scoffed at that ridiculous question. "You do not understand. If Rising Eagle could neither see nor hear he would still know Elizabeth."

Undaunted, Stephanie attempted to make her meaning clear. "Do you understand what I mean, Elizabeth? We are nearly the same size. If I wore my hair down, wore your clothes, your perfume, if the room were dark, would Andrew know the difference as ill as he is?"

Elizabeth's face brightened immediately. "Stephanie, would you be willing to do it? Would you?"

"Elizabeth!" Red Tail hissed his disapproval. "Rising Eagle is dying and you would trick him?"

"No, not really trick him. I want to save him, Red Tail. I just want so badly to save his life I will try anything. Any deception is worth a try if it will help him want to live." Elizabeth turned away to hug Stephanie and whispered as they bent their heads together to plan what the young woman should do.

Red Tail sat down again on the comfortable bolt of cloth and put his head in his hands, his disbelief clear. "Elizabeth, this will never work, never."

As Elizabeth lay in Clayton's arms that night, she thought the sound of his rumbling snore delightful. As long as he slept soundly, her husband and Red Tail were safe and she prayed Stephanie would play her part well enough to fool Andrew, to make him want to grow strong and live forever.

At that same moment, Stephanie MacFadden sat in the Jordan kitchen. She'd slipped into the house late that afternoon dressed as a maid. The staff of the household came and went so frequently she caused no comment among the guards when she arrived in a dull brown cape, the hood hiding her face, and her basket filled to the brim with onions and carrots. Mrs. Blackstone, however, had been as appalled as Red Tail by the girl's story.

"Is it not enough to have the young master and that savage under arrest here? How will you ever accomplish your errand? You look nothing like Elizabeth. Surely you must realize that."

"I know we'd never be mistaken for twins, but don't worry. I will do what I must to help Andrew." Stephanie was scared to death. She hadn't expected the soldiers to be inside the house as well as surrounding the residence and was not nearly so confident as she wanted the housekeeper to believe. When Red Tail moved soundlessly up behind her, she almost shrieked in alarm at his touch.

"Come, I will show you up the stairs," he whispered softly and, taking her arm, led her up the back staircase, one she'd never had occasion to use in her many visits to the Jordan home. He nodded toward one room, waited for her to enter, then went into Andrew's bedroom and came back through the connecting door. He opened the wardrobe and tossed her one of the cotton dresses Elizabeth had made herself. "Wear this."

"Aren't you going to leave?" Stephanie's apprehension grew as she realized he meant to stay right where he was while she changed her clothes.

Red Tail swore impatiently, grateful the woman had no idea what he'd said. "There is no time. The soldiers do not play cards all night. One may come soon!"

"Turn around then." Stephanie held the pretty dress in front of herself, as if she were nude rather than fully clothed, for truly she did feel his gaze was far too curious and she was terribly embarrassed.

"I have seen women." Red Tail shrugged, unsure of her reason for hesitating.

"Not me, you haven't, and you won't either, now turn around!" Stephanie stamped her foot impatiently and when he turned she slipped out of her own dress and chemise and pulled on the blue gingham dress quickly. "Where is her perfume?"

Red Tail gestured toward the dressing table but the collection of bottles mystified Stephanie. "Which one is it? Do you know the name?"

"I do not read your writing," the Indian confessed slowly, but seeing she thought no less of him for that admission, he began to sample the aromas. He tried several, then reached for the smallest bottle, withdrew the stopper and instantly recognized the scent. "This one."

"Thank you." Stephanie put two quick dabs of the perfume behind her ears then replaced the bottle upon the dresser.

Red Tail scoffed at her effort. "Give the bottle to me." When he extended his hand she placed it in his grasp. He sprinkled the fragrance on his fingertips then ran them through her long hair and slowly down her arms. "There. Elizabeth smells this good all over."

"Thank you," Stephanie stammered again. She was surprised by the gentleness of his touch. It was light, so delicate, like the summer breeze upon her skin, not at all what she'd expected from an Indian and she blushed deeply, shocked by the thoughts which flooded her mind.

Red Tail left his hands upon her shoulders. "Do you know how to kiss a man?"

Stephanie shrugged nervously. "Is there some trick to it?"

The Indian chuckled at her innocence. "Yes. Elizabeth knows how. You saw her kiss me."

"Oh, like that." Her courage was fast disappearing. "I didn't think Andrew would be well enough to kiss me, but if he does, would you please show me what to do?"

"I do not frighten you?" Red Tail's expression was serious, without the trace of a smile. As he stared down at her, his dark brown eyes appeared black in the dim light and their gleam was not warm but cold and calculating as he assessed her chances of fooling his friend and found them not good.

"Yes, you do, but I promised Elizabeth I'd try and

481

do this and if Andrew should kiss me, I don't want him to know I'm not her." She licked her lips and tried not to be frightened but truly what he was was far more terrifying to her than he was himself. He was an Indian and she had never even spoken to such a man before, let alone kissed one. She closed her eyes as Red Tail moved his hand up to tilt her chin. His lips were soft, but she drew away when his tongue caressed her mouth.

Red Tail issued a disapproving warning. "You will never fool him if you are afraid."

Stephanie gathered what little courage she had and placed her hands upon his shoulders. "Please, show me again." Her lips met his and she relaxed this time, letting his tongue slowly explore her mouth as she clung to him, fascinated by the tenderness of his lesson. This time he was the one to draw away.

"Now you must kiss me," he whispered invitingly.

Stephanie took a deep breath and leaned against him. His touch was so gentle as he drew her hips to his she didn't realize what he'd done until the heat from his loins seared through his buckskin britches and spread through her slender body with an electrifying current. Shocked by the blatant nature of his advance she pulled away. "Red Tail!"

"You do not like me?" He chuckled, and not waiting for her reply, he pulled her along into Andrew's room.

The blood was pounding in Stephanie's ears. She felt as if her whole body were on fire as she stood trembling with the desire the handsome young Indian had awakened, yet it was obvious to her what he had done. He'd only wanted her for Andrew, not for himself, but she was stunned by the power of her own

482

response no matter what his purpose might have been in arousing it, and she could not deny she had enjoyed it.

Red Tail drew her close and whispered softly in her ear, "Say nothing. Kiss his face. Lie down beside him and hold him in your arms as though you loved him."

Stephanie followed his directions but whether Andrew realized she was there she couldn't tell. She let her long hair brush his face as she bent down to kiss him. Red Tail had snuffed the candles and she could see little of the ailing man's expression. She nestled against him and put her arms around him but he seemed much too warm, too feverish to feel her tender affection, yet she hated to go. She waited, nearly frightened to death until finally Andrew stirred from his sleep and whispered, "Elizabeth?"

She kissed his lips lightly once more and he drew her close to his heart, spreading her scented hair out over his chest with his fingertips as he returned her gentle kiss. She let her hand move across his chest and down his arm as she buried her face in his shoulder, her tears genuine, her sorrow far too great to hide. She thought only of how dearly Elizabeth loved the man in her arms and hugged him tightly as she wept.

"Elizabeth, do you love me still?" Andrew's hoarse whisper was filled with the anguish of doubt.

Stephanie answered so quietly she knew he would not be able to recognize her voice. "I will love you forever." She held him clasped warmly in her embrace as he again fell asleep and, when she was near sleep too, Red Tail took her hand to pull her away and led her back into Elizabeth's bedroom, the room she'd used only to store her clothes. Stephanie was shaking all over and could not stop. "I didn't know it would be like this, so very sad. He loves Elizabeth so. It should have been her here with him. It should have really been her." Stephanie threw her arms around Red Tail, the erotic effect he'd had upon her forgotten.

"Stephanie, you must go now. Do not cry. For him you were Elizabeth. She was here in his heart." Red Tail unhooked the soft cotton dress and rehung it in the wardrobe as Stephanie struggled to don her own garments once again. That he had seen her nearly nude seemed unimportant to her now. "Henry is waiting. The housekeeper will tell the guards you are ill and going to your parents' house."

"Yes, I know the plan, but I can't seem to stop crying. I'm sorry to be so foolish, but what will happen to you two? Is Andrew really dying?"

"His heart is gone. If he remembers when he wakes that Elizabeth was here, I will tell him that she was. It cannot harm him to have the hope she will return."

"No. That's cruel, for I can't keep coming back! I'm not really his wife. If he were to, well, to want to make love to me, I wouldn't know what to do!" Stephanie pleaded with him to see her dilemma.

"I will teach you. It is easy to learn, like kissing." Red Tail laughed at her embarrassment.

"It is not! I'm no fool and I think I better leave here right now." Stephanie pulled on the drab cloak she'd borrowed from Esther's cook and started for the door, but Red Tail caught her arm. "Yes?"

"If my friend dies, I will be hanged swiftly. Have you no good-bye kiss for me?"

Stephanie gasped sharply and reached out to take his hands. "No! God forbid that he should die, but if it happens you must flee immediately. Do not tell the guards he is dead. Tell them only you need more herbs, then come to me." Stephanie whispered the directions to her cousin's home, then made him repeat them until she was certain he understood. "I will hide you until you can escape the city." She saw him incline his head as he bent down, but she did not draw away. She wanted more of the deep kisses he gave so sweetly and clung to him again as his hands moved slowly down the hooks of her bodice so he might caress the soft fullness of her figure as she stood in his arms, hungry for his taste and touch, knowing all the while she should not be there, yet she could not draw away. When Mrs. Blackstone suddenly came through the door, she pulled her cloak up to her throat to hide her state of undress from the woman's keen gaze. "Do not forget, Red Tail. You must come to me."

"I will come." Red Tail smiled broadly, his promise given with calm assurance.

"Whatever you two are plotting must cease! Hurry, Henry is waiting!" Mrs. Blackstone grabbed Stephanie by the arm and hustled her out of the room, but not before the shy girl turned back one last time to smile and wave at the Indian brave.

Elizabeth paced nervously in front of the windows. She would not be able to meet Stephanie until the end of the week, but found the suspense of worrying over how things had gone nearly unbearable. Andrew couldn't die. He just couldn't! It was all so terribly unfair that he should lie so ill and think she would not come to tend him if she could. She could not bear for him to think she had deserted him, and prayed that Stephanie's plan had worked well. When Clayton slammed the door she turned instantly, but her fright grew when she saw the wicked looking whip in his hand.

"That brother of yours thinks he can slip his mistress in and out of his uncle's house at will. You're coming with me while I teach him just how wrong he is!" Clayton grabbed for her wrist and pulled her along behind him as he went through the door.

"A mistress! Clayton, surely you don't mean it? He was so ill. How can such a thing be possible when he has been so badly injured? He can't possibly have the strength for such a thing as you suggest." Elizabeth grabbed the sleeve of his uniform and tugged violently to make him halt and listen to reason.

"His driver was observed returning from the young woman's home last night. I will not have men under my protection flaunt my rules so openly!"

Elizabeth planted her feet firmly on the scuffed wooden floor of the hall and whispered, "You made no mention of women other than me, Clayton. You did not forbid Andrew to have visitors."

"What?" Clayton cried out in astonishment.

"Well, you didn't! If every woman in town wants to visit my husband, how is he to blame?"

"Elizabeth!" Clayton found her use of such piercing logic exasperating in the extreme.

Elizabeth turned to go, but he reached out to take her arm again. "I didn't plan to stop with Andrew. I'll flog that Indian and the driver, too. I want to know that woman's name!"

"You need not beat anyone for such a secret. Come

into your rooms and I will tell you who it was." This time when she moved away he followed her without protest. "Just sit down and drop your whip, please. I do not wish to see anyone flogged over this incident, myself included."

Clayton tossed the weapon aside and snarled, "Well, who is the bitch?" He sat down quickly, impatient to hear the tale.

As always, Elizabeth found just looking into his eyes made the most fantastic lies spring from her lips. "She is the daughter of a prominent Loyalist, a woman you have courted yourself I believe. At least I did see you coming from her house one afternoon. Of course, that was some time ago."

"What?" Clayton leapt to his feet. "What nonsense is this?"

Elizabeth lowered her gaze as if she were mortified to repeat her story. "I'm certain it was not Andrew she went to see last night, but his friend, Red Tail. She had this curiosity about savages, about what they would be like, and I'm sure that's who she'd go to see."

The color drained from Clayton's tan features as his mind raced frantically to decide which of the young women he knew she must mean. "Surely you can't be referring to Esther Nolan!"

"As I said, she was so curious about Indians, pestered me for the most intimate details of my relationship with my husband. You must not be too hard on her, for she is a very spoiled young woman, used to getting what she wants. Red Tail was probably afraid to refuse her, for if she got past your guards then he must have thought you gave your permission for her to be there in the house."

487

"My God! Esther!" Clayton covered his eyes with his hand for a moment, as if he could shut out the erotic images which quickly filled his mind. "This must not be allowed to continue."

"I quite agree. Red Tail is far too modest a man to refuse her, but should there be a child—" Elizabeth left her sentence hanging in midair for his imagination to complete and she could tell by his expression she had been successful.

"This is horrible, Elizabeth. I was expecting to catch some pretty barmaid, some whore I'd toss to the guards the next time she showed her face at that house, but Esther!"

"Yes, your problem is a far different one now for undoubtedly Mr. Nolan will blame you for any consequences of this affair. You must not blame Red Tail, though. Do not punish him for Esther's insatiable lusts for savages." Elizabeth watched the thoughts fly through her captor's mind and stepped forward. "She was probably badly disappointed after being with so fine a man as you."

"Me?" Clayton's dark eyes widened in disbelief. "I never slept with her. I thought her a respectable young woman, a virgin!"

Elizabeth shook her head knowingly. "How could she have fooled you, deceived you so completely, Clayton?"

"Enough of this whole business. No one will enter or exit that house, absolutely no one! Most especially no women!" Clayton stormed out of the room but he left his whip behind. Elizabeth kicked the blasted thing under the dresser and when he asked later if he'd left it there, she replied innocently that she'd not seen it since he'd gone out the door with it in his hand.

Elizabeth stood for her fitting while Stephanie wrung her hands and cried. "You mean Clayton found out I was there? Oh, no, what will he do to me?" The poor girl was terrified and Madame Dupré called for more tea. She had plenty thanks to the generosity of her British customers.

"Nothing. I told him there was a certain young woman he knew who had a passion for savages and he drew his own conclusions. Stephanie, you needn't worry that he'll ever discover you were there."

Stephanie stared at her friend's mischievous smile. "You mean he thinks it was—"

Elizabeth put her fingertip to her lips in warning and Stephanie fell silent. When the French seamstress had stepped out of the fitting room, they again discussed the evening and how the ruse had gone.

"Red Tail thinks I should return." Stephanie helped Elizabeth to dress, but her hands shook so violently the blonde pointed her toward the chair and dressed without assistance.

"No, that is impossible. Clayton has stopped all visitors from entering the house. He swore to give Andrew's 'mistress' to the guards should she ever again appear. Red Tail did not know Clayton would find out about your visit so soon. I warned him that the Englishman was a crafty devil, but I don't think he believed me."

Stephanie chewed her lip nervously, then confessed shyly. "I let him kiss me, Elizabeth."

"Yes, that was why you went, to fool Andrew. I knew you would kiss him. I'm not jealous, or angry at what took place, only grateful for your friendship and bravery."

Stephanie shook her head. "No, that's not who I meant. I know it was all right to kiss Andrew."

Elizabeth bent down beside her friend and took her trembling hands in hers. "Red Tail, you mean? Oh, Stephanie, why shouldn't you if you like him? He is handsome, and very nice."

"He is an Indian, Elizabeth, a real Indian." Stephanie's eyes swept Elizabeth's face but found no trace of understanding. "I should never have kissed an Indian."

Elizabeth leaned her forehead against her best friend's for a moment as she gathered her thoughts. "Red Tail saved my life more than once, Stephanie. He was with me when I lost Andrew's child. I have no better friends than you and he. The British and the Patriot's both value their Indian allies for their bravery and courage. He is a fine man and you should not be ashamed he kissed you if you wanted him to do it."

"I didn't want him to do it at first, but then I did not want him to stop." Stephanie brushed away her tears with her fingertips and continued. "I am not pretty like you are, Elizabeth. Men like you so much better than they like me and I know so little how to please them."

"Which is why I am Clayton's whore and you are not!" Elizabeth stood up quickly and picked up her cloak. "You are pretty, Stephanie, truly you are. What good is Esther's beauty when she has the heart of a snake, or mine, when it has brought me so much pain?"

490

"But you have Andrew!" Stephanie protested instantly.

"Yes, I do and thanks to you he is still alive, or at least I pray he still is. Now, I must hurry back to the inn before Clayton returns and finds me gone."

"Elizabeth?"

"Yes?" Elizabeth stopped as she pulled back the curtains which provided privacy to the small fitting rooms.

"If the very worst thing possible happened, if you were to lose Andrew, would you take Red Tail as your husband?"

Elizabeth's breath caught in her throat at the horror of that thought, yet she understood why her tearful companion had to ask such a question. "No, for Andrew will always be my husband in my mind, and heart, and Red Tail would know that, too. That would be agony for both of us. No, do not worry. I will not be your rival for Red Tail, not ever."

"I can think of no way to see him again."

Elizabeth laughed. "Do you wish to see him? Make up your mind!"

Stephanie laughed too then, realizing how silly she sounded. "I would like for him to kiss me again, to hold me in his arms as he did. I have never felt so wanted, so loved. He treated me as though I were beautiful, Elizabeth."

"Oh, Stephanie, you are! In so many ways, you are a beauty. Now, I must go. This war cannot last forever. It is rumored the French will join our cause soon. You will be able to see Red Tail when the hostilities cease. If not before, surely then."

Elizabeth had been back at the inn for no more than five minutes when Clayton returned for the midday meal. She told him the riding habit was nearly completed, but absolutely nothing more. She laughed to herself, remembering Stephanie's tears over kissing an Indian brave. Surely being Clayton's whore was a far greater sin. She had not even the end of the war to which to look forward, if the British won, Clayton would remain in the Colonies and she'd be his captive for years to come, all her babies his. If the British were defeated, then she had no hope either, for what and who she was was so well known she'd be tarred and feathered for certain!

Twenty-Six

The winter of 1778 was a severe one. After his defeat at Germantown, George Washington set up his winter quarters in Valley Forge, but Elizabeth hoped the dire reports Clayton gave on the fate of the Continental Army were exaggerated. She believed little that the British officer told her, even doubted his comments that Matthew's failing health was deteriorating more rapidly until one afternoon he arrived with the news her uncle had died in his sleep the previous night.

The early spring rain was no more than a light mist as the mourners left the church to accompany the casket containing Matthew Jordan's body to the freshly dug grave in the adjoining cemetery. Elizabeth kept her hand on Clayton's arm, her devotion to the tall Englishman plain in that simple gesture. She stood close to his side. Her eyes averted from the sharp gaze of the man she still called husband. They were standing upon Phillip's grave, she realized with a shudder, and read the man's tombstone silently, welcoming the distraction from the exquisite torture Andrew's presence brought. The man had been only thirty-four when he'd died, she noted with sorrow, then her eyes swept over the dates again. She bent down and looked more closely. Phillip Jordan had died on October 12, 1758, a full eleven months before she had been born and no matter how fine a man Andrew's father had been, he could not have done the impossible, and most assuredly he could not have fathered her four months after he had died. She had been premature, born after only seven months, conceived in February, the month her parents had married. She counted the months again and again in her mind, but each time the answer was the same. She tried to recall what Matthew had shown them to prove she and Andrew were related. He'd used only the date of her parents' marriage and the date of her birth, but he had lied about when Phillip had died. He had lied to them! She was furious with what the man had done to end her marriage. No wonder he had suffered a stroke. The weight of his own guilt must have crushed him when Andrew had fled his home. She could scarcely contain her happiness and the smile which lit her face as she looked up at Andrew was radiant, glowing with the love which filled her heart, for at last she had all the proof she needed to be his wife. His eyes widened in surprise as she mouthed the words, I love you, so plainly everyone present could see except for the finely uniformed man at her side. Andrew began to grin then looked away quickly as Clayton St. James turned to look down at her. She glanced up at the colonel, her expression blank, completely innocent and he turned away, impatient for the lengthy service to end. When at last the Angelican priest intoned the benediction, he took her arm firmly in his grasp.

"We should speak to Andrew, don't you agree, dearest? Tell your brother how deeply we share in his tragic loss." Clayton's voice dripped with sarcasm as he tightened his hold upon her arm.

Elizabeth could barely contain her excitement as she responded demurely, "If you insist, Clayton." They waited until the crowd had thinned, then approached Andrew, but before her escort could speak, Elizabeth reached for her husband's hand and spoke rapidly. "I hope you were able to find a skilled stone mason to make your uncle's tombstone in the same style as your father's. Phillip's is magnificent, especially the dates, and I hope you will take the time to study it closely this morning, if you have not done so." She gripped his fingers in a quick clasp and prayed he would understand her meaning. His eyes clouded with pain as he looked down at her, but he nodded and squeezed her hand as it slipped from his.

Colonel St. James' arm closed firmly around Elizabeth's shoulders. "Your uncle was a fine man, Andrew, a true friend of the Crown, and I will miss him."

Andrew's expression changed instantly to reflect his unbridled hatred. "I'll see you in hell yet, you bastard. Save your sympathy for yourself!"

Clayton scoffed at the younger man's insult. "I have no need of any sort of sympathy when I have a treasure such as Elizabeth to show me all I need of heaven." Clayton lunged to the left as Andrew's fist tore by his cheek. He slammed his boot into Andrew's still mending left leg with a vicious kick and laughed loudly when Red Tail had to catch his friend before he fell face downward into the mud.

"Come, Elizabeth. I fear your brother lacks your refinement. Shall we leave him to mourn alone?" He turned to gesture casually. "Guards, return these prisoners to their quarters."

Elizabeth looked back as they moved away. Andrew had not cried out under what must have been the most agonizing of blows, but she had known he would not. He was Indian through and through, stoic and proud. He would die well no matter when his fate overtook him, but she prayed he would continue to live with the same fierce determination he had shown in the face of that excruciating pain.

Once seated in their carriage, Elizabeth removed her bonnet and shook out her long damp curls. She felt drained, too tired to resist as Clayton put his arm around her waist to draw her close.

"I am sorry Andrew is not stronger. He limps badly. Did you notice how slowly he walked as we left the church?"

"Yes, I did." He had once moved with such masterful grace, but now he limped like a tired, old man, stiff with the pain of advanced age. "Why should that concern you, though. Surely it is to your advantage if he never regains his former health and strength."

"No, my pet. I have plans for that brother of yours, and I want him to be well as soon as possible."

Elizabeth sat up and stared intently at Clayton's shining eyes. They glowed like two black diamonds, chilling her to the bone. "What plans might those be?" She held her breath, afraid to imagine what ghastly ordeal the hateful man might have dreamed up for her husband.

"He is going to escape and return to fight again with the Patriots. I have heard LaFayette has Indian scouts with him. Perhaps I will send him to join them."

Elizabeth was astounded by his remark. "You'd set him free to fight against the British?"

Clayton chuckled at her lack of insight. "No, of course not. I'll set him free to spy for me."

"Andrew would never turn traitor!"

Clayton lifted an eyebrow quizzically. "Aren't you forgetting he is already a traitor to his king? To ask him to turn his coat again is only to set him upon the right path."

"Never! He'd never spy for you. You can't actually believe that he would!" Elizabeth was outraged at the man's conceit.

"We'll see. Shall we lay a small wager upon the outcome of this argument? I say your brother regards your life as highly as you prize his. He will obey me eagerly when he understands the consequences should he refuse."

"When I have come to you willingly, have done all you have asked, you would forfeit my life as if I were nothing to you still?" Elizabeth was sickened by the evil man's lack of honor, then cursed her own stupidity for even expecting such a virtue in him.

Clayton leaned forward and pulled Elizabeth close, his tongue ravaging her mouth as he kissed her with a savage abandon. He held her so she could not escape his forceful passion until he was ready to release her. "You are the most fascinating of amusements, Elizabeth, but do not credit yourself with having won my heart."

"That would be impossible, for you have none!" Elizabeth turned away as she wiped her bruised mouth on the back of her glove, but that was not enough to remove his bitter taste from her lips and she forced herself not to gag and retch right there upon his spotlessly clean uniform.

"Elizabeth, you are a great prize, one I shall not risk losing foolishly. I would not kill you simply to spite Andrew Jordan, but there are so many truly horrid things I can threaten to do that will convince him to do my bidding as readily as I have bent you to my will."

Elizabeth did not respond. She despised the man for his evil lusts. He would stoop to any degradation to get even with Andrew and she would never understand why nor would she inquire as to his reasons since he had none other than his own passion for meanness, of that she was certain. "It is a tragedy General Howe leaves you here to defend the city when he goes out to challenge the Continental Army. A man with your drive to conquer must be magnificent in battle!"

Clayton grabbed Elizabeth's shoulders and shook her soundly. "I am as fine a commander as any, and I do not question my orders! If I am needed here, then this is where I will be! I suggest you show the same obedience to me!"

Elizabeth replied in a vicious whisper, "Have I ever refused your attentions? Please tell me if I have not been as obedient a mistress as any man could ever hope to find!"

Clayton shoved her away rudely. "Your hate is preferable to any other woman's love. I have told you that repeatedly."

Elizabeth held her tongue. Why had Andrew not taught her how an Indian brave bears agony in silence? Had he never imagined what horrors she would find when he had left her to fend for herself in the world? She clenched her fists tightly in her lap, but spoke not another word. She knew only too well what Clayton would want when they reached the inn, but he shocked her by drawing her close as he began to loosen his belt.

"Draw your cloak around us, Elizabeth. I can wait no longer to take you again. Your defiance is a greater aphrodisiac than any wine or perfume."

"Clayton, this is a public street!" But her sense of modesty meant nothing to him. His hands moved under her skirt, stripping away her lingerie as he pulled her upon his lap. His left arm held her waist in a firm clasp as he forced her slim thighs apart with his right. "You never refuse me, do you?"

Elizabeth closed her eyes as she wrapped her arms around his neck in a warm embrace. "No, I will never refuse you." She whispered her promise in his ear. "As long as you keep Andrew alive I will gladly be yours." She blocked out all sensation as he wound his fingers in her hair and forced her head back so his mouth could again plunder hers. She could escape him in her mind if not in her body, but nothing mattered to her except saving Andrew. His life was worth a hundred of hers. When they arrived at their destination, she pulled her torn undergarments back into place as best she could and walked into the crowded inn ahead of him, her head held proudly as if she were the finest of ladies returning from a pleasant ride rather than the young woman who was fast becoming the city's most gossiped about whore.

Although her head throbbed painfully, Elizabeth completed the complicated figures of the dance gracefully, then smiled sweetly at her partner. She'd forgotten the lieutenant's name. He was very young, not much older than she, his well tailored uniform new, his confidence high, but she wondered how fast his smile would vanish should he realize her husband was responsible for the deaths of countless numbers of British troops. She felt out of place, as if she were the enemy in plain view, yet none saw her. Clayton was the only one who knew where her sympathies lay, but he was careful never to reveal her true feelings to his friends.

"Thank you, Mrs. St. James. You are as lovely a dancer as you are a woman," the officer complimented Elizabeth as he returned her to the side of the man he mistakenly believed to be her husband.

Clayton grinned as he watched the color flood Elizabeth's cheeks. "Now there's a thought I'd not even considered, Lieutenant. I doubt Miss Peterson would have me though, would you, my dear?"

Elizabeth was appalled by that question and had no idea how to respond as she was careful never to embarrass the arrogant colonel in public. She went out of her way to be charming and pleasant wherever he escorted her since he was the one who should be ashamed of their liaison, not she. "Is that a proposal, Clayton? Surely a man with your pride would not wish to be any woman's third husband." Elizabeth smiled coyly as she watched the anger explode in the man's dark eyes. She'd never told him the truth about Red Tail so since he counted two husbands, so would she.

The startled lieutenant interrupted before his senior officer could reply. "Miss Peterson? I'm sorry,

I must have misunderstood your name when we were introduced, but why are you called Miss if you've been married twice? You are so young to have been widowed."

"Miss Peterson may well be a widow if she's not more careful!" Clayton took her arm to lead her back out onto the dance floor, but his anger continued to mount in spite of the soothing music to which they moved. "I could force you to marry me. You know that I could." He whispered his threat as he drew her close.

Elizabeth's emerald gaze swept his stern scowl slowly. "Why would you wish to complicate our relationship with a legal tie, Clayton? I know my place now, but as your wife things would have to be entirely different."

Clayton looked askance, intrigued by her words. "In what way? You would still have to obey me."

"Yes, but you would have to promise to love and cherish me. Surely you could not bring yourself to swear to so preposterous a lie." Elizabeth held her breath. She was pushing him and shouldn't. She knew that well. It had been over a month since the funeral. Was Andrew strong enough yet to flee the prison his home had become? She did little but think of him, think of him, pray for him, hope he was growing stronger with each passing hour so he might soon elude Clayton's grasp and she would be free then, too. That day couldn't come too swiftly for her. The fight to free the Colonies from English rule was a small squabble compared to the battle she waged daily in her heart to be free of Clayton's dreadful power over her.

501

"Do not mention the subject of marriage to me ever again, Elizabeth. It is a far too dangerous one for us to discuss."

"As you wish, Colonel."

"Do not address me as colonel. How many times must I remind you to use my name?"

"I have not forgotten, Clayton." Elizabeth's smile tempted him further, but they were interrupted before he could begin.

Stephanie approached them shyly as the music ended. "Good evening, Colonel St. James, Elizabeth. I wonder if you might come and help me a minute, Elizabeth. I'm afraid I've torn my petticoat and—"

Clayton gestured impatiently. "Elizabeth is no servant, Miss MacFadden. Surely there is a maid here to see to your needs."

Stephanie stammered as she reached for her friend's hand. "None is good with a needle, Colonel. I can repair the damage myself, but I will still need Elizabeth's assistance."

Clayton watched the tears fill the soft spoken young woman's eyes and relented. "Oh, take her. I can do with some more agreeable company for a few minutes, but do not be long."

Elizabeth tapped Clayton's sleeve lightly. "I will hurry. This should not take much time and I know there are many young ladies present who would appreciate the opportunity to dance with you." She smiled as the man blushed. He was very vain and she could not resist catering to that vanity when it suited her purpose. He nodded and she hurried to follow Stephanie up the stairs, but she soon realized they were not going to do any mending.

Stephanie looked around the small bedroom quickly to be certain they were alone, then locked the door and drew Elizabeth down beside her upon the bed. "I will try to be brief. Please do not interrupt me. You undoubteldy know Red Tail is every bit as clever as Andrew, as crafty an Indian as was ever born, and he has gone in and out of the Jordan house almost at will since the day Clayton brought him there."

"Stephanie!" Elizabeth's lashes nearly swept her brows as she realized what the young woman was admitting.

"Just listen! The first time he came to my cousin's house he told me only that he wanted to be certain which one it was so he could find it if he needed to hide."

Elizabeth swallowed her anger as she asked sharply, "He just came calling at the Nolan residence one afternoon? Is that what he did?"

"No, of course not. He came in the middle of the night, found my room and woke me to tell me he was there."

"Said good evening and then left?" Elizabeth was furious with her friends' stupidity.

Stephanie blushed deeply. "He only talked with me for a while, Elizabeth. Andrew was so very ill. Had he died Clayton would have had no reason to keep Red Tail alive. I told him where to find me so he'd have somewhere to hide, some way to get out of the city before Clayton could hang him. He came just to talk to me at first."

Elizabeth sighed impatiently. "It has been months, Stephanie, months! Red Tail has been visiting you all this time and you never told me?"

"I didn't want you to worry about us when you have been so frightened for Andrew. But now things are different. Red Tail wanted me to give you a message."

Elizabeth gripped her friend's hands tightly. "From Andrew? He sent a message for me?"

"Yes. He wants you to know he will come for you as quickly as he possibly can, that he won't leave Philadelphia without you."

"Oh, no, oh, Stephanie, you must tell Red Tail not to let Andrew attempt such a foolhardy act! If he can escape, then he must go, think only of saving himself and not of me."

Stephanie shook her head. "Do you really believe he can do that? Leave you with Clayton when he loves you so?"

"Yes. If he loves me at all, then he must leave me behind for he cannot take me without fighting Clayton and he can't be well enough to beat him. He'll only die trying to save me and I won't have it! You must make Red Tail understand, Stephanie. You must! He and Andrew will have to leave alone, just leave Philadelphia and not stop traveling until they are safe."

"They are not cowards, Elizabeth. Neither would leave you here with Clayton."

Elizabeth leapt to her feet, then began pacing nervously as she spun a tale she hoped the naïve girl would believe. "I have not forgiven Andrew for deserting me so callously. I know what I told you, that I loved him still, and I did until I went to live with Clayton."

Stephanie's eyes widened in alarm, then overflowed with tears as she cried out in disbelief, "I know you love Andrew. Don't say that you don't!"

Elizabeth lifted her chin defiantly. "I despise the man for leaving me alone, for leaving me to have his child without once caring how I might survive without him. Clayton spoke of marriage only this evening. It is a very real possibility between us. I would be happy to marry the man and return to England as his bride for he has far more to offer me than Andrew. I am finished with that man and you must make Red Tail believe it."

"But that's all lies, Elizabeth!" Stephanie was aghast at the enormity of Elizabeth's suggested deceit.

"It is the truth! I am going to marry Clayton St. James and return with him to England! I absolutely forbid Andrew to attempt to take me from Clayton when it would cost him his own life. Now, you make him understand that. I won't go with him, not ever!" Elizabeth's eyes blazed with anguish. "Please, Stephanie, you must convince Red Tail I want never to see Andrew again, never! Tell him I'm deeply in love with Clayton and plan to marry him soon." She unlocked the door and ran down the stairs, straight into Clayton's arms.

"I was just coming upstairs to find you. Was the petticoat in such shreds that it has taken you this long to mend it?"

Elizabeth tossed her fair curls coyly. "No, the tear was a slight one. Stephanie wanted my advice in a matter of romance more than she wanted my help with sewing. Your officers are all so dashing, the silly girl cannot make up her mind which one to love." Elizabeth smiled her most charming smile as they returned to the party, but her heart was racing wildly, her breathing far from even. She could not let Andrew throw away the freedom she had sacrificed everything to buy him. She glanced up at the tall officer and knew she would have to marry him, and soon. That would be enough to make Andrew hate her, and then he would be able to escape without stopping to take the risk of rescuing her. Yes, she could do it. She could entice Clayton into offering marriage and she'd do it, as soon as they returned to his inn.

Twenty-Seven

At Clayton's insistence, they were the last to leave the party and it was long past midnight when they returned to their inn. Elizabeth stopped by Naomi's room to pick up her sleeping daughter. Clayton held the door open as she carried the baby into her crib, but as Elizabeth turned to leave the darkened room, she saw a shadow move stealthily across the wall and froze. She knew instantly who it was and why he had come. It was too late to send him away for the knife blade gleamed in his hand and she knew there had been no time for her message to reach him and she could not speak the lies she'd told Stephanie to his face.

Andrew stepped silently to her side. "Stay here. That bastard will hide behind you if he has the chance. Don't give it to him." He was gone then, disappearing into the other room and she heard him call Clayton's name in a low whisper, no louder than a sigh, but the Englishman's response was an angry shout of surprise.

Elizabeth clamped her hands over her mouth to keep from screaming. The inn was filled with British officers. Was Andrew out of his mind, so consumed with a lust for revenge he did not realize what he had done by coming there? She was sick with fright, but the suspense of not knowing what would transpire was far worse and she moved to the doorway. If she could not prevent her husband from fighting Clayton, then she could at least see he didn't lose. Her mind raced frantically for some way she could assist him. She had no weapon, no way to aid him without adding to his problems, but she watched closely as the men moved, circling each other warily. Clayton had found his own knife. He had outsmarted himself, she realized, for he kept no other weapons in the room for fear she would use them against him so now had no sword or pistol to use on Andrew.

Clayton kept up a steady stream of insults, all filthy, exactly what she would expect from the man, yet he did not succeed in making Andrew lose his temper. He said every vile thing he could possibly say about her, but Andrew did not even blink, let alone respond in kind. He moved slowly, with a deadly grace, then sprang upon the Englishman in a flash of buckskin that sent the gray-haired man sprawling. They may have been near equals in strength when last they'd fought, but Clayton was now clearly superior and threw Andrew aside easily, but the younger man leapt to his feet and the officer's blade tore through thin air rather than flesh. As the fight continued, the men seemed to be only toying with each other, playing with weapons far too deadly for such sport, then Elizabeth realized Clayton planned to simply wait it out, to avoid Andrew's knife and make him exhaust the energy he possessed until, too tired to defend himself, he would make an easy prey. Andrew was faster, more agile, better with his weapon, but no longer stronger, and Clayton now had greater endurance if not more skill on his side. Soon each had slashed the other, inflicting no serious injury but drawing blood which splattered about the floor in bright red drops. Elizabeth gasped in terror as Andrew slipped, his left leg giving way but as Clayton lunged, his knife raised to strike a lethal blow she kicked open the door behind which she stood and the edge of the wood struck his elbow, knocking him off balance for the split second Andrew needed to rise and move out of danger. She had surprised Clayton with the speed of her action, jolted him out of the complacency of a sure victory against his old enemy and when he turned in the next instant to check her position, Andrew saw his chance and took it. In the split second Clayton had let his eyes move from his target to her, he lunged swiftly to drive his blade deep into the Englishman's chest.

Andrew withdrew his knife with a fierce upward thrust and Clayton staggered backward against the table, then slumped slowly to the floor. His breathing was ragged as he clutched his pierced chest. His eyes had never left Elizabeth and he tried to speak to her, his lips moving, but no sound coming from his throat.

Elizabeth stepped into the room hesitantly, repelled by the grim spectre of death, yet Clayton's pain-filled eyes implored her to come near. She knew him far too well to trust him, however, and first removed the knife from his hand and tossed the evil weapon upon the table before she knelt down at his side. She placed her hands lightly upon his shoulders and leaned close to hear what he was trying so desperately to say.

"I have always loved you. It was all for love, only for your love."

Elizabeth sat back, staring wide-eyed with disbelief

as Clayton tried to smile. His face was relaxed. The stern mask of hatred he'd always worn in her presence was gone and she saw for the first time what other women had always seen. He was a handsome man. Perhaps once he had been kind and good, before his heart had become twisted with the lust for vengeance and power. The light faded from his dark eyes as he slipped into unconsciousness and she lay his hand gently upon his bloody chest.

Andrew knelt beside him and reached for his thick thatch of gray hair. "Get the child, Elizabeth. Hurry. We must go quickly!"

"Dear God, you would scalp him before he is dead?" She was horrified by what Andrew plainly meant to do.

"Yes! Now get the babe!"

"No, I will not go with you if you do this. No purpose can be served by mutilating Clayton now. Come with me and leave him to die in peace." Elizabeth got to her feet and waited for her husband to rise.

"What did he say to you?" Andrew did not move. His left hand held Clayton's hair while his knife rested against the fallen man's scalp.

"That he loved me. I had never known that, not even suspected he cared for me. There had only been his lust and my hatred between us, no other emotions as far as I had known. Come, leave him be. You will dishonor only yourself with what you wish to do. Clayton had none for you to steal with his scalp." Elizabeth prayed Andrew would give in to her, but the flame which burned in his light eyes did not abate.

"If he had killed me, what would you have done?"

"Waited my chance to plunge your knife deep

510

between his shoulder blades! I would have avenged your death swiftly, but I would have left his blasted scalp on his head. Now, let us go!"

Andrew frowned as he weighed her words against what he wanted to do, then rose to stand beside her. His left leg throbbed painfully and he limped as he reached for the door. "Hurry. We'll go out over the rooftops as I came in. Clayton's body won't be found until morning, and we'll be far away by then."

Elizabeth swept past him into the adjoining room. She grabbed up her daughter's clothes and jammed the tiny garments into a small bundle before lifting the still sleeping child from her cradle. She followed Andrew to the window and looked out.

"Don't be afraid. I will carry the babe. You must follow me closely, step exactly where I do."

"I am not afraid," Elizabeth replied calmly. "I will do whatever we must to leave these accursed rooms behind." She wrapped her cape around herself to avoid tripping and crawled out of the dormer window and onto the ledge below. She did not once look down, only watched as her husband had told her to do and followed him on small sure feet over the roof. When they came to the edge of the tavern roof, Andrew lay down to drop the baby into Red Tail's waiting arms. The Indian caught Andrea and hushed her cries as Andrew swung down to the pavement, then turned to catch Elizabeth.

"The carriage is hidden nearby where it will not have been seen." Andrew took her hand as they traveled silently down the alley then turned down a side street. Elizabeth saw nothing she recognized and was out of breath and gasped for air when at last they reached the battered old carriage. It was covered with baggage and bundles, as if some poor family had loaded all its belongings upon the ancient vehicle to flee their farm for the safety of the city.

"Where did you find this wreck?" Elizabeth whispered as Andrew lifted her through the door. He waited until she was seated, then handed her the child and climbed in beside them. Red Tail leapt to the front seat and gently urged the team to pull the creaking conveyance down the street toward the nearest route out of town.

Andrew sat back and grinned happily despite the sharp pains which continued to shoot up his leg. "It is too early to rejoice, I know, but I have set you free and that is enough for now. Let me hold my daughter. Is she pretty?"

Elizabeth handed the baby to her father. "Yes, she is very pretty, fair like me and she has our green eyes."

Andrew kissed the small girl's chubby cheek, hugged her tightly, then reached for his wife's hand. "I don't think the annulment was valid since it was based upon a deception, but no matter, legally wed or not, you are still my wife."

Elizabeth turned away as she was overcome with sorrow. "If only you had believed me, Andrew, or not cared, as I did not, should it have been true every last drop of blood we have is the same. I can no longer bear to look at myself in the mirror and recall what I have done. I have become the finest of whores and although I would scrub my skin each morning until it was the same bright shade of crimson as Clayton's coat, I never felt clean." She pulled her hand from his and moved to the far side of the carriage. "I told you once no matter what I suffered I would live only to return to you. I was so terribly young then, and so very wrong. I no longer want to live with the memories I have. As soon as we leave the city I beg you to use your knife upon me. I would rather be dead than have to live another hour with what I have become."

Andrew was stunned by his wife's bitter words, shocked by the hollow sound of her once musical voice. "Elizabeth—"

"You must kill me or I will do it myself!" Elizabeth hissed back at him. "I stayed alive only to guard your life and Red Tail's. You will both be safe now and the need for me to survive is over. I want only the peace of the grave. I wish you had killed me after you'd stabbed Clayton, then I would already be dead!"

Andrew sat clutching his child in his arms and tried to speak calmly to the woman he adored. "I will not kill you nor allow you to be alone for one second if you would destroy yourself so eagerly. I will not risk such a death for you."

"How can you want me to live when I am filthy from that horrid man's touch? He took me again and again, Andrew, a thousand times perhaps. I meant to count, but lost track of the times he used me to satisfy his vile lusts. He took me in the carriage on our way home from your uncle's funeral. He could not wait to put his mark upon me again after I'd seen you. I will never feel clean again, and I do not want you to touch me! Just kill this empty shell. It is all that is left of me. My heart went with you when you left me more than a year ago."

Andrew sighed sadly. His own sorrow was as great as hers. "I should never have gone, Elizabeth, never. I was just so damned angry, furious you had not trusted me with a secret you'd kept the entire time we'd lived in my uncle's house. We had been so close I didn't understand why you would have hidden such a thing from me unless it were true and you were terrified of what my reaction would be." Andrew reached out, hoping again to draw the slender young woman into his arms, but she shoved him away.

"Don't touch me! I'll scream if you do! Leave me be until we are far enough out of the city for my body never to be found, then slit my throat quickly!"

Andrea began to whimper, tired and hungry. She flailed her clenched fists and kicked angrily at her father.

"The child needs you, Elizabeth. She needs her mother."

Elizabeth slowly unfastened the bodice of her gown and reached out to take the unhappy little girl. "I can leave her a full stomach, if nothing else. Give her to me." But as she felt the baby's anxious mouth at her breast, she shuddered for she felt only Clayton's hot breath as he had covered her body with unwanted kisses and she began to gag. "Dear God, I'm going to be ill!" She thrust the child back into her father's arms and leaned out the carriage window to retch. It had been too much for her, the fury of the knife fight, the bright red of Clayton's blood upon the snowy whiteness of his shirt, the horror of her own wish for death. Had Andrew not grabbed for her as she fainted, she would have toppled out of the carriage onto the cobblestone street below.

The sun was high above the carriage as it passed through a thick grove of trees. It wobbled and rocked as the wheels crossed over the gnarled roots and jarred Elizabeth awake. She was stretched across Andrew's lap, his strong arms holding her firmly even though he was still sound asleep. Andrea lay nestled against them, sucking her fingers noisily as her deep green eyes curiously studied her father's handsome face.

"My poor baby. What a night you must have had, my darling." Elizabeth managed to straighten up and finding the child's belongings, swiftly changed her sopping diaper. She drew her pretty daughter to her breast and tried to recall how they had come to be traveling with Andrew. Then it all came back to her with blinding clarity and she began to sob softly, her tears spilling down her flushed cheeks to splash upon the baby, but the child scarcely noticed her mother's sorrow as she slurped away on her breakfast.

Andrew opened his eyes slowly and found Elizabeth wiping her face on the hem of her yellow satin gown as she tried to hold her daughter securely at the same time. He moved over and drew his wife and baby into his arms. "Please do not cry so, Elizabeth. There is no reason for you to weep now that we are together again."

Unconsoled, Elizabeth continued to sob. "Oh, Andrew, what an awful mess I've made of my life, and yours, too!"

Andrew laughed at her words, too happy to have her in his arms to believe her statement was true. He yelled out the window for Red Tail to stop. "We'll rest here, Elizabeth. Red Tail can watch our daughter. What is her name? I neglected to ask you last night."

"I named her Andrea, for you. I am sorry she was not a son."

515

"Elizabeth, we will have plenty of sons. Andrea is a beauty just like her mother and I love her already. I told you once I would love all the daughters you could give me. Didn't you believe me? Now, adjust your dress before Red Tail opens the door."

Elizabeth blushed as she straightened her clothes. "Red Tail has seen me without a stitch, Andrew. Did he never admit that to you?"

"He would never tell me that and neither should you!" Andrew teased his wife playfully as he helped her down from the high carriage and, carrying Andrea, led her around to the horses.

"Oh, Andrew, you brought Lady!" Elizabeth hugged her mare's neck ecstatically and the horse snickered in response, recognizing her mistress' gentle touch and sweet scent instantly.

"She could not be left behind. I hope she has not gotten too tired. We'll let the horses rest a while, then leave the carriage here."

Elizabeth looked up toward the sun, shading her eyes with her hand. "It must be noon, Andrew. Where are we going?"

"We're heading southwest. If the British come after us at all, they'll go north believing I'd go home to the Seneca. They'll never find us. They could not track a bear through the desert let alone an Indian through the woods." Andrew withdrew his knife from his belt and stuck it's sharp blade into the roof of the old carriage with a savage thrust. "Now come with me. I want to talk with you and I do not want you to suspect I might stab you at any moment. That is something I'd never do." He took Elizabeth's arm, but she turned back to speak to Red Tail.

"I'm angry with you. You must know that, Red Tail. Stephanie told me how often you went to see her. What do you think will become of that sweet child now that you have left her?"

The Indian shifted their lively infant in his arms and smiled slyly. "She does not have your spirit, Elizabeth, but she is learning. We agreed to meet at the full moon in a place that is safe. If she wants to come with us and be my wife, then I will take her."

"Oh, you will?" Elizabeth laughed at his plan. "You won't try to sway her decision in your favor?"

Red Tail nodded as he grinned. "That is all I have done."

Andrew tugged on Elizabeth's arm impatiently. "You two can discuss Stephanie later. I want to speak to you now." He pulled her along beside him through the knee-high grass which blanketed the floor of the woods.

"Where are you taking me?" Elizabeth looked up at her husband. He was smiling happily at her as they moved into a small sunlit clearing.

"This will do. We need go no farther. Now come here to me, Elizabeth." Andrew pulled her close but she stiffened in his arms and turned her face away to avoid his kiss.

"No, please don't, please."

Andrew's voice was soft and low as he drew her close to his heart. "Elizabeth, you have always been mine, only mine. What is wrong?"

Looking up into the green eyes that matched her own so closely, Elizabeth could barely form her question. "How can you still want me, Andrew, after I have been so long with Clayton? How can you possibly want me still?"

Andrew raised his hand to trace the soft curve of her cheek. "I remember the day you traded Lady for me as if it were yesterday. You saved my life then and when the British caught me you saved me once more by going with Clayton. Why would I ever fault you for what you have done out of love for me? Clayton loved you, too. You have never been with any man who did not prize you more highly than his own life. You have never been a whore, my dear wife. Never."

Elizabeth shook her head sadly. "You are only trying to be kind to me, Andrew. I know what I am."

Andrew said nothing for several minutes. He held his wife in his arms and stroked her soft blond curls lightly. He could feel her tension, but could think of only one way to ease it. He stepped back and pulled off his buckskin shirt. "Put your hands on my chest, Elizabeth. Just touch me as you used to do. Your hands are so soft, your fingertips as light as a butterfly's wing upon my skin."

Elizabeth sighed as she turned away. Her shoulders shook with her sobs and she wrung her hands as she answered. "I'm sorry that you did not bring your knife. I can't make love to you any more, Andrew, and I do not want to live without you. I cannot."

"Was it rape with St. James, endless rape? Was that how that monster treated you?"

When Elizabeth turned back toward him he saw once again the wild creature he'd found living in the small shack in the forest. Her eyes had the very same vacant yet terrified stare and he felt the same pain of helplessness he'd known then.

"No, it was never rape. I made love to him, Andrew,

or allowed him to take me in any way he chose. I never fought him, not even once. I was too frightened he would hang you just so he would have the pleasure of watching me cry."

Andrew reached out to take her hand and drew her trembling fingertips to his lips. "I am alive, Elizabeth, and so, my dear girl, are you. The very first time I made love to you, you were not so frightened as this. Why are you so afraid of me now?"

Elizabeth attempted to offer an explanation, but there were no words to adequately describe the torment which tore at her soul. "I am not afraid of you, only sickened by what I have become. I felt nothing with Clayton, no trace of any emotion other than the revulsion I did my best to disguise. It was as if I were dead and he had found my body before it had grown cold and stiff. I could not bear to be with you if it were going to be the same."

"It is nothing to die bravely, Elizabeth, no feat at all. What is difficult is to live with the courage you have always shown. It will not fail you now and neither will I. I will wait for as long as it takes for you to want me again. I will never force you with threats as Clayton did, never take from you what you would not freely give." Andrew placed her small hands upon his warm chest and kissed her forehead tenderly. His lips traveled slowly down her cheek before softly caressing her moist mouth. His touch was light, so gentle upon her pink-tinged lips before his tongue began playfully to tease hers. Not since he had first taken her as his wife had he moved so cautiously, so carefully, to arouse the passionate nature he knew held such fiery warmth within her slender body.

519

It was difficult for him to be so considerate when he loved her with such desperation, ached with longing to possess the loving woman he had known. "I will never leave you, dear sister, dearest wife. Never will I allow us to ever be parted again. I will take you so far away no man ever sees the sun rise or hears the song of the birds. I will take you away until we find paradise again as we did so long ago in the peace of the forest near your parents' farm." When he sank to his knees she came with him. Her arms wound around his neck, pulling his mouth down to hers so she might return his affectionate kisses. She was crying softly still and he licked the tears from her cheeks, making his lips salty when they returned to hers.

Elizabeth wound her fingers in Andrew's long curls. The softness of his hair delighted her and she smoothed the waves back from his forehead. His skin was only lightly tanned now, pale after the long winter months when he'd not left his bed. Her kiss was easy and light, sweet, as she simply enjoyed the sight of his gleaming green eyes and wide smile.

"Elizabeth, I meant to come back for you, once I'd gotten over my anger. I cared no more than you that we had the same father, but there was always one more fight, one last battle which kept me from returning to you. Red Tail was not the only friend who came to find me when they heard I had joined the Patriot's side. There were many who were there only because they would fight beside me and I hoped we would make a difference." Andrew paused, wanting her to understand his anguish. "I do not want to see the Iroquois punished when the war draws to an end. If I could not keep them out of the fighting, I wanted at least to see peace would not be hard on them. Washington is a just man. I am convinced he will look after the men who were my brothers and deal with them honorably. But I worried constantly that you had married another. That was my greatest fear, that I would come back too late and find my precious wife belonged to another man. The prospect of death never compared to the terror of that thought in my mind."

Elizabeth kissed her husband's face lightly as she replied, "I did not see you for almost a year, the longest year of my life, and you thought only of me? There were no others?"

Andrew moaned in frustration as he could no longer restrain the desire which surged through his veins. He tightened his hold upon his fair bride and did not slacken it as his mouth caressed hers softly, conquering her small shudder of resistance easily while his hands moved swiftly to remove the layers of clothing which separated them. He was gentle, patient, yet moved with a strength of purpose she couldn't resist. She was his and he meant to make her feel his love to the depths of her being. That she had been with another man mattered not at all to him for she loved only him and he whispered every sweet phrase he could summon to mind as his lips moved over the soft swells of her figure, drawing her into the realm of pleasure from which he hoped never to release her. She was so slender, her delicate beauty as fragile as her spirit, and he cradled her in his arms, tenderly holding her body pressed tightly against his until the rhythm of her heart matched his own, pulsating with the vibrant beat of his love.

Elizabeth trembled, but did not pull away, nor did

she close her eyes. She wanted to watch her husband, to see his smile as he made love to her. She wanted only to remember how dearly she loved him. He was life itself to her and she no longer wished for death when he was there to give her the exquisite joy of living. His arm, strong body joined with hers so perfectly, and she gasped with the pleasure which filled her loins. His loving heat burst within her in delicious waves, spread through her slender body with the same sweet surprise he'd given her the first time he'd taught her what love between a man and his bride should be. She called his name softly as her arms locked around his neck to hold him near. She was so lost in his affection she wanted never to let him go. She was dizzy for his deep kisses left her no time to breathe, and as she lay enveloped in the security of his embrace she could recall nothing save the joy of knowing his love. He held her enfolded tenderly in his grasp until she had grown calm, quiet and serene, at peace with herself once more.

"The answer is no, Elizabeth. Did you understand that?" Andrew nibbled her ears playfully as he hugged her.

"No what? I've forgotten my question." She reached up to touch his cheek and he drew her hand to his lips, lightly kissing her fingertips before releasing her.

"There have never been any others for me since the day I first saw you. I have missed you so terribly this last year, hated myself for the blind anger which drove me away when you meant the world to me. That we have a daughter is such wonderful news. I am sorry I could not be with you when she was born. How old is she?"

"She was born last July 11. She is nine months old now. She's a very bright baby, very sweet and fun. She'll take her first step soon now. I know she will," Elizabeth boasted proudly.

"July?" Andrew's expression became somber as he questioned her again, "Then you knew before I left, didn't you? You kept the news of a child from me, too? But why? What had I done that you no longer trusted me, or wanted to confide in me?"

Elizabeth's eyes grew bright with tears as she told him the truth. "I did not want you to be hurt as you had been when our son died. Had I lost Andrea too, you would never have known of her existence. I meant to tell you I was pregnant only when I could no longer keep the secret."

"Oh, Elizabeth." Andrew moaned softly. "I was such an awful fool then. I'll never fail you so completely, not ever again, nor will I leave you alone. I want only to share your life, with all its joys and sorrows. Do not hide your pain from me when I can help you bear it." Suddenly a thought came to him that he could scarcely relate fast enough. "Do you remember the first time you came to see me last fall when I was so ill?"

Elizabeth was puzzled. "The first time?"

"Yes, I was so sick I couldn't even sit up to eat. My leg felt like it was on fire, then you were all over me, hugging me and kissing me. Your perfume still filled the air when I awoke the next morning. I knew then I hadn't lost your love and tried with all my strength to get well. The next time you came I—"

"Andrew, I really must tell you the truth,"

Elizabeth interrupted shyly. She hated to spoil the beauty of his memories, yet knew she must.

"No, you needn't explain. I understood why it was too dangerous for you to stay, but you came to see me and that was all that mattered. It gave me hope when I thought I had none."

Elizabeth inclined her head thoughtfully and tried again to make him understand. "Andrew, you never left my thoughts, my prayers, but it was only my love which you felt, for I was never really there with you. It was Stephanie whose kisses you felt the first time, but there were never any other visits."

"Elizabeth, Red Tail always told me what you'd said, and the perfume you always wear, the lovely scent of fresh flowers, it remained on my pillow for hours!"

Elizabeth began to giggle and couldn't stop. They lay with their nude bodies entwined, sprawled in a meadow filled with spring grass and wild flowers, surrounded in lush beauty, and she howled with laughter until the tears ran down her cheeks and Andrew could not make her stop. "He is really a devil, Andrew. I don't envy Stephanie one bit! You could never have found a better friend, but he tricked you, and several times too from what you say for I left my perfume in the Jordan house and it sounds as if Red Tail made very good use of it."

Andrew laughed in spite of his embarrassment. "I'll find a way to repay him. Don't worry, I'll think of a way."

Elizabeth snuggled back in his arms, her mood still loving. "When we do have a son, I would like to name him for Red Tail, but I know Indians never honor their

524

friends with such a tribute."

"We are not Indians any longer, Elizabeth. How can you have forgotten that?" Andrew teased softly.

Elizabeth opened her mouth to argue that point then thought better of it. They would have the rest of their lives to decide just what they were and where they truly belonged. "He is named for the Red Tailed Hawk, is he not?"

"Yes, he is. What are you thinking? That we'll call the boy Hawk?"

"Why not? It would make an intriguing name, Hawk Jordan. I rather like the sound of it, but it would remind me only of you. Only of Silver Hawk, the Indian I adored when I didn't even know his true name."

"I don't care what name you call me, Elizabeth, Hawk or Eagle, or simply Andrew. I will always answer you."

As Elizabeth lay content in her husband's arms, she was filled with the joy of being alive. The spring day was warm, the breeze a lazy caress upon her smooth skin and she began to wonder aloud. "Andrew, what do you suppose really happened between my mother and your father? Some nights as I lay sleeping in his bed, I would wake suddenly, certain I'd heard their voices or laughter. It was almost as if they were there with me, watching over me while you were away."

"Yes, you would be able to hear spirits laughing if anyone could." A rakish smile played across Andrew's handsome features as he bent down to kiss her shoulder, then let his lips move up to her lips once again. "I think my father loved your mother with all his heart as I love you, and this is what happened between them." He drew her into his arms as he deepened his kiss, filling her body with a loving abandon which drove all doubt from her mind. She understood the beauty of love was meant to be shared forever. Lover, husband, brother, friend, he would be all things to her as she was to him. Truly she could see her destiny in his eyes. She would never be alone again, for as long as they lived, his promise was certain. They would live their whole lives together, then spend eternity in each other's arms, enjoying the most precious gift of paradise, love's timeless rapture.